# EVERY THING COUNTS

## (THE AKASHIC READER)

**by Jim Curtiss**



ISBN: 978-0-578-01668-9

**Published by Gallivant Multimedia**

*For Jarmila*

**Author's Note**

Even as a younger and more foolish man, I was vaguely aware of a higher plane at work, and though I actively ignored it for a long time, to have done so indefinitely would have been just plain silly.

My eyes were finally wrested open when I lived in the Czech Republic. There, time and again I was confronted with happenings so sublime that I could only attribute them to the divine, and my doctrine came to be: There are forces at work that we simply cannot comprehend. Some call it Jehovah, some name it Allah or Brahma. Some call it the Tao, while others know it as Fate or Luck. But for me, the big secret is this: *They're really all just facets of the same thing.* People of different cultures and faiths naturally have different words for it – or concepts of it – but if you open yourself up to Tao/Allah/God/Buddha/Brahma, positive things can happen.

It's not always simple or easy, and I'm not even sure how you yourself would do it because I've only got my own limited experience to draw upon. But if a screwup like me can become the relatively engaged and aware person I seem to have become, there's no reason other screwups can't do it as well.

It is my sincere hope that Elijah's journey sheds some light on this life's possibilities and helps screwups of all stripes as they progress on their own spiritual journey.

PS: Though inspired by real events, this book is not an autobiography.

Jim Curtiss — Spain, 2008

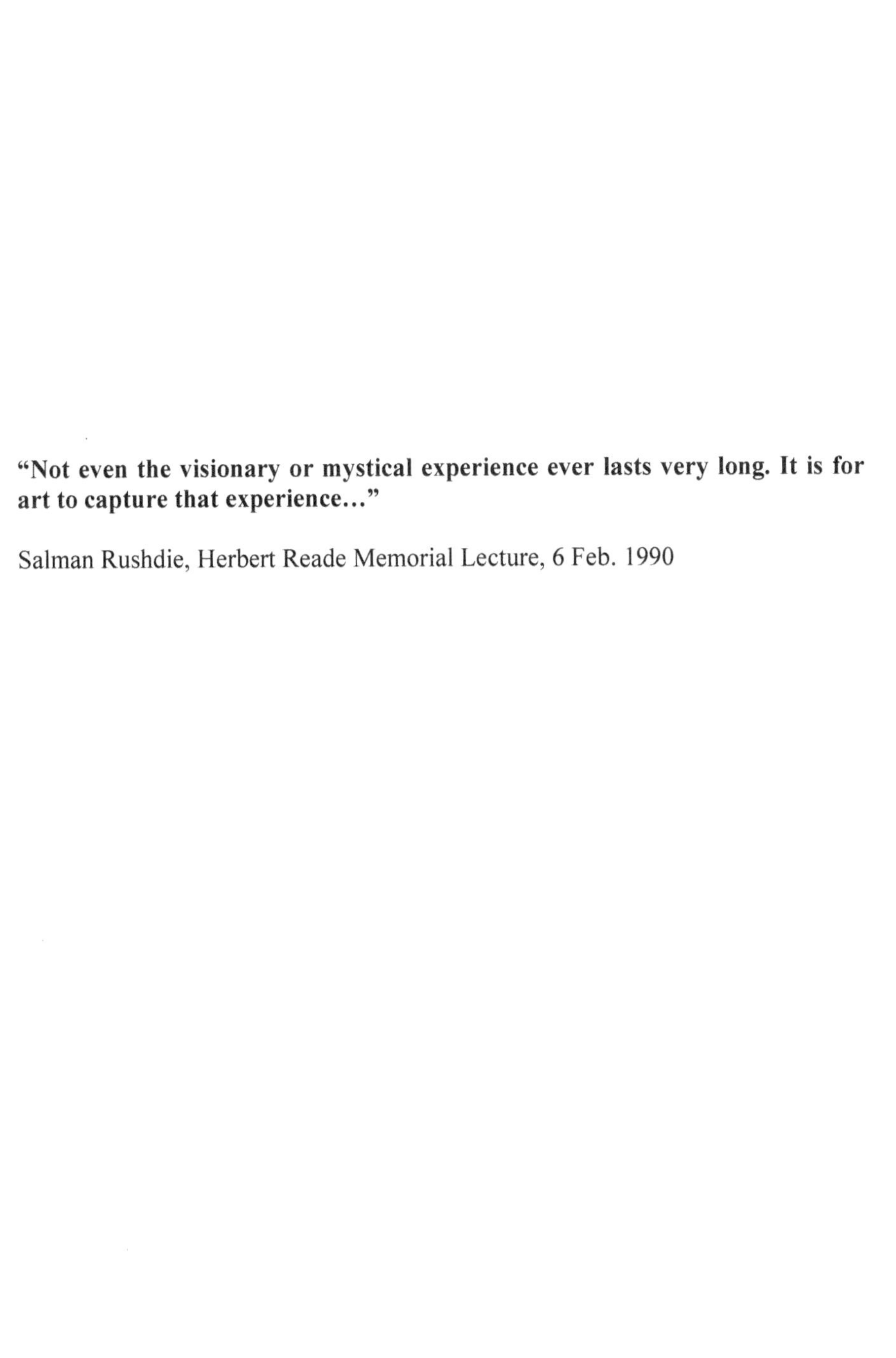

**"Not even the visionary or mystical experience ever lasts very long. It is for art to capture that experience..."**

Salman Rushdie, Herbert Reade Memorial Lecture, 6 Feb. 1990

# Book I

# Every Thing Counts

# Preface

When I was in graduate school I attended a fascinating slide presentation given by a black-haired female alumnus who had been on a Space Shuttle mission. She delivered exuberant commentary and engrossing pictures of the earth and Shuttle lifestyle, and we in the audience rewarded her with a standing ovation.

In the lobby afterwards there was a heap of free NASA goodies, among which was a poster that portrayed the Milky Way galaxy as a wavy horizontal line. But the poster didn't contain just one line: It was a stack of 5 horizontal lines, each one of the Milky Way, each one in a different color and pattern. One couldn't tell, just by looking at them, that they were images of the same thing because they were all portrayed by sensors that detected various portions of the electromagnetic spectrum: Gamma rays, x-rays, ultraviolet radiation, and so on.

Each of these sensors refined their images of the galaxy in a drastically different manner, sometimes showing bulges where others showed narrows, sometimes showing brightness where others showed its absence.

I took the poster home and put in on my wall, and one day while staring at it instead of studying, it occurred to me that our 5 senses are pitifully limiting. Indeed, the fact that our galaxy appears so drastically different when viewed through various filters convinced me that we have about zero understanding of different dimensions, ESP, or even the spirit.

And why?

Because essentially, we humans are really only a set of filters, and we understand just as much of reality as those filters permit.

If we wish to see beyond that, we need to somehow increase our perceptual abilities.

# Act I
# Golden Prague

I first met her at the Internet café nestled in the art nouveau Prague Municipal House. It was a relatively expensive Internet provider, but its central location and the atmosphere of gentility it exuded were such that I didn't mind the price. There were crystal chandeliers, sumptuously padded wooden booths, and also an English-speaking staff – namely, Magdeline – who brought coffee, Pilsner Urquell, or cigarettes as required.

During my third visit in early September, Magdeline told me she was a senior at one of the city's art high schools, and that she lived with her parents quite close to me at the university where I'd be teaching English. As we spoke more and more, it also came out that she was 18 and had spent a year in Virginia as part of an exchange program.

Magdeline's American experience had enhanced her language skills to the point that, as many young Americans do, she peppered her English with well-placed variations of the word fuck. Sentences with *fucking, fuckhead, fuckwad, mother-fucker, rotten fuck, stupid fucker, shitfuck* – they all rolled smoothly off her tongue. She even used *fuckingly* in new and creative placements, and that she did this cursing in the middle of the highbrow Prague Municipal House struck me as a terribly interesting juxtaposition. I was attracted to her despite (or perhaps because of) her brazen youth.

Oh, I know – being 27 and interested in an 18 year-old girl makes me a weirdo, right? Well not exactly, because it was legal in the Czech Republic, at least it was then, to have relations with a girl of 15. (Magdeline herself is the one who told me this, and I later verified it with a Czech colleague.) In the eyes of society, then, I was Mr. By-the-book.

At any rate, on my fourth visit to the Internet joint, Mad, as she liked to be called, invited *me* out on a Friday night. She knew of a great party if I wanted to come along, and we could get to know each other better.

I gladly accepted and was early for our bus stop rendezvous. And my goodness, when I saw her walking towards me through the twilight, I had to catch my breath. She was a sexy little thing, dressed in a short mini-skirt, boots, and tight sweater. Moreover, she came on to me from the start, and her flirty brashness was at once titillating and – truthfully – unsettling.

On the bus ride into town, Mad told me we were meeting two English guys at the Metro station. At first I was disappointed I wouldn't be alone with her, but after thinking about it, I saw that it was probably better this way – maybe I wouldn't be so preoccupied with her legs. Or any other parts of her, for that matter.

At the Metro station Dejvice, Colin and Tim had already arrived, and after brief introductions we all boarded the Metro and began chatting. Right away I saw that Colin and Tim were great guys; funny, open, and most importantly interested in the world around them. Later at the party they were full of questions and jokes, and the night turned out *swimmingly* (a word I picked up from them). In fact, we got along so well that when Mad had to leave, I stayed instead of accompanying her home. I did walk her to the Metro stop, though.

"Will you stay out late," she asked as we walked.

"Just a couple more beers."

"Uh-huh. Well, when I get home I gonna…" she looked meaningfully at me, "I gonna touch myself."

I blinked.

"And I will fantasize about you helping me..."

"Uh…."

Mentally and physically, I took a deep breath.

"Well, I… I like helping people," I responded.

"Uh-huh… so maybe you help me sometime?" She moved close to me, rubbing against my chest, and kissed me on the neck.

She stood back and smiled at me again. Turning and walking towards the Metro, she shook her hips at me and then quickly turned to see if I was watching.

Of course I was watching.

We waved goodbye, and as I walked back to the party I could not stop grinning.

Colin, I discovered later that night, had a connection that he was willing to share, and next Sunday at noon, we rendezvoused with Priestly underneath The Horse at the top of Wenceslas Square. Priestly told me that he was from Sudan and was living in the Czech Republic illegally, hoping to one day gain asylum status. In the meantime, he'd been making money this way.

The three of us walked together down the square and turned right onto Na Přikope. We walked all the way up to the Powder Tower and then turned left onto Celetná ulice. On the right-hand side we found a small café and went inside. We sat down and had a drink and talked about life, and by the end of our meeting, Priestly had taken to calling me "my friend." He did this to Colin as well.

At the end of the meeting, there was a slippy exchange of the grass and the money, and I was given Priestly's phone number. It was implicit that I no longer needed Colin to come along.

The other Brit, Tim, was a funny, thoughtful kid, and we began to keep in touch almost daily.

Two weeks after we met, Tim began a Big Boy Job as a Marketing Director with a Czech firm, but on the fifth day he hit some sort of wall and resigned – just walked out at lunch and didn't go back. Further, he decided to move back to London. He'd had enough of Prague and needed a change. Or money. Or both.

An interesting thing about the people I was meeting: We all seemed to need constant variation, and to find it, we no longer thought in terms of cities or states, but in terms of countries, continents and hemispheres.

The world that our parents had inhabited – full of Iron Curtains, Cold Wars and well-entrenched prejudices – was gone.

In its place stood countries to be explored, customs to be discovered, languages to be learned. Never mind that going in, most of us had no in-depth knowledge of our adopted countries. It was the adventure, the wanderlust that courted us and placed us fully in the midst of the hardy expatriates – the Global Village Idiots – who gypsied our way across the globe, seeking *experiences*, short-term under-employment, and a type of fulfillment that could never be provided by the grist-mill of efficiency- and profit-seeking corporations.

It was a rainy autumn afternoon when Mad knocked on my door for the first time, and when I opened up I simply had to admire her a moment before letting her in. Spread apart was a long, black jacket, and underneath was a white sweater short enough to reveal a svelte, pierced stomach. She was also wearing a plaid miniskirt and over-the-knee white stockings. I simply couldn't believe how hot she was, and my sudden sexual energy convinced her to… well…

Afterwards, Mad lay on top of me under the covers.

"Mmm. We do this again?" she asked.

Twenty-seven or not, it seemed just a little quick for me to consider. "Uh… *now*?"

"No, no, I have to go home until 5 o'clock. I think another time…"

"Oh, PLEASE," I enthused. "You just tell me when."

"I come back tomorrow if you like…"

"Absolutely… say, 4 o'clock?"

"Yes, 4 o'clock. I will finish fucking school then. Tell me, you like me in this skirt? I can wear another…"

"Mad, it doesn't matter what you wear – I'll just take it off you!"

We laughed and kissed, then she threw off the covers and stood up, both of us shivering from the relative coldness of the room. I covered back up and propped up my head with a pillow. My eyes danced over her as she collected her clothes from around the room.

Sitting on a chair opposite the bed, she pulled on her stockings, then stood up and slid on her skirt. She found her shoes and slipped them on, and then as she was putting her shirt on, a hand-lettered sign on the wall caught her attention. She read it aloud: "Pride. Envy. Lust. Gluttony. Anger. Ava… avarice. Sloth. What the fuck is that?"

I considered telling her about my recent dream, but realized I didn't feel close enough to her, which was odd given what we'd just done. I gave her the stock version instead.

"Well, in Christianity, those are the seven deadly sins – the things that everybody has to avoid to live a good life."

"I don't fuckin' believe in God," she asserted as she buttoned her sweater.

"I can understand that – I myself was an atheist until a couple of days ago…"

I took a deep breath and again considered telling her about it – and decided not to.

"Anyway, those 7 sins are pinned on the wall to remind me to try and be a better person."

"A better person? Isn't it too fucking late for that? I mean, you're almost *30*!"

"Uh… *no*, it's not too late to be a better person. It never is."

She looked back up at the wall and said, "Well, one word I do know is lust! I am full of it, and you will continue having problem with it when I am with you! You know this, yes?"

"Oh, I know it. I'm having problems right now."

Mad looked at the blanket and said, "I see it. Want me to suck your cock before I go?"

I winced at the harshness of the offer. But harsh or not, I still let her.

Much like Mad, I considered myself an atheist for quite a long time. Just one of the many drawbacks of, let's say, Christianity, is the age-old postulate that humans are the only inhabitants of the universe. I mean, ok, perhaps God placed us here on Earth, but when you consider the sheer vastness of space and the number of stars that are out there, it becomes an exercise in buffoonery to really maintain that earth contains the only life in the whole of creation.

Which is probably why the Vatican recently stated that God may indeed have created aliens as well. But still, for thousands of years the church asserted that we were alone in the universe, which drove me crazy for a number of reasons, but chief among them was this: What we call the Milky Way Galaxy contains approximately 200 billion stars. That's 200,000,000,000 stars, which by any reckoning is a boatload. Moreover, what we call the Milky Way Galaxy is *only one of the billions* of galaxies scattered about the universe's rumpus room. Now, I'm no mathematician, and I still can't convert Fahrenheit to Celsius, but when we start to talk about this many stars… well, far from being the only life out there, I think we merely lack the sophistication to detect all the others.

But back to the religion thing – right before I met Mad, I came to see – rather, was *made* to see – that atheism is completely wrong.

And I know this may be hard to swallow, but I can't stress enough that it's the truth: I was given a message that there is something out there higher than we can perceive – something that unmistakably plays a hand in the Big Scheme of things.

Which naturally begs the question: Why would a sexed-up fool like me be the one to receive such a message? My only answer, the one I arrived at after careful consideration, is this: Who better than a sexed-up fool to be shown The Way?

And anyway, even assuming that the dream *wasn't* a message from God, it had a big impact on me. At the very least, it pushed me into a phase of spirituality in which I realized that my soul was blessed, and no harm – aside from my own neglect – could come to it.

I giggled when I first put it into words, but the simple, pure truth is that I found God in Prague.

Or rather, God found me.

It took awhile amid the total traffic chaos, but I finally recognized Mad on the massive roundabout of *Vítězné náměstí* (Victory Square) at 5 p.m. on Friday. She was on the far side of the bustle and from there we walked, holding hands, through progressively quieter parts of the Dejvice quarter. We were going to her cousin's birthday party, then Mad had to work at 8 that evening (in addition to her Internet café job, she was a part-time waitress at a disco).

During the walk, because I didn't want to do it in front of an audience at the party, I gave Mad the small gift I'd made the previous evening. It was a dream catcher, the sort that Native American Indians used, and I had collected the various components in the forest. There was no occasion for the gift – I had just always wanted to make one. Anyway, as I gave it to her, I saw the girlish light flash in her eyes before she kissed me.

We arrived at the party early, the only other people being the Birthday Girl cousin and Mad's older sister. The cousin was in her early 20's, black-haired, and spoke a bit of English. Mad's sister Simona was in her late 20's, had short red hair, and wore tight jeans and a slightly-cropped t-shirt that revealed a healthy midsection. She also spoke a bit of English.

Introductions were friendly and I was led to a cozy chair and brought a glass of whiskey on ice while Mad and Simona, on either side of me, tried to include me in their sisterly Czech conversation as much as possible. More people came in, and in less than an hour the party was going strong.

During one of the many periods when the girls were speaking Czech and I couldn't understand a word, I looked around the studio, taking in the party and my surroundings. We were in the lobby/bar of a fashionable fitness studio operated by a blonde Slovak man. I knew this because the week before I had walked by this very same fitness studio, and upon seeing that they gave massages, had gone in and made an appointment. It turned out to be a mistake, as the owner had a horrible Iron Grip philosophy when it came to massaging, and I walked out feeling terribly crooked of back. Because of that, and also because my Gaydar had gone through the roof there, I promised myself never to return. So it was with a feeling of smug confirmation that I looked over Simona's partially-bared shoulder and saw a young, cross-dressed boy twirling around, wearing a skirt and a bleached-blonde wig.

Later, on my way up to the bar, the same boy approached me and said something in Czech.

"I'm sorry, I don't speak Czech," I replied.

"Oh, you're American," the boy said. He continued dancing, getting closer to me. "What I said was, 'You're really hot.' Are you a fairy?"

"Uh… no… But thanks for asking."

The boy's smile dimmed and he said, "Pity," before dancing away.

For who, I wondered, and continued up to the bar. I ordered three more whiskeys from the now-bartending cousin, and secretly hoped that Mad wouldn't want hers because of work.

When I arrived back in the sisters' midst carrying the drinks, my hope was confirmed. Mad was already thinking about leaving and didn't want hers, so it sat on the table untouched. The girls talked a moment more in Czech and then Mad got up to go to the toilet.

When she got up, Simona slid closer to me and asked, "So, you like sister?"

"Your sister? Oh, sure. And you?"

"Yes! He's my sister! But tell me – who is my English?"

"It's good – like your sister's English…"

She smiled and looked downward. "You do fun."

"No, really. We're talking, aren't we? That's good English for me."

She looked back up at me. "But I need a help. I need teacher too, like Mad. She said me I ask you for lesson…"

She looked at me expectantly, and I responded just a bit *too* quickly through the whiskey, "Oh, sure! I'll be your teacher."

"Fine! Tonight after Mad go – you stay by me."

I hesitated, already feeling vaguely guilty at being alone with her. "Uh… I'm sorry, but I promised Mad I would walk her to the Metro station."

"No problem. We tell her it." Simona sat back and smiled, apparently satisfied things had been worked out.

I took a drink and then Mad came back and sat on my right. Simona was on my left and they spoke over me in Czech – a second or two later, Mad asked me, in English – "So you'll stay with Simona tonight, yes? Perfect. She likes you."

At the mention of her name, I had looked over at Simona, but at Mad's last statement, I snapped my head back to her and said, "No … I'm going with you."

"No, stay with my sister – she will be lonely if you go."

"Mad, I don't want to stay. I'm more comfortable going with you."

"You don't like my sister?"

"Of course I do, but-"

"Then what's the fuckin' problem?"

"I just don't want to stay."

"But she will think you don't like her."

"Tell her I do like her, but I don't want to stay – I can teach her next week. In the daytime."

I sat back and the girls spoke in Czech again. I watched their non-verbal cues, trying to see how Simona was taking the news – she was clearly disappointed.

Mad turned to me. "She says it is a pity for her, but good that you like me."

She smiled, pecked me on the cheek, and asked if I was ready to go. We all stood and walked over to the cousin, wished her well, then Mad and I said goodbye to Simona.

"We have English, not forget," said Simona as we shook hands. "Last week, ok?"

"I will call you next week," I said, shaking her hand.

The sisters spoke in Czech and laughed, and then Mad and I walked out of the party and into the still-sunny streets.

After the door closed behind us, Mad led me around the corner and hungrily kissed me. She looked into my eyes. "You want to fuck my sister, don't you?"

"*What?*"

"You like her and want to fuck her."

"Uh, no… I like you."

She smiled when I said this and kissed me deeply again.

*Czech girls… so refreshingly simple to deal with,* I thought.

Then we walked, holding hands, to Hradčanska metro station. I was relieved I didn't have to be at the party anymore and that I had the whole evening – with a nice buzz, to boot – in front of me. But just as we got to the stairs that led to the underground station, Mad stopped and said, "Shit! I fuckin' forgot your gift! Someone will throw it away now!"

I looked at her for a second, then sighed and shook my head.

"They won't throw it out. I'll go get it."

"Will you? I'm so sorry… and I'll pick it up when I visit on Monday! Will you really go back?"

"Yeah. Don't worry about it."

She smiled, kissed me again and said, "I'm so sorry. I'll make up on it on Monday, ok?"

She started backing away.

"You'd better!"

"I promise I will! See you Monday!"

"See you Monday."

She turned and quickly walked away, and didn't look back as she hurried down the stairs. I watched her go, disgusted that I had to go back to the party, before I turned and walked up the street. It was only a five minute walk back, but it took me 15 heel-dragging minutes. It was early – not even 8 o'clock yet, which meant it would be difficult to extract myself from the party again.

I breathed deeply before I opened the front door. There were a lot more people there, and my entrance went unnoticed by everyone but Simona, who at once saw me from across the room. Our eyes met and we smiled.

I worked my way to where we had been sitting before, and Simona met me there.

"Mad forgot something," I said.

"I know."

"What do you mean, you know?"

"She said me."

"*What*? She told you she was leaving the gift here?"

"Yes. We plan. Now you mine for night."

"Simona, I-"

She put a finger to my lips and said, "Yes."

I sighed deeply and looked at her.

"Yes," she repeated, and arched her eyebrow.

I took off my jacket and sat down. The glass of whiskey Mad had left was still there among some empty glasses, and I picked it up and drank it in one go.

When I looked up at her, Simona smiled and went to get me another.

Two hours of whiskey, dancing and flirting later, Simona got up to use the toilet, and while she was gone, from out of the crowd the black-haired cousin materialized. She walked over to me and said, "What's your relationship with Simona?"

"Uh… I like her sister. I just met Simona tonight."

"Good," she said, and melted back into the party.

I sat there wondering about the question and then Simona came back and sat on a chair to my left. She looked at me provocatively, ensured that I was watching her, and then leaned over to get her drink. As she leaned, her loose neckline dropped low enough to expose her chest. I saw this out of my peripheral vision but struggled to maintain eye contact with her. I swallowed hard. After a moment Simona sat back with her glass in hand, smiling.

I looked at her and covered my mouth and cheek with my hand. I breathed deep, feeling the smoothness of my freshly-shaven face, then stood up. I indicated that I was going to the toilet, and walked back the darkened hallway. The music faded slightly as I went.

Opening the door to the toilet, the light was already on and I looked at myself lazily in the mirror against the far wall. Then my eyes shot open when I saw, behind my own reflection, that of Simona.

I whirled around and saw her sultry smile wane when she realized I hadn't intended to invite her in with me. She became terribly red and apologized all over herself as she backed out the door and scurried up the hallway.

I slapped myself on the forehead and shook my head. After I closed the door, I looked at my reflection. How did I get myself into these situations?

I found that I didn't have to masturbate any longer, which was the reason I'd gone to the bathroom in the first place, and when I returned to the party, Simona had apparently left.

Relieved but still feeling guilty, I finished my glass, picked up Mad's gift and slipped out the door.

*Czech girls are so simple to deal with,* I chided myself.

I was peeved at Mad for her little games. She'd pretty much lied to me about leaving the gift at the party, and overall she was a negative influence on me that night – I ended up drinking too much and getting to bed late. Plus, there was the whole scene with Simona, which still felt like a punch to the gut.

Nevertheless, when Monday rolled around, I planned on hiding my negative vibes because I wanted to… well…

The knock on the door came while I was still arranging things, so I yelled "Moment," and hustled about. I was thinking about the dust in the corner when I opened the door and found both Mad and Simona standing there.

Smooth me, I said, "Uh…" and looked between them.

Mad leaned over to give me a kiss. She looked very happy, and asked if they could come in.

"Uh. Sure. Of course."

I stood aside. Mad went first, followed by Simona. When they passed me up, both were smiling.

After they sat down, Mad on the bed, Simona on the reading chair, I offered them beers. Both accepted, so I went back to the fridge and opened three, wondering what was going on. I returned to the bedroom, we toasted, and then I couldn't wait any longer.

"So," I ventured, and sat on the bed.

"Elijah," Mad started, "we want to apologize…"

"Yes, we very sorry," nodded Simona.

I looked between them and said, "Oh, don't worry. It was my fault, too."

"Yes," laughed Simona, "you confuse me with toilet!"

"I am *so* sorry for that! Really. I didn't mean to–"

Mad stopped me and said, "It's all right, Elijah. We already spoke about it and it was just a confusion. But we wanted to apologize in person…" She looked at Simona, who nodded, "…and we want to apologize in a special way."

I looked at Mad and said, "It's ok. I accept your apology. Really."

I drank my beer and watched them over the bottle. They put their beers down and then Simona stood and moved cat-like towards me.

I swallowed all wrong and coughed, then asked, "What are you doing?"

"We want apologize," said Simona.

"You already did," I said, standing up and backing away.

Mad, still on the bed, grabbed my forearm with both hands and pulled me towards her.

Simona suddenly pulled her sweater over her head and threw it onto the chair. I gaped and strained at Mad's hold while Simona came over and took the beer from my hands. I watched her naked back and jeaned bottom as she walked over and put my beer between theirs.

Having both hands empty allowed me to pry my hand free from Mad's grip, and when Simona started back for me, I held both my hands up in front of me.

"Wait, I – "

Mad grabbed at my arm again, getting a hold and pulling me towards her. Seeing me off-balance, Simona pushed and hipped me until I fell onto the bed. I curled up fetal with both of them on top of me, laughing and saying they needed to apologize.

I stayed curled up, feeling Simona's breasts against my bare arm and kinda liking it, until they started tickling me.

Writhing around and giggling, I tried not to hurt anyone as I pushed them away, but holding back just got me further underneath. Finally they had me on my back, Mad straddling my chest and arms. Simona was sitting over my knees and pinning my hands.

I looked up at Mad and said, "Ok, really! Let me up and I won't have to hurt you."

She smiled and said something in Czech, and I felt Simona's hand begin to unfasten my jeans.

As Mad was pulling her shirt off, I looked up at her fullness and wondered if I should freak and muscle my way out, or just…

The face-to-face student placement interviews that took place in October were the beginning of the semester for me and my three English teaching colleagues at the Czech Agriculture University. They were actually an occasion for fun and socializing, but I was taking my job seriously and approached the interviewing process as such. For example, while none of my colleagues had even dressed smart casual, I showed up wearing a tie.

That's not to say my colleagues were somehow less engaged – they merely had varied approaches to things. Katherine – Kat – was from southern California, had studied art, and had the whitest smile in the city. She lived up the hallway from me, and on her second day in Prague had gone to Ikea to dress up her foreigner-ghetto room. She was the most naturally sociable of all of us.

Ryan was also from California, but further up the coast. He was the real Bohemian of the group: He and his girl had been traveling around the coastal cities of the world, surfing and taking work wherever they could find it before ending up in Prague.

Andrew – not Andy – was the lone Brit among us, and was the most depressed, depressing individual I'd ever met. A recent breakup and move-out, coupled with his talk about how crappy Prague was, convinced me to avoid him wherever possible.

The classroom we used for the interviews was very 1950s, outfitted with straight-backed wooden chairs, tables made of painted particle board, and a 30-grit green chalkboard on the front wall. We conducted the interviews at the rear of the classroom, two of us per table asking questions of the prospective students. A sample interview might include, "Where are you from? <present tense diagnosis>, Have you studied English before? <present perfect tense>, "What did you do last weekend?" <past tense>, What will you do next weekend? <future tense>, and so on.

I was paired up with Andrew and making the best of a bad situation; to my right were Kat and Ryan, having a ball. At the front of the room was the waiting area where between five and ten students stood at any given time.

We had been there for about two hours when she walked into the room.

Just a glance was enough for me to be impressed – she had long, chestnut hair, was wearing a stylish blue suit, and was beautiful in a wholesome, natural way.

I couldn't ignore her presence, couldn't concentrate on our interview, and luckily Andrew picked up the slack until it concluded and the student walked away. I dearly hoped it was the beautiful girl's turn, but instead another boy came to our table, bright-eyed and talkative. The lovely girl walked back to Kat and Ryan's table and I simply could not keep my eyes off of her.

As Andrew conducted our interview without me, I listened to and watched Kat and Ryan speak to my sparkling beauty.

"Elijah… *hellooo…*"

It was Andrew.

I turned and smiled sheepishly at him. "Hey, can you handle this one alone?"

"What? Uh…"

Both Andrew and the interviewee looked at me blankly.

"Thanks," I said, and scooted my chair over next to Kat. Andrew, abandoned yet again, returned to the interview. At Kat's table, my chair-skidding had taken everyone aback.

I took it in stride, gave them my Big Smile and said, "I thought you might need some help."

Ryan shook his head at me, Kat smiled, and the beautiful girl held out her hand and said, "Liliana."

Shaking hands with her was like licking a 9 volt battery. I actually stuttered my name.

"Uh… Elijah. Nice to meet you, Liliana."

Kat giggled at me and said, "Liliana is looking for a private teacher…"

"Oh, really," I almost sang.

"...and Ryan can't do it because he lives so far away. That leaves me or you, because we both live here on campus."

Genius me asked, "Do you live here on campus, Liliana?"

"Yes, I live in campus but I am away too often for normal classes, so I need private teacher." She smiled.

Ears ringing, blood pressure skyrocketing, I sat and gaped.

Kat nudged me on. "So... do you want to teach her?"

I spun on her quickly and blurted out, "I can't teach her!"

Ryan and Kat looked at me as if I'd deliberately poked myself in the eye, and when I looked back at Liliana, her smile had drooped slightly.

Kat ventured, "Are you sure?"

"Yeah... uh... I just don't have time for private students. I'm sorry Liliana, but Kat is a great teacher, you'll really like her."

Liliana smiled politely at us all, and made the necessary arrangements with Kat. Standing up, she shook all our hands and walked toward the front of the room. As she walked out, she turned back for a final goodbye and was away.

I sighed in relief; bells were still ringing somewhere in the distance.

Ryan leaned over and looked at me, "Are you a idiot, or what? She's a fox, dude! Why don't you wanna teach her?"

I swallowed hard and said, "Man, I'd just slobber at her the whole time. How could I concentrate on teaching?"

Ryan shook his head again. "Dude, you're a fuckin' *idiot*."

"Well," said Kat, "I think you were sweet."

A sweet idiot.

That's me all right.

Around mid-October, Colin, his American friend Josh and I started playing hoops in the skating/basketball complex across from Letna Park. We played mostly on Sundays, after I visited St. Vitus' Cathedral.

On this particular Sunday, we joined the full court – it was a serious game, but all three of us contributed well. Colin, especially, was built for hoops – long and lanky, with about zero body fat, he could run and jump all day. Still, he wasn't the most coordinated fellow, and fell or tripped more often than anyone I'd ever known. Josh was middle-sized stocky but fast, which is always a plus on the court.

After the game petered out, the three of us sat on a bench in the weakening sun, guzzling water.

"So," I asked, "what's happening the rest of the day?"

Colin went first. "I'm cleaning and then going to bed early," he said. "I have a meeting with the police tomorrow."

"Whaddya mean a meeting with the police," Josh asked.

"That's just it. I don't know. I only got this letter telling me to come round to the station tomorrow morning."

"Do you know what it's about?"

"I've no idea."

"Are all your papers in order," I asked.

"Oh yes, I'm all legal."

"Hmph. Good for you."

Josh turned to me. "What? They didn't help you with your papers up there?"

"No, no. It's all very under the table."

"Man, that's pretty dangerous… they'll deport you if-"

"Yeah, I know… but the job is just so cherry! I make a respectable living by working 20 hours a week!"

"Yeah…"

I looked at Colin. "But what about this copper thing? You really have no idea about it?"

"No, man. No clue."

We sat a moment and looked at each other before I blurted out, "Dude, I'll bet you it's about Priestly! We haven't been able to reach him this whole month."

"Ah… he's probably on holiday or something."

"No. It's definitely him. You get summoned by the coppers out of the blue and you haven't done anything wrong? 100 bucks it's about Priestly." I chugged at the water.

Colin looked pensively between me and Josh and finally nodded, "You may be right."

"I hope I'm wrong, man, but… let's assume it is Priestly. Could they bust you for anything?"

"I don't know. Only if they caught me buying, I guess. Or for the having of it."

"Have you got any at home?"

"A bit."

"Dude, this is gonna sound funny, but you gotta give it to me-"

Josh started laughing and said, "No, no, give it to me!"

"Seriously," I continued, "I'll take it and hold it just in case – I don't know – maybe the coppers want to search your place or something. I sure wouldn't want to be holding, especially being a foreigner."

Colin breathed deep. "Yeah, ok. We'll swing by my place and you take it. If something goes wrong I'll call you and you can flush it or something."

"It probably won't come to that, but you never know."

We gathered up our stuff and walked to the front gate, making vague plans to meet Josh for weekday beers before walking the 20 minutes to Colin's one-room apartment in Dejvice. After getting inside and settling into two beers, Colin rooted around in a drawer and took out his stash.

Instead of handing it directly over for safekeeping, he rolled a fattie for the two of us, sprinkling it with tobacco and grass, and we smoked it together while watching the Czech news.

Perhaps it was the weed – more likely it was the strange circumstances – but the joint did nothing except open up the door for Mr. Paranoia to come in and hassle me, and I in turn hassled Colin. We found ourselves obsessing over worst-case police interrogation scenarios and creating the most improbable situations. Finally, in a move of pure avoidance I blew out of there after the first beer, leaving Colin in a worrisome tizzy.

On the crowded bus ride home my mind continued to work: I had called Priestly from the pay phone of the Foreigner Ghetto a number of times. And if the cops were able to track down Colin through Priestly's mobile, they could sure track down the pay phone number and then send up the dogs. It wasn't an unreasonable assumption, and as I stood on the crowded bus I felt the dark monkey of paranoia chewing on my neck.

Standing there with the throbbing, obvious-to-everyone bag of marijuana in my backpack, I must have bumped into the thing lying there, because a German Shepherd suddenly erupted into an unholy barking fury right under my feet. I tried crawling up the leg of the woman next to me, but the bus was packed and there was no room for maneuver. Luckily the dog had a muzzle and couldn't bite. Still, it freaked me out completely, and the barking of the dog, coupled with my profusion of vulgarities in English, ensured that the entire bus was staring at me – the very worst of my paranoid fears had come to fruition.

It took forever to get to the university and when I finally entered my dorm room, I drew the curtains before I turned on the lights. After unpacking my bag, I carefully wrapped the stash and hid it in the only place I could think of that people wouldn't want to look – the toilet tank.

I was a nervous wreck, could barely concentrate on reading, and all that night had dreams of endless pursuit.

I nicknamed our dormitory the Foreigner Ghetto for two reasons. First, it's where the university placed all foreigners – student or instructor, it didn't matter, that's where we all lived. Secondly, it was just plain shoddy. The fixtures, the lights, the windows, the furniture – you name it. Shoddy.

Shoddy I found I could live with, but that the Foreigner Ghetto had no in-room phones was a major pain. Unable to afford a cell phone just yet, I lived with this tele-inaccessibility for awhile before enlisting the service of a voice mailbox company – this way people could leave me messages that I could access from any phone.

The morning of Colin's police interview, I held my breath when I checked those messages. To my great relief there was nothing, and I went through my morning classes without worry.

Still, I hadn't slept much and was nervous about sitting on Colin's big fat stash – I don't know what I had been thinking when I volunteered to hold it for him, because I was majorly freaked by the situation.

When classes finished for the day, I checked the voice mailbox again and this time Colin barked at me, "Hey man! You know that *book* I lent you? You can take it back to the library. And you might want to do it quickly. Like *immediately*. I think someone is listening to your messages."

Just one minute prior, I had been in my Upstanding University English Instructor mode, but Colin's message totally wrecked it. I was suddenly Paranoid Fugitive Elijah, and as I made my way back to my room, I imagined opening the door and seeing the coppers there waiting for me, holding up Colin's bag of marijuana and a set of handcuffs.

Instead of keying open my door, I knocked on it; if someone answered, I thought, I would pretend I was looking for myself there. I knocked once but there was no answer. I knocked again, louder.

A moment later my bathroomate Marcel, a French Instructor, opened up his door and looked out. He seemed surprised to see me and said, "Ave you forgotten zee key?"

I walked over to him and quietly said, "Uh… yeah. That's right. Can I get in through the bathroom?"

"Of course – come in," he said, and backed into his room. I followed him into his small foyer, and then turned into our shared bathroom. The door opposite, which led into my own foyer, was locked but easy to break into, and I did it quietly and carefully.

I inched the door open and slowly poked my head in, fully expecting to be attacked by the drug dogs, but instead I was scared witless when Marcel loudly asked, "What are you doing?"

In my frantic mindset I had forgotten about him standing behind me and actually jumped, in the process squealing like a little girl.

When I landed, I said, "What the fuck, man? You'll give me a heart attack!"

Marcel looked at me through widened eyes and said, "Uh… I need zee toilet."

I walked into my room shaking my head. The jig was up one way or another, so I resigned myself to going inside. I was relieved to find no coppers or drug dogs waiting there for me, and I sighed deeply and sat on the bed, plotting my next move.

After I heard the flush, followed by Marcel exiting the toilet, I went in to collect the stash. Marcel saw me going into the toilet and warned me, but I was immune, this day, to his pungency. Once inside, I stood on the seat and fished around in the high-mounted toilet tank, pulling out the dripping parcel. It was no bigger than a mobile phone.

As I carried the stash back into my room, a year of my life was taken away by each of the three loud knocks on my front door. I froze. In my hands was my ticket to Czech jail, to eventual deportation and complete and utter disgrace. I didn't breathe. The three loud knocks were repeated and I stood there completely frightened. I swallowed hard. Drymouth and desperation.

The visitor must have placed an ear on the door because I heard the slight bump as it pushed against the frame.

It was a cop. It had to be.

At length, I heard a heavy set of footsteps retreating up the hallway, and I finally breathed. Paranoid or not, I was sure I was in deep shit. I shook my head at the stupidity of the situation and placed the stash deep into my backpack. I had to get the hell out of the university setting and bury the hot potato somewhere.

But then I thought, wait a second. Here I am going through all this bullshit, I might as well enjoy some of it, right? I hoped the grass would calm my nerves, somehow sedate me so I could deal with things a bit better, so I packed up a pipe and took a couple hefty hits with Marcel – in *his* room – before packing it away.

When I eventually opened my front door to leave, a folded note fell to the ground. I picked it up and opened it – it was from Mad. The beginning was sweetly worded about missing me, but the gist of the message was that Simona's period was over two weeks late and she was probably pregnant. She asked me to call soon and she signed it with love.

Forgetting to close the door and holding the note down low, I breathed deep and stepped back into my room.

The hooch had left me unable to think straight, and I found I could only obsess about my problems. Individually they were serious enough, but when combined they formed a set of unenviable imaginings about Simona having a child and me being deported on drug charges. Or marrying into their trashy family. Or moving back to the U.S. with Simona and receiving a lifetime sentence of vulgarity.

I sat on the edge of my bed, head in my hands.

After a time I collected myself, washed my face, and headed out into the world. Unlucky for me, the campus was full and I bumped into no less than 10 acquaintances, five of whom stopped me to ask language questions. I repeatedly stumbled over my words, unable to find coherence. Also, the paranoia I'd hoped to smoke out had only entrenched itself. And from the odd looks I was getting, people knew something was up.

Fifty yards from the bus stop I ran into Ryan, my teaching colleague. He looked at me with a face full of concern and sincerely asked how I was doing. I meant only to giggle, but from somewhere deep inside a manic chortle escaped into the light of day.

Ryan flinched at the force of it, and with wide eyes he repeated the question, “Elijah, are you sure you’re all right?”

I put a hand on his shoulder and said, “We’ll see, Ryan. We’ll see.”

I turned to cross the street, and almost got hit by a bus before skittering across.

I took the bus to Dejvická Metro stop, and from there walked up the hill to the side entrance of Prague Castle. Once inside St. Vitus’ Cathedral, I sat, closed my eyes, and tried to calm my mind.

The dream came back, just as vivid as the first time I had it…

*I entered a room in which I could sense three other beings. I encountered the first figure as I entered the door. He motioned me forward. The room was completely ensconced in wood, and opened up to my right. It was wide and deep, with high cathedral ceilings.*

*The second figure I encountered was in the far corner of the room. As I approached it, I found I wasn’t walking, but swimming towards it in the corner. It was a gargoyle, evil and green, his face contorted. As I drew nearer, the water between us began to roil and turn green. The gargoyle grinned and pointed at me. He was chanting, “Green water, you die! Green water, you die!”*

*His pronouncement didn’t seem to scare me as the water swept me around the floor and to the long wall beside the entrance door.*

*Even when I stopped in front of this last figure, who gestured at me and brought me to a mid-air float in front of her, I wasn’t so scared.*

*This last figure was a woman, the actress Elizabeth Shue, and she was naked and tempting me. In the process of tempting me, I knew she was going to deliver judgment on my soul. As I floated in front of her, the mist that slowly gathered below my feet alarmed me and I became aware that this was really it – Judgment Day was upon me. The mist at my feet was whirlpooling, pulling my soul downwards, and I was filled with fear.*

*I screamed and screamed in helpless fury until the previously naked Elizabeth Shue was suddenly clad in overalls and had called off the proceedings. I was also now clothed, and the room had produced a long wooden pew upon which we sat.*

*Ms. Shue looked at me intently and said: “When I was told about your coming, I felt that you were one of the good ones. You shouldn’t worry about the decision. It has already been made.”*

*She then made me to understand that my soul would have made its way to the next, upward level had I let the dream progress.*

*But apparently I wasn’t ready.*

Emerging from the castle complex awhile later, I walked over to the Strahov Monastery, along the top of the orchard overlooking Malá Strana, and then into the forest. I appreciated this forest because of its accessibility and peace, but as I walked through it this blustery afternoon, I appreciated its desolation – there was nobody about to witness me.

Approximately midway between the monastery and Prague's Eiffel Tower replica is the Hunger Wall. I went through one of its archways and followed the trail for about a minute before I came to a large, fallen log. At the upper end I began digging a hole with a spoon I had brought. I dug nice and deep, unloaded my burden and then covered it, camouflaging the ground with sticks and leaves. It wouldn't be a problem to locate again.

Feeling liberated, I sat on the stump and breathed deep, smiling slightly.

And then I remembered Simona.

That evening as I was preparing lessons for the following day, a knock on my door made me jump. I thought about ignoring it, but then I heard Edmund, a student from the Ivory Coast, calling my name.

I opened up and after some small talk, Edmund said he was applying for a position with Camping USA, a summer camp outfit that recruits foreigners to work on temporary visas, and he needed help with his application – could I spare some time? I invited him in.

Edmund had made copies of the job application and had already completed one by himself, so together we looked for ways to improve it. The obvious errors were no problem, but we had some difficult moments when discussing what to write in various sections.

In the bit that asked him, "Why would you be a good counselor," Edmund had written, "Because I really want to visit the United States."

In the part that asked him, "What is your greatest personality weakness," he had responded, "I am very lazy and enjoy sleep."

After reading those two passages with raised eyebrows and a slight smirk, I switched into teacher mode and said, "Ok Edmund. Both you and I know that you are lazy, but we cannot tell *them* that."

He cocked his head and asked, "Why not? It is the truth."

"Yes. But if you want the job, you cannot say you're lazy. You are competing for this job and if you tell them that, you will not get it."

He looked at me for a moment and then asked, "I have to lie?"

"It is not really *lying*. It is more like… bullshitting."

He laughed at hearing his teacher use the word "shit" and then asked, "What is this bullshitting?"

"It is a type of lying that is not *really* considered lying. For example, instead of saying that you are lazy, you write on the application something like, 'I realize the value of harmony in life and I try to achieve that in everything I do. This personal harmony is something that children respond to."

He laughed again. "No, no, I cannot say this. This is *really* lying."

"No, not really, it is just a different *approach* to the truth. You are coming at it from a different angle – highlighting the positive – because you want the interviewer to think that you are the right person for the job."

"But lying is wrong."

"Yes, it is, but..."

We continued on like this for a long time and I felt as if I were trying to convince an honest man to do a dishonest thing. But really, if I were reviewing applications and came across one where the applicant had written that they were lazy and like to sleep, I'd pin it up on the wall!

Anyway, it was an interesting cultural interaction: The honest Ivory Coast man being told the slimy facts of the hiring process by the slick American; the slick American being right about how to negotiate through the process, but on a higher, moral level, being just all wrong.

Honesty was definitely displaced, and I got the feeling that Edmund was disillusioned by it all. As well he should be, because trickery and deceit can get you a lot of places, but it all adds up in the soul department.

"Of course it was about Priestly," said Colin, "I don't know why I didn't think of it sooner."

We were sitting across from each other in a smoky Czech pub.

"But man, it was a terrific pain in the ass. The cops really hazed me, trying to intimidate me into telling them any information I could think of. Other buyers, for example."

"Did you give any names?"

"Just yours."

I hesitated a moment until I realized he was joking.

"Ha-ha."

"Seriously, I told 'em I was friends with Priestly and smoked with him from time to time, but never bought anything from him. They didn't seem to believe me, but I kept saying I didn't know he was a dealer. They were completely skeptical and kept asking me about his dealing over and over. Finally, after hearing me lie enough, they produced this list – I have no idea how they got it – of EXACTLY how much grass I'd bought from him in the last two years. I had no idea I smoked so much."

"How much was it?"

"They said I bought over 100 grams from him."

"Wow! Uh, wait a second... how much is a gram?"

"What you bought last time was a gram. A hundred seems like a lot, though."

"Man. How did they know how much you bought?"

"Uh... apparently they have my phone tapped."

"WHAT?!"

"They must have, because they also showed me a list of how often I called Priestly. My guess is it's been tapped for like a year."

"A year?! You didn't call me about ditchin' the stash from your *house*, did you?"

"Er…yeah…"

"Oh, man! They're gonna track my ass down!"

"No, they shouldn't be interested in you. I didn't tell them anything about you, and you don't have a phone registered to your name. Plus, we were talking about a book... you did get rid of it, didn't you?"

"Yeah, I buried it in the forest. Do you want it back?"

"Shit no! I'm finished for awhile."

"Me too. Plus, the last time I smoked, I was a total paranoid freak. It wasn't any fun at all."

"I was paranoid, too! I think it was that batch we got from him."

I took a gulp of beer.

"Anyway," he continued, "at the end of the interview I had to sign a letter saying that I bought all this weed from Priestly. And they had four affidavits from other people… I don't know exactly what the others said, but mine detailed how much grass I had bought from him."

"What if you hadn't signed?"

He took a slug of beer and then sighed.

"They told me they could put me in jail, they told me they could deport me if they wanted, they told me they could make my life difficult..."

"Man. That's rough you had to sign on him, though."

Colin's eyes flashed and he said, "Whaddya expect, man? It was either him or me!"

I held up a conciliatory hand. "You're right, daddy. You're right... I'm just sayin' it was a hard position to be in."

After a silence, I asked, "And what about Priestly, anyway?"

As Colin finished his beer, the waiter thudded two full mugs on the table without asking if we wanted them, made two chits on our receipt, and walked away.

Colin wiped his mouth with his hand. "Apparently he's in deep shit. They have a huge file on him but they haven't charged him with anything. They won't let him out on bail because they think he'll try to leave the country… So I think he's gonna be in for a long time. And being black in a Czech jail is no situation to be in."

"Man. He's got kids too, don't he?"

"Three."

After a short silence, I took a deep breath and said, "Well, maybe this'll cheer you up… Simona thinks she's pregnant."

"Wait, I thought you had to reach *puberty* before you could get pregnant."

"That's Mad, ya prick. Besides, she's 18. It's all legal."

"Yeah, but does that make it – wait a second... *Simona's* pregnant?! You told me you fought your way out of the double-team, ya fuckin' git!"

I took a slug of beer and looked over my glass at Colin, who was shaking his head. I continued holding up the glass but not drinking, stalling for time.

He leaned towards me and burst out, "Come *on*! I almost went to jail this morning! Gimme some details!"

I relented and put the beer down.

Funny thing: It was the first sex story I ever told that didn't require embellishment.

Mad's first visit after she left the note began rather... uneasily. On the one hand was The Issue, which we carefully tiptoed around, and on the other hand was the seeming removal of any sexual tension between us.

The latter was especially odd, because it was only then that I discovered how little, aside from the sex part, that I actually *liked* her. As we made small talk, I began to see that her concerns were really those of a kid – girlfriends' antics, parental interference, *grades*. I'd outgrown that stuff years before and it was hard to grant it credence, even though to her it was all of reality.

In fact, she didn't even take the whole pregnancy thing seriously. When I asked her if Simona had tested herself, she said, "Hey! That's a great idea," as if they hadn't even thought about it. Since the topic was finally broached, I took a deep breath and reached out for her hands. Taking them in my own I said, "Listen, if Simona's pregnant, I'd like to help her with the baby any way I can – money, babysitting, whatever. I've given it a lot of thought and I want to do the right thing. I don't-"

"Are you fuckin' crazy? She doesn't want a baby! If she's pregnant, she's gonna kill that little fucker for sure."

I went slack-jawed and blinked at her.

Now, as a sociological issue, I'm all in favor of abortions. That is, I agree abortions should be available for those wanting to have them, or those who were victims of rape, or for whatever other good reason there may possibly be. But I found myself keenly emotional about the issue when it was MY baby under threat, and upon hearing Mad's latest vulgarity, I strenuously suggested that Simona consider the possibility of keeping it.

But Mad continued her line about Simona killing that little fucker until I finally said, "She'll have to do it herself then, because I don't want anything to do with killing a baby. I'm not helping with that."

Mad screwed up her face and said, "That's the most selfish fucking thing I ever heard." She was suddenly all pissed off and putting on her jacket, and I really couldn't think of anything else to say or do, so I just watched as she stormed out and slammed the door.

After she left, I paced around the room wondering if I was really being selfish or if Simona and she were the ones. Either way, I knew the abortion was wrong and wanted to avoid it.

I stretched and meditated, which only reinforced my intention to avoid the repercussions that playing part in an abortion might have in the soul department. Eventually I went to bed half-wired and when sleep finally came, my dreams were filled with blood and I couldn't for the life of me convince Simona to keep the baby away from the spiders.

Four days later, at 04:30 on Friday, the radio switched on and I immediately got up. I made my bed – a simple task because I slept with a sleeping bag – and shuffled into the shared bathroom. The water wouldn't warm up, and I cursed my way through a very short shower before emerging, my wet feet slippy on the dirty linoleum floor.

Wide-awake now, I stood in front of my sink mirror shivering, towel around my waist, and brushed my teeth. Marcel fumbled into the room with scrunched eyes and said, "What in 'ell you doing up zo airly?"

"Holiday, baby! Holiday!"

"What? I teach anoz'er two weeks before 'oliday! What is zis shit?"

"Early Christmas gift! I was a good boy this year!"

"Yes, zis is typical, no? The French work and the Americans holiday."

"Ha! More like the French go on strike, isn't it?"

Marcel gave me the French stink-eye me and finally said, "It is too airly for arguing. We drink good *French* wine when your return, yes?"

"Mais oui, mon ami!"

"Now move – you block zee toilette."

I giggled and let Marcel by, then hustled back into my room. I had to dodge around my suitcase lying on the ground, and in so doing banged my knee on the corner of the bed. I grabbed it and cursed in Czech. I looked around as I rubbed it, thinking that I wouldn't miss the room at all.

The rent was cheap – less than 30 USD per month – but the space itself was a bit of a hole. When I first saw the room, it was arranged as a type of mirror of itself – the twin beds set against opposite walls, the two student's desks as well – and I had been too lazy to re-arrange it. The one bit of home improvement that I had engaged in was the lounge chair I'd "borrowed" from the lobby.

In the room's entry foyer was a wall of closets and beside that, a nook where the hotplate lived. Under that was a small, dirty fridge, which I had unplugged the night before. In all, the room covered the bare essentials. Style I could do without.

I dressed quickly, putting on the smart clothes I had prepared for myself the night before. I had even tied the necktie the previous night, and I slipped it over my collar and tightened it up. I normally travel casually, but the buddy pass I held demanded a certain standard.

I put my U.S. Dollars in one pocket and the Czech Crowns in the other. Looking at the clock, it was already 04:55 when I unplugged it. I looked around the semi-clean room and turned off the light, pulling my bags out into the hallway. The clack-clack of the wheels on the tiled flooring made horrendous noise for 05:00.

The idling taxi was waiting for me in the darkness.

A friend of a friend of dad's had provided me with my first-ever buddy pass for the trip home that Christmas. A buddy pass is a lovely thing: It entitles the bearer to purchase a vastly discounted ticket for a given airline. The catch is that one has to fly stand-by: That is, one must show up at the gate and wait for the plane to fill with normally-ticketed passengers. The remaining seats are then allotted to stand-by ticket holders.

Furthermore, buddy pass holders are assigned priority based upon the seniority of the airline employee who gave them the buddy pass in the first place. So it can very well be that one goes through the hassle of check-in and security and waiting for the plane to board only to discover there's no space on the plane because the president's son got ahead of you, and you have to try a later plane or come back the next day. It's not a very good means of travel if you're on a tight schedule, but it is very cheap, and the benefits can be enormous.

For example, upon boarding the Swiss Airlines 737 from Prague to Zurich, I was assigned a first-class leather seat. Since 737's are not long-haul planes, the seats aren't that much more comfortable than coach – there's more leg room, they're a bit wider, but that's about it. The seat itself wouldn't be worth the extra cash.

But the service! The stewardess was with me before I was even settled in, asking if I wanted orange juice or champagne. I blinked in surprise not only at the offer, but also at her beauty. She was in her early 30's, had long, curly blonde hair, and creamy smooth skin that rivaled Mad's. She was smiling widely at me.

"Uh… could I have both?"

"Of course!" She gave me a Big Smile and then walked back to the front of the plane with my eyes glued to her bottom. She returned directly, with both the champagne and the juice.

"Here you are. Enjoy!"

"Thank you!"

"You're welcome, sir. I'll be back shortly." Again with the Big Smile.

As I drank the champagne and the juice, the stewardess performed her survival theater primarily for me – I was the only passenger in First Class – and she was giving me that Big Smile the whole time. I felt a pleasant glow, not only from the champagne, but also from her.

After we took off, I was looking at the pictures in *Le Monde* when the stewardess approached again. She smiled as she walked by and drew the curtains closed between first and economy class. When she returned, she stood beside me and asked if I would like more champagne and juice. I accepted, and again watched her walk up the aisle.

When she returned and gave me the drinks, she struck up a conversation. And since I was her only passenger, she sat on the armrest across the aisle and we spoke amicably, sometimes flirtily, for the bulk of the trip to Zurich.

As we were preparing to land, the stewardess said she often came to Prague… would I be open to meeting with her when she next flew in?

I smiled like an idiot and said, "That would be great."

I took out a pen and paper and wrote down my phone number and email address, and as I handed it over, we smiled our Big Smiles at each other. Later, when she walked forward to take care of landing preparations, I was so full of myself it was disgusting.

On the flight from Zurich to New York, the staff had no idea I had lucked into Business Class by virtue of a buddy pass – all they knew was they had a passenger to please. I continued with the champagne before takeoff and occupied myself with discovering the full range of motion of the reclining seats.

When we were again in the air and the "fasten seat belt" sign went off, a flurry of activity began. A wide variety of wines and liquors were made available and I was given various choices in the entertainment and culinary fields. To my delight, the fold-away entertainment screens had movies or video games available in a continuous stream, and the music selection was broad. Warming to my role, I listened to classical music, chugged red wine, and looked through the luxury goods catalogue for imaginary Christmas gifts.

After the first meal was finished, I decided to have a chew, and, nicely drunk, shuffled to the toilet wearing the slippers the airline had provided. And my goodness, was the bathroom huge! I did a jumping jack just to prove it could be done and then rooted through the beauty products neatly placed around the sink.

I came across a disposable razor wrapped in plastic, and looked at myself in the mirror – I had a pretty good scruff going. Resolute, I took off my shirt, hung it on the door, and ran a sink full of hot water. When I discovered no shaving cream, I sighed and looked at the door, wondering if I should call the stewardess. But that would mean spitting out my chew and re-dressing. I decided to use the hand soap.

Ten minutes later I shuffled out of the bathroom bleeding heavily from the several gashes I had drunkenly laid into myself. The other passengers stared as I passed them. I slumped into my seat and bled.

Moments later the stewardess came by and acted very concerned, offering to help somehow – aside from bringing more wine, that is.

Declining her "assistance", I let my alcohol-thinned blood flow, no longer feeling so damned full of myself.

Coming back to America was a strange thing. For the previous six months, Czech had been the main language I was exposed to. And since all foreign languages were still just one continuous stream of nonsense to my ears, I had therefore walked around in my daily life oblivious to the utterings of those around me. On a certain level, I heard what was being said, but I simply didn't pay any attention to it. And on those few occasions when I did attend to what was being said, I couldn't understand it anyways. So I had become accustomed to, and had even started enjoying, not having to listen to other people's banal stories, opinions, or concerns. Most of the time I inhabited the world of my own mind, by and large ignorant to those around me unless they wanted something from me, or I from them.

So it was odd when I got off the plane in Pittsburgh, still half drunk, and understood every single word of the people around me. I understood the conversation of the people walking behind me, the advertisements on the wall, the PA system. It was an information-rich environment, and I suddenly realized how alienated I had become while living abroad.

I walked toward the main concourse, my curiosity overwhelmed by the reawakening of dormant familiarity and a disconcerting onslaught of overabundance. I marveled at the number of magazines available at the newsstand – whereas its counterpart in Prague contained only a handful of English titles, this one must have offered over 500. And the snacks! I could have eaten for a month on just what the magazine stand offered! Candies, cookies, chips, sodas, gums, mints – the cornucopia was shocking enough, but the effects of this abundance were also immediately clear. As I stood in the middle of the busy corridor and absorbed the scene around me, a horribly obese woman walked by, the first I'd seen since I'd left the States, and I marveled at the sheer elasticity of the human organism and the extremes we're capable of.

As I watched her trundle past, I tuned in to a man behind me speaking inappropriately loudly. I turned and saw that he was on a cell phone, telling everyone around him how the party he'd been to the night before was "insane". He didn't remember how much they drank, but he did remember how many people were there – four in total. Based on the man's description, the four of them were apparently quite the group at their insane party, which lasted until he didn't remember when. I was relieved when the crazy partier finished his narrative and hung up; he spoke only in superlatives, exclamation points, and italics, and after traveling all day I was in no mood for his brand of enthusiasm.

Walking on, I discovered I was unable to drown out the noises and voices around me. I was attuned to 20 cacophonous sounds simultaneously, whereas in Prague I had been attuned only to the soothing calm inside of my head.

I took the people mover over to the landside terminal, and once out of the train, rode the escalators down to the baggage claim and finally spotted mom at my flight's designated area. We were all hugs and after she began crying, I had to start as well.

Dad was by my luggage and came over barking where the hell have I been, I was the last one out. After his initial barrage, though, he softened up and we had a three-way hug, then chatted about the trip. As we walked towards the car with the baggage, I suggested that we take the elevator and wheel my stuff out to the parking lot, no sense in waiting by the side of the curb for dad to fetch the car.

So I led us across the street to the elevator, which turned out to be on the blink. I punched the button a few times and suffered the looks of my parents – leading them somewhere and my plan having failed. It was such a simple thing, not even my fault, but nevertheless illustrated how being around mom and dad always seemed to annul whatever progress I may have made.

In the end, dad went to collect his big SUV as he'd wanted to do in the first place.

When we got home, mom and dad were all geared up for a night of banter, excited at having their erstwhile son home from Europe, but I simply couldn't hack it. Instead, I ran to bed and embraced it. Stretching out felt like a gift, my legs sending coos of pleasure to my brain and making me groan in relief. I actually broke into giggles it felt so good.

I slept the sleep of recent arrivals and it was blissful.

Unfortunately, it was also short. At 05:05, I woke up fresh and invigorated, looking for things to do. Which was all well and good until 3 hours later when I had to crash again.

Christmas Day I was awakened, hung-over on the downstairs couch and with a sore throat, at 07:30 by the nephew (sis and her family had taken over my old room for the night). He was hazing me to get up and open gifts.

"Eveyone's up aweady," he yelled.

I struggled through the morning trying to muster the appropriate enthusiasm, but the weakish coffee wasn't doing the trick. My loot: Slippers and money from mom and dad, a nice watch from sis and her husband Dave that made me feel guilty for having gifted them so little, and socks from the nephew. Later, after the big afternoon meal, we watched football and even with everyone around me having a great time, I had to crash early.

Next afternoon I met the boys at Mr. Pockets and played pool for a few hours. It was good to catch up with everyone, and afterwards we drove down to the South Side of Pittsburgh, where I spotted a Pilsner Urquell sign in the front window of a bar. I promptly freaked out and we had to go there to sample my favorite Czech Beer. But it turned out that the place had no Pilsner Urquell, hadn't for a long time, and didn't expect to anytime soon.

Slightly deflated, we headed to the Grand Concourse, the lovely old train station next to the Monongahela river. I had a great conversation with Rob, who lives in New York City, about our hometown and how it's filled with people who desire very little change or mystery in their lives. We were both happy and a little proud that we had gotten outta that place.

Things caught up to me on December 29th and I weirded out a little bit. The compression of time and emotion that accompanied my trans-Atlantic visit had weakened me. I wasn't exercising, I was sleeping poorly, and I was drinking way too much. Plus, I was in a limbo between where I belonged and my own home, and it was a confusing feeling.

Mom, dad and I went to Frank Lloyd Wright's Fallingwater House that day. On the whole we behaved well, and shared two meals and culture together. But still, we had small tiffs that centered around my goals, my relationships, my future. The long and short of it was that my parents just didn't get me, and they never would because they couldn't integrate into my life.

And even when I tried to explain to them how my life was going great, I had to hold back so much information that what I did give them had to be scrubbed and spun. For example, I told them I was dating a girl named Mad, that she was nice, a student, and that she had spent a semester at the University of Maryland. They took this information and envisioned romance and love blossoming. Truth: I was in a short-term sexual relationship that made me feel dirty when I thought about it.

On the drive back home, listening to KDKA spew drive-time brain candy, I looked ahead to my upcoming visit to Happy Valley for New Year's and Raquel, an old friend from Penn State who was now in graduate school. She and I had been trading emails and phone calls, and were both showing more romantic interest than we ever had. Even better, she was thinking of a Spring Break trip to Europe.

*Dear Raquel,*

*The turbulence is acting up again – this big-ass plane has been shimmying all over the place and I'm not encouraged at all. I was lucky to get a seat today – the geniuses at the airline overbooked by 40 people and it wasn't certain until the last second that I'd get aboard. In the end I got the nod, but instead of flying in the lap of luxury like before, I'm in coach with a screaming Italian child behind me.*

*I was real surprised at the good-bye between me and the parents today – we had a meal and then they scatted after a quick farewell. All three of us were teary-eyed, and the quick goodbye saved us a lot of pain. They say hello, by the way. They like you.*

*I'm on my third drink and it isn't enough. Not enough at all. I wanted to get good and loopy before I drifted off for a nap, but I can't see it happening. I guess I'll just have to re-live our Happy Valley time together...*

*Man, once upon a time I was a calm flyer. Now, tonight, anxiety and turbulence are going hand in hand. We're shakin', baby. Elvis would be proud of this bird's gyrations.*

*You know, the anxiety has hit me at the same time during both of my trans-oceanic flights. Midway across – no man's land. A limbo that must be suffered through. Will we make it or not? Where's the sense of a bunch of humans in an aluminum contraption being thrust through the air by highly flammable liquid? Being entertained and fed at 35,000 feet above terra firma?*

*I'm sorry this is such a crappy letter. I'll try to make the next one better, ok? I miss you.*

*Love, Elijah*

Arriving in the States in late December, I felt strong in more ways than one. Physically, I was happier with myself than I can remember ever being: I weighed 177 lb. and was energetic as hell. I had been really dedicated to a job for once. I had been learning Czech and French, and feeling pleased with my progress. I was extending myself – reaching out in many areas – and even began to believe in God. In short, I felt like a person who was making genuine progress in multiple areas. I felt good and strong. Virile and lucid. Peaceful and open.

These feelings were not to last long – less than a week after arriving in the U.S., I began to delude my body and mind with alcohol. My friends used booze as a social crutch and I hobbled along with them, telling stories, laughing, drinking late into the nights.

As Christmas gave way to New Year's, the friends who were visiting PA from distant cities began to return back home. Left alone, I had only family issues to deal with, I wasn't exercising, and I was still drinking too much.

Especially disturbing is that I began drinking whenever I was around my family: I needed the elixir to dull the edges of our personalities and to keep my tongue under control as my sister moaned about my parents and my parents moaned about my sister; I needed the booze to feel funny; I enjoyed who I became as I drank and I fell into a shitty and unhealthy lifestyle.

But after being in the Czech Republic for three full days, my good habits were slowly returning. Drinking slowed down. I jumped back into reading full force, and almost finished three books in as many days.

I was eating healthy again – lots of vegetables and soups; sleeping well enough to dream vividly; stretching while listening to calm music; praying up at the cathedral. I finally bought a Bible. Overall, I felt great to be back where I belonged, doing what I needed to be doing.

It was still Christmas break and nary a soul, aside from the Africans and Vietnamese, were in the Foreigner Ghetto. I spent my days in the city, exploring Prague's beautiful Old Town or visiting the cathedral. In the late afternoon I'd visit the British Council, where I borrowed The Brothers Karamazov, The Great Gatsby and The Fountainhead. I spent quiet evenings reading, chewing, and drinking wine.

I did this for two weeks, which brought me back into a more peaceful, introspective demeanor, and when the students began trickling back to the dormitories and the semester began again, I was feeling fit.

Two calm, uneventful months of teaching later I was waiting at Prague Ruzyné airport at 10:00, grinning at the thought of smiling, beautiful Raquel coming out of the arrivals gate and giving me a big hug. I wondered if she would cry like she had when we said goodbye in January, and decided that she would.

The sliding, frosted-glass windows of the international arrivals gate produced a steady flow of people, and I stood in the expectant crowd examining them. I continued smiling broadly, picturing the upcoming night with ex-cheerleader Raquel, and then a girl emerged that looked exactly like Mad. I stopped grinning and seized up until I realized it wasn't her. I didn't want to think about Mad and Raquel meeting, and reminded myself that Mad was out of the picture anyway.

I had been staring at the Mad look-alike so intently that I hadn't seen Raquel actually come out of the arrival doors. She must have spotted me in the crowd and walked towards me when I was looking at the other girl.

"Hey, don't you even recognize me anymore?"

I looked down and there she was – Raquel in Prague via the great Northeast. I shook my head and said, "Hey! Where'd you come from?"

I reached out and hugged her, the flowers in my right hand tickling my nose, and apologized. I said it was great to see her, and she said, "You too."

Feeling her slight distance, I wondered how much should be chalked up to post-flight torpor and how much I had just brought on myself. At any rate, I decided to ignore it and produced the spring bouquet in a flourish. Raquel smiled and accepted them slowly, seemingly unaccustomed to the practice.

Sensing she didn't feel talkative, I switched into Tour Guide Mode as I took her bags and we walked out to the taxis. I punctuated the 20 minute ride back to the Foreigner Ghetto with anecdotes and asides about the area, as well as a brief itinerary of planned activities.

Once on campus, we dropped her bags off in my room and went for a quick walk. After some coincidental meetings and introductions, we retired to back to the room and had some surprisingly reserved discussion over Czech beer. It took awhile before we started to completely open up to each another again, but for my part it was a pleasant process to go through.

The ensuing week was filled with the wonders of Golden Prague and lots of beery nights in smoky pubs. Me and Raquel spent a lot of time alone tramping through the city, but a few nights we spent with my friends, all of whom seemed to enjoy her randy wit.

For example, upon hearing about Colin's police problems, she asked him, "How did you like the cavity search?"

When Josh said he thought Czech women were beautiful, Raquel shot back, "You've never seen me in my cheerleader outfit."

There were also some poignant times of romance, like on the Charles Bridge when Raquel convinced me – though I'd never done it – to swing dance in front of the ragtime band. To the delight of the small crowd, I stumbled through a dance with her leading.

But a week is short, and by the time we'd completely warmed to each other again it was her last night. We went to an early dinner and were back in my room by 20:00. We were lying in bed and talking when Raquel hit me with a proposition: Rent-free living at her Happy Valley, PA apartment during the upcoming summer. We might try being a normal couple for awhile, she said, and if it worked out, maybe I could move back.

I was tempted by the idea and looked far off as I imagined living in the Unites States again. Somehow, though, the thought of going back wasn't altogether comforting. In fact, it felt… *limiting*. Like a regression of sorts.

I was searching for a positive way to explain this feeling when a knock on the door shifted our attention. We were naked under the covers and Raquel asked, "Are you gonna see who it is?"

"Nope. I don't need to see anyone else right now."

She snuggled deeper into my neck and I tried to ignore the idea of a person at the door.

Then a few seconds later Mad's voice rang out, "Elijah, I know you're in there."

My eyes snapped open.

Raquel brought her head up and asked, "Who's that?"

As coolly as I could, I said, "Must be a student. I can't place the voice."

Her eyes narrowed and she said, "If it's a student, shouldn't you answer it?"

"No - I'm naked!"

"Fine. I'll go see who it is." She started to pull the covers off, but I stopped her.

"No, no. I'll go."

I kissed her softly on the forehead and got up, putting on my vintage leopard-skin robe. The knocking came again and Mad said, "Elijah, I want to tell you about Simona's pregnancy test."

I grimaced as Raquel looked at me with a furrowed brow and asked, "Did she say *pregnancy test*?"

Shaking my head, I avoided Raquel's accusing eyes and picked up the half-empty beer from the desk. I turned around and walked towards the front door.

Once out of Raquel's sight, I chugged the beer and put the bottle down by the hot plate.

I stood behind the door hoping Mad would go away, but she knocked again and yelled, "Elijah, open the fuck up! I want to tell you about Simona's pregnancy test!!"

With one hand on the door, I stood there with my head bowed penitently, wondering what I'd done to deserve this.

Soon after Raquel left (don't worry, we'll come back to that) I started reading a lot of new age stuff – mostly Dan Millman, as well as *The Celestine Prophecy.* I found a lot of good in both sources, but the soul stuff in *The Celestine Prophecy* didn't sit well with me. Specifically, the book talked about other dimensions where the soul supposedly originates from, and eventually, if all goes well, returns to.

In practical terms, the book claimed, this means that a soul is sent from a place of benevolence and light, where other such souls have been living for time immemorial. These souls are given a set of instructions when they enter the child at birth, and if these instructions are realized during that person's lifetime, the soul returns back to the place of Benevolence and Light to consort and eventually get a new assignment – after some blissful soul-lounging, one would assume.

What's always bothered me about this system is that the soul is told what the human needs *before* the human is even born. Now, assuming that the human is a *tabula rasa*, then why would it need to be taught a specific "soul" lesson? Wouldn't any old lesson do?

To my way of thinking, isn't it the soul itself, that entity which is going through all of these "lives", these instructions and lessons, these returns to benevolence and light – isn't *that* the entity which is really the one benefiting from all of these trials and errors?

What makes more sense to me is that we humans are simply vessels for the divine that temporarily resides within us.

*I was strolling around Amsterdam on wide avenues, feeling fine. I turned a corner to enter the non-existent Amsterdam metro and suddenly found myself in the middle of pitch blackness. I felt my consciousness constrict as an absolute void swept over me like a disease. It surrounded me, suffocating me.*

I woke up petrified and lay awake in bed thinking for a very long time. I decided that I don't ever want to go back to the Blackness, wherever it was.

# Act II
# Universe (-ity)

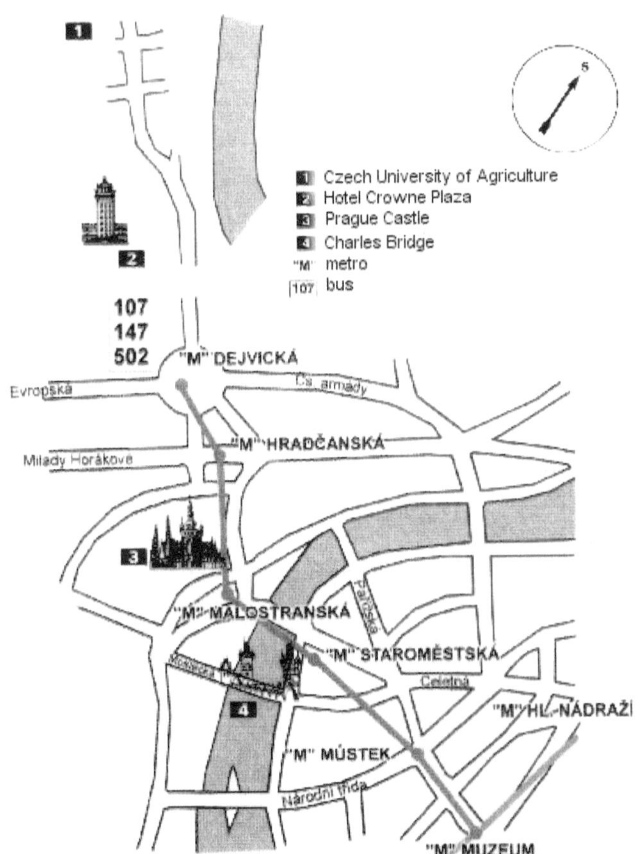

**Late April**

The knock came a little after 21:00, and I finished reading an idea in Kerouak's *Desolation Angels* before shluffing to the door in my slippers. I opened up just as the second knock came, and there, shockingly, was The Fox. She was dressed in jeans and a tight maroon turtleneck that highlighted the reddish glow of her long hair.

I stood there a second too long before I finally said, "Hi, er…" *I had forgotten her name. How could I forget her name?* "… Liliana, wasn't it?"

"You remember."

"Lucky." I smiled and put a hand in my pocket. "So…how are you?"

She frowned, but the glow in her eyes still transfixed me. "I'm good, but I have a problem."

"Yeah? Can I help?"

"I hope yes. I'm searching for Kat… is she maybe here?" She looked over my shoulder into the room.

"Kat? No, I haven't seen her today."

She nodded. "That's my problem – we have class in her room at nine, and she isn't there."

We both looked up the empty hallway in the direction of Kat's room.

I hesitated while the sickening wave of nervous energy passed through me and then said, "Well… you can wait here if you'd like... she might be back soon."

She smiled and said, "I'm not disturbing?"

"No, no – I was just reading."

"Ok, but can we have a note on Kat's door?"

"Sure."

I turned and went back into the room, making happy faces to myself as I walked. Rustling around in a messy drawer, I found some paper, a pen and tape. I turned around and was surprised at the surrealism of seeing Liliana waiting to come in – we hadn't seen each other for months, and now she was coming in for a chat!

As I walked towards her holding the paper, Liliana looked down the hallway and waved, then turned back to me with a wrinkled forehead.

"Kat is here…"

*Well, shit.*

"Oh… well," I said, "that's cool… I'm glad she showed up,".

I popped my head out the door and saw Kat sashaying towards us in her green corduroy jacket and bell-bottom jeans. She was yelling down the hall. "I'm sorry I'm late, Liliana. The bus broke down and we had to wait for another to come pick us up…"

"It's fine. I was just talking to Elijah."

Kat drew up to us and looked at me with a knowing gleam. "Is that right?"

"Yeah, thanks for ruining it," I said.

Liliana blushed as Kat smirked. "I didn't ruin it *for* you… I saved Liliana *from* you!"

We all laughed, Kat the hardest, and then they were sending non-verbal, we're-ready-to-go-signals, so I said, "Liliana, I'm glad I could help you with your problem. Have fun in your lesson, you two."

The girls smiled and said good bye, then turned and walked up the hall. My eyes were glued to their bottoms until they reached Kat's room, when I yanked my head in so they wouldn't see me leering.

I closed the door and sighed, then slumped back into my reading chair and picked up the book.

It was a long time before I could concentrate on Kerouak's ramblings again.

Compared to the student unions of my American university experience, the Czech university's equivalent, the Mensa, was a bit disappointing in its lack of recreational facilities. Instead of being a place to meet and recreate, the Czech Mensa was simply a place to meet and eat.

The Mensa's cafeteria was divided into two sections – one for the students and one for the faculty and staff, and between classes on a bright May day, I made my way to the faculty cafeteria. After choosing from a slim variety of the starchy entrees, I carried my tray out to look for a seat. Just nearby was Alena, an English Instructor who I'd helped with some paper corrections, and another girl I didn't recognize. Alena was a pleasant Czech girl with brown plastic spectacles and straight black hair – her colleague had short red hair and a tough look about her. Alena waved me over.

"Hi, can I join you ladies?"

"Certainly," replied Alena. She spoke British English and behaved properly formal. "Elijah, this is Karen. She's also an English teacher here. Karen, Elijah."

After placing my tray down, I extended my hand for a shake, but Karen's tone of voice when she said, "So *you're* Elijah," made me lower it.

I sat down as Karen continued, "I met a friend of yours a couple of days ago. He came into the language department looking for a girl named Eva. He said she was going to hire him."

I blinked in confusion and said, "Who was it?"

But then I remembered. Three weeks previously I'd told a friend of a friend, Fred, about my job at the Czech University. He was keenly interested, so I told him I'd ask about openings with Eva, the student in charge of organizing the English Courses – courses which fell outside the auspices of the university's language department (this is why I had six months vacation time, a four-day work week, and more pay than "normal" university teachers like Karen and Marcel.)

As Alena looked sheepishly at her food, Karen stared at me for a moment before continuing. "Yeah, he was this British guy looking for work, so I took him to my supervisor."

I chuckled at the absurdity of Fred going to the director of the university language department and asking to work for the illegal English courses – courses which she knew about but most likely disdained because it took away private students, and therefore additional income, from the university lecturers.

Apparently upset at my giggle, Karen barked at me, "You think it's funny?"

I tried to remain calm and said, "I do, because it's perfectly in character with that guy who came up. He's not a friend, by the way. Just an acquaintance."

"Well, he mentioned your name over and over and said you told him that we were looking for teachers. My supervisor explained to him that you don't really work for the university at all, that you're an illegal worker and an illegal resident and that the English Courses only operate because she doesn't report them to the police."

My amusement at the situation disappeared when she said "illegal worker and resident". While it was true that I was both, it was also true that I would have preferred to be legal – but any time I broached the topic with Eva she'd rebuff me, saying that if I applied for residency status, the whole program would likely be shut down. Once the Czech bureaucracy got involved, she said, it would be too complicated for the students to run any longer.

"So why do you prefer to work like this," Karen asked.

"Like what?"

Her eyes narrowed. "Without residence permits! Without work permits! You do this in America, you go to jail! You're an illegal alien! An illegal worker!"

People from the surrounding tables were now looking at us to see what the ruckus was all about.

"What are you, a cop?"

"No, but I *respect* the law! Unlike you," she sneered. "You think you live in the jungle, eh? Law of the Jungle, perhaps?"

I don't raise my voice very often, but when I do, its deepness helps people get my point. I used it then, saying, "Listen, you can pay taxes without a residence permit. In fact, you don't even know me and you're accusing me – in a public place I might add – of being illegal! They sure teach you good manners here!"

I took a deep breath and continued, "I have an idea, Karen. Why don't we pretend you're not a rude bi-"

I stopped and looked around at the onlookers before turning back to Alena.

"... Alena, I'm sorry, but I didn't start this."

I got up, ignoring her meek protests, and walked away, leaving my tray of food untouched. As I stalked out of the cafeteria, I noticed someone waving at me from a back row. It was Kat and Liliana. I tried to put on my happy face and went over.

Kat looked at me critically and said, "Hey, what's wrong? Where's the smile?"

I grunted and said, "You know a girl named Karen, works in the language department?"

"No. Why?"

"She just jumped all over me for working under the table! She was actually yelling at me, making a huge scene, peoples' heads turning… you didn't hear it?"

"No! Did it just happen?"

"Yeah, I just walked away from them – they're right over there." I pointed at them until Liliana said, "Oh, I know that girl – she's very unpleasant."

"Tell me about it."

Kat asked, "What business is it of hers, anyway?"

"Exactly!"

"I know that girl from a long time," Liliana said, "and she is very mean. It is not just to you, but to everyone."

"Well, she ruined my mood all right."

"But you know," said Kat, "I really does suck that the university won't sponsor us for living and working permits. It puts us in a difficult position."

"Yeah… but really, who's gonna check on us?"

"You don't have any permits for working or living here," asked Liliana.

Kat told her that Americans had no-visa necessary, three-month access to Czech soil. These three months were often used to take low-paying, black-market teaching jobs, but very often private language schools would sponsor the teachers for long-term documentation. This was not the case with us, however.

Liliana nodded as she took this in, and then smiled at the two of us. "So you're criminals – how *exciting*!"

We laughed and Kat said, "Yeah! We're dangerous, too. Especially Elijah."

Liliana raised her eyebrows and turned to me. "Oh?"

"Oh yeah. You wouldn't believe it."

"Tell me how bad you are," said Liliana, squirming in her seat.

I was about to talk some bullshit when Kat looked dramatically at her watch and said, "I'm sorry, but I have to run. Will you two be all right together?"

I eagerly, and Liliana shyly agreed, and as Kat stood up and collected her belongings, she said, "Liliana, 9 o'clock tomorrow, right?"

"Yes, at 9."

"Ok. See you then. *Bye*, Elijah." As she turned away, she held my eyes long enough to let me know that I owed her big time. I winked at her.

And then Liliana and I were alone, smiling awkwardly at each other. My mind raced through a hundred different questions before settling on a neutral topic – her work at the university.

She told me she was working on her doctoral dissertation in economics and also had a few international projects that she worked on – one that took her to Austria four or five times per year. That reminded me about my arrival in Vienna – when I got lost and headed to Poland instead of the Czech Republic – so I told her the story as she ate.

When she had finished her meal, we spoke easily for perhaps ten minutes more and then she apologized – she had to get back to work. I was in no hurry to part ways, so after we left the Mensa I walked her to her office.

At the front door of her building I told her I had enjoyed speaking to her and asked, "Maybe we could do it again sometime?"

"I'd like it," she said.

We smiled big at each other and then Liliana said, "But I have to go now, really. Bye, Elijah."

"Bye."

With that, she turned around and immediately bumped into the closed glass door. I grimaced and asked if she were all right, and she turned and smiled at me. We both burst out giggling then, and I reached around to open the door for her. "I'm sorry. I should have done this in the first place."

Red but still smiling, Liliana thanked me and hurried inside.

Letting the door shut, I turned around and reveled in the brightly shining sun. Closing my eyes, I breathed deeply and then walked back to my room to prepare for next class.

Naturally, I smiled like an idiot the whole rest of the day.

Karel was one of the many Czech students I knew who'd spent a summer working in the U.S. as cheap labor. Short and well-built, he'd lived and worked in the state of Washington picking strawberries the year before.

Anyway, at the beginning of the second semester, Karel had begun inviting me to the pub or to the gym a few times a week, and these meetings were beneficial to the both of us – Karel got to practice his English and I got to learn about Czech culture from a native.

One evening at the pub, Karel mentioned a boat trip on the Vltava River that he was organizing in mid-May. "I've done it for three years now and it's always fun – there's singing, drinking, and the river is really nice. Maybe you could bring Mad." He smirked and stifled a laugh.

The Mad story had slipped out once and now he always teased me about it.

"Funny. But how about you be my date instead?"

Karel couldn't stifle his laughter any longer and we both giggled, toasting each other's jokes. As we drank, I pictured Liliana and myself on the boat ride, drinking wine and getting to know each other better, maybe dancing...

Karel asked me if I wanted to reserve a place for myself, but optimistic me said no – I wanted two.

The next afternoon, still bleary from the night before, I went to the computer lab and searched the university database for Liliana's email address. Then I spent 45 minutes writing a 3-line invitation to the boat trip, agonizing over whether to adopt a subtle but forward, funny but reserved, or simple but sweet voice. In the end, I opted for all the above, and threw in gently macho for good measure.

Pressing "send" spurred my mind to obsessive thoughts of rejection or acceptance, the reasons behind those possibilities, how I'd react to them, or even if Liliana would write back at all.

I left the computer lab and meandered across campus back to my room, my head filled with alternating visions of delight and disturbance. As I walked along the narrow, pot-holed road that led to the Foreigner Ghetto, a soft voice floated to me. I looked up the empty road and then into the parking lot on my left. As always, I was amused to see it filled with old beater Škodas and Ladas, but I found no body to match the voice.

I continued walking towards my dorm and heard the voice again. This time I was able to put a direction to it – it was coming from the dormitory next to mine. Looking at the broad façade of the socialist-style dorm, I saw movement in a third-floor window. Someone was waving. Then I recognized her – it was Liliana, leaning out the window and calling me over.

*Well, well.*

I cut through the parking lot and walked into the overgrown grass in front of the building, sustaining eye-contact the whole time. When I was perhaps 50 yards from the window I yelled, "Hey, Liliana! I didn't know you lived here… I live right next door!"

Leaning out of the window, her long chestnut hair falling to one side, Liliana's smile penetrated me.

"I know! I visited you, remember?"

I blinked a moment before answering.

"Right! Sorry…" I looked down and kicked at a clump of grass.

"I just got your email," she said.

I looked up suddenly. "Yeah? Already?"

"Yes, I have a computer in my room."

"That's convenient."

"Yes, I like it very much. I wrote you back… did you get my message?

"No… uh…" my stomach exploded but I still managed to ask, "What did you write?"

"I'd love to go on a boat trip with you!"

*YES!*

"That's perfect! I'm really happy you can come!

"I too."

"Yeah!"

We smiled and nodded and I could find nothing to say. I was just basking in the delight of it all.

Then Liliana said, "Well, I have to work some more now... but why don't you visit sometime? My room number is 313."

"Great! I will!"

After we said goodbye, I floated back to my room grinning like a dumb shmack at the prospect of a date with Liliana, and when I sat down at my desk I realized I couldn't concentrate at all on my lesson preparations.

It was still early in the day, so I readied my army-green backpack and struck out for a walk in the town – there was a park on the map that I'd never been to, and I headed for it, bringing along the Bible and a copy of the Tao te Ching.

I was a giddy mess the whole day, like a little boy looking forward to Christmas.

The Chechov Bridge, which spans the Vltava River in the shadow of the giant metronome, is my favorite Prague bridge. For starters, it isn't nearly as touristy as the Charles Bridge, so one can sit underneath it with a good book and truly experience calm there. Secondly, it's architecturally wonderful in its own right. Whereas the Charles Bridge has its statues and arches, the Chechov bridge is lined with bright yellow pillars mounted with winged goddesses and is majestically lit up at night. And lastly, the Chechov bridge is where Liliana and I met for our first date.

I arrived under the bridge at 17:00 and stood on the outskirts of the group of 50 or so students waiting to board the long riverboat. Scanning the crowd for Liliana, I instead spotted Karel's back and waded into the crowd. Coming up behind him, I unshouldered my heavy backpack and set it carefully beside me. Inside were three bottles of white wine, cheese, apples, crackers, and the necessary utensils. I tapped him on the shoulder and he turned around.

"Hey Elijah! Where's your date?"

"She'll be here. Where's yours?"

"Don't have one."

"What?"

"Too much work with organizing. I didn't have time to – *Ahoj, Liliana!*"

I turned around and saw her walking towards us. I smiled as Karel took a step over, kissed her on the cheek, and they spoke Czech to each other.

Karel turned to me and spoke in English, "Elijah, do you know each other? This is Liliana."

I smiled and held out my hand, "Nice to meet you, Liliana."

She took up the act and said, "Nice to meet you, too."

Just then, Karel's name was called and he apologized before running off to deal with something. We were alone in the middle of the crowd.

"You know Karel," I said.

"It's my seventieth year at university. I know a lot of people now."

"Wow! And my parents said *I* was a career student! Are you sure you don't mean *seven* years?"

"OH! Yes, seven... oh, my English is terrible... and I still have some years before I finish my PhD!"

"So you'll be a doctor, eh? What's your field again?"

"Economics."

I nodded my head, inside of which I yawned widely. "That's impressive. Is it difficult?"

"Not after time."

Karel yelled something in Czech over the boat's PA system and everyone in the crowd except me laughed. Moving towards the steep gangway with the crowd, Liliana asked, "Do you speak any Czech?"

"Not really. I can order a beer, but otherwise not much."

"We'll have a little lesson tonight, then."

It took ten minutes to board, and Liliana found us a bench on the top, open level. We sat facing each other across a table, the warm breeze tousling our hair and wafting sea gull calls our way. We opened up the first bottle of white, drank a toast, and fell into a short, comfortable silence as the boat pulled from the dock and fought upstream. As we rounded the bend, the late-afternoon sun was eclipsed by the castle's bulk, which was outlined in a gilded cloud that slowly disappeared as we motored upstream and out of its shadow.

We shifted our attention to the green domes of Malá Strana before Liliana pointed out the statues on the Charles Bridge, and we waved at the multi-colored parade of humanity that leaned over and waved as we passed underneath.

As we approached the locks, smaller boats dodged out of our way and the scenery's drama faded enough for Liliana to ask me, "So, Elijah. Why did you come to Czech Republic?"

I raised my eyebrows. "Good question."

With this, I told her how I'd become somewhat bored in America; how I'd had a well-paying public relations job with the State of Pennsylvania that didn't really demand much of me; how I'd gotten tired of driving everywhere; how mundane everything had started to seem, and that I wanted to do something with my life when I was still young. This discussion lasted through the first bottle of wine, during which time we had passed up Vyšehrad castle. We had also broken out the apples and cheese when Karel and another kid joined us. The other kid, who also seemed to know Liliana, sat beside her. Karel crowded in beside me.

"This is my roommate Honza," said Karel.

As we shook hands, I noticed a severity in Honza's greenish eyes that didn't seem to match his laid-back demeanor.

"Nice to meet you, Honza."

"You too," said Honza. "You're American, eh? Where from?"

"Pennsylvania. Near Pittsburgh."

"I've never been there. I was in Washington with Karel last year… have you ever been?"

"No, never the Northwest."

"Well," said Honza, "you have to go there. It's really beautiful."

"What were you doing there?"

"I was picking up strawberries with Karel. Shit work, but good money."

I noticed the boys eyeing the food laid out on the table, and as soon as I offered, they dug in.

"Thanks," said Karel.

"We call this an American Picnic," said Honza. "Every American packs the exact same thing, don't they?" He smiled at Karel with a mouthful of food.

"Well, you seem to be enjoying it," I said. I didn't like him very much.

"Don't worry about Honza," said Karel. "He had an American girl break his heart, and –"

"Bitch!"

"– and now he says he doesn't like Americans."

Honza looked at me and said, "I think Czechs should stay with Czechs, and Americans with Americans."

"That's silly," said Liliana, causing all our heads to turn in her direction. "If the people are in love, why should it matter where they come from?"

"But geography can be big problem," Honza said. "For example, what if you and Elijah were together, and you had to live in the USA? Could you live so far from your family?"

Blushing, Liliana replied, "I don't know. But if we were in love, our families would have to understand."

"Or," I said, "we'd live half the year in America, and the other half in the Czech Republic."

"Right," said Karel. "and you would fly back and forth on your private jet."

"I *told* you not to mention I was rich." I smiled and winked at Liliana.

"The point is," said Honza, "geography can be a problem. You start to care for other people if you don't live close together. That's what The Bitch did."

Karel nodded at me, "And what you did with Mad and Raquel, Elijah."

I turned and gave him a full-on stink eye.

"What? It's a good story! Tell Honza about how Mad came to your room while Raquel was there… Honza, you have to hear this!"

I could not believe this was happening.

"Who is Raquel," asked Liliana. "And the other one…"

"Mad," volunteered Karel.

"Yes, Mad. Who are these women, Elijah?" Her left eyebrow was lifted.

I took a drink of wine and looked at them.

"I don't want to tell that story."

"Come! I want to know about all your women," said Liliana.

I shook my head.

Karel said, "Ok, I'll tell it…. It all starts with Elijah and Raquel, his girl from America-"

"She's *not* my girl."

"… his girl from America who came to visit a week ago. While he was naked in bed with her…"

"All right, shut up. I'll tell it myself!"

Karel took a smug bite of his cheese and they all looked at me.

"Ok, it's like this. When I lived in the U.S., I was friends with a girl named Raquel, and we kept in contact."

"Did you sleep with her," asked Honza.

I looked at him.

"In the States, I mean."

"Yes."

Liliana asked, "And here?"

I looked at her and said, "Also."

"How often," asked Karel.

"Fuck you. The–"

"Yeah, how often," asked Liliana.

I looked at her and said, "You too." I hoped she wouldn't be hurt by the strong joke, but I also felt cornered enough that I didn't care all that much.

"So anyway, we kept in touch and she came over during her spring break. She stayed for a week, we got along well, and she'd like to be together. The problem is, I'm not ready to go back to America. Now that I'm here, I want to stay as long as I can…"

"Ok, but who is Mad," asked Honza.

"Mad is a Czech girl I met last year. We see each other on and off."

"How old is she," asked Karel, laughing.

I looked over at him and said, "I'm gonna get you back, you know."

"Yeah, how old is she," asked Liliana.

I looked at the riverbank on my left and wiped my mouth with my hand. I avoided looking at Liliana and turned instead to Honza.

"Eighteen."

"Wow," said Honza. "Good work, dude!" He reached over for a high-five, but I left him hangin'.

I looked over at Liliana, who was smirking and shaking her head. "*Eighteen*? Elijah, she is a child."

"It's all legal," I said, perhaps a little too defensively.

Liliana continued shaking her head but she seemed more entertained than appalled.

"That's not even the best part," goaded Karel. "Tell them about her coming to the room."

I took a deep breath, trying to calm the kicking child of absurdity in my womb.

"All right. The thing is… we thought Mad was pregnant."

(I had lied to Karel and told him that we thought Mad, not Simona, was the pregnant one.)

I looked around at all of them and nodded. Liliana and Honza had big eyes but Karel was smiling like a proud daddy.

"So, just to recap, I'm 27, sleeping with a girl who's 18. We think she's pregnant, but aren't sure. Into the middle of this situation comes Raquel, who wants me to move back to the States and be with her."

"Shit," said Honza, taking a drink of his beer.

"Yeah, so Mad promised she'd stay away during the week of Raquel's visit, right? But in the end she said she *forgot* the day Raquel was leaving and instead of coming over on Sunday, she came over on Saturday night, which was Raquel's last night here."

"Man! Is she a little dumb, or what," asked Honza.

"Poor girls," said Liliana. And then, "Wait a second… Mad knew about Raquel and didn't care?"

"She didn't have much choice, did she?"

"And did Raquel know about Mad?"

"I mentioned her, but I doubt she thought we were sleeping together."

"Poor girls…"

"Yeah, yeah. Anyway, Raquel and I were in bed and there was a knock on the door. Of course it was Mad, yelling through the door that she had to tell me about her pregnancy test. Raquel wonders why she's yelling such things to me, and I'm trying to stay in bed so Mad will go away, but Raquel wants to open the door naked to see what the hell is going on, why this girl is yelling about pregnancy to her man…"

"Did you open the door?" asked Liliana.

"Yeah, but not before Mad yelled that "WE" weren't pregnant, which is when naked Raquel jumped out of bed and jumped all over Mad and me. Mad seemed legitimately shocked that Raquel was still there, but after being called a whore over and over, she got all vulgar and nasty back to Raquel. It woulda been a catfight but I closed the door on Mad and let her pound and scream until she went away. Meanwhile, Raquel was stomping around, packing her bags, cursing me out."

Honza asked, "Have you seen Mad since then?"

"No, I've been afraid to go to her house. Her dad would probably kill me."

"And what about Raquel?"

"She had me call a taxi. She said she'd rather sleep in a ditch than with me, which I personally find hard to believe. Her flight didn't leave until the next day, so I reckon she stayed in a hotel, but I don't know. I tried calling her parents, but they just act cold and take my messages. She doesn't answer my emails and its been over two weeks now, so I reckon that's the end of that."

The boat was executing a 180 degree turn, using the current instead of its engines.

I took a drink and looked at them. Honza wanted another high-five but I declined. Telling the story had left me empty – the emotional scars were still close to home and the duplicity of dating both girls at the same time made me feel genuinely bad about what happened. For her part, Liliana didn't turn cold as I'd expected, but seemed to have enjoyed hearing the tale. After the food was gone, the boys went to another part of the boat and we continued drinking as the twilight surrounded us.

"So I've told you all of my dirty secrets, Liliana. Now it's your turn."

"I don't have secrets like yours. Not so dramatic."

"Good for you."

"But I do have one…" She looked at the table. "Like your Raquel in America, I have a man in Austria."

*Shiiiiiiit.*

"You do?"

"Yes, but we see each other seldom. Perhaps once per month. Sometimes less."

"How long have you been together?"

"Seven years."

"What!?!"

"Yes, it's a long time. But we don't speak about me now. He isn't here, so let's speak about us."

"Uh… fine with me."

But as often happened when I didn't have enough information, my mind started making things up, and before long I was having random images of the Austrian and Liliana together. I had to fight them away just to remain conversant.

We chatted about our travels and families for the rest of the trip and finished the third bottle of wine just before we docked at 22:00. When we disembarked there was a lot of loud milling around on the dock; some groups were continuing out into the town, some were taking the metro home, and others decided to walk across the Chechov bridge, up the wide stairs to the metronome, and then through Letna Park.

Liliana and I joined the last group, which numbered about ten people. The others must have had a lot more to drink than we had because they were unsteadily lurching all over the place as we crossed the bridge.

One of the boys, very drunk, was weaving his way along the edge of the sidewalk when he stumbled. He had one leg out into the road, about to step out onto the street, when an arm from his group grabbed his collar and yanked him from in front of a bus that was speeding by.

Both me and Liliana went slack-jawed – the boy's life had literally been saved before our eyes, and the boy didn't even know that he'd almost been killed.

That happening, plus the wine, stimulated me to speak about spirituality, and I began to hold forth about the value of living every day to its fullest. Liliana agreed and this complicity spurred me on to a half-baked definition of love, which she agreed with up to a point but then refined, adding several important aspects that in my inebriation I had overlooked.

The 45-minute walk to the bus station was over far too soon, and I hoped to continue the discussion about love on the bus. However, once aboard, Liliana fell asleep on my shoulder, which was probably more endearing than any amount of chatting could have been.

When I woke her up at our bus stop, Liliana was no longer exhibiting the feeling of closeness we had been enjoying and acted only tired. I had planned on inviting myself in to her room for some more concrete examples of love, but instead I gave her a kiss on the cheek at her door and retired to my room for a chew.

For two days I walked on clouds remembering our date. And then that weekend, with the mood I was in, the weather – cool twilight beginnings – the sun almost down and everything positively *glowing*, I moseyed around Kampa park, digging on the Vltava and the opposite riverbank with the National Theatre and the amazing soft white glow bouncing off of everything and everyone and I suddenly was struck by the LOVE OF LIFE and EVERYTHING in it.

I walked, glowing and empty, across Kampa to where the stream is, digging the moving water, some girls as well, and then finally, before walking over the bridge and away from the island, I watched two puppies cavorting with each other and everyone around them in openness and joy.

And then across the small pedestrian bridge, up past the John Lennon wall and into Malá Strana, where the streets of eternal Europe opened up to me and spilled out secrets of architecture, texture and peace as I stood in front of a Ministry Of Culture building and listened to cello music pouring out of the open windows. I stood there and dug the crazy, still glowing light of European splendor and I knew how lucky I was to be there.

I walked around the quarter passing perfect buildings and villas and churches and falling in love again with Prague, the beautiful twilight city of my dreams, until, in front of the Greek Embassy, I walked under a flowering tree and got hit full in the face by the crisp night air saturated with heady fragrant white blossoms, just closing up shop for the night and giving one last burst, petals of spent blossoms petalling the ground. I stood there smelling flowers for the first time of the year and life was perfect.

I caught the tram over to Colin's, where he and Josh were hanging out and we joked and laughed and drank beers and smoked some of Josh's hooch. Then Colin broke out his saxophone and Josh surprised the hell out of us by playing these unbelievable tunes of blues and jazz. He played one he called, "Mad, Elijah and Raquel", and it was all chaotic and jittery – he nailed the relationships on the head, ok.

Man, he was blowing awesome and me and Colin would look at each other and acknowledge that here we had us a genuine saxophone angel blowing us a sweet song on a Saturday night – everyone full of booze and laughter.

It was a perfect night until the neighbors came round to complain – only 11:15 on a Saturday night, and complaints about wonderful music being played – just beastly.

So then we listened to CDs and laughed and I bummed a smoke and left – at the bus stop smoking the butt I was one step away from visibly intoxicated but felt like I was in good control. Then the bus ride home swayed me to sleep and I woke up at the end station – a 15 minute extra walk on unlit streets until I got home and crashed.

What a day, what a day.

Liliana and I went out to dinner and had a wonderful time the next night. She was funny, charming, and entirely positive. We laughed a lot, had great conversations about our travels, our past loves, our current relationships, our futures.

It ended with a walk home through a Prague Spring night filled with the moon, stars, crisp night air and the tortured scent of blossoms waiting for the dawn. A perfect night, she even paid, and we had plans to go out soon.

Life!

And then the Siren's Scream of my uncertain future began howling. Eva bumped into me on campus and told me that our classes were up for review and might not be around the next year, and that no one knew when the word would come. Thrown into turmoil, the following possibilities hurled at me:

1. Remain in Prague, try living from the meager wages I would get from private students and sporadic business classes.
2. Go to Poland for the summer.
3. Go back to the States for whatever summer work I could find.

I had in mind a two-year stay abroad and it was still feasible, but my lovely university position was apparently in jeopardy. So the question was: Continue feeding the wanderlust or pack it in? Go back to the States and hope to muster the *cajones* and the resources to make it out again, or stay out of the box and remain poor (but not of spirit)?

❂

Liliana and I settled into a twice-weekly dinner schedule. Both of us enjoyed her cooking more than my bachelor cuisine, and after a few of my botched experiments we agreed that dinners would henceforth take place in her room.

Compared to my place in the Foreigner Ghetto, Liliana's room was a slice of heaven – it had carpeting, posters, throw-pillows and was totally cozy when her roommate wasn't there. In fact, for the first two weeks of my visits, Liliana arranged with Marek, her roommate, to stay away when I came over.

And yes, to my American sensibilities, Liliana having a long-distance Austrian boy was troubling enough. That she also had a male roommate was simply beyond my comprehension; I had to work hard to control my feelings of jealousy. And my negative vibes were not soothed when I finally did meet him.

It was around 20:00 on a school night, and me and Liliana were sitting close as we corrected a letter on her computer. In fact, Liliana was sitting on my lap when we heard Marek's key enter the lock.

Scrambling to avoid being seen on my lap, Liliana was a touch too slow. Marek, tall and with short-cropped blonde hair, opened the door and stopped short. Liliana finally succeeded in standing up and introduced us, so I stood up and held out my hand. Instead of taking it, however, Marek turned his back and went into the bathroom.

As me and Liliana looked at each other blankly, Marek called her into the bathroom.

"I'm sorry," she said, "but he's very protective. I'll be right back." She went into the bathroom and the door closed behind her. I heard an animated exchange in Czech.

*Protective my foot*, I thought. *You're together, and if you're not together, then he wants to be. No way can you live together and there's nothing going on, especially when he reacts to me like that.*

I sat back down at the computer and corrected the same sentence ten times as they argued in the bathroom. Sometime later they emerged.

When Liliana came over and sat on my lap again, I felt Marek's hate-rays drill into my back. Trying to ignore him, we worked on the paper for a few more minutes and when we finished I stood and said, "Ok, I'm gonna go."

"You don't have to leave already. Forget about him."

Marek apparently didn't speak English.

"No, I feel uncomfortable. But why don't you walk me home?"

She agreed, and as we stood up from the desk we heard the ruffle of newspaper. Turning around, we saw Marek lying on the bed, pretending to read the magazine he was holding in front of his face.

I said goodbye in Czech and Marek responded by grunting.

*Nice manners*, I thought.

As she closed the door behind us, Liliana apologized for Marek's behavior.

"Don't worry about it," I said, "I'd be jealous, too."

"He's not *jealous*. He's angry because he knows Manfred and he doesn't want me to do something bad with you."

"Is that what he said, that we're doing something bad?"

"Yes, but I told him that it's not his worry – I'm a woman and I can make my own decisions."

"Right you are," I said. We fell into silence as we walked out the building's front door and through the parking lot.

When we reached my building we stopped and I said, "Still, he doesn't seem to like me very much."

"Oh… he'll be fine. He just doesn't know you. He only sees you're a foreigner, and he wants me to find a good Czech boy, not an Austrian or an American."

"What's wrong with foreigners?"

"Some people don't like them. But no worry, you don't have to be with Marek, you have to be with me!"

She reached out and hugged me and as we embraced, I said, "Why don't you come in for a minute?"

She smiled at me. "I want to, but I have to stand up early tomorrow."

"Just for a second," I said, holding her hand.

"I really can't. But next time, ok?"

I nodded and said, "Ok, next time we have dinner here, yeah?"

"Yes. And I'll bring the wine."

With that, I leaned in and kissed her, our first kiss.

After we opened our eyes, she said, "Hey! That was no friendship kiss!"

"Nope," I grinned. "I think you like me."

Smiling, she turned and walked away.

I watched her walk, and when she got to her building she looked back and waved.

Back in my room, I leaned back against the front door and sighed in the darkness. My heart was so full and yet so empty. I felt indescribably light and unbearably burdened all at once.

What a kiss.

During the next date in my room, after the meal had been eaten and the dishes cleared away, Liliana sat across from me drinking red wine. She was in the reading chair and I was sitting on the bed.

We were speaking about ex-lovers once more, and she was speaking about a boy that we both knew when I said, "Wow. You've got so many options for men – it must be nice!"

She scrunched up her face and said, "It's actually not so good, because I find myself alone."

"But… then it must be your own choice to be alone…"

"Yes, because of my situation… my friend in Austria…"

It hurt to even hear the country's name now. I looked at her deeply and asked, "So where do I fit in?"

She began to blush and said, "What do you mean?"

I cocked my head and said, "I mean, what are your intentions for us?"

"Intentions? I don't know this word."

I got up, produced my Czech-English pocket dictionary and looked up the word "intention." I showed her the Czech translation and she smiled at me.

"I don't know my *intentions*. I… I don't even know your feelings…"

"*What*?"

"I don't know how you feel about–"

"You don't *know* how I feel about you!?"

She puckered her lips and said, "Maybe you should tell me…"

"Oh, I have to start, do I?"

Liliana nodded while I drank my wine. I placed my glass down on the table and rubbed my hands together.

"That seems unfair, but ok. So, how do I feel about you? Hmm… Well, I'm happy when I'm with you and – What are you smiling at? – I want to spend as much time together as possible… you really didn't know that?"

Liliana moved her hand away from her mouth and said, "Well, I hoped you did."

We looked at each other with a soft, calm affection that went on until I couldn't stand it any longer. I stood up and kissed her on the cheeks and forehead before sitting back down across from her.

"You really didn't know I feel that way about you?"

"Well, people from different countries act differently… I wasn't sure…"

"Well, again, I really like spending time with you…" I laughed. "In fact, today after I walked away from seeing you, three people asked me why I was smiling so much."

Liliana looked at me for a full five seconds before she stood and came over to the bed. She embraced me for a long time before returning to her seat and we were both feeling it and it felt wonderful to have the feelings confirmed.

As she took a drink of wine, however, her look darkened.

"But it can be dangerous," she said.

"Dangerous how?"

"What if we fall in love? Then I have hard decisions…"

"Well, life is full of them…"

"But... I'm afraid of such decisions."

"Well, we won't talk about them."

She looked at me with a grin and said, "What will we do if we don't talk?"

I held out my hands for her and she came to me, leaning over, enveloping me in her hair, a protective Lillian canopy where I felt no harm could befall me.

It was 21:30 when we started kissing, and 00:30 when I walked her back to her dorm. After saying goodnight, I floated home and went to bed, smelling the pillows where Liliana had been laying just minutes before. I lay there remembering and shivering in anticipated ecstasy before falling into a sleep of blissful infatuation.

The next day, in one of my last English classes of the academic year, I wanted to reward the students for having put in a good semester of work by filling their last class with fun activities. One of the games was this: I cut paper stock into small cards and wrote important words on them that we had learned over the course of the semester. Each student had a card pinned on their back and showed this card to the other students. The student with the card on the back would then ask questions of others to discover what he or she "was."

On one of the student's backs was the word, "Love."

He had already circulated to the other students and finally walked over to me. He showed me the card and his first question was, "Is it good?"

Dreamily thinking of Liliana, I purred out, "Yeeeaahhh."

The student, a big macho type, blinked for a moment and then mimicked me, "Yeaaaaahhhh."

The class, which had been watching, all laughed and one of the students asked, "So who's the girl?"

Struggling to maintain my composure, I said, "I'll tell you next semester."

As I walked through the parking lot, I heard the wind carry my name and looked up to Liliana's room. She was there waving at me, so I walked over through the grass, again beguiled as she leaned out the window. When I was within hearing distance, she asked if I'd be in my room at 17:00.

"I'm sorry, but I won't... I sent you an email and I left a note on my door – I forgot about a meeting with Karel to play billiards."

"Oh... well... can I come?"

"Absolutely! But can we meet at the pub? I'm already late."

"Fine. I'm working, but am over soon, ok?"

"Great! See you soon!"

We looked at each other for a long smiling moment of shared glow and then I turned away.

Walking into the pub five minutes late, I saw that Karel already had a table, so I ordered myself a beer and walked over to him.

"Hey, did you bring your money," he asked.

"No. In fact, I told the barman you'd pay for this one."

He laughed and I went over to choose a stick. Karel had been practicing and the balls were scattered. I returned and shot a few for practice, then racked the balls for Karel to break.

Midway through the first game, Karel asked, "Why do you keep looking at the door?"

"I'm not."

Smirking, he went back to the game and I went back to watching the door. Before long, I had lost three straight games.

Finally, Liliana came in the door and as I watched her walking towards us, Karel said, "Hey Elijah! Your shot!"

"Wait a second, willya?"

Liliana came over and shook our hands, accepting cheek kisses from both of us, and asked how we were playing.

"He's a bit distracted today," said Karel.

"Karel's just playing well," I said.

Liliana looked at us skeptically and then asked if we needed another beer. We both said yes and she went up to the bar.

During the time she was away I scratched on the eight ball, making it four straight losses to Karel, who I normally dominated.

Shaking my head, I gathered and racked the balls. Karel broke. He didn't sink any, but set up the solids in an unbelievably simple pattern – I immediately spotted the order in which to proceed and set about sinking the balls. By the time Liliana had come back with the beers, I had potted five. Still deep into the game, I heard Karel and her speaking in Czech, but continued to shoot until I sank the 8-ball in the proper corner.

With that, I looked up to see the glow in Liliana's eyes as she clapped – and the disgust in Karel's as he drank his beer.

We played once more and I spanked Karel so badly that he said, "That's enough for me. You'll win your money back if I don't stop now."

"I guess I just needed the proper motivation," I said.

"I see that."

After Karel said his goodbyes, Liliana and I sat at one of the nearby tables.

A placard on the wall advertised the rock group "Laura and her Tigers", which led the conversation to dogs and cats, and Liliana said that she really liked dogs. I agreed but also said that I liked the independence of cats. Liliana said that's exactly what she didn't like about them, and wrapped up the topic by saying, "Well, we'll have a dog for me and a cat for you, then."

I looked at her with a smile. "And where will we be living when we have these pets?"

"That depends on when we–"

And there she stopped, apparently realizing that we weren't even officially girl/boyfriend and she was already planning out our future. She flashed me a lovely, demure smile.

I smiled back and said, "It's ok. I have thoughts like that too."

"You do?"

"Of course."

"But it's strange you would think such things – you're from so far away... What we do for the future?"

"How should I know?"

"Don't you care?"

"Yeah, but in a vague sort of way. Like, I'm reasonably sure that the future will be good, but we really have no idea – maybe it will be dark and horrible."

"Exactly. And that doesn't worry you?"

"Why should it? It will be horrible if I worry or not."

"Because if you worry about it, maybe you can *do* anything about it."

"Maybe. But the only thing I can *really* do is be the best Elijah I can be. And if I'm a good person, I'll naturally do good things in the world. That's all I can really worry about and that's why I don't worry about the future or what it will bring. For now, I'm just happy that you and I are able to spend time together. In fact, I think being with you is the best thing I can do."

She blushed and shook her head. "You hardly know me..."

"True, but the more I know, the more I want to know. Now, about the future... tell me, what are you doing this weekend?"

Her smile faded and was replaced by a wrinkled-forehead expression. She sighed and looked at me a moment before saying, "I wanted to tell you before, but... my friend from Austria is coming."

"Oh... yeah? Huh." I looked away and drank some of the beer. Just a moment before I had been feeling so very into this thing we were creating, and now I was being reminded that this thing wasn't the only one that Liliana belonged to, that basically I was the other man.

"Elijah, talk to me."

"What do you want me to say?"

"Anything. What you're thinking."

"Ok. I think it's unfair."

"But you had your Raquel and Mad, didn't you?"

I looked at her for a long moment.

She continued, "And I didn't plan for us to feel this way. I really don't know what to do."

"Neither do I, but here we are."

"It's unpleasant, isn't it?"

"You know, I hadn't really thought about Mad and Raquel's feelings before you mentioned them just now. Those poor girls if I made them feel like I do now."

"But you didn't tell Mad to come visit you then – that was her thing."

"Yeah, but I was the one two-timing."

"Two-timing?"

"If someone dates two people at the same time, like..."

"Me and Manfred?"

"Well... yeah. That makes you a two-timer, sorry to say."

"I don't like being a two-timer."

"Me neither."

There was a long silence and then I asked, "How long will he be here?"

"Six days."

*Shiiiit.*

"When does he arrive?"

"Tomorrow morning."

"*What?*"

She looked at me, sad, and said, "I couldn't think of how to tell you."

I sighed and asked, "Is he staying with you?"

She looked down at her beer and nodded.

I looked over her shoulder and imagined seeing the two of them – my girl and some Austrian fungo – walking across campus, kissing, making love – and it felt like someone had kicked me in the stomach. I had never felt such intense jealousy – it actually pulsed – and the heaviness in my chest wouldn't go away with any amount of deep breathing.

Finally I stood up. "Well, I'll just see you next week after he leaves... you'll come and see me then, yeah?"

Liliana looked up at me and asked, "Where are you going?"

"I have to meet Josh in town," I lied.

"Oh… But don't you want to– "

"No. I'll just see you after… I'll see you next week."

I walked out of the pub without looking back and cursed my feelings, cursed Liliana, and cursed the dirty Austrian all the way back to my room.

I entered my front door and looked around – I wasn't nearly calm enough to read. I could drink but that would just make me more jealous. So I packed my bag, took the bus into town and started walking.

I hoofed around town completely obsessing, and even praying at St. Vitus' was only marginally soothing. I read the Bible and prayed and prayed, but couldn't unburden the heaviness in my chest.

After tramping all through the town – I walked for like four hours – I was finally so exhausted that I wasn't thinking of Liliana anymore. I headed for home and jumped in bed.

Around midnight there was a knock on my door. I was tempted to ignore it, but eventually answered. It was Liliana, saying things like, "I had to see you… I was lying there feeling so lonely…" and so on.

It was such a relief seeing her, but at the same time it was so damned hurtful knowing her boyfriend was coming the next day.

After a few moments of standing in the doorway, she said she had to get up at 06:00 and really had to get to sleep. I asked if she'd like to stay the night, mostly as a joke, but to my surprise she accepted!

Just hours before I had been so terribly jealous (wasted energy) and now Liliana was here wanting to sleep with me. We pushed my single beds together and for the first time were skin-to-skin – spooning, nuzzling, snuggling ourselves to sleep. It was totally fulfilling, but at the same time completely sorrowful.

We awoke several times during the night and dreamily re-snuggled into position. When 06:00 came, we had a long hug good-bye that was so much better than my hasty, hurt rush out of the pub.

But it was still awful picturing them together.

The following week was one of distressing contrasts. Thinking I'd run into Liliana around every corner with her dirty Austrian made me edgy, so after classes I'd rush across campus and into town, not coming back until the shadows concealed me.

Beset by jealousy and anger on my walks, I'd rage against my situation, feeling as if Liliana were the most vile, duplicitous girl I'd ever known. The insidious pleasure of these thoughts was that I could gnaw on the same idea over and over and in the end she was *always* wrong and I was right. It was obvious. I walked around having imaginary quarrels with her, trying out various lines of argumentation until I found the proper threads. I anticipated retorts and refuted them brusquely, defending my feelings to the utmost, pressing the idea that she was making me feel bad, that she was being inconsiderate of my feelings, insinuating that *she* was the one responsible for my misery and I myself was the victim.

In short, I blamed Liliana for the sum total of my unhappiness.

And yes, there was a seed of truth in my over-constructed labyrinth of self-deception – she *was* with another man, was she not.

But I wasn't always so distressed, and during the clear moments I tried to rationally analyze why I was feeling like I was.

Eventually, it all boiled down to my high school years.

It sounds ridiculous to put it so simply, but the roots of my jealousy tree seemed to be a high school episode that ended badly. The short story is that a cheerleader dissed me, but hard.

The long story is this: As so often happens with American boys, I was infatuated with a blonde, pony-tailed cheerleader. But unfortunately for teenage me, I was not athletic and not one for socializing, so popular wasn't a label that ever stuck. Oh, I had plenty of friends, but I was never part of the "in" crowd, which placed the cheerleaders, especially Karmie, out of my league.

I admired Karmie from varying distances during high school, and we even got to be friends of a sort after having a class together in our junior year. But my continued obsessing was, ironically, counter-productive, and I succeeded only in pushing her away. Then in our senior year, a breakthrough: One of my friends planned on asking Karmie's good friend to the Senior Prom, so between classes I approached Karmie and pitched the idea of double-dating – the four of us could have a really fun time together, blah blah blah.

She reacted skeptically and told me she'd think about it. Then at lunch a few weeks later, after I had pretty much given up on an answer, she glided over my table surrounded by her entourage, and agreed to go with me.

Delirious and grinning, I stood and asked her to shake on it. She shook her head and with a wry smile took my hand, thus validating my long-standing obsession and allowing the seed I'd been tending for so long to sprout and grow.

Now that I'd finally secured a date, I knew I could convince her that we should be together. I looked past the Prom, past a number of summer dates, and envisioned the day when Karmie and I would consummate our relationship, preferably with her wearing her cheerleader outfit.

But the Prom was still to be attended to, and the flurry of planning and sense of urgency that leads up to them was entered into. Karmie took the lead in planning: She made the dinner reservations, came with me to choose my tuxedo, and even chose her own bouquet.

I was naturally beside myself with pleasure. My four-year affliction was being rewarded as Karmie and I spent more and more time together, and I was ecstatic to be privy to the cool crowd buzz, that illusory grapevine the underclasses hear about but are never allowed access to. I was becoming popular by association.

Alas, teenage alliances are capricious, and despite my frenzied objections, my friend backed out of the foursome plan in order to go with a cheerleader of his own. Thus, two weeks before prom my worst fears were realized: I simply didn't have enough mojo to keep Karmie as my date, which she cheerfully and cosmetically explained to me in the hallway between classes.

Externally, I tried to take the news well, hoping that being a good sport would keep a window of opportunity open. But internally I was a volcano of obsessive anger and insecurity. I'd been presented with the awful truth, The Cheerleader's Verdict – I just wasn't mojoed enough.

In the ensuing years, like a dumbass, I used Karmie's assessment as a guide when dealing with women. And since insecure and obsessive are rarely traits that people seek out in their mates, my early romantic past became a sort of wasteland in tribute to Karmie's pronouncement.

But of course I had ~~not~~ managed to outgrow all that and had ~~not~~ become self-assured. Yes, Karmie had put a hurting on my self-esteem, but I'd ~~not~~ gotten past it.

Bad Karmie.

"*And now Liliana is doing the same thing*," wailed the Banshees. I listened to their screams, wallowed in the remorse and self-pity they brought as gifts, and my mood would grow foul.

For brief spells, however, I would let go of my black, chaotic emotions and succumb to periods of calm and lucidity. These were mostly brought about by spending time in Kampa park playing hacky sack, smoking grass, and reading the Tao, the Bible, or some other philosophical text.

One book I read during that time – in a *day* – was called *Siddhartha*, by Herman Hesse. Of particular interest was the description of Buddhist meditation from an internal point of view, and I decided to replicate the meditation techniques to help me through my current turmoil.

In the late evenings, then, I sat in my room in the dark trying to meditate away my frustrations and afflictions. And though I came nowhere close to enlightenment, I did become sufficiently calm that I could, sometimes, examine my situation from a more objective standpoint.

The end of the academic year arrived and I was faced with the bittersweet pleasure of saying goodbye to classes full of people of whom I'd grown terribly fond. Many of them would be around the next year, but others were graduating and would be gone for good, which brought out a nostalgic sadness.

Four of my five classes were filled with hard-working students committed to learning English, and this helped me form solid relationships with most of them. And the progress they made! For example, I had a class full of beginners who on the first day couldn't speak a word, but at the end of the semester were capable of *conversing*! Their progress, and the accompanying pride I felt over their efforts, was more fulfilling than I would have thought possible. I honestly loved seeing my students become more proficient, and found it rewarding to have a job wherein I could help people achieve a goal such as learning. I knew I'd miss it over the summer.

But as sad as the end of classes was, even worse was when my bathroommate Marcel moved home to France. We had become close over the year, so when he asked me to help get his luggage across the city to the bus station, I was happy to oblige. The bus left at 14:00, so at noon on the pre-arranged day, I went through the bathroom to see how his packing was progressing.

His door was open and I found him in the middle of his moving-out inspection. A brusque, matronly Czech woman was bustling around the room, scrutinizing the shoddy furniture for signs of damage.

"How long until we leave," I asked.

"I don't know," he snapped. "Until this cow finishes – she has already fined me 500 Crowns for not cleaning the refrigerator!"

"Really? Is it dirty?"

"Look at it."

I walked over and opened it – there was black mold growing on the sides and it smelled awful. I started laughing and said, "It should be a *thousand* Crowns! Did you shit in there or what?"

He fixed me with a French stink-eye and said, "Perhaps you have something else to do?"

"Only help you. Come get me when the inspection is finished."

"Yes, yes."

I walked out his front door to see what we had to carry and stopped short. I counted four overstuffed backpacks, two overflowing crates, two duffel bags and a mature plant.

I went back into Marcel's room and asked, "How much of that you taking?"

"All."

"How will we carry it?"

"Oh, Mr. Optimistic American, you say we can't do it?"

"I–"

"We must try it. I need these things."

"Right."

The lady finished up her white-glove inspection and presented Marcel with a bill for 500 Crowns, payable immediately.

"*Merde*," he said. "What a stupid cow."

"Marcel," I said, "the fridge is a nightmare!"

He looked at me petulantly, then turned and paid the lady. She gave him a receipt and he turned the key over to her. These last two actions were done in a snappy, reciprocally discourteous manner and when I began giggling they both eyeballed me, which made me giggle even more.

We were all in the hallway and as the lady walked away, Marcel cursed her in French. Then he was suddenly in a tremendous hurry. I left him in the hallway, collected my small rucksack, and returned to see him strapping on backpacks. He already had a huge red one on his back and was putting a blue one on his front.

It made him look like a pregnant turtle, and he looked at me indignantly when I told him so. I donned my two assigned backpacks while Marcel picked up two duffel bags and found his hands full. After I got the two backpacks on and picked up a crate in each hand, I looked at him standing there. We were both horribly loaded – if we fell we'd jostle around like we were wearing Sumo wrestler suits.

With our two backpacks and heavy objects in both hands, he looked at his houseplant for a moment before he said, "Fuck eet. It's yours."

He turned up the hallway and waddled slowly, the heavy duffel bags pressing against his legs and making him walk knock-kneed. My crates weren't so heavy, but I still had to rest them against my legs as I walked.

This is how Marcel proposed to walk the 15 minutes to the bus stop, then later switch to the metro, then take another bus to get to where his coach was departing from. We struggled out to the foyer of the Foreigner Ghetto, where we ran into Remy, a student from Mali.

Remy and Marcel had a spirited exchange in French, after which Remy said, "Elijah, don't you think it's a good idea to take a taxi?"

"Absolutely. I'll even pay."

"No," Marcel said. "I will pay it. Remy, will you call?"

As he unloaded his burden, Marcel looked at me sheepishly and said, "We should be so smart."

The taxi came 10 minutes later and we packed the trunk full. I rode in back next to two backpacks and Marcel rode in front.

As we drove across town I peppered Marcel with questions about France, hoping to wheedle an invitation out of him, but he seemed concerned about the time and was untalkative until he asked, "And what about you? How does it going with your red-haired girl?"

I looked out the window and sighed.

"Oh, we're ok, but... man, she's got this long-distance boyfriend who's visiting, and it's just terrible."

He turned his head around and asked, "How long are they together?"

"Yeah. Seven years is all."

"*Merde*. When did he arrive?"

"Last week."

"Ahhhhhh... I see. This is why you have been depressed, no?"

"Whaddya mean?"

"No music, no stupid bathroom joking."

"My jokes are *not* stupid."

"Yes, well, I saw her on campus with someone not you and thought you might have broken up. I am happy it is only temporary."

"Yeah. Although happy might be too strong a word."

"But it will be over soon, no?"

"Yeah..."

"Elijah, just be yourself. If she doesn't like that, then she is not worth it."

I blinked at him.

"W... was that a compliment?"

He smirked and turned back towards the front. "The only one you will ever get from me."

We drove for a bit and I said, "You know, Marcel, I think I'll miss you..."

A silence stretched out and I added, "Or not," to which we both giggled.

When we arrived at the bus station, the taxi driver (who'd been visibly peeved that his fare was two foreigners) parked, walked back to the trunk and started to heave the duffels onto the sidewalk until Marcel cursed him in French and motioned him away. The driver appeared happy to be relieved of his work and stood there watching us unload. Marcel paid but gave him no tip.

I stood guard over Marcel's mountain of goodies while he went to search for his bus among the 20 that were parked nearby. It turned out to be just meters away, and we relayed the stuff to the coach, where the driver was wrestling with the passengers' baggage. When Marcel handed him the third bag, the driver said something to the effect that Marcel would have to pay an additional freight fee.

After their discussion, Marcel turned back towards me and loudly cursed the driver in French. Then, to his surprise, the driver hustled over, got in Marcel's face and began barking at him. Marcel stood there wide-eyed until the driver walked away fuming.

"What was *that* all about," I asked.

Marcel looked at me impishly and said, "I forgot he understood French. I have been cursing the Czechs in French for months, no problem. Now I have to be more careful."

"You sure will! Someone might teach you some manners!"

Marcel grunted and then said, "We stop now, yes? We say goodbye like friends."

He extended his hand to shake.

I took it and said, "Marcel, we *are* friends."

We shook and hugged at the same time, then pulled back.

"*Bon courage*, Elijah. Say hi to your red-haired girl for me."

"Sure will. *Bon courage*, Marcel."

He climbed aboard the bus, took a seat, and we had a final wave before I turned and hoofed it back home through summertime Prague.

The next day I saw Eva on campus and she broke the news about the English Courses. They were continuing for another full year!

Having lost my Mary Jane connection to the Czech police months before, I was forced to find alternative sources. After a period of spending too much for too little, or for the poor quality provided by the random dealers who would approach me on the Charles Bridge at night, I finally asked Standa, one of my hacky-sack buddies, if he knew of anyone.

He did indeed, and agreed to get a bag for me, deliverable the next day at noon in front of the Anděl metro station.

Next day I arrived on time and waited on the busy corner, nervously thinking about Priestly being in jail and hoping this deal would be an extremely low-key affair.

Ten minutes later Standa showed up, carrying, to my bewilderment, a huge bag of grass in his right hand.

After saying hello, Standa held up the baggie and said, "It is enough? Do you want to smell it?"

I looked around suspiciously and said, "No, man! Uh… I'm a bit nervous about you holding it like that..."

"E, don't worry. Nobody cares. Look!" He held the baggie over his head and did a giggling pirouette.

I looked on, thinking, *Wow. That must be some good shit.*

I was nowhere near as amused as Standa was and finally said, "Hey man, let's go somewhere else and do this."

"Sorry, E, no time today. Here, take it."

He held the bag out and I snatched it, shoving it into the cargo pocket of my shorts.

"E, relax… So what about the money – do you wanna pay me later at the park or what?"

"No, I have it now." I fished out and handed over a sealed envelope with the money inside.

Standa took the envelope and smiled. "See… wasn't that easy?"

"Uh… yeah. Thanks, man."

We shook hands, promising to see each other in the park, and then said goodbye. Seconds later Standa blended into the crowd, leaving me with my pulsating bag of marijuana on the busy street. I hurried over to a window ledge and with my back to the pedestrians, rested my backpack there, steadying it with one hand. I wanted to bury the grass as far down as possible. I unzipped the backpack with my free hand and then retrieved the grass from my pocket. Then, as I brought the baggie up to the backpack, someone touched my right shoulder.

I jumped and lost my grip on the backpack, which began falling from the ledge. Fumbling for it as it tipped over, I then dropped the bag of grass, watched it fall towards the sidewalk, said fuck, fumbled some more with the bag as it turned upside down and then held onto it pitifully as it spilled its contents out onto the pavement.

"Fuck!"

I squatted down and scrambled to put everything back in, and while I did, the person who had touched me began speaking in Czech.

I looked up at him – he had short black hair and was wearing a white shirt, black tie and dress pants. The perfect detective.

I shit myself and said I didn't speak Czech. I put my attention back to re-stuffing the bag in the hopes that the person would just give up and move on.

But the person didn't leave. Instead, he asked me, in English, "Do you believe in God?"

I stopped hustling my belongings into the bag and looked slowly up into the man's eyes.

"What?"

"Do you believe in God?"

I swallowed. "Yeah…"

"And do you think he'd approve of what you're doing?"

"What?"

He squatted down beside me and pointed at the bag of grass.

"Do you think God approves of what you're doing?"

I looked into his steady blue eyes for a moment and shrugged.

"I don't know."

"Well, *I* know. You should cast that away now, just throw it away…"

I stopped listening, unable to consider throwing the bag away after I'd just paid good cash for it. I began packing my bag again.

The man stood up and continued, "So if you believe in God, maybe you'd join us?"

"Join who?"

"We're a non-denominational church group. We meet every Sunday, have a little picnic, talk about The Bible… most of us are English speakers."

When I finished packing my bag, I stood up and found the man holding out a business card.

He looked deep into my eyes and said, "God is reaching out to you. If you take one step forward, he'll do the rest."

I hesitantly reached for the card .

The man smiled then, and said, "Join us sometime – we'll talk some more."

I nodded and said, "Yeah, I'll think about it."

"Do that. And God bless you."

Turning and hustling off, I said, "You too, buddy."

That experience really shook me, and soon after I started reading a lot of spiritual books. One of M. Scott Peck's books – all of his books helped me immensely – mentioned a C.S. Lewis book called *The Screwtape Letters*, which I found in one of Prague's English language bookstores.

The book's premise is this: Each human has a soul which naturally endeavors to reach Heaven. In order to prevent this from occurring, the Devil assigns a demon to tempt, very subtly and without the person's knowledge, each human into making choices which will eventually place him or her on the Highway to Hell.

In the book, Screwtape is a senior tempter who writes a series of letters to his nephew, a trainee tempter, telling him about the infernal ways employed to trick, beguile, and twist humans away from thinking about spiritual issues.

The tricks are devilishly clever and when one reads the book, one can see very easily how, if the premise is accepted, each of us could very well have a little tempter poking at us.

One trick goes like this: When the "patient" begins to think about spirituality, the tempter whispers something in the patient's mind – the topic doesn't matter, what matters is that it must be distracting to the patient. For example, if the patient loves cooking, images of cooking should be whispered; if the patient loves running, thoughts of that should be whispered, and so on.

Thus distracted by some interesting "worldly" topic, the idea of spirituality is abandoned, but the same *import* one would normally feel when considering spiritual issues is transferred onto the distracting worldly thought, thereby tricking the patient into placing an inordinate amount of import onto the worldly thought at the expense of the spiritual issue.

What I found utterly fascinating about this transference is that after being confronted with the idea of it, I noticed that it actually *happened* to me!

For instance, on my walks through town, I would often think about what is written in the Bible. Quotes or ideas of compassion and patience might run through my mind for a bit as I tried to remind myself to be a better person. Then suddenly, a random scene from a movie would flash in my brain and off I would go, playing through the scenes, trying to remember the lines, the scenery – sometimes even repeating the lines to myself as I walked.

And the thing is, the segue into these movie thoughts was so seamless that I actually attributed the same solemnity to them as I had been doing to the spiritual thoughts of just moments before. Sometimes after realizing my drift, I'd be able to realign my thoughts back to spirituality. But other times I would never realize the shift had occurred, and instead I'd just keep on thinking about whatever movie had hooked me in the first place.

The important thing, though, is that I realized my mind (or a little demon tempter) distracted me when I tried to think clear-headed, spiritual thoughts, and I found that disturbing.

A noteworthy quote I read during that time came from a book by Carlos Castenada titled *A Separate Reality – Further Conversations with Don Juan.* The quote is this: "With my ally or with Mescalito I am only a man who knows how to SEE and finds himself baffled by what he SEES; a man who knows that he'll never understand all that is around him."

This quote really touched me, for I too am baffled by some of the things I've seen. Indeed, more often than can be termed coincidence, seemingly normal situations have coalesced and taken on a gravity that I could neither deny nor comprehend.

One of the most vivid examples of this took place when I was in my senior year of college. I spent a lot of time exercising back then, and I would normally finish my workouts with a warm-down jog on the indoor track. On this particular day I was really tired and intended to run less than usual, but something strange happened to me in the middle of the first lap – for no apparent reason, I began talking to myself.

I started out by saying, "Because I run, I am a runner... Because I am a runner, I run." Looking at someone else, I said, "Because she runs, she is a runner. Because she is a runner, she runs."

I gradually but deliberately increased the magnitude of this cyclical mantra until I was saying – and this is the important part – *envisioning* things like, "Because we are from Earth, we are Earth-dwellers. Because we are Earth-dwellers, we are from Earth..."

I maintained this mantra with everything that popped into my head – words that I don't really remember – and ultimately I ended up somehow expanding my awareness past the solar system, into what we call the Milky Way Galaxy, out into our section of the universe, and… well, that's when words began to fail me.

I had no words left, but my *mind* was still there, somewhere out past the boundaries of everyday thought, and while "seeing" the stars and nebulas, I was able to grasp the sheer inter-connectedness of it all. By and by, I was filled with a sort of transcendent compassion for everything and everyone. "I" was no longer there as an individual thing, but as a part of it all, belonging to reality as much as an ant or a star or even time.

Even more astonishing was that during this… mental journey, I was still running, and dimly realized that my stride had taken over for itself. I was no longer bodily concerned – my mind was a completely empty vessel and there was no concern over breathing, speed or technique at all. But I was like the wind! Long striding and arms pumping, I didn't feel A THING because my mind was elsewhere; my body had taken over and I entered into a state of pure involvement – and it was simply beautiful.

After a time, however, my concentration began to wane, and I found my mind constricting backward. But it wasn't the gradual process it had been when I'd expanded there – instead, I found myself back in the mundane in a matter of seconds. I slowed to a jog, then began walking around the track. Checking the time later, I discovered that I had run for over *60 minutes*, and never once did I feel out of breath or fatigued. Quite the opposite, I felt supercharged – like I was all starlight and nebular dust!

I felt extremely… vivid. And when I looked at my hands, they had tiny electric trailers, like I had taken some wicked LSD or something. I walked around the track for maybe 5 more minutes and noticed people staring at me. I looked back at them questioningly, but they just continued to stare.

After I dressed, I drove home precariously, scared that I would crash into someone because I still felt one step removed from my surroundings – as if I were just an observer. And when I happened to catch myself in the rearview mirror, I realized why people had been staring – my eyes had a strange glow, and the pupils were completely dilated. That's probably why I had trailers.

Back then, I didn't know what to make of the experience, but in my need to catalogue it, I decided it must have been something close to illumination.

Whatever it was, my mind was part of the big picture, and I understood it all in a way that began to fade almost immediately.

To get my mind off Liliana, I accepted Colin's invitation to take a road trip to visit a girl he knew in Kroměřice, a town in southern Moravia. On a Saturday afternoon we took the rusty, lime-green Škoda that Colin had borrowed from his company and commenced to shimmy down the highway on balloon-like tires. The weather was fine and we were happy to be watching the rolling landscape for a change.

Two hours later in Kroměřice, we wrong-turned our way through town before finding the girl's apartment. It was a strange introduction – I guess she had only expected Colin to show up, and was a bit cold to me until we left for that night's party in a wine cellar. Moravia is a wine-producing region, and the girl, Jill, had organized a party in one of the well-known cellars. Unfortunately, I had packed what I'd normally wear to a summer party – shorts, t-shirt, sneakers – while everyone else we met were wearing ties and dresses. Awkward.

Now, among wine cellar circles it's apparently a given that the cool underground air reduces the effect of alcohol. So if you drink a whole bottle and still feel fine, once you reach the normal temperatures above ground, you're going to feel the alcohol in a hurry. I didn't know this at the time, and since the wine was really delicious, I kept right on drinking. Also, since Colin and Jill were into each other, and because the others were non-English speakers, I was left alone for long stretches of time.

A few hours into the evening we were given a very serious tour of the wine-producing facilities. The Czech-speaking tour guide was obviously absorbed by the process of wine making, but I couldn't understand a word of what was being said, didn't care to, and the whole situation suddenly struck me as excruciatingly funny. It wasn't funny, of course. It was a nice, cultured evening. But I got a case of the giggles over nothing and they went on for at least a minute. As it went on, the others shot me ever more hate rays, which only aggravated them. I covered my mouth but the giggles burst through. I held my breath but the giggles imploded my lungs. Finally I walked away from the group and around the corner. There, leaning against the wall, I suddenly had no reason at all to laugh. Instead, I remembered how sad I had been lately and I stared at the wall until the group streamed back towards the party room.

I stood there fielding more hate-rays until Colin came up to me and said, "Hey, are you all right?"

"Yeah, but I'm sorry to be so embarrassing."

"Hey, it's no problem. You'll never see these people again and they're boring anyways."

"Yeah…"

"Seriously, I've had enough. You ready to get out of here?"

"Oh, hell yeah!"

I let Colin do all the talking and minutes later we were climbing the stairs out of there. When we opened the door, the hot June air hammered me on the head, the late evening sunshine warmed me, and I was suddenly, staggeringly shitfaced.

I don't remember how I got there, but I woke up the next morning lying in a bed between Colin and Jill. My head hurt so bad it cancelled out my need to pee, so I went back to sleep.

When I woke up again Colin and Jill were smoking a joint, so I sat up with them and took a hit. We passed it back and forth as we sat in bed and after awhile my headache went away. Then Jill started in on me.

"Elijah, what's wrong with you?"

"Whaddya mean?"

She poked me gently in the gut and said, "Come on, sometimes it's easier to talk to people you don't know real well. Besides, you owe it to me after being so drunk and strange at my party."

I winced at the memory. "Sorry about that. Great wine, though."

"Yeah, yeah. Now tell me what's wrong."

So I regaled her with the whole sordid tale of Liliana and Mr. Austria, my uncertainty, my jealousy. She listened with a sort of bemused fascination and when I finished she said, "Wow. I thought only girls had these problems."

"I wish. Got any advice?"

"I'm sorry, but… I'd say you have about zero chance of breaking up a seven-year relationship."

"But it's so perfect when we're together!"

"Listen," Colin said, "If you want to be with her, you'll have to accept this Austrian for now. It's the only way. Maybe she'll break up with him. I doubt it, but…"

I lay down, covered my head with the pillow and screamed into it.

Giggling, Jill pulled the pillow from my head and said, "This is great! I've never seen a man torture himself over a relationship – do all of you do this?"

I put the pillow back over my head and heard Colin answer for me: "Certainly not!"

On the highway back to Prague that afternoon, a summer downpour skulked upon our joke of a car and exposed its many weaknesses: Water leaked down through the doors and up through the floorboards, the ventilation couldn't prevent the windows from fogging up, and the wipers just smeared things around. Also, from Colin's sawing on the wheel, I could tell it wasn't handling the wet roads very well. Nevertheless, Colin kept it well over 100km per hour, passing up other cars like *they* were the old Škodas.

My instincts were urging a slower tempo, so I asked Colin to ratchet it down a bit. He acted like he didn't hear me, so I sat there scared for awhile and then asked him again. This time he slowed to 90kmh. But we were still passing up the other cars – more modern and well-built cars, I might add. The rain was just horrible.

And then as we were passing yet another car, our balloon tires lost their grip on the road and we hydroplaned sickeningly towards the middle guard rail. I held on for dear life as Colin jerked the wheel, which lurched us in the opposite direction but failed to correct us. He jerked the wheel again and we spun out of control. I was screaming "Jesus! Jesus Christ!" over and over, and during one of our spins, as we were going sideways, we felt the two left wheels lift off the ground like it wanted to roll over, but then it didn't and we spun and hit the car next to us and spun around some more. We finally came to a rest facing backwards and I thought we'd get smashed head-on, but the cars behind us had all slowed and stopped.

We got out of the car and exchanged "Are you all rights?" with the other motorists – luckily everyone was ok, if worse for the wear. As the deluge continued I erupted into a teary-eyed, "Colin! We're ok! Oh, sweet Jesus what a perfect thing! We're ok!"

We hugged and then, harried by the traffic jam we'd caused, we pushed the car to the side of the road and kicked the glass away. It was raining hard and we worked with our heads down, the adrenaline pumping like mad. Finally there was enough room for cars to pass through and gawk at us.

There was damage to the front and rear of our car – we'd hit the divider-rail and two other cars, one of which had a trailer. I eventually realized I was wearing shorts, so I ducked into the car to change into long pants. After I had dried and dressed properly for the weather, I got out of the car and discovered that I was alone.

Confused, I cast around for the others but our car was the only one left on the side of the road, and it was facing the wrong way. I got back in and tried to think of what to do, but the cars rushing at me were simply terrorizing. I got out climbed over the guardrails in the rain.

I paced for 30 minutes until a flat-bed truck came and parked in front of the car. The driver jumped out and I attempted a conversation with him, but he had no patience for pidgin Czech and went about winching the car up a set of ramps and onto the flatbed.

After the car was up and secure, the driver put the ramps back into their little cubby holes but one was bent to hell and had to be jammed in hard. After he had done this, he realized it was probably stuck and tried with a four-way lug wrench to pull it out. He struggled for awhile and then shrugged at me – looked like an SEP – somebody else's problem.

I got in the truck with him. I didn't know where we were going, didn't know where Colin was, didn't know a thing. We drove for 10 minutes to a gas station and there was Colin being all buddy-buddy with the police. It was somehow all taken care of and it seemed there'd be no jail time. Still, I didn't relax until a different driver had us halfway to Prague in the flatbed and the police weren't on our tail.

The man drove slowly – as we should have done in the first place – and it took us four hours to get back to Prague. The thing to do then was to leave the car in front of Colin's company. (Imagine his boss coming in first thing Monday morning and seeing the smashed-up car!)

We pulled into the parking lot to unload the car, and as the driver struggled to free the stuck ramp, a police car rolled up. Two cops got out of the car and made their way over to us. The big one walked ahead of the other. They said they noticed we had parked in the grass and demanded a fine of 1,000 Crowns (about $50). Our driver tried to explain that he had to park that way to get the crashed car into the parking lot, but the police wouldn't hear any of it. Obviously disgusted, our driver turned his back on them and continued trying to jimmy out the ramp.

Which brought the big cop's attention to us.

They demanded Colin's passport and upon discovering he was a British national, upped the fine to 1,500 Crowns.

They asked if I were British, too.

"No, I'm American," I said.

The second policeman grunted and the one holding Colin's passport said, "2,000 Crowns."

I had maybe 200 Crowns in my pocket.

Colin had no choice - he had to get his passport back. He paid them the money and they returned the passport. As they walked towards their car, Colin asked for a receipt for the fine. The big cop looked over his shoulder, smiled, and said, "Of course. Just a minute."

Then they got in their car, started it, and drove off.

We stood there dumbfounded and fuming until the driver called us over – he said he could put our anger to good use. We all three pulled and strained at the ramp until it abruptly became unstuck and we toppled backward in a heap. It was the only semi-funny moment of our whole absurd adventure.

We unloaded the car, said good-bye to the driver and hopped the underground. After a strained farewell to Colin, I took the bus home. I finally got to campus at 23:00, tired and jittery. On the way to my room I looked up and saw the light on in Liliana's. I wanted desperately to stop, but knew I couldn't.

In the long, hot shower, after finding calm for the first time that day, I had a moment of realization: Colin was a Dark Angel who brought me just too much negativity – car crashes, near arrests, and so on – so I promised myself to hang out with him less in the future. Even the thought of it was comforting.

That night: Horrible dreams of the crash.

On my way home from the city the next evening, I passed up Liliana's window. Though tempted to yell up for her, I knew Austro-Bastardian was still there so I walked on, kicking rocks and grumbling my way across the parking lot. And then she called to me.

I looked up and saw her framed in the window, waving me over. Instead of happiness, I felt a surge of tumultuous emotions. I walked over to the window and saw her smiling broadly at me, as if nothing had happened, as if she had merely been away for awhile.

I said hi and was again struck by her loveliness as she leaned out of the window, and even though I still wanted to feel sorry for myself, I have to confess some fondness crept back into my heart.

Looking down at me, Liliana asked, “Elijah, is it all right if I visit? Marek is here, or I would invite you up…”

“Fine, but give me a few minutes to shower.”

“Oooh. Or I join you?”

“Uh… maybe you should wait just a bit.”

“Ok. But I will come over soon.”

“Ok.”

We nodded at each other and I turned away, cutting through the edge of the bushes to the front of the Foreigner Ghetto.

Once in my room I tried to stop my stomach turning over on itself by breathing deep and taking a long, hot shower. Unfortunately, my mind wouldn’t let me relax – it was filled with images of them together. I was drying off when the door buzzer rang.

A minute later I answered the door shirtless, my hair frumpy, and there was Liliana – in a long blue dress, smelling of soft perfume. Her reddish hair was falling into her eyes, which widened upon seeing me without my shirt. She smoothed her hair back and then reached out to grip my arm, saying, “You look good!”

I smiled wanly and made a muscle, which she held tight. I invited her in and closed the door. As she walked back into my room, I put on a t-shirt and snuck into the bathroom for a comb. My stomach was still churning and I looked in the mirror, telling myself to calm down. When I went into the room, Liliana was sitting on the reading chair and I sat across from her on the edge of the bed.

She asked about my previous week – what had I been doing, had I seen anything interesting and so on. When we had talked around the topic long enough, I asked about her visit.

“It was ok. But hard, you know?”

“Hard? How could it be hard for *you*?”

Her eyes flashed. “You think I like this? You think you’re the only one having problems?”

Well, yeah. That’s exactly what I’d thought.

“What do you mean,” I asked.

She sighed heavily and said, “I was so bad to him the last week…”

She continued speaking but I missed a part as I internally celebrated her being bad to him the previous week.

"… and he'd only be nicer, but I'd just somehow be meaner. Oh, it was so bad…"

She started to cry then, and I reached out to her.

"And I was angry I had to be with him when I really wanted to be with you!"

I moved over and we hugged. Resting on my shoulder, she said, "And now he thinks he will lose me."

I struggled between my glee over what she'd just said and legitimately feeling sorry for her sadness.

"Is that what you told him," I asked, hoping the bubbles didn't float their way into my voice too obviously.

"Yes… I told him he will lose me and he says he doesn't want to…"

She sighed and wept lightly. "Oh, it's so hard… why don't you just forget about me?"

"No. I won't forget you. We just have to get through this together – and I'll be here for you all next year, too. Eva told me she wants me to work here again next year, so I'll be here whenever you need me…"

She looked up through wet eyes and said, "Really? You're staying for another year?"

"At least."

"What about your trip home?"

"I'm still going, but then I'll be back again and we'll be together if you want. But this situation with Manfred can't go on. It's too painful for all of us."

"Yes, it's painful. That's right." She paused and said, "He wanted to make love – we were sleeping together," – I saw red and fought to control it – "but I had to keep telling him no. And he didn't understand why, only that I was saying no and that made the situation even more unhappy."

The utter rage I'd been feeling just a moment before was replaced by joy over her not sleeping with him.

"You didn't make love?"

She looked up and shook her head.

I smiled my Big Smile at her, but this time I felt it had something extra, a new glow that adorned it – and I said the words that we'd been feeling but not wanting to express.

"I love you, Liliana. I'm so happy you weren't with him."

I actually teared up as I saw her start crying again. "And I don't know what's going to happen, but I'm so happy now that – "

She looked up and kissed me then, and I felt a depth charge of love exploding in our lips as we sighed and kissed over and over. Then she was pushing me back on the bed, crawling on top of me.

"I love you, too."

We were looking into each other's hearts now and both saw the same desire and longing.

She said it again.

I smiled at the novelty of the words and we came closer and more hungrily together and then we did together what she had refused to do with her boyfriend of 7 years.

The next few days were rapturous. Liliana and I spent nearly all of our time together, making love and washing away the ill-will created by the introduction of Manfred into our love equation. More and more discussion was given over to whether and how she would break up with him.

Holding hands on campus, which Liliana had forbidden before Manfred's visit, was now encouraged. We were finally a couple and it's no exaggeration to say I was proud to be seen with her.

That summer, Liliana worked and I basically shirked. She always spent a full day on her research, while I would spend my time tramping around the city, ending up reading in Kampa park. The first time Liliana met me there, she was fetching in a tight tank-top and loose summer pants. And when I saw her carrying a bottle of wine, I knew she was the coolest. After greeting each other, we held hands over to the stone wall that banks the river. There we sat, feet dangling over the water, taking in the beauty of the buildings on the far side of the river.

The sun was going down behind us and the light was at once brilliant and soft. When Liliana's attention was occupied by the shining wonder of the National Theater, I rummaged around in my sack and brought out the bottle of wine I myself had brought. She laughed when she saw it and I said great minds think alike. We sat there toking on the wine talking about nothing until I told her I wanted to discuss "us".

"Uh-oh," she said.

"What do you mean, 'uh-oh'? What could be better?"

I took a long swallow and looked down to the Charles Bridge in the sunlight. The sound of the river running over the weirs was soothing.

I wasn't looking at her when I said, "You know, I respect your decision one way or another, but if you don't break up with him-"

"But I've been with him for so long! I know he would be so hurt…"

She took a drink of the wine and looked at the nearby island.

"But still, I know I can't be with him."

I wanted to yell, *YES, BREAK UP WITH HIM*, but instead I heard myself talking sense.

"Liliana, I know what you're saying. But everything you mentioned is in the past, and you've got to focus on the here and now. In sparing his feelings, you're torturing the both of us."

I guess it was a lot to put on her plate, because we didn't speak then for a long time. Instead, we watched the moon – a full moon to boot – rise out of the distant clouds over the cityscape of Prague. We looked at each other and kissed before returning to our silences.

After finishing the bottle I asked, "So… should I wait for you or not?"

She sighed and said, "Ok, so this is where I was." She put her arm straight up. "Manfred on one side, you on the other. 50-50."

"And now I'm here." She leaned her hand maybe 45 degrees to the side and smiled at me softly.

"And which side was mine?"

Her eyes flashed and she said, "The one I'm leaning to! But now only this much!" She moved her hand more upright and I reached over and tried to pull it more to my side.

We giggled and I said, "Seriously, that's wonderful."

We smiled at each other and kissed, then collected ourselves and slowly walked out of the park. We were holding hands again and walked the back streets to a nearby pub where I knew the barman, Michal (he was one of my students).

More red wine led to more questions about the future.

What if I moved to South America to teach? Would she come?

Yes.

And what about if we lived on the beach?

Yes, but only for a short time before we moved to the mountains.

And what if she got a position in Germany, would I come with her?

Yes.

But what if she stayed in Prague, would I stay?

Of course.

And to think: Dark Angel had convinced me that she would never break up with him!

Over the next two months I was giddily happy, and my energy level was soaring from eating healthy, sleeping adequately, and not boozing too much. These basics taken care of, I tried, really tried, to devote time to learning Czech. And even more than that, I tried to develop myself more spiritually by reading various philosophical texts while I sat in St. Vitus'.

Applying these readings to my life experiences, I came to believe more and more in the interconnectedness of things. When I was upbeat, open and contributing positivity and light into the big Karmic web, that's exactly what I got back. And after experiencing all this positivity, I knew I'd never go back to non-belief, because life seemed so much more *rewarding* as a believer. And that's why I was convinced being with Liliana was right – the way she affected my life was positive on so many levels. She helped me become stronger and more…

grounded, I guess. I noticed, for example, that I cleaned a lot more than I had previously. I shaved more regularly. I was more courteous. I tried to think of others before myself. I was more helpful. More compassionate, somehow.

And I became convinced that Liliana was a wonderful teacher in my life – a physical embodiment of the belief system I was coming to hold as true. I suppose it's a sense of integrity that I'm speaking about – how *knowing* the right thing is different from actually doing it. Anyway, one night as I was meditating on these issues, a memory flooded over me that perfectly illustrated the concept: One evening at college I was jogging around the portion of campus where the stadium is located. Normally the run would take me about 45 minutes, but that day I was stopped short midway through by the spectacle of flight.

As I came around a stand of trees, I looked up and saw over 20 hot air balloons filling the sky. Some had just lifted off from the field in front of me and were very low, even nudging each other, while those that had taken off minutes before were following the wind to the right. A long line of colorful and multi-shaped balloons (including a winged angel) stretched to the hilly horizon.

The balloonists were taking off from the middle of a huge field, and as I walked closer I noticed a man sitting at a bus stop. He was a middle-aged guy, kind of dirty. Even without his hand cart, I would have guessed he was homeless. But as he sat there watching the balloons, I could see the same wonder in his eyes that I was feeling, and I went over and sat on the far end of the bench.

Even the most taciturn of people would have been forced to comment on something like all those hot air balloons, and soon we were making small talk while the balloons took off. After about 10 minutes of watching the spectacle, I got up to resume my jog and when we said goodbye, the man gave me a two-fingered peace wave.

As I trotted off, my mind began to ponder things I could do to help the guy. I envisioned buying him a meal or giving him a ride somewhere – anything to help him out. Thinking these thoughts made me feel somehow altruistic, and I continued my run feeling like a prince.

But the weird thing was that in the end, I didn't help the man at all. Instead, I just returned to my comfortable life. Ok, maybe *not* helping him wasn't so strange. In fact, I'd probably been socialized to look down on him and his non-conformist ways – I mean, he looked healthy enough to work, so why didn't he?

Anyway, what especially puzzled me is that the feeling of benevolence I experienced persisted, with my feelings of positivity stemming from the very *thought* of helping him. And even though I chose the easiest, most selfish path of inaction, I continued to feel good about myself for even *considering* lending him a hand.

This made me wonder which is more important – intent or action? I'd always thought that action was the most important – that is, one can have negative thoughts but do good deeds – and those good deeds end up creating good karma.

But revisiting the episode with the homeless man made me reconsider it; perhaps it's not an either/or situation, but both.

☯

A cultural tidbit well-known inside the Czech Republic but little-known abroad: Many Prague-dwellers find their city crowded, littered and dangerous. True, most pay lip-service to the architectural wonders of *Zlatá Praha* (Golden Prague) and acknowledge that Prague is where the work is. But then they'll warble on about the cleanliness and safety of the small town or village they hail from. Which explains why so many Czechs leave the capital *en masse* for the countryside every Friday and return *en masse* every Sunday.

And the Czech countryside *is* lovely. The forests are well-preserved and managed, and as a legacy of socialism, readily accessible. A privately-owned lake, for example, will be used by the surrounding community for all sorts of recreation because there are very few "NO TRESPASSING" signs. It isn't anarchy, of course – private property exists and yards and houses are not entered without invitation, but most of the forested land is utilized by all.

Despite these selling points, when Liliana asked me to visit her parents for the weekend, I balked. Why go to the country when I had Prague? I liked tramping around the city. I liked not having to answer to anybody – especially to parents.

Liliana countered my concerns by saying that a country's capital is a different animal than its outlying areas, and if I really wanted to learn about my adopted culture, I'd have to brave the wilds of Bohemia and go home with her.

So on a Friday afternoon we drove Liliana's Škoda Favorit through the rolling Bohemian countryside to meet her folks. We traveled west out of Prague, the sunlight in our eyes, through progressively smaller villages and larger fields until all the other license plates denoted the same county of origin.

"How far to your home," I asked as we passed up a farmyard littered with wooden and iron relics.

"Still another 10 minutes."

We finally ran out of field and entered a forest. The road was lined by pine trees with bare, reddish-brown trunks until high up, where the branches formed the sparse canopy. There was a relative lack of underbrush. Instead, there were meadows of low, green grass. Very peaceful. Very inviting.

A few minutes later we arrived at Liliana's village, Svatý Hubert (Saint Hubert). Instead of following the bend in the road off to the right, we plunged straight ahead, onto a grassy lane that cut into a wall of shrubs and trees. Seeing me stiffen, Liliana patted my leg and said, "Don't be scared."

"Humph."

Through the thick shrubbery (the village was surrounded by it) I caught glimpses of a large building, which, when we came onto the round village green, materialized into an old but refurbished lodge. Off to Liliana's left, three houses hunkered under the trees.

The village's salmon-colored central lodge had two levels and mammoth windows on each of its eight sides. Perched on the ceramic-roof was a watchtower topped with a jaunty stag. (I later learned that the lodge's octagonal design was a necessary feature; it had previously been used as the local Lord's hunting lodge, and the womenfolk needed a view down each of the paths the men might return on. From an aerial perspective, Svatý Hubert forms the hub of an eight-spoked wheel – minus the tire, of course).

But the trees are what really defined Svatý Hubert. Towering oak, pure white beech, lime and chestnut trees ensconced the glade in which the settlement was situated, making it postcard idyllic.

Of the three houses, only one wasn't shuttered up, and we drove towards it. A low dwelling, it nevertheless had a steeply-pitched, red-shingled roof and a small balcony on the second floor. A woman's behind was bent over the small flower garden.

Halfway across the village green, a golden lab erupted from the forest on an intercept course. Out of her open window, Liliana yelled "Doktor – ahoy," and he escorted us to our parking place in the yard. He was jumping up to see who was in the car, wagging his tail furiously.

"What do you think?"

"Lovely," I answered. "Really beautiful."

She smiled at me and then spoke out the window to her mom, who said something as she slowly straightened up. Her dad came around the side of the building wearing blue coveralls.

"Mom says she is happy you like it here," she translated. Turning to me, she added, "I, too."

We looked at each other and she asked me if I was ready.

"Sure."

Liliana opened the car door, which was instantly filled with Doktor trying to climb in on her lap. He had a pitiful look on his face as she pushed him out and then struggled to stand up. As she stood, he nearly knocked her down and then ran over to inspect me with a chewed-up stick in his jaws. I roughed him up and tried to get the stick but he skittered away. I chased him a ways before Liliana called me back over.

I poked my head in the car to get the bunch of flowers Liliana had advised me to bring, then walked over.

Her mother was short and robust, and had a powerful grip when we shook hands. She beamed when I gave her the flowers and kept shaking my hand as she spoke to me earnestly.

She maintained her grip and gaze as Liliana translated that mom was happy to have me visit, that it was an honor to have an American stay with them and that she hoped I would enjoy my time in her house.

I said thanks, that it was lovely, and I was sure I would like it there.

Still shaking hands, Liliana translated.

Her mom and I went through two more rounds of polite greetings and well-wishes, all the while shaking hands. I couldn't have wrenched free of her grip had I tried.

This process was repeated with her dad, who was built just the same as mom – short, with powerful hands and legs. The hand shaking and smiling was still there with him, but fewer words were exchanged because apparently everything had been said.

After unpacking and settling in, Liliana and I went out to build a fire in the village green's fire pit. Later, her mom and dad joined us and asked about life in America. Hearing about the plentitude of consumer life was fascinating to them, just as their stories of living under the scarcity of socialism were fascinating to me.

We drank beers and ate roasted sausages (I snuck pieces to Doktor when no one was looking) as we told our stories, and I could have kept it up all night. But I sensed that Liliana was getting tired of translating, so I left them and went upstairs to read in the guest room. They stayed up late around the fire.

Next morning after brunch, I was given a lounge chair in which to soak up the three hours of direct sun that permeated the forest glade. Liliana sat beside me and from time to time her mom or dad, between chores, would sit nearby and pepper me with questions. Then, with Liliana translating, I would ask them about their village, their work, (both retired now), their four-bedroom house (built it themselves), and Liliana's most embarrassing childhood stories, which were somehow lost (intentionally, I think) in translation.

After lounging, Liliana and I rode bikes through the forest to a nearby lake, where we swam and played with Doktor. On Saturday night we had another bonfire and I drank all the beer that was thrown at me. Long story short, that first weekend was enchanting and I was oddly disappointed when we returned to Prague on Sunday. Indeed, that week during my walks, the city seemed different – somehow less interesting than before. Was it nostalgia for the previous weekend? Already?

Anyways, when on Thursday it was extended, I jumped at Liliana's weekend invitation and felt all the better for it.

Alas, the quiet forest laze of my first visit wasn't to be repeated. That weekend, the whole of Liliana's family showed up – her two brothers, their wives, and children to boot – 12 in total (having grown up with one sibling, the size of this family was unnerving). To complicate matters, none of them spoke English, which largely left me to my own devices when Liliana wasn't available. And she often was unavailable due to Czech familial demands, which I learned a great deal about that second weekend.

Because the family was so large, feeding them was a serious task which mom approached with an apparently unalterable plan. Unfortunately she wasn't able to communicate this plan very well, nor to delegate. So if you stepped foot in the kitchen, you had better know exactly what was expected of you, do it well, and do it without getting in mom's way. Otherwise you'd get browbeat back to wherever it was you had come from.

Liliana was the youngest, knew what her mom expected and knew her way around the kitchen, so she was lost to me during mealtime preparation and cleanup; during these times I would go into the garden to read or play with Doktor, both of which were fine occupations.

But Liliana was obviously struggling to balance the tensions involved with familial expectations and her own needs, not the least of which was spending time with the potential boyfriend she had brought home. This tension is probably what she wished to appease that Saturday night when she suggested going to a pig roast that her brother knew about. Of course I agreed, since being alone with her was the only time I was able to fully open up; because I still didn't speak Czech very well, I was forced to nod and smile dumbly as the family laughed and carried on.

That evening as she drove us to the pig roast, Liliana and I joked about family matters as I enjoyed the beautiful scenery of the lush pine forest through which we passed. After some time we emerged from the main forest road, the trees abruptly stopped, and we were surrounded by rolling, uncultivated fields. Soon after, we turned right onto a small lane that led through a golden field – the high, mid-summer grass waving at us in the breeze. The air was alive with the sounds of insects, and at the far side of the field we drove into a small opening in the trees that obscured a narrow way leading steeply downward. The road was paved but potted, and it was dark inside the tree canopy. When we reached the level ground of the basin, the trees opened up on the right side to reveal a wide, lazy river with willow trees leaning out over it. Across the river, cabins ran along the bank and the land rose steeply behind them to form a high, rocky hillside.

We parked in a nearby field next to the other cars and got out. We had noticed Liliana's brother and nephew kicking a soccer ball in the field beside the bonfire, and were walking towards them when a man staggered over to us. He had salt and pepper hair and a heavy mug of beer in his hands. When he and Liliana greeted each other, they kissed and he hugged her for what I felt was just a *bit* too long. After their greetings in Czech, Liliana introduced the man as Pater, who smiled broadly at me and said, "Hey! It's good to have someone I practice my English with! How long you been in Czech Republic?"

"About six months."

"Really? You like our country? So many beautiful girls, eh? Like this one!"

Liliana blushed and brushed her hair behind her ears. Just then, her brother came over and shook hands with me, then spoke in Czech to Liliana. After a moment, brother and sister went off to get beers and me and Pater were left alone.

It was on the dark side of twilight now and the hues of the huge fire were getting brighter.

I was looking at the bonfire when I thought I heard Pater say, "Fucking Americans."

I turned to look at him. Never taking his eyes off of me, he took a slug of beer, then continued.

"You Americans, you come here, you take our women. I fucking hate that you have a chance with Liliana!"

I thought he was making a bad joke, so I smiled at him. But the unflinching gravity of his bearing convinced me otherwise. I started to say I wasn't taking anything, but right in the middle of my sentence Liliana came walking towards us through the grass. She was smiling and holding two beers, and both Pater and I stopped to look at her.

She handed me the beer and after we toasted, Pater turned to me, nice as pie, and asked, "So, how long you know our Liliana, Elijah?"

I paused before I answered. "About three months."

"Oh, that's nice. And what about you, Liliana? How is school?"

Liliana answered Pater in Czech, and they spoke very animatedly and full of laughter. I didn't understand much and tried to act interested in their conversation, but found myself thinking about other things and drinking the beer too quickly.

After awhile someone yelled for Pater, and he took Liliana's hand and led her up to the house's wooden deck. Walking off, I felt Liliana look over her shoulder at me, but I was already in the process of looking away. When I looked back at her, she was looking ahead to the party.

I walked over to the fire and stared into it. I also needed a beer but didn't want to get into the middle of all those people. Standing across the bonfire was a tall, skinny man with wide shoulders. After making eye contact, he spoke to me in English, "You speak Czech?"

"A bit. I have only been here a few months."

"What you doing here?"

"I'm an English teacher. You?"

"I'm in army with Pater. You need a beer?"

"I sure do," I said, and put my empty glass into his outstretched hand. He smiled and went up the hill.

I stood there looking at the fire before Liliana came back five minutes later. We talked a little about the party and the beautiful nature surrounding us, and Liliana was telling a story from her childhood when the army man came back holding a beer. He only had one in his hands, half full, and he wouldn't look at me. I quietly told Liliana about the beer issue and she said he must have misunderstood, that we'd just go ourselves.

As we walked up the hill, I noticed that the army man was looking sideways at me and smirking. Of course Liliana did not see this.

Mixing into the middle of the party on the deck, I was introduced to the 10 or so people surrounding the keg, and then finally to Pater's wife. She was in her mid-forties, good-looking, and very flirty.

"How you like Czech women, Elijah?" Her eyebrow was arched.

"As much as I can," I said.

Liliana, standing beside me, laughed and so did Pater's wife. They got me a beer and we stood there talking until I finished it. Then they got me another and Liliana and I went back down to the fire.

Liliana's brother was sitting on the smoky side of the fire, playing the guitar and singing. He was horribly off-key in both, but he was very absorbed by it. Liliana said he had been drinking all day and also the cigarettes had given him a raspy voice. I didn't understand his words but was happy to sit there and watch him.

After a few songs, Liliana went to get us more beer and a blonde woman sitting next to us spoke to me. "He's a little off tonight."

"Yeah, but it looks like he doesn't care very much."

"True. Uh… can I ask what you're doing here in the Czech Republic?"

"Sure. I'm an English teacher at the university."

"Oh, that's great. I love English. I read a little Hemingway from time to time."

"Is that right? He's one of my favorites. In fact, I have a book of his short stories in the car."

"Which one?"

"The 'First 49 Stories' or something like that."

"Really? Can I see it?"

"Sure, I'll go get it."

I got up and walked over to the car. Since I was already up, I also walked into the bushes to pee. After, as I walked back towards the fire, I met Pater. He was staggering.

"You pig American fuck." He said it low, so no one else could hear. "What you still here for?"

"You want us to go?"

"Liliana no. But you, yes. Back to America!"

He made to get in my face but I backed up a step and said, "Stay away from me."

I started to walk around him and as I passed by he said, "American pussy."

I stopped and sized him up. It would be a massacre because he was drunk as hell. I shook my head and walked away.

When I got back to the fire, the army man was staring at me. He had probably seen the episode with Pater and it was obvious which side he'd take. Liliana was at the fire again and I sat down beside her. Then the blonde woman asked me about the book and I suddenly remembered the Hemingway collection. I apologized and went to the car to fetch it.

Returning back to the fire, I stood beside the blonde woman and spoke about Hemingway and after awhile I relaxed a bit and forgot about Pater until he staggered over, sat next to Liliana and put his arm around her shoulders. Liliana coolly accepted it and even laughed from time to time. Pater got up and walked over to where the army man was standing. The guitar was laying nearby and Pater took it over to Liliana. She didn't want to play. Pater insisted. So did Liliana's brother, and finally so did the blonde-haired woman.

As she reluctantly began playing, I went over and sat on her right. Pater was on her left.

Liliana's playing was rudimentary but precise, and she played a soulful, yearning song while singing in Czech. I didn't understand the words but was deeply stirred. When she finished, I told her that I was continually impressed by her and she leaned over the guitar to kiss me.

She started another song and wasn't halfway through it when one of Pater's friends, a man in his 50's, staggered over with a folding chair and tried to nudge his way between me and Liliana. I gave him a nasty look over my shoulder, but he was drunk enough that it didn't matter what kind of look I gave him. He wanted to sit close to her.

So we had Pater on Liliana's left, sitting very close and putting his hand on her left leg from time to time. And now, on Liliana's right side, almost completely between us, was this other drunk letch who from time to time would reach up and put Liliana's hair behind her ear, sometimes stroking her cheek on the way down.

"Are you ok," I asked her.

She nodded yes.

"Are you sure?"

Again the nod.

I didn't believe that she was all right. I drank more beer and stewed.

The letch on my left reached up again and stroked Liliana's cheek. I exploded inside and asked her once more how she was.

Again the nod.

I sat forward in the folding chair, finished my beer and looked across the fire. It was now only me, Liliana, Pater, and his two buddies.

Sitting up and alert, I decided I would get things rolling by giving the letch on my left an elbow to the face. That would send him over backwards on his seat and probably take him out of the fight. The force of the blow would also help me stand up quickly and get to the half-burnt log in the fire. I'd pick that up with my right hand – that was the side the army guy would come from – and with my left leg I'd kick that son of a bitch Pater square in the pie hole. Then it would only be me and the army guy and I'd have my heavy beer glass and a torch that I'd burn that bastard with if he got anywhere close.

*Yeah, that's how it would go.*

I sat there on the front of the chair perfecting the plan, placing my feet properly to stand up. I even thought that by bending over and pretending to tie my shoelaces, I'd be able to start the elbow lower and thereby pack it with more force to hit that dirty letch with.

I was actually bent over, doing a shoelace when I realized Liliana was standing in front of me with her hand extended. I finished my shoe and then she led me over to the car, where she asked me straight out what was wrong. Not wanting to overly alarm her, I told her I was bothered by those guys touching her. I mentioned nothing of starting a brawl, but did say that I was probably just tired and ready to go whenever she was.

She said ok, but I could tell she thought there was something more to it.

Still, we went back to the party to say our goodbyes and were met with a chorus of "You can't leaves." Liliana was flattered. Another set of songs was demanded and when she agreed I disgustedly went up to get another beer.

Halfway back to the fire with my glass, I met Pater.

"Asshole," he muttered.

I didn't say anything, but gave him a hard shoulder as I passed by. I heard his heavy glass hit the ground, followed by strong words in Czech. I kept walking, half expecting a tackle from behind, but it never came.

Liliana sang the last song wonderfully – I really loved to watch her play – but I loved it even more when she finished and we could leave. On the ride back to Svatý Hubert, we fell into a silence and I was having angry black thoughts about Pater until one clear thought percolated upward: *If you can control your anger and jealousy, being with Liliana will be the reward.*

I don't know where this thought came from, but it sure gave me something better than dirty Pater to think about.

When we arrived home that night, I told Liliana what a great time I'd had. Luckily for me, she didn't catch the irony and seemed pleased to hear that I got along with her friends

Manfred's weekly calls were becoming increasingly difficult to take. Twice I was in her room when he phoned and she started speaking in German right away; a laughing, happy Fraulein. Of course I couldn't understand a thing and had to leave immediately or I'd start breaking furniture.

So although he was fading, Austro-Bastardo was still in the picture and each phone call either led to a suppression of the issue, or to a heated discussion that always ended the same way; she just wasn't ready to break up with him.

And because I so wanted to be with her, I had no choice but to deal with my anger and jealousy, which was no mean feat.

So when Manfred would call, I would ~~sometimes~~ calm myself by thinking, *Yes, they're still in touch. But he lives in Austria, and you're here. In ten minutes the phone call will be over and you'll spend the night with her again. You know that she loves you. Two months ago you had no chance. Now she's yours. Just stay cool. At the very least, you've been able to spend two months with an incredibly lovely person.*

If someone would have asked me the meaning of life during one of those more lucid moments, I would've said, "To minimize the negative and maximize the positive."

Life is just that simple.

Ok, ok.

Life is not really that simple.

But wouldn't it be great if everybody lived that way?

Oh, but July was such a blissful time of being in love in Prague! Liliana and me went to the parks and lay in the grass together, we went shopping – we just did stuff as a couple, and it was SO GOOD I couldn't stand it… sometimes I'd be overcome with sophomoric gushiness and burst out giggling.

Towards the end of the month, Liliana went home for a week and I packed to go back to the States on a long-planned trip. Naturally, I began to miss her before I even left CZ, and called her at home. We spoke all happy until she asked me conspiratorially if I had checked my messages. I hadn't. Well, I should check my messages and then call her back.

Ok…

So I called my messages and she had left the following: "Elijah, I miss you already and wish you a safe trip. But I want to tell you something before you go – I'm not with Manfred anymore. I broke up with him. So make sure you come back to me!"

I freaked out and did the pogo dance like a six-year old, chanting with every hop, "She! Broke! Up! She! Broke! Up! She! Broke! Up! With! Him!"

I called her right back and was all delirious but I felt something interesting as well – I was genuinely concerned about how she was feeling, whether she was having difficulties with the decision to breakup, and so on.

She said breaking up with him was easier than she thought it would be and we spoke all happy, couldn't wait to see each other, it would only be a month, I'd call when I got to the States.

And I hung up completely giddy – my beautiful lovely girl was no longer my beautiful lovely girl with an asterisk beside her – she was now my girl ok, and I was a sloppy happy cat because of it!

An American buddy in Prague told me that the last time he'd traveled home, he'd eaten a chunk of hash before getting onto the airplane. He said that the subsequent flight had been awesome, totally calm and relaxing, and that I should try it sometime. So on the way to the airport at 05:00, I did just that. In the taxi to the airport, I swallowed a chunk and thought myself quite the cool cat. Mr. Edgy, that's me.

The hash didn't manifest itself straight away, and I was able to check in and get my stand-by tickets without incident. But waiting in line at passport control, I started getting shaky. Literally. I was becoming jittery and agitated, and couldn't concentrate very well.

My pupils must have been huge, because the passport officer did a little double-take as he compared my mug with my photo. He scrutinized and questioned me in Czech, and although it took a great deal of concentration, I managed to talk my way through.

The paranoia and worsening shakes helped me decide the hash might not be cool after all, so I headed for the bathroom to pull a bulimic.

Locking myself in a stall, I hung my backpack on the door, bent over the bowl and shoved a finger down my throat. I felt the gag and my eyes teared up, but nothing came out. I shoved the finger further down and gagged harshly, but only saliva came. The third time a series of dry heaves racked me, but again there was nothing but saliva.

I stood up slowly and closed my eyes while the world spun. I was still jittery, but now exhausted as well. I wiped my mouth and glanced at my watch – I was on the cusp of lateness and had to hustle. The hash would have to stay.

I went through security completely expecting a gorilla to shove a flashlight in my face or offer to do a cavity search, but nothing happened. I was cleared and stood waiting in front of the window looking at our plane in the early light as the ticketed passengers boarded.

*Amazing thing, planes. How can something so big –*

They called my name and I lurched down the boarding thingie and into the plane. It was a relief to finally plop down in my seat, but that's when the hash really started to hit me. The shakes galloped over me and I had to ask the flight attendant to bring me a blanket. She did, and I cuddled up and tried to relax.

But the takeoff was a nightmare, being in the air was a nightmare, and every slight noise or bump, to me, was an indication that the plane was going down. I felt like William Shatner or John Lithgow in those Twilight Zone skits. Come to think of it, they were probably hopped up, too.

When we landed in Zurich I hustled to the next gate, power walking and dodging between people on the way because I was paranoid I'd miss the flight. But when I arrived, the plane was still boarding; hurry up and wait, hurry up and wait.

I took a seat next to the terminal counter and waited for my name to be called. I was sitting straight up, almost standing as I watched everyone around me receive a ticket. I wrung to death the piece of paper in my hands until I realized it was my ticket voucher. *Shit.* When I was finally called, the flight attendant couldn't read the thing and the whole process was further delayed. I was the last one to board the flight. I had again lucked into a business class seat and planned to just lean back and quietly suffer the whole trip.

Much to my annoyance, however, there was a hot girl in the seat next to mine. I was almost incoherent with my hello but it didn't seem to matter – she was a chipper little thing.

When I closed my eyes after strapping myself in, she asked, "Are you tired?"

I kept my eyes closed.

"Yes."

"I always have trouble sleeping on a plane because I'm so excited to fly."

"Oh, I'll sleep."

"Hmm. That's good. I wish I could sleep."

"Me, too," I said.

"What do you mean? You said that–"

"I mean *now*. I wish I could sleep now."

"Oh… ok…."

When I awoke from my distressing half-dreams, my mouth was pasty and tasted like bile. A look out the window gave me a great view of the topside of puffy clouds and I didn't give a damn. I frowned over at the girl on my right and she smiled brightly.

"Did you have a nice sleep?"

I grunted and looked away.

'I'm sorry for saying this, but you don't look so good. Are you sick?"

"Kinda."

"I can see it. My name's Ivana, by the way. And you?"

She was holding out her hand so I shook with her.

"Elijah."

"Nice to meet you, Elijah. Where are you from?"

"Pittsburgh."

"Oh, *really*? That's where I'm flying to! I'm going to visit my Aunt and Uncle!"

"Huh."

"They moved from Lithuania to Pittsburgh 30 years ago. That's where my whole family is from – Lithuania. Have you ever been there?"

"No."

"Oh, you should come to visit me there. It's a beautiful country."

I'd had enough of her already. "Uh… will you excuse me? I need to get up for a moment."

As she stood up to let me out, she said, "Ok, but we'll talk more when you return, yes? I need to practice my English!"

I nodded and went to find the toilet, wondering how long I could manage to stay there.

Ten minutes later I stood in the bathroom, sweating and jittery. A loud knocking on the door made me jump out of my skin.

"Are you all right, sir?"

"Yes… thank you."

When I emerged into the fresh air of the cabin, lunch was being served. At my row, Ivana, smiling broadly, handed me her tray and then stood up to let me back in. I handed her back the tray and slid over to my seat by the window, then she handed me the tray again. It contained a big piece of meat that made my stomach churn. I handed it back to her after she sat and then closed my eyes again.

The flight attendant came by and asked if I wanted beef or chicken. She mothered me when I told her I wasn't hungry.

"You don't want anything for lunch?"

"No."

"Elijah, you should eat something," said Ivana.

I looked at them both peevishly and then said to the flight attendant, "Do you have anything vegetarian?"

She gave me a pasta dish to go along with my salad and rolls, and both women smiled after my tray was filled.

Problem was, my stomach was a mess and I couldn't fathom the pasta. I tried the cake. It went down ok, but started hassling me once it was there.

I leaned back in the seat and closed my eyes.

"Elijah, you should eat."

"I'm not hungry."

"You will be hungry later."

I didn't say anything.

A few minutes later her voice jolted me awake. "Elijah?"

I opened my right eye at her.

"Are you going to eat your pasta? Because I –"

"Take it."

After she traded our plates, I rang for the flight attendant. When she came I told her to take my tray and then I stretched the seat out as far as it would go.

Lying in an ultra-comfortable seat next to a sweet Lithuanian girl who wanted to chat, I couldn't have been more miserable.

When Ivana and the stewardess woke me for the next meal service I gruffly told them I didn't want anything and went back to sleep.

The last time I woke up we were an hour away from New York. Seeing me awake, Ivana asked me how I was feeling.

"Eh."

With effort, I was able to speak in a polite tone and we chatted for awhile. But the conversation drained my energy and I was soon thinking gruff thoughts that I had to polish as they passed over my tongue. After a period of acting interested and polite, I leaned back and closed my eyes again. I felt Ivana looking at me but ignored it.

"Elijah," she finally asked, "can we exchange addresses? Or maybe we could –"

"No."

After that she was finally quiet and remained so for the rest of the flight. After landing, when the plane parked, she even stood up and crossed to the other aisle so she wouldn't have to stand near me.

Can't say that I blame her.

The interesting observations and feelings of homecoming I had experienced the year before were not to be duplicated. Instead, I was oblivious to my surroundings – even actively uninterested, if that's possible.

I made my way through the airport feeling shitty and dark. not happy to be back, not excited about seeing my parents, not even healthy.

When we finally did see each other, my parents made shocked faces and peppered me with questions about my health – did I eat something bad or what?

It was a convenient explanation and I ran with it. Yes, I had packed a tuna sandwich that must have gone bad.

There was only the ride home to get through, but I managed that by laying on the back seat. When we got home dad carried my bag upstairs and I got a hot shower before jumping into bed to sleep it off. It was 14:00.

I woke up at midnight ready for action, so I went down to the family room. I had a couple beers and chews, watched American television (wrestling, b-movies) and by 05:00 was ready for a nap.

When I shuffled into the kitchen the following afternoon, both mom and dad were at work. I showered again, fixed myself a big meal and ate on the deck in the sun. I was feeling happy to be back, and the familiarity of being in the house I had grown up in was comforting. After reading the county newspaper (Local Man Arrested), I rooted through my stored belongings in the garage and by the time mom and dad got back from work the only thing I had accomplished was choosing two books to take back.

"Well, are you serious about her?"

It was one of mom's standard questions and was most frequently delivered in a private consultation in the back bedroom.

I looked at the wall and squirmed. "I don't know, mom. What's serious, anyway?" I sat down on the bed and watched her root around in one of her drawers. "I mean, we haven't even been together for two months yet."

She looked around at me and said, "Yeah, but for you that's forever."

"That's not true."

She returned her attention to the drawer and said, "You know what I mean… you haven't even had a girlfriend since that last piece of work…"

"I still can't believe you didn't like her! She was nicer to you than she was to me."

"That's only because she wanted to trap you."

"Yeah, right."

She stood up and faced me. "Anyway, this is the reason I called you back here." She held out a small blue jewelry bag that was cinched at the top.

"It's Gramma's wedding ring. She told me she wanted you to have it."

I looked at mom for a pregnant moment. I still hadn't visited Gramma's grave. My throat was tight when I finally said, "I think you should hold onto it for awhile."

She continued holding it in front of me and was misting up. "Just in case?"

"No. I don't need it. But I'm glad to know it's here."

I wiped my eyes. "At least now I won't have to pay two months' salary! What's two times nothing, anyway?"

She lowered the ring and said, "Elijah, don't even joke about that. And please, don't – I'm serious, now – don't joke about that in front of your dad. He's having a hard enough time with you away. He doesn't need to know you're not working."

"I'll be careful. And thanks for paying my rent over the summer. It's really great you're helping me out so much."

"Well, 200 a month isn't that much, but don't tell your father!"

"Fine with me."

She looked like she had a question but was hesitant.

"What?"

"How long you think you'll stay over there," she ventured.

At that moment I wanted nothing to do with living in the U.S. again.

"That's the question, mom. That's the question."

I'd been home for less than a week when the 4th of July rolled around. It's customary in the Counts family to have a cookout at mom and dad's on most holidays, and since I was eager to show my family some things I'd learned in Central Europe, I volunteered to plan the menu.

Hamburgers and corn-on-the-cob were non-negotiable, of course. But in addition, I wanted to bake a potato, chicken and Parma ham casserole and also whip up a blueberries and cream dessert, both of which Liliana had taught me.

So I worked all afternoon in the kitchen as the family played outside in the sun. Oddly, I was really enjoying myself – putting all the love that I could into dishes from Europe that I could share with my family. It was a new experience for me, as I had never been a recreational cook; I also never appreciated how long it takes to prepare a meal for a large group of people. Luckily the beer kept me company.

Finally everything was on the table, the cats were rounded up and we all dug in.

My brother-in-law Dave was the first one to comment on the cuisine, saying, "Hey, Elijah, the burgers are great."

"I cooked those," barked dad.

"Oh, sorry, Gary. Hey Elijah, which one is the Czech dish?"

My 8 year-old nephew said, "That nasty potato stuff."

"Jacob! Be nice," said sis.

"But look at it."

"I said, '*Be nice*!'"

Dave put a scoop on his plate then handed me the spoon and I loaded up my plate. It was one of my favorite dishes and I started in on it.

When I looked up, everyone was staring at Dave. He was making a strange face and then spit his mouthful out. He made a noise and rinsed his mouth out with beer.

"Christ! They eat that stuff?"

"What's wrong," I asked.

"It's horrible! It tastes all… funky!"

"That's the Parma ham – it's a specialty from Italy. Like Parmesan cheese."

"Well, I've had enough of that."

The rest of the family looked at me. They didn't want any funky potato nasty.

Later on, dad took a scoopful and said, "Not bad," but didn't finish his portion.

No one else tried the dish, opting instead for the burgers and corn. I pretended to be hugely happy to have it all for myself, but internally I was disappointed my hard work had been a waste of time. Not one of them had thanked me for exposing them to the new dish, nor had they expressed any interest in where it came from.

In fact, that family dinner was indicative of a larger lack of interest I was beginning to bump my head into. Here I was, the first of our family to travel or live abroad, fresh from a year of experiences that had been incredibly transformative, and what did our conversation consist of? Shopping. There were big sales on, and mom and sis were coming up with a plan of attack.

And between that, Dave and dad spoke about lawns and lawn mowers.

Finally, after they all turned up their noses at the blueberries and cream, sis asked me something about living abroad. The family all looked my way and I began to speak about one of the differences between CZ and the USA. But it couldn't have been more than a minute before I started to see their blank looks (as a teacher, it's my business to spot boredom). They started nodding and grunting when I'd mention something they weren't familiar with – and instead of asking a question, they just nodded and pretended to follow.

Basic concepts that I took for granted seemed beyond them – not in terms of intelligence, but in terms of exposure. For example, when I mentioned that my favorite Czech beer was Budweiser, Dave said, "Budweiser? Did they steal the name or what?"

"No, they were brewing the beer first," I said. "In fact, they'd like American Bud to change *their* name."

"But it's always been Budweiser."

"Yeah, but if another company had the name first, it's also called trademark infringement."

I found myself wanting to lecture.

"It's the same thing with original Champagne… the original is specially produced in the Champagne region in France. But here in the states, a lot of companies call their product champagne when it's really sparkling wine. In most European countries they make a labeling distinction between the two so consumers know what they're buying."

"I've never heard that before," said dad, "but it sounds like a bunch of baloney. Champagne is champagne – it's just bubbly wine."

"But the issue is," I continued, "that original champagne is a specialty product and should be able to demand higher prices."

I saw them lose interest, but I sallied forth anyways.

"If you have two bottles of champagne – original French Champagne and a bottle of… uh… American champagne side-by-side, and the original costs $20, and the imitation costs $9, which one will you buy?"

No one answered, so I answered for them. "The $9 bottle, of course. But then the French company is cheated because an inferior product took their name."

"Why don't they just call it 'American champagne'," asked sis.

"That's still using the French name, isn't it?"

"Well, I wouldn't drink that French crap anyways," said dad, eliciting laughter. He got up and started to clear the table, and others followed his lead. I looked at all of the untouched bowls of blueberries and lamented their waste.

As they ferried the dishes into the house, I sat there eating my dessert, enjoying the freshness of the berries mixed with the richness of the cream, and thought about the discussion we'd just had. All my points had been rationally tenable, but were still rejected out of hand. And why? Because they flew in the face of 4$^{th}$ of July patriotism? Because they weren't the accepted way of approaching things?

I looked out over the freshly-mowed lawn and realized that the things I found so terribly interesting about living abroad – foreign languages, traveling to different cities, cultivating an interest in world affairs – all these things were starting to separate me from my family. I found their conversations somehow uninteresting, just as they likely found my topics of conversation somewhat irrelevant.

It was that 4th of July when I first felt the extent of the changes I'd been going through. I wanted to share my new knowledge and experiences with my family, but they just didn't seem to care for it. So what to do? Beat them over the head with it?

Feign interest in home improvement?

I was probably difficult to be around that month – filled with stupid new ideas and at the same time depressed over Liliana. She and I spoke on a weekly basis, and while we missed each other terribly, one large difference existed between us; Liliana thought nothing of hanging out with other guys while I was away. The pattern was always the same: She would casually tell me about the pleasant evenings she'd been having and I would tighten up, blistered by the fact that she was out with her guy friends.

So while it was gratifying to talk to her, it was also tormenting to hear that she was regularly out on the town, and after our conversations I'd spend the following day or two worrying about what was happening all those thousands of miles away.

Then I'd finally succeed in reminding myself that her behavior was out of my sphere of influence – that I could only control my own actions, not hers. This simple reminder would allow me to realign my attention to where it belonged – the here and now. The pure present – what was in front of me and not so far away in Europe, out of my control, causing me to fret.

And naturally I toyed with calling my old partners, but ultimately it would have been out of spite, not desire. And that just isn't the proper motivation.

Freeloading in Suburbia, PA sucks cheese when compared to freeloading in Prague, CZ. Compare:

| **Prague** | **PA suburbia** |
|---|---|
| Largest castle in the world | White Castle |
| Architectural wonders | Strip malls, big-box stores |
| A city made for walking | A lack of sidewalks |
| Beautiful, friendly women | "What kinda car do *you* drive?" |
| (cheap) Czech Budweiser | American Budweiser |
| Naked weathergirls | Joe DiNardo |

Most reasonable people would agree – Prague is the better place for a young man more interested in idling than in earning money.

In addition to the above issues, I began to be overly critical of the U.S. in general. I was bored with spending time in the car. I was bored with television, bored of fast food, bored from a lack of intellectual stimulation. Bored, bored, bored.

Even a trip to our cabin on the Clarion river – something that had never failed to excite me – left me feeling empty.

My parents couldn't understand my depression, and to tell the truth, neither could I. The only thing I knew was that I was ready to return to Prague.

When I finally got back to CZ at the end of July, Liliana was still at her house in Svatý Hubert, so I had some time to kick around by myself. I was disappointed that she hadn't met me at the airport, but on the other hand, re-entry to Europe always seemed more difficult than re-entry into the U.S. and I used the time to adjust. So after a two-day nap, I began enjoying something beautiful: No work until the beginning of October. The late summer stretched before me as a jolly feast – the beauty of Prague in all of her splendor was mine once more and I renewed my walking regimen with abandon.

It was wonderful being back in *Zlatá Praha.* In Czech grammar, the city's name is feminine, and like any foreign woman she has mysterious ways. But ironically, I felt more at home in Prague than in PA. I knew Prague, enjoyed what she offered, and had developed a strong taste for her. PA was fast becoming just the place where my parents lived.

When we telephoned, Liliana told me she'd first come back to Prague the following week, leaving me to wonder why the hell she didn't rush to Prague to see me – I mean, I *had* been gone for almost a month. But she was just pulling my leg, because the next night I spotted her car in the parking lot and immediately ran over to her window. We went through the Rapunzel routine again and she agreed to come meet in front of her building. I kicked around, waiting, and when I saw her silhouette running towards me it was a dream – a vision of joy and love and when we came together I couldn't hold her enough.

We spent the night in bliss, up all night, our kisses electroshock therapy. I didn't ever want to let her go, the fullness in my chest only expanding when she was within reach.

We spent four lightning days together and we were so into each other that only speaking about it, sharing our feelings with one another, was adequate to quench the building infernos that were in our chests, our bellies, our thoughts.

Liliana was working on her dissertation in a Bohemain-summer kind of way. She'd be in her office for about 5 or 6 hours and afterwards we'd meet in a pub or in town somewhere. I think she would have worked longer if I hadn't been around, but I cannot say she would have had more fun. The time we spent together was so full of happiness and peace that to describe it fully would only take away from its import.

We were falling in love in a beautiful city, we had plenty of time at our disposal, and we knew this much at least – geography wouldn't become a factor in our relationship for another year.

The only snag during that time was her 5-day trip to Warsaw for an academic conference. I volunteered to drive her to the airport at 06:00, which was a real show of love in my book.

After we had packed up the car that morning, I started to get in myself, but Liliana said we had to wait for her colleague Vlada. Alarm bells went off in my head, because when I had been away for the month, Vlada and Liliana had gone out drinking at least once per week.

"You didn't tell me *he* was going."

"I thought I – "

"You didn't."

"Hmm. Oh, here he is."

They exchanged cheek kisses, which drove me crazy, and then spoke to each other in Czech. Vlada spoke English but knew I didn't speak Czech, and he used this to his advantage the whole way to the airport. Even after we had gone inside to check in, I was kept to an outsider position and had to succor myself with the hug and short kiss Liliana gave me.

I fumed back to Liliana's car, which was mine for the week, and drove home. I got back to my room at 07:30 and got in bed, but of course couldn't sleep. I could only obsess about Vlada and Liliana in Warsaw for the 5-day weekend. I didn't even have a phone number or contact information.

This was not a good start to the week.

In the evening, after a day of preoccupied walking through a city that I vaguely recognized as Prague, I finally reached this line of thought: *You've examined everything except the worst case scenario, which is what? Worst case, she sleeps with him. Yes, that would suck and would lead us apart, but why should that frighten me? People sleep together every day. Why should I be frightened of something as natural as that? Ok, I'm in love and it would hurt to be cheated on. But before we met, I was reasonably happy and I'm sure I could be reasonably happy again if Liliana and I were to split up. That's the worst case.*

The kernel of it was this: Why worry about something I could not control? Something that was outside my sphere of influence? Should I worry about a bridge collapsing when I'm walking under it or should I assume it's going to hold? Should I worry that every car I pass on a narrow road is going to hit me or should I assume otherwise? In short, should I dwell on worst-case scenarios or should I primarily consider what I myself can influence?

I thought that if I concentrated on what I had in front of me at any given moment – really concentrated and did my best with the task at hand instead of daydreaming about illusory ideas, figments, hopes or dreams – including people – then I could attune with the way things are meant to be. Taoism has a phrase for it: "Doing, not doing", meaning that by embodying the Pure Present, one effortlessly slips into the activity of that moment. For example, if I'm with my child, I'm completely available to the child, not pre-occupied with my work problems. Conversely, if I'm angry with someone, the best thing to do is to feel that anger completely, release it, and move on. This approach is far better than being peeved at someone for weeks, harboring negativity, breeding black thoughts.

Dan Millman says there are "no ordinary moments", meaning that each one of them has the potential to be life-altering – each moment offers ultimate positivity and ultimate negativity. The choice is ours – do we want to wallow in negativity or bathe in the light?

In the end, I allowed myself to be angry with Liliana for not telling me about Vlada. But I also chose to examine my anger, to really feel *why* I was angry. And of course the root of my anger was my Self. I was scared to lose her and in the end the only thing I had to be angry at was my stupid jealousy. My pitiful, insecure Self. My poor feelings.

But being afraid isn't the proper way to live, and I decided I wasn't going to do it anymore. Oh sure, the negativity skulked about and would strike when I was least expecting it, but at least I was taking conscious steps to fight it. What more could I do?

When I picked them up at the airport 5 days later, Liliana, completely happy to see me, hugged and kissed me all over in front of Vlada, showing him I was her man. And then and there I realized that time spent worrying is the ultimate of losses.

The next month was again idyllic – we spent long weekends at Liliana's, swimming and biking and walking through the forest. But on the other hand, her mother recruited me as a grass cutter and her dad nabbed me as a wood-chopper, so it wasn't all relaxation. In fact, Czech villagers put the Protestant Work Ethic to shame.

Then in September, Liliana asked me to go mushrooming with her.

"Say again?"

"Mushrooming. We'll mushroom in the forest."

I had learned to reserve judgment on foreign customs, but really wanted to be clear on this one.

"Do you mean, like, eating mushrooms and having funny visions?"

"NO! I mean looking for mushrooms in the forest."

"Uh-huh. What for?"

"To eat. You don't look for mushrooms in America?"

"Uh. I'm sure people do, but I never have. Unless they're hallucinogenic, of course."

"*What*? You haven't done that, have you?"

"Oh…"

"Are you really so bad?"

"Hey! They're completely natural."

"Hmph. Well, Czech mushrooming is different. Here, we just walk through the forest and look for mushrooms."

"Sounds exciting."

She narrowed her eyes at me and said, "Fine. Stay and chop wood."

So we went mushrooming.

My holiday just ran by and before I knew it we were conducting placement interviews for the English classes again. Kat had decided to come back for another year as well, and we two, amusingly, were now the senior teachers who the others were to come to for advice and support.

One of the best things about being a second-year teacher was that we already had a fairly set curriculum from the year before, which meant class preparation took less time. But I needed that extra time to juggle the competing occupations of work and girlfriend. Gone were my long walks in the city; they were replaced by long conversations and dinners, followed by nights of... things which weren't so hard to adjust to.

With my bathroommate Marcel gone, it was sure that a new lecturer would take over the room next to mine. To my lasting regret, though, it turned out to be Richard the American.

Yes, I know, I'm American. So's Kat. And yes, I sometimes went to an ex-pat place to watch Friends and eat brownies. I admit it. But mostly I steered clear. I mean, why eat American food, drink American beer and talk to other Americans about America when you're in a foreign country? I traveled outside America to learn more about the world.

Which is why I was so disappointed that Richard moved in next door. True, there was no language barrier to deal with, but that turned out to be the only plus.

On the down side, Richard was a talker – the type of guy who once started was difficult to stop. The type of guy who thought everything he had to say was intensely interesting, even if it was about, say, tree bark or stick pins.

I swiftly came to loathe him.

My definitive Richard story: One evening I opened up the door to the bathroom to see him shaving at his sink. I said hello, was polite, and he started in on the topic of looking for work in America. He was looking for a job for the next year and wanted to tell me where he was applying. Now, the reason I'd gone into the bathroom was to do a Number 2, and I danced in place for twenty seconds or so trying to get the message across. But since Richard was oblivious to others, I finally excused myself and ran into the toilet room.

"No problem," said Richard, who continued to talk to me through the door. From the topic of work, he moved on to internet access, my bicycle, his past roommate, Star Trek, his old boss, two former colleagues, a past landlady, and then a past roommate's girlfriend.

I sat on the commode listening to all this with dismay.

I mean, really. Who talks to someone through the door when they're shitting?

I came out of the door and he was standing right in front of it. He continued talking, but backed away a step. I washed my hands and then said, "Hey Richard, I'm really tired. 'Night."

And even when I shut the bathroom door behind me, the guy continued talking!

Not being rude to him was almost impossible.

When I was 13, I started chewing Copenhagen snuff because everyone else did it. It's a disgusting habit, really – you pinch a wad of tobacco between your lip and teeth and then suck on it. Results: A nicotine buzz, a swollen lip, and having to spit tobacco juice. Though it depends on your station in life, it's not really a socially-accepted form of tobacco use. Also, there's the inevitability that at least once per year, any given chewer will spill a spittoon over things not designed to be flooded with tobacco juice – and a spilled spitter never fails to repulse. (Though it is rather funny when it happens to someone else.)

Nearly fifteen years after my Copenhagen habit began, I came over to Europe with high hopes of quitting tobacco altogether. But then when my chew ran out and the withdrawal symptoms commenced, I found myself at the *Tabák* buying Marlboro Lights at 11 p.m.

So I smoked for three months until I discovered a tobacco store in Prague that sold Swedish Snus, a product very similar to Copenhagen. I quit the smoking and again took up chewing. I was only doing it once per day, but still.

Liliana was fiercely anti-tobacco, so telling her wasn't an option. And as we became closer and closer, we spent most of our evenings together – which previously had been the only time I would chew. Having that opportunity taken away from me was making me extremely nervous. Sometimes we'd be lying together and I'd think, "When can I go back to my room and have a chew?"

I eventually resorted to my high school method of hiding in the toilet to chew. This worked for awhile, but after a few weeks of sneaking off for a chew whenever I could, I began to see the absurdity of the situation – I was with a kind, affectionate and beautiful woman and all I could think of was how soon I could leave. Stupid.

I don't know exactly when I had enough, but once the plan to quit came to me I knew it made sense.

Here's how I did it: I enjoyed one last relaxing chew, then got up my nerves and went to the bathroom. Standing over the toilet, I swallowed down a disgusting mouthful of tobacco juice and sludge.

It didn't take long to come back up, and for the rest of the night my gut was tobacco-lined and achy. It was just an awful bit of shock therapy, but after chewing for 15 years, how does one muster the self-discipline to stop? I couldn't think of any other way.

The good news is that it worked. The gag reflex was strong when I buried my nose in the disgusting spitter the next day and I was able to go a whole day without.

Two nights later the monkey came to visit and I had to constantly remind myself of the puking bout. But the monkey was strong, and talked to me in harsh tones, saying things like, "Oh, come on – have one more chew and then do the puke thing again. You know you want to..."

And when he saw that I was trying to ignore him, he'd get meaner and meaner: "Yeah, like you've got the courage to quit… I've heard that before! What do you expect to substitute chewing with, anyways? Whatever it is, I guarantee I ain't gonna cooperate! Who do you think runs this show, anyways?"

And so on.

Oh, sick, dirty little monkey! He'd torment with me all night long, sometimes leaving for short stretches only to pounce on the bed again and hassle me, allowing me to only toss and turn somewhere between semi- and fully-conscious.

I actually spotted that little rascal once in the middle of the night and jumped up to throttle him, but he morphed into a jacket draped over the back of a chair before I could reach him.

Next time.

The only good thing about quitting tobacco was my surfeit of nervous energy. When Liliana wasn't around, I took longer workouts, and when she was around, we'd invest it in… longer workouts as well.

"Lovely, precious nicotine," whispered the monkey.

In early November my parents asked if I was coming home for Christmas. I told them yes, but that I also wanted to bring back Liliana. Problem was, we couldn't afford tickets for the both of us.

"Any suggestions?" I fished.

By our next conversation, mom and dad had scored buddy passes for the both of us.

Problem: I wasn't exactly sure Liliana was ready for a trip home. I mean, we'd only been together for six months, and exclusively for just three. A trip to meet with the parents therefore seemed like a huge step. But things *were* going great and it was hard to deny our intentions.

Once, for example, Liliana borrowed the key to my room when I was teaching and scattered "I love you" notes all over the place. In my books, the refrigerator, the bed – you name it. Took three weeks of melty discovery to find them all.

The question of mutual attraction and suitability seemed pretty well answered, and I decided not to get hung up on the gravity of the situation. So after dinner and a movie one evening, while walking across the Charles Bridge I asked her to come home with me. It was freezing cold and windy, and we were snuggled close together.

"Sure! It will be wonderful to meet your parents," she said. "Thank you so much for asking."

"I can't be away from you for another month, you know?"

"I'm happy you want to keep me close!"

We snuggled again as we walked and then a moment later she stopped short.

"But where will we sleep?"

I hadn't thought about that. Mom likely still thought I was a virgin.

"We'll sleep in my bed," I bluffed.

"*Together*? You said your parents were conservative."

"I'll just tell them there's no alternative. I mean, I'm 29, you're 25… we're adults who sleep together."

She cocked her head and squinted at me.

I shrugged. "They'll just have to accept it."

That weekend I called mom and dad and told them we were coming home the day after Christmas (we wanted to spend time with both families). They were disappointed that we wouldn't be home for the big day, but were also excited about me bringing home a woman, and began the planning right away. The big question was what to buy Liliana for Christmas. I told mom that gold is always appropriate, to which she said, "Uh-huh."

But the meat of the phone call was the sleeping arrangements. I had to be diplomatic.

"Mom, you know Liliana and I will sleep together, right?"

"Oh… uh…"

Standing next to me at the pay phone, Liliana pinched me in annoyance.

"I mean, we've been practically living together for the last six months, and suddenly we're going to pretend we're not together? We're all adults here, aren't we?"

Liliana walked away shaking her head.

"Well…" mom stalled.

She sighed, probably exhaling a huge cloud of smoke.

"… I'll have to ask your dad."

Put through the Mom-Decoder, she'd really said, "Not in *my* house."

# Act III
# Hrad (*Castle*) Krakovec

During the weeks leading up to Christmas, carp vendors started appearing on Prague street corners or public squares where pedestrian traffic was high. The vendor stations consisted of three-foot high fiberglass pools containing scores of fat carp, a long butchering table, and a scale. When a customer reached the head of the line, (s)he chose a fish from the vat and the carp seller, wearing a rubber apron but hardly ever wearing gloves, fished the carp out with a net and placed it on the table. After whacking it on the head until it stopped moving, he'd gut it. Then he'd weigh the fish and the customer would pay for it.

For freshness, the only way to beat the sidewalk method is to take the fish home alive, where it spends its last hours in the bathtub before someone from the family prepares it themselves.

This last was the system in Svatý Hubert, where we were spending Christmas Day, and Liliana's father, after learning I'd never gutted a fish, was keen on teaching me how. After being handed the club, I looked at the fish suffocating there on the counter, then back to her father who was encouraging me to whack it. I shook my head no and he encouraged me further. I again declined and he continued encouraging me so much that I finally screamed for Liliana.

Her father shook his head, making a *you-big-girl* face at me until she arrived in the kitchen.

I had Liliana translate for me: "The only thing I want for Christmas is to be released from *this*."

After a brief but intense negotiation, her father made a grudging face at me and to my great relief assigned me to Christmas Tree Duty. Instead of getting my hands bloody, I was to carve the trunk down so it could fit into the undersized, archaic tree stand that was waiting for me when I went out into the garage. I got to work, shuddering at what must have been happening up in the kitchen.

Five minutes later as I was sitting on the cement floor, pitifully hacking away (I'm about as handy as a foot) Doktor snuck up behind me, got me into a hump-grip, and commenced to pump at me. I squealed and tried to fight my way out of it, but his grip around my shoulders was simply too strong and it took me ten seconds of panicked struggle to fend him off. I jumped up and chased him off, but the damage to my dignity was already done.

And I'm not sure if they bought it, but when the Christmas tree collapsed the next day when we were all gathered around exchanging gifts, that's the story I dredged up.

Otherwise, there were lots of happy visits, both at home and to distant family members, and the best thing about Christmas in the CZ that year was my realization that the holiday spirit is the same in CZ as everywhere else – people just want to be happy, to enjoy their families, and to eat well.

The story about Doktor humping me proved popular, especially when Liliana told it to a table full of my relatives during dinner on New Year's Day. Still hurting from the night before, I was admittedly a bit irked at its retelling, and it reminded me how challenging it sometimes is to bring home a new partner.

Happily, my brother-in-law Dave kept the ball rolling.

"So, Lillian, are you a communist?"

"Don't be a jerk," I snapped. "At least she didn't hoard half the Wal-Mart for Y2K."

He opened his mouth but nothing came out. He narrowed his eyes at me.

Liliana looked over at Dave and said, "No, I'm not a communist... but I am an atheist."

My eyes darted around the sudden silence at the table until my 7-year old nephew said, "You don't look so old."

Liliana smiled at him and shook her head. "Not '80-ist.' A-thee-ist."

Mom put her glass down and closed her gaping jaw. "Now seriously, you're not really an...?"

"Mrs. Counts," replied Liliana, "I'm a scientist. We believe in what we can see and measure, and since I haven't seen God, technically I am."

"So you don't believe in God."

"Well, I think there's something out there that may help us sometimes, but I don't know what it is."

"I don't believe in God, either," pronounced my nephew, grinning at Liliana.

"Shut up. You do so," said Dave.

"What about your family," mom asked.

"I think they are, too. But we are all baptized."

"Oh, ok," dad jumped in, "Then technically you *are* a Christian."

She hesitated, then said, "Yes, but for us it's more complex than that–"

"Whaddya mean, complex? Either you're Christian or you're not."

"Yeah, ok," I interrupted. "But no one here went to church on Christmas, and over there we all did."

We hadn't really all gone. It was only Liliana and me for Midnight Mass – I just wanted to put him on his heels a bit.

Dad glared at me a second and then turned to Liliana.

"But if you're an atheist you shouldn't be in church anyways, right?"

"Maybe we're the ones who need the most help," she said.

He considered this a second, then announced he was getting ice cream and stood up.

I gripped Liliana's hand and whispered to her, "I like it when you're ornery."

"But now your family hates me," she whispered back.

"They don't hate you – they're just scared of your evil, foreign ways!"

"Ha-ha."

"Just don't put a hex on them, ok?"

She squinted at me and said, "I'll do it to *you* if you're not nice."

An hour later as I was zealously explaining the college football bowl system to a politely listening Liliana, mom asked me back to her room. Leaving a visibly relieved Liliana with a kiss, I followed her back. As she always did for these conferences, mom sat me on the bed, lit a cigarette, and paced.

"So what's up, mom? It's pretty late in the game…"

"Is Liliana really an atheist?"

She was looking out the window at the glowing, snow-covered ground.

"Maybe, but she's still nicer than all of us put together."

"Yes, I noticed that. She's very helpful. And kind."

"Sure is."

"And you're serious about her, aren't you?"

"I guess."

She turned, put her cigarette in the ashtray, and faced me.

"Well, then it's time you took this."

She held up the small velvet bag and arched an eyebrow. Smiling at her, I stood up and took it from her hands.

"What's this?"

"Don't play dumb. And don't get married without me!"

I hugged her and promised not to.

She guided me back onto the bed, and I untied the knot of the bag. I hadn't seen the ring in ages and was stunned when I got it open – it was white gold, with a tastefully large but understated diamond.

I looked up and said, "That's really nice!"

"It is. You're lucky Gramma liked you."

"…I miss her, you know?"

I put the ring back and tied the knot. I was already nervous to think about it and just wanted to hide it away.

"Just be sure," she said.

"Thanks, mom. I promise."

I kissed her, put the ring in my pocket and turned to the door.

"I'll just be a second," she said.

I nodded, then went out the door and into Bedlam Central.

Liliana was playing a game of hallway soccer with my nephew and brother-in-law, all three of them knotted together, jostling for the pillow-ball in the narrow space.

When she saw me, Liliana said, "Out time! Out time," which forced the boys to look at each other for a puzzled moment before they realized she was calling a time-out.

They stopped playing and Liliana pushed me into our bedroom and closed the door after us.

"What were you talking to your mom about? Does she hate me?"

"Of course not. She just wanted to speak about your Christmas gift."
She scrutinized me and said, "I don't believe you."
"Ok, she wanted to speak about your Name Day gift."
"She doesn't know about name days."
"Are you saying my mom is stupid?"
"No, I – *what*?"
"You think she's just a stupid Christian!"
"..."
"I'm gonna go tell her!"
I feigned my way around her and she jumped on my back, then wrestled me onto the bed.
"Tell me! Tell me! Tell me," she chanted.
"We spoke about your birthday gift!"
"Oooooh!"
She was roughing up my hair, pulling my ears, tickling me.
I quite like being tickled, but eventually I had enough and started muscling her around until she called a truce. "Ok," she said, "Enough. But now tell me."
"Ok, I'll tell you, but not here. It would be best to show you in mom's room."
She frowned and said, "Mom's room?"
"Come on – I'll show you there."
We disentangled from the bed and I stood up and opened the door for her. When she walked out, I quickly closed the door and locked it behind her. She banged and protested, but I didn't let her in until I'd hidden the ring in my secret hiding spot beneath the carpeting where I'd used to hide the Playboys.
When I opened the door, she gave me the Czech stink-eye and said, "You sleep on the couch tonight!"
Mom, who was just coming out of her room, overheard this and quipped, "That's the best news I've heard all day!"

There's not really that much to do at my parents' house in the winter. Of course with my friends home for the holidays there were visits to make and bars to frequent, but everyone eventually trickled back to their distant lives and the world again shrank back to my parent's house.
After a week of indoor emptiness, Liliana and I had to get out and my bright idea was to take her to our mountain cabin in Clarion County. It's beautiful countryside up there, a river runs nearby, and we'd finally be alone.
"Why are you gonna take her up *there*," asked mom, who hadn't slept there since I was 8.
After much lobbying, dad reluctantly parted with his SUV and Liliana and I excitedly packed up and drove the three hours on back roads, feeling road-trip happy until we stopped at a diner and ate fried *pickles* for the first and last time.

Further on, the roads got darker and narrower, and we were feeling the positivity of the pine countryside.

We arrived at the cabin in the 20:00 winter darkness. Like many of the neighboring cabins, ours was shuttered up. Plus, the exterior remained unfinished, so Liliana's first impression of the place was tar-paper flapping in the January wind.

I turned off the engine and looked at her expectantly.

"So? What do you think?"

She looked at me warily, so I answered for her.

"Great, isn't it?"

Leaving the headlights on, I puppy-dogged out of the car, excited to be at the cabin after so long, and even peed on a nearby tree.

The headlights illuminated a stand of leafless Maple trees on the riverbank, and Liliana walked towards them.

When I caught up to her she said, "The river is so close!"

"Great, isn't it? We swam and boated here all the time when we were kids."

We stood, looking out at the wide bend in the Clarion that I will always have as my archetype river memory, and breathed in. The air was painfully clean, made crisp by the smooth, unfrozen river, and we breathed deeply.

But the wind was whipping at us and I said, "Come on, I'll show you the inside."

We carefully navigated the snow-covered steps and opened the lock. Finally I could show my baby the best place in the world!

But when I opened up the door, an invisible intruder pounced directly at my face, causing me to recoil; it was the reek of refined petroleum, overpowering and industrial.

"What's that," Liliana asked.

"Kerosene," I said through my hand.

I didn't want to introduce electricity to the fumes by turning on the lights (you never know up there) so we retreated to the truck for a flashlight.

Once inside the cabin, the penumbra of the flashlight revealed no monsters or large animals, and we walked into the wood-paneled main room. The cabin contains furniture discarded over decades: A 1950's-era sink, stove and fridge line the far wall. A natty green fold-out couch lounges against the right wall, and a long rickety table with chairs stands against the left. The brown heater squats in the far corner.

On our way over to inspect the heater, we felt the brown, threadbare carpeting simultaneously squishing *and* crunching under our feet. I swung the flashlight down onto the carpet. The squishing came from the liquid that had saturated it. The crunching noise was from ladybug carcasses – thousands of them. There had been some sort of ladybug massacre and they lay on every flat surface in huge colonies. If it's true that ladybugs are lucky, whoever had done this was headed for some serious trouble.

"Poor beetles," said Liliana.

Crunching across the swamp, we discovered the source of the kerosene. The fuel valve had broken and an unimpeded stream had flowed into the cabin until the outside tank was empty. It may have been recent, it may have been months before. There was no way of knowing.

My disappointment was tumorous. Not only because of the consequences for the cabin, but because I had *so* planned on impressing Liliana with a romantic, secluded weekend of semi-roughing it; no TV, only candlelight and love, love, love.

When we emerged and breathed easy again, Liliana said, "Your mom told me a hotel would be better anyways."

I smiled at her bleakly and looked out at the river in the darkness.

"What should we do," she asked.

I sighed.

"This sucks."

Ten minutes later we burst out of the building dragging a roll of most of the carpeting that had been saturated. We struggled our way over to the fire pit and heaved it on.

"We can either burn it now, or tomorrow," I said.

"Tomorrow. It's late."

We locked up the cabin (as if it were necessary) and went to look for a hotel.

We drove back to the cabin around noon the next day, fat and happy from a Bob Evans breakfast. None of the neighbors' cabins were occupied and we walked around the neighborhood poking our noses in windows, inspecting the riverbank and finally returning to the truck.

"Are you sure you're ok with staying here," I asked for the $100^{th}$ time.

"It's nicer as that dirty hotel."

The hotel's bathroom had been horrible, but at least it was indoors. The cabin boasted an outhouse that now smelled better than the cabin itself.

I climbed into the truck and came out with two beers. Something about being at the cabin made drinking at noon acceptable. We toasted and then fished out the bags of cleaning agents we'd purchased.

Once inside, Liliana started cleaning up the ladybugs and mice pellets while I tried to fix the fuel thingie. Whereas her work went well, mine went nowhere. The fuel thingie needed a rubber whatsis, but a larger one than we'd been able to purchase at the general store. They'd had a commanding beef jerky selection, but the heater repair section had been pitiful.

Because I was unable to fix the central heater, we had to rely on a kerosene space heater for warmth. The sticker on the side claimed it was "Clean Burning" but the cabin smelled so nasty we couldn't tell if it was kicking out more fumes or not.

We regularly popped outside for fresh air until it turned dark (Liliana was afraid of bears) then opened a window. We taught each other card games until bedtime, then moved a mattress to the floor and burrowed – fully dressed – into our sleeping bags.

When we woke up in the morning, we discovered that the heater had stopped burning and it was so cold that the condensation on the window had frozen. But that wasn't what bothered Liliana – when she saw the mice pellets on the surfaces she had scoured clean the night before, she called uncle.

"I told you she wouldn't like it."
"Mom, it was only because of the kerosene."
"She didn't like it, though, did she?"
"No, but – "
"Told you."

A couple of days before our return to Prague, we were invited to a friend's house for a get-together. Matt, an old high school buddy, had just finished renovating an old house and wanted to show it off. A three-story Victorian affair from a bygone era, the house had a cozy and lived-in feeling to it. One of the many endearing touches was an automatic player piano squatting in the corner of the dining room – its music really added a sense of jauntiness as we said our hellos to the 10 or so people who'd come.

Liliana was taken up by the girls straightaway, and Jake, myself and some other guys were led downstairs by Matt to "see his home gym". This was really an excuse to smoke a joint – as had been our custom for years – and as it circulated, my friends were surprised at my refusal to smoke. Cries of traitorship, sissyness, and other attacks on my masculinity were parried and dodged until the thing was gone, and when they eventually tired of poking at me, we piled upstairs for refreshments.

I wandered into the dining room and found Liliana talking to Matt's wife Sarah, and somehow the idea of playing Trivial Pursuit came up. This was met with enthusiasm by most everyone, and soon afterwards the game commenced. Liliana and myself were a team, and there were four other couples as well.

Prior to that I had never given it much thought, but the degree of cultural specificity that Trivial Pursuit embodies is downright scary, with the questions being an absolute and deep exploration of American culture. Example questions: "What brand of trucks was made in Mound, Minnesota for 46 years before a move to El Paso, Texas?" (Tonka); "What state gave birth to more than half the members of the 1980 U.S. Olympic hockey team?" (Minnesota); and "What type of plants did the U.S. Supreme Court affirm the rights of states to ban in 1983?" (nuclear power plants). Which is all well and good for most people, but the upshot is that Liliana and I got absolutely pummeled in the game, coming in last with just two wedges. Losing wasn't such a problem for me, but Liliana got upset because she felt the game unfairly cast her as being ignorant and backward – the poor girl from the ex-socialist country – and no amount of me speaking of the cultural specifics of the game could appease her.

But later, when we were sitting on the couch, Jake and Sherry started a conversation about Liliana's PhD dissertation, which lightened her spirits somewhat. And whether or not it was intentional on their parts, it also revealed that Liliana was actually the most educated and worldly among us.

Nevertheless, we have not played Trivial Pursuit since then.

When I had come home the previous summer, I couldn't *wait* to get back to CZ.

But this trip was different. Mom and dad's house, with Liliana inside, was so full of life for me – it wasn't just a place where my parents lived, it was where *my home* was.

And that was the thing about our trip home that winter – I realized that my home was no longer a static geographic location, but rather that place where Liliana and I happened to be.

It was late January by the time we were back and settled at the university. As usual, my classes didn't start for a couple more weeks, but Liliana jumped right back into her work. We were early to bed and early to rise in the winter darkness.

We mostly slept in the Foreigner Ghetto, but when Liliana had to work we spent the evenings apart, which was fine for my reading. I was again tackling philosophical texts: Iris Murdoch, Carl Jung for the work he'd done with dreams, Dostoyevsky, more M. Scott Peck.

Much as I hate to admit it though, all these readings didn't help me a whit during my frequent examinations of Gramma's wedding ring. (The ring itself was instrumental to my musings, the physical embodiment of the idea. The talisman of togetherness.)

*Marriage to a Czech girl.*

*Could I live without her?*

*If she said yes, where would we end up?*

*And the children - what language would they speak?*

*Would I be content with one woman for the rest of my life?*

*Could selfish, lazy, boozed-up, drug-addled, jealous me be a good husband anyways?*

Liliana's Feb. 4 Name Day, when I planned on asking her, was drawing ever nearer, and since I had no other gift it was basically all or nothing.

☯

When I wasn't examining it, I carried the ring in my pocket. I thought of it as a charm, a type of connection with my grandmother's spirit. It had been her ring, after all, and perhaps it would bring me some of her wisdom. Perhaps it would even see me through the turmoil of deciding between tying myself to a Central European lady or remaining Mr. Freeandeasy.

Both paths beckoned, and the situation really didn't need exacerbated by the re-appearance of one of Liliana's old boyfriends. But sometimes I guess these things happen for a reason.

The story: On Feb. 1st I told Liliana I was going into town to meet Josh. No problem, she said. She had a lot of work. So into town I went. After two beers and no Josh, I called my message service and he'd left one saying he couldn't make it. Great. So, being the in-love fool that I was, I hurried back to spend a quiet evening with baby. But when I knocked on her dorm room there was no answer.

Ok…

Since I didn't have to teach the next day, I headed over to the big campus bar to see if Karel was there. Maybe we'd play some pool.

I went in, got a beer, and looked around the large hall. There were perhaps 30 square tables in the middle of the room, the pool tables off to the right. It was sparsely peopled, and thus easy to pick out Liliana. She was sitting with a man I didn't recognize; her back was towards me, the man to her left. I could partially see his face.

Like an idiot, I skulked over to a nearby table and watched them. They were enjoying each other's company, and every now and again they'd explode into laughter.

I chugged at the beer and watched, my throat burning, constricting as they carried on. I was finished with the beer when Liliana stood and turned in my direction. She was carrying two glasses, and as she walked away from the table I noticed that the guy was watching her. She must have felt it too, because she spun around to bust him. He smiled. When she turned forward again, she looked… pretty happy.

The bile had never been so thick in my gut, and as Liliana came closer to my table and recognized me, she stopped short.

I stood up and nodded toward the bar. "I'll come with," I said.

When I got there, I turned and saw her trailing behind. I ordered three beers and she came to stand beside me, placing her empties on the bar. I watched the barman fill the first glass.

"I thought you were working tonight."

"Tomaš surprised me."

Second glass.

"You seem to be having a good time."

"He's just an old friend."

Third glass.

"*Just friends* don't watch your ass as you walk away."

Silence.

I paid for the beers before saying, "So enjoy yourself. I'm outta here."

"Wait. Come join us."

"Yeah, right."

As I walked around her she said, "Don't be like that."

My only comeback was too ferocious to voice, so I choked it down and walked out the door feeling a lot shittier than when I'd gone in.

Nothing can plunge me into blackness as quickly as the jealousy can, and I was neck deep in it, my breathing shallow and inadequate. I couldn't think past how happy they looked together.

It was too late to go back into the city and the pub was now out of the question, so I went for a long walk. In the middle of it, like a clever boy, I bought a pack of cigarettes at a vending machine and set about chain-smoking.

As I walked, I jumped to the conclusion that I had been given a perfect illustration of what to expect from marriage to Liliana.

I mean, hadn't I once been the other man in her life? Hadn't I caused her to end a seven-year relationship?

*Can't trust her.*

*She's sleeping with him.*

After walking to exhaustion, I returned to my room. A note was stuck between the door and frame. I snatched it down but didn't read it, and went inside to obsess instead.

After fitful sleep, I got up at 07:30 and read the note from Liliana. It was apologetic. She said she missed me and could I please come and get her – anytime – when I returned from wherever I was.

I crumpled it and threw it out. I wasn't ready yet. I knew she had to teach at 08:00 and that's when I wanted to slip off campus.

I was in the shower when I heard the knock on my door – it had to be her but I didn't have anything to say.

Plus – and I know this is wrong – I wanted her to feel bad as well.

St. Vitus' opened at 10:00, and I was in a pew shortly thereafter. I needed counsel, but bad. Just 12 hours before I had been ~~relatively~~ sure about asking Liliana to marry me. Now I wasn't even sure I trusted her.

Shaking my head and being pissed off, I unpacked the Bible from my backpack and all I could picture was Liliana flirty and happy with that dude the night before.

I obsessed for a long spell until remembering where I was, and that I was actually there to cut that shit out. I closed my eyes and began to breath deeply, berating my nasty self until I was able to drive it into the corner and back into its trunk. I shut the lid and tried to affix the latch, but again realized there isn't one. When I opened my eyes I looked up at the far end of the church's stained-glass windows and relaxed my shoulders, placing my hands in my lap.

My mind finally empty, I took the ring from my pocket.

It hadn't lost any of its beauty, but it had somehow lost a great deal of its allure.

Marriage to an unfaithful partner was the last thing I needed. It would drive me to a number of things I'm predisposed to anyways.

Did I *really* want to get involved with a woman who saw no problem in evenings out with old boyfriends?

I pressed the ring between my palms and closed my eyes.

I prayed for forgiveness.

I prayed for Liliana and I prayed for the strength to act with integrity – to dispel my doubts and fears and to replace them with courage. I prayed for the ability to minimize the negative and maximize the positive.

Courage.

Compassion.

Patience.

I asked for help in determining whether Liliana and I belonged together. I pressed the ring harder and asked that it be blessed with the wisdom of my grandmother and the caring and love a proper marriage should possess.

When I opened my eyes again, they struggled to adjust to the sun streaming through the stained glass, and I blinked until I could see properly.

I sat there, holding the ring in my hands and breathing calmly until my mind was again empty.

Then I repeated my prayers.

At length I opened my eyes and appreciated the beauty of the church's architecture before I packed and stood to bundle up. Donning my pack, I walked out, pausing only to anoint my forehead with the holy water. I left the church, went through the long, dark passage to the second courtyard, and then turned right toward the side exit of Prague Castle.

I felt a solemn lucidity as I walked out of the plain arched passage. There were very few people about as I exited past the cloaked castle guards and strolled across the high earthen bridge and past the gates of the closed summer garden. At the corner of the castle proper, on a whim I ducked into the touristy café there.

It was cozy inside. The seating area was small, perhaps five tables, and the walls were painted a warm orange. I ordered a cappuccino and sat down.

As I waited I took out the Bible, turned to the Book of James, and commenced to reading. By the time the coffee came I was halfway through. I put the book down and sipped at the coffee, which burnt my tongue.

Suddenly the entrance door burst open and an older red-haired lady exploded into the room. With my cup suspended in mid-air, I couldn't help but stare at her. She was wearing a long, reddish fur coat with a high protective collar, and the wind-burnt red of her cheeks and forehead gave evidence of the nasty weather. Her cheeks were doing a Dizzy Gillespie thing as she fought for air.

She grabbed the back of a chair and put her weight on it, breathing heavy. Looking at me as if I were an old friend, she started speaking in German and I understood nothing. I looked around to make sure she was speaking to me and when I looked back at her, she nodded theatrically.

I smiled at her, puzzled.

Behind her, a tall, grayed gentleman came in and closed the door. He was wearing a long navy blue trench coat and carrying an umbrella. He took off his cap and came over to the red lady, who continued her gesticulations.

The man smiled and asked if the table next to mine was free.

I said that it was and they took off their coats.

The woman spoke quickly and the man translated, "We just walked up the hill. She says I am trying to kill her."

I smiled, and when they started to discuss what to order, I placed my cup down and picked up where I had been reading. I got through two sentences before I realized the woman was speaking to me again.

I put the book in my lap and looked up at her. The man walked around the corner to order and she continued jabbering away at me.

As I was shaking my head and shrugging my shoulders at her, the man came back to the table. He asked if I spoke German.

"Not yet," I replied.

"Ha! That's a good answer!"

The man said something to his wife that made her stop yammering at me, and I gratefully took up the book and started to read.

They spoke in German for a moment and then the man said, "Excuse me..."

*Sigh.*

Why fight it? I closed the book, put it on the table and gave them my full attention.

"Yes?"

"I'm sorry to interrupt... but my wife doesn't speak English. Do you permit me to translate for her?"

"Of course."

The woman spoke for awhile, then the man asked me how to get to the castle's National Art Gallery. I gave him the directions and he translated for her. Then he asked me if I were a tourist. I told him I lived in Prague, and he seemed very pleased by this.

"When I was a young man," he said, "I also lived in Prague..."

The woman reached over, patted my forearm and rolled her eyes.

"... and I had the nicest Czech girl. The Czech girls are beautiful, aren't they?"

"They are."

"We were going to get married but I was in love with another girl, a German girl, and I went back to her."

"Really? Is this her?"

"Yes. This is her."

The lady spoke while looking at me, then gestured that her husband would translate.

"Well... she wants me to ask the name of your Czech girlfriend."

*How did she know I had a girl?*

I looked at her and said, "Liliana."

"*Wunderschön Name*," she said.

The man asked to see a picture of Liliana, and I dug around for the snapshot we'd made in a photo booth.

He looked at it, nodding a long time before passing it over to his wife.

She nodded vigorously and said, "She is beautiful!"

I looked at the picture after she handed it back and nodded. "She is."

The man took off his glasses and leaned close to me.

"You must not lose her," he said.

I blinked at him.

"Pardon?"

"Do not lose her," he repeated.

I looked at his wife, who broke out her English again. "God is with you," she said.

I looked at the man for clarification, but the lady patted my arm to get my attention again.

"God is with you," she repeated.

I nodded dumbly. I probably should have been overjoyed and celebratory, but the whole thing was just too direct, too crazy strange for me to handle gracefully. I stood up and excused myself, saying it was time for me to go. They nodded at me, smiling indulgently.

As I bundled up, I offered my hand to the man. He shook it and smiled. "Remember," he said.

"I will."

I turned to the lady then, and as we shook she patted me on the cheek and gave me a little cherubic smirk.

I backed off and went around the corner to pay the waitress. On a whim, I paid for their drinks too, and walked out of the café amazed at how stupefying life can be.

On my way home after meeting the "Germans," I convinced myself that I had to forgive Liliana for her meeting with her friend the night before. But I also had to be sure that she had such things out of her system.

I went straight back to her room and knocked, halfway wanting *him* to answer the door so I could simply turn my back on what lay before me.

But no. She was there, alone.

Her puffy eyes turned on when she saw me and she hugged me so hard I stumbled backwards.

It was a nice re-affirmation, and when she said, "I'm so sorry! I didn't sleep at all last night," I knew everything was going to be fine.

On my previous birthday we'd gone to a French restaurant called Chez Moi. Located in Malá Strana near the Wallenstein Castle, it was unique among the many dark and romantic cellar restaurants in Prague because I knew the owner. I taught him English, and in return he fed me and a guest once in awhile (without drinks). It was thus the natural choice for Liliana's Name Day dinner.

After we were seated, the blond waiter greeted us by name and gave us the wine list. Liliana skimmed it and chose a bottle of French white.

"Oh, very good choice," gushed the waiter. When he returned with the bottle, he presented and opened it with a flourish, making a big show of it.

The wine was delicious, as was the food. Nevertheless, neither sat well in my stomach. My right pocket was full to bursting and I needed to unload the ring. After the plates were cleared, I excused myself and went into the bathroom for a pep-talk.

Looking in the mirror at my nervous eyes, I told myself over and over to calm down. I tried to deep-breathe the irregular heart beats away, but nothing doing. There was only one way. I practiced my lines again, reviewing the main points I knew I'd forget most of.

Another patron came in and went into a stall behind me. I continued practicing, and after he emerged and washed his hands, he winked at me and said, "Good luck," before walking out.

That left me alone again, and a short time later I came out of the bathroom feeling like a football team taking to the field after halftime. The ring was in my right palm.

Liliana looked beautiful waiting there for me, and after I sat and guzzled my wine, I put the ring between my legs. I took a deep breath, reached across the table for her hands, and then launched into the marry me spiel.

I don't recall exactly what I said, but I started with how happy I'd been since being with her, how she helped me be a better person, how I couldn't imagine living without her and how much fun we had together.

About midway through, her eyes widened in recognition, but that didn't stop me from finishing. Nor did I stop when she began crying.

I finally ran out of words and reached down for the ring, but in my haste clumsily pushed it back between my legs. There was a moment of silence when the ring should have been produced, but instead I had to give her a Big Smile as I dug under my bottom for the ring. I finally found it and held it up to her.

With a smile I asked her.

She shook her head and said, "You're crazy."

*Uh...*

Time stretched on as she shook her head at me. And then, after a gut-wrenching perpetuity, she finally smiled and said, "I will."

We stood up and embraced then, kissing away each other's tears, and when the waiter came to see what was happening, we gave him our camera to record the event, tears and all.

After he'd gone away, the serendipity of our togetherness was made obvious once again; as I slipped it onto her finger, we found that Gramma's ring fit Liliana perfectly. And though it sounds incredulous, we both felt, very strongly, that we were simply fulfilling something foretold, that it was the most obvious and natural thing in the world to get married.

PS: At the end of the evening, after a second bottle of the French white, we made a less serendipitous discovery – the wine cost over $80 per bottle.

On my first weekend visit to Liliana's the previous summer, before the chore-filled weekends had commenced, she took me to see Krakovec Castle. Located atop a narrow plateau that overlooks rolling fields, a pine forest and the confluence of two streams, the castle ruin has seen far better days. It has no windows, no roof, and is missing its south-facing wall.

But for all that, the light brown walls that remain standing embody more than what an intact castle ever could. For me, functioning castles are urbane and exclusive. Snooty, even. But castle ruins are something else – they remind me that things fall apart, that even things built to withstand time are subject to its rigors. In ruins I'm reminded of my mortality. In ruins I feel the weight of time, the lives that came before me. Indeed, in ruins I feel history as I feel it nowhere else.

This was especially so at Krakovec during our first summer evening there, when the sunlight illuminated us, rendering our auras visible and showing us how they could merge as two clouds would – slowly, the edges mingling until after a time it was not possible to distinguish where one began and the other ended.

In a mood of jubilation that first day, Liliana took my hand and showed me the secrets of Krakovec Castle, with its grassy inner courtyard, its once-proud tower and its windowless panes overlooking fields of cut hay across the valley.

We explored for over an hour and when I took her photo in the golden light and saw that her eyes outshined the sun, I knew our being together was just a matter of time. It was because of this magical first experience at Krakovec that we agreed to have our wedding there.

It doesn't matter who you are or who you hire, planning a wedding requires months of logistical involvement. Ours was no exception and bore the extra burden that the Czech and American bureaucracies, respectively, place on those of its citizens who wish to marry a foreigner.

Massive, far-reaching and embarrassing in its scope, the paperwork necessary for us to acquire, fill out, send to the American authorities, have translated and then officially reviewed by the Czech national authorities took most of our time that spring and early summer.

It didn't help that we intended to get married so quickly – I asked Liliana in February, and we decided to get married on July 6$^{th}$, Jan Hus Day. (Aside: Jan Hus was a religious figure in Bohemia during the 15$^{th}$ century whose burning at the stake led to the Hussite wars. Hus' beliefs, among which were that Catholic Church officials shouldn't hold positions in government and that wine as well as bread – the blood and body of Christ – should be provided during Communion, were cornerstones upon which the Protestant Reformation were later built.)

Partially due to my fledgling spirituality, but also because of my American background, I thought we should be married by a church representative, so we approached the Catholic priest from the nearest town.

Sitting on his little gilded throne, he first hectored us for not attending church regularly. I didn't catch most of what he said, but I sure understood his mannerisms – he was all furrowed brow and flailing robes until he calmed down and thought seriously about our proposal. For perhaps a minute he looked us over before grudgingly agreeing to marry us in his cathedral. Pending completion of eight weeks of marriage counseling, of course.

After we thanked him for the decision, Liliana and I smiled at each other. Then she asked him to marry us under the free sky at Krakovec Castle.

As soon as she pronounced it, the priest actually scoffed. Not only did he *not* do outdoor weddings, he said, there was *no way* he'd do it in Krakovec because of the Hus issue.

Liliana, who had been politely respectful throughout, abruptly thanked him for his time and stood up to leave. Confused, I stood up with her.

The priest's contemptuous look was instantly erased and he said one or two things that seemed conciliatory, but Liliana wouldn't be stopped. She thanked him again and hustled us out of there. On our way out, she told me all the arrogant and disrespectful nonsense he'd been spewing, and we agreed it was a good thing I hadn't understood it because I would've snapped on him. I respect all people, but those who try to abuse their power over others I have no stomach for. The priest had actually told Liliana that he would marry us only if we made a large enough "donation" to the church.

There were no other denominations in the vicinity, so with a church service being out of the question, the next week we petitioned a provincial mayor to wed us in a civil ceremony at Krakovec, which fell under his jurisdiction. Upon hearing the idea, he vacillated, then tried to convince us to marry in his completely unhip wedding hall. But our dedication to Krakovec was unwavering. We bluffed and said we'd use his hall as an alternative if it rained, and he rose to the bait. Krakovec it was.

After the meeting as we drove to our next bureaucratic appointment, Liliana offhandedly told me that the mayor was a member of the communist party.

"He is? He didn't look communist." I realized it was a stupid comment even as I pronounced it.

She laughed at me. "What does a communist look like?"

"Uh... Stalin?"

"Yes. All communists are like Stalin... Now serious, did you know that most of this region are still of the communist party?"

"Really? I –". My American dogma was about to bark furiously, but I kept it at bay. I smiled, savoring the irony.

Real live communists... I'd sure have to keep that one from dad.

The details were overwhelming. Visitors would arrive from America, the Slovak Republic, Germany, Great Britain, France, Poland and Prague. And since hotels did not exist near Svatý Hubert, it was agreed that prior to the wedding everyone would just find a spot of floor.

After the wedding, upon the recommendation of the communist mayor, we would all stay in a hotel in his hometown (doubtless he received a kickback). When we first went to inspect the place, we were impressed with the outdoor pool, the dance hall/bar, and the main pub with billiards. But the banquet hall was a sore spot, because all along the top portion of the walls were deer and wild boar heads. There must have been 30 of each, and Liliana was adamant – no way we were going to eat there with those dead animals staring at us. After some haggling that I didn't quite follow, the hotel manager agreed to take them all down and the deal was struck. We had our venue.

It should be mentioned that throughout this process, Liliana was not only dealing with scheduling and speaking to the bureaucrats, she was also dragging me along, acting as my translator. Without her, I would have been hopeless. I mean, I tried to understand, and perhaps got about 25%, but it always seemed to be the least important quarter.

For example, when Liliana was dealing with the hotel manager, I understood the following: The venue was secured but we'd have to pay a deposit before June.

When Liliana translated, it turned out to be: June was booked, so was July, but luckily July 6 wasn't a weekend so we could have it then. We didn't have to pay a deposit.

Big difference, eh?

So I was very grateful to Liliana for her patience with me during those stressful months when the rest of my life was merely filler between planning and doing things for the big day. Indeed, before we knew it, it was the week of the wedding and the stress of last-minute details and errands had to be dealt with. We were all on Full Steam Ahead as we raced against time, trying to complete preparations before the visitors arrived.

When Liliana and I arrived at the airport, we discovered that my parents' flight had been delayed by an hour and the prospect of waiting irritated us both because we could have been doing a hundred other things. Lucky it wasn't anybody's fault; Liliana was on edge because of last minute details and I was on high voltage because mom and dad were coming. They had never been out of North America prior to this and had never met my in-laws, my friends or my life in CZ, and I was nervous at the impending cross-examination.

After an hour of discussing inane details, (*Do you really think white is ok for the boutonnieres?*) mom and dad finally emerged from the sliding glass arrival doors. Waving, we worked our way through the crowd and as I hugged mom, she whispered in my ear, "Those stupid planes!"

It was the first time she'd flown in over twenty years, and our wedding was probably the only thing that could have gotten her in the air.

We changed partners and I hugged dad, made small talk, and then into the taxis we went – Liliana and me in one car, mom and dad in the other. Hindsight tells me it was wrong to have put my parents in with a Prague taxi driver; we could see him honking and spewing obscenities the whole while. When we arrived at their hotel on Kampa, near the Charles Bridge, they were visibly happy to be out of the car. After carrying up their luggage (*What, no elevator?*) we left them to get settled.

A dozen errands and a few hours later, we returned and found they still hadn't left the room.

"I'm beat," said dad. "What time is it, anyways? I called the manager but I couldn't understand his English."

"Lunch time," I said. "Are you ready to explore?"

Mom inquired about room service.

"Room service," asked Liliana. "Mrs. Counts, you're in Praha! We want to show you our lovely city!"

Liliana and I were chomping at the bit to get out, but mom lit another cig. She needed to approach the idea from afar, I guess.

Thirty minutes later we were sitting in a nearby restaurant conducting a Czech language lesson for mom and dad, trying to figure out what they wanted to eat.

"Kned – what," asked dad as we explained what a *knedlík* was. (It's a dumpling.)

When their selections eventually arrived, mom and dad looked pleased, probably because the Czech cuisine didn't differ much from their own – meaty, saucy and plenty. They had no trouble cleaning their plates.

There were still two prices for most services in Prague then – one for Czechs and one for foreigners. Liliana and I could tell which one we were being charged when the bill was presented, and we didn't like it.

But before we had a chance to pay, Michal, my barman student, came in and started chatting to our waiter at the bar. I went over to say hello, and a minute later we came back to the table.

After introductions and an explanation of our dilemma, Michal picked up our bill and walked over to the waiter. They had a short conference and afterwards the waiter came to our table with a new bill, this one for half as much. He apologized for the "mistake" and set down four shots of Becherovka.

After paying and drinking, we walked over to Michal, now sitting at the bar, and thanked him. No problem, he said. Also, he was going to work soon after and invited us to come visit – he'd set us up with drinks.

So it was a nice first outing for us – my folks saw that we were somehow connected and we were half-drunk to boot. We walked out of the restaurant at 14:00 feeling no pain.

We strolled over Charles Bridge, pointing out things that we knew about and answering their questions as much as we could. Both of them were perhaps overwhelmed by the scene – so many people, so many things to take in. The historic architecture everywhere, the art, the statues, the river. Mom clutched both her purse and dad as we crossed the bridge among the summer crowds.

We popped into Old Town and the narrow streets that are so romantic to Liliana and I, but to our surprise, they seemed dingy and disquieting to my parents. Mom said, "I'm not going down that alleyway," no fewer than five times. In fact, she said it so often that Liliana and I knew we'd use it someday when telling stories about them being in Prague.

Still, they were impressed with parts of the city, and were curious about things, so we did our best to give them good tour guide monologues. (*Actually, that one's Roman, not Gothic. The one across the street there – that's Gothic.*) But the walking was taxing on them and when we arrived at the New Town Brewery at dinnertime, they were just about to collapse.

At dinner we introduced dad to Czech stinky beer cheese (*Now that's good!*) and tried to hustle through the meal because they were visibly waning – dad actually started nodding off at the table. I realized I had to get them home quick, so we paid, left, and walked towards the tram stop.

The word taxi kept popping up, but I was stubbornly convinced that Prague taxis were criminally overpriced, so we walked three blocks to the proper tram stop, got on the tram, rode 15 minutes over to *Malostransé náměstí* and walked them down to their hotel.

They were dead on their feet when we said goodnight, and it was only on our way home that Liliana helped me realize we really should have gotten them a taxi.

Next morning at 09:00, Liliana drove home with a car full of wedding paraphernalia. She still had a lot to organize, things I couldn't be of use with, so I was left to entertain my parents and pick up Jake from the airport. Like my sister, most of my buddies weren't able to make the trip, so Jake and my parents were the lone U.S. representatives.

Coming out of the sliding-glass doors after customs, Jake's first words were, "I'm here to talk you out of it, dude."

"Don't even think about it," deadpanned mom from behind me.

Hugs all around and then back into the town for tourism. As we walked across the Charles Bridge again, mom and dad tried to teach Jake the Prague ropes, but were getting things a bit turned around. (*Vaclev Havel was the King of the Holy Roman Empire*). I had to take him aside and whisper corrections every now and again.

Truthfully, I probably couldn't have handled more visitors from the U.S. because while it was interesting for them to be in Prague, mom and dad were also full of comments like, "It's great the buildings here are so old, but imagine how many people died in them," or "Don't they have any light beer," or "Why is all the water bubbled," and so on.

Things they were most surprised at: The number of tourists, what passed for English, the size of the castle, the number of beggars, the artists on Charles Bridge, being able to drink beer on the street, seeing a man helping his little girl pee in the gutter, the tight-fitting clothes Czech girls wear, narrowly avoiding getting pick-pocketed on the metro, the McDonald's on Wenceslas Square, and the old age of the trams.

After an early dinner at another good but touristy place, we kicked around up at the castle, and in the evening went to visit my barman student. He worked right around the corner from mom and dad's hotel, and since it was their second night, they were ready to stay up a bit later.

Problem was, I still had to drive home in the rental car and couldn't drink. Instead, I got to watch my parents becoming progressively giddier, and when mom turned all heads in the pub by knocking over a barstool and dismissing it with a hearty laugh, I'd had enough. I left them in Michal's hands and dragged Jake home to glorious sleep.

What I forgot was that Jake snored like a logger, and his self-composed symphony kept me awake far too long.

I was peevish when I opened my eyes the next morning. I'd barely slept, my parents were meeting Liliana's parents later that day, and the wedding was in two days.

After ablutions and packing the car, Jake and me drove down to pick up mom and dad. Of course they weren't ready yet, and when I returned to the car a confused Jake was being hassled by the police for parking in front of the hotel.

I didn't even speak – just got in the car and started it up. Jake hopped in a second later and said, "Holy fuck, dude! I thought they spoke English here! It sounded like they asked for my penis!"

I giggled. "They probably said *peníze.* It's the Czech word for money. They wanted your cash, Mr. Rich American."

"I gave them *your* name, by the way," he said.

I cruised around the block three times until mom and dad were standing in front, then we parked again and brought down their luggage. It barely fit into the rented Ford Mondeo.

On our way out of the city there was a generalized critique on the small size of European cars relative to American cars. This led to a very pointed critique on the quality of Czech roads and drivers, especially on the outskirts of the city where the cars were creating dangerous situations when they'd pass.

Overall, getting out into the wilds of Bohemia was proving to be very foreign, and mom and dad weren't completely at ease. Plus, their discomfort was translating into stress for me; each negative comment they made – and there were plenty – compounded the tension.

Halfway to Svatý Hubert, we stopped to tour the medieval Karlstein castle. It was fascinating for all of us, but there was a portion of the interior that was closed for repairs and would open first the following week. So naturally on the walk back to the car dad didn't speak about how interesting the castle tour had been, but rather of how disappointing it was that we weren't able to see the other (2) rooms.

Anyway, we passed up dozens of shops on the way back, but only when we had returned to the car did mom mention she was running out of cigarettes. Would I go back and buy her some?

*Sigh.*

"Sure, mom. What do you want?"

"Five packs of Brand X. Menthol."

"Ok. I'll be right back."

I left the three of them chatting at the car and as I walked away, was enveloped in a glorious feeling of freedom. I breathed deep and relaxed, enjoying the silence and the lovely view of the castle fortress up in the narrow valley. Buying the cigarettes was quick and when I returned they were all standing under a nearby tree.

I handed mom the cigarettes and she frowned. "But I wanted menthols."

"I know, but they don't have them."

"Elijah, you know I smoke menthols."

"Yes, I know, but they didn't have any."

"Fine."

Dad jumped in. "Here, I'll exchange them for you." He took them from her and looked at me. "Which store were you at?"

Not taking my eyes off dad, I said, "Jake, could you do me a huge favor and exchange those for…" I looked at mom with raised eyebrows.

"Anything with menthol. Brand Y if they don't," she said.

"Would you do that for me, please?"

"Absolutely." He also seemed relieved to walk away.

I waited until he was properly distant and then said, "Listen. I'm all freaked out here and I need a little help. You having to smoke normal cigarettes, not menthol, is the absolute least of my worries. You're gonna meet my future in-laws in an hour, and I'm nervous about–"

"What, are you ashamed of us," asked dad.

"No, I'm not *ashamed* of you! Jesus, it's not only about you, ok? And it's definitely *not* about menthol. It's about my wedding and us helping each other through it, and if you have to make the dreadful sacrifice of smoking a different brand of cigarettes for a few days, then *please*, *please* don't make me feel guilty about it, ok?"

Jake came back then, which probably prevented a full meltdown. He said they didn't have any menthol cigarettes and mom said, "Fine. These will be fine."

We piled into the car again, and the drive to Svatý Hubert was the last quiet time we'd experience for days.

When we finally pulled in, the village was alive with activity. There were ten cars parked in the grass opposite the house, and people I both recognized and didn't were milling around. There was a game of horseshoes going on, a pig was roasting in the fire pit, and most of the people had beers.

Liliana came rushing over all sweaty and hugged me. It felt like we hadn't seen each other in a hundred years. Then hugs all around, chatting, introductions to family members both distant and near, children running around, laughter.

We took the luggage up, then adjourned to the fire pit for beer and pig. The Slovaks had brought a five-gallon jug of *slivovice* – a moonshine product they call brandy – and we all did shots until even Jake called uncle.

The *slivovice* helped my Czech considerably. I provided rudimentary translations and was surprised how far my limited vocabulary took me. When Liliana wasn't around, I was the bridge between the two sides of the family, and even managed to translate a joke my father told. Then Jake wanted me to translate a joke for him, but he started out, "Ok, there's this midget on a highwire getting a blowjob," so I didn't.

But overall, everything was happening just as we'd hoped – people were getting along, there was no tension and we were all having a great time.

Then the clouds rolled in.

It was 21:00 when the rain started, forcing most of us inside. The remainder, of which I was a member, had to ferry all the crockery and cutlery inside and to construct a shelter for the pig and pig-master. Before long all but the pig-master were inside, and although he had only the keg and the pig to keep him company, he seemed content.

Inside it was wall-to-wall action. Liliana's parent's house is large, but it was past the point of comfort with the 15 guests all jockeying for a spot on the floor. My parents scored a bed, but the downstairs living room was full, the hallway was becoming so, and the three Slovaks were waiting for the kitchen to be vacant so they could stretch out on the floor there.

Liliana and I went to bed at 02:00, too exhausted to even share the events of the previous days with each other.

One day to go.

Liliana was awake at 06:00 and abustle by 06:05. Breakfast had to be prepared before a thousand other things were taken care of, and bride-to-be or not, she was the youngest girl in the household and the duty was hers.

I myself slept until the noises of the house forced me out of bed, and then slouched downstairs to pick at the leftovers.

Soon everyone was up and outside, despite the intermittent drizzle. Family members scattered over the countryside to deliver or pick up things and people, to confirm services and venues. Dad, and partially mom, were cleaning up the cars.

And poor Jake was gathering wood for the bonfire when he happened to brush against a thatch of stinging nettles (they burn like crazy but are essentially harmless). I saw him run into the kitchen doing the I-gotta-pee dance amid the cooking Czech ladies.

I stood behind him in the doorway a second later and heard him say, "...and now it's burning so fuckin' bad!"

When he spotted me, he barked, "Dude! I just brushed against a bush and it's all burning! Is it gonna stop? Can we make it stop?"

The ladies were closing in on Jake and peppering me with questions because they didn't understand the nature of the emergency. Seeing the severity of his mannerisms, they were prepared for a severed artery or something. When I told them he'd gotten into the stinging nettles, they all burst into laughter.

Jake stood there crestfallen, and I told him not to worry, that the pain would go away soon.

"Tell him it's healthy," Liliana's mother said. She was grinning.

"She says it's healthy."

Jake looked at her blankly, and then the ladies' second burst of laughter shamed him out of the house.

Outside, the men were trying to drink the keg dry and avoid work. Periodically, one of the women would poke her head outside and assign a project, and the men would argue over who would do it. Then a higher-ranking lady would poke *her* head outside and demand the task's completion. It seemed better to be outside in the rain than inside with the stressy ladies.

The mayor called in the afternoon. He was concerned about the rain and wanted to move the wedding to his hamlet's wedding room. We told him to go ahead with the castle preparations – we could always move the venue the next day.

Time plunged on and we didn't have space to be nervous anymore. We were simply orchestrating a series of events that would culminate in our marriage.

We again went to bed late, listening to the rain.

When I woke at 07:30, Liliana was already up. A quick look outside revealed a worst-case scenario of steady rain and low gray clouds.

I stumbled downstairs and discovered everyone eating breakfast, abuzz about the weather. I took a cup of coffee and went to find Liliana.

In the upstairs living room, Liliana was having her hair done and we spoke about the upcoming day. We hadn't had much time together and questioned each other on how we were getting along. After assuring each other everything would be fine, I left her and went into the bathroom to get ready.

Once inside, I finished my coffee while shaving and got into the shower. The hot water was relaxing and energizing all at once, and I breathed the steam deeply, clearing my lungs. With the water coursing over me, I closed my eyes and began to pray.

As always, I prayed for integrity – for the ability to put my beliefs into practice – and I also prayed that our wedding would be blessed, that the people who attended would make it home safely and that Liliana and our parents would have the strength to get through the emotional day we had ahead of us.

I can't properly explain the feeling that shot through me then, but a jolt of... I guess you would call it ecstasy, raced through my back and a fullness I had never felt before entered my body. The fullness persisted, and as I tried to continue my prayers, I found I was no longer able to pray as I was accustomed to, using words and dialog.

I was still concentrated on the idea of prayer, but words were no longer available to my mind. Instead, a vision of sunny skies filled my consciousness and I concentrated on it until I knew, without reservation, that the day would be sunny and bright. I continued meditating on the sunny sky idea until concentration ran away from me, then I got out of the shower and dried off.

I can think of no better illustration of the relativity of time than our wedding day. The morning simply flashed by and I was barely able to even scarf a roll, but when I accidentally saw Liliana in her plain white wedding dress, sprigs of baby's breath in her hair, all of time imploded. What was left were only we two, a shining, binary system floating among the stars.

When I left her and her entourage, time sped up again. I went to another room to change into my suit and overheard several people saying the rain was letting up. As I buttoned everything up, I heard someone downstairs yelling that the rain had stopped. A look outside confirmed this and I closed my eyes to pray in thanks and humility.

Soon everyone was gathered in front of the house admiring each other, discussing the logistics of getting to the castle and the inexplicable change in the weather. The clouds were thinned, the sun was actually out, and a warmish breeze was gusting.

And then time halted again when Liliana came out of the house in her wedding dress, looking only into my eyes.

Beautiful.

The breeze danced with her gown as the rhinestone pattern on the hem flashed in the sunlight as it dodged through the forest leaves. And then an odd thing happened – the 20 or so people actually applauded her. She looked around shyly and yelled at them to stop, but they didn't for a moment of infinite time. It was pure, spontaneous affection and it produced tears in more than just the womenfolk.

After an eternity, the applause subsided and we piled into the cars and headed over to the castle. My car was driven by a neighbor and he drove fast, leaving the rest of the six caravanning cars in the dust. I kept asking him to slow down but he wouldn't. Time dragged until the other cars caught up to us.

There are a heap of Czech customs which I think are great (most of them tend to include alcohol) but there's one which I do not embrace, and it's this: At some point during the wedding day, a group of the bride's family or friends kidnap her and take her away to some faraway pub. There, they chat and booze until the groom, after having combed the countryside looking for his lady, shows up and pays the bill for all the drinks.

I was resolute that Liliana wasn't going to be kidnapped. We had asked her brothers and friends not to do it because I wasn't comfortable with the custom, but upon learning of my discomfort they only redoubled their threats.

Krakovec Castle is approached by foot. Parking is in the middle of town, so the wedding party had to parade through the narrow streets toward the castle green. Along the way we passed dozens of onlookers, and when we got to the field that lay in front of the castle, there was an uncharacteristic crowd of perhaps 20 come to see the show.

At the foot of the high wooden bridge that leads to the castle entrance, we met the mayor's assistant. She was in her early 40s and wore a tasteful gray dress. Her first words were congratulations about the weather: We had really gotten lucky with that, she said.

She was to be the orchestrater of the wedding, and proceeded to go over the details of the march and ceremony with Liliana. All around us people were milling about, joking, taking photos in the sunshine.

I listened to the mayor's assistant with increasing alarm. There was a big problem, she said: The interpreter hadn't arrived.

"How big a problem is it," I asked Liliana.

"Without him, we cannot be married."

"*What?*"

"Without a translator, you cannot understand the mayor. Perhaps he is converting you to communism."

I looked at her.

"That's a joke, Elijah. Relax."

"*Relax?* You said we can't be married if he doesn't come! What time is it?"

"10:50. Do we have his phone number?"

"I don't think so." I looked at the numbers on my cell phone. No interpreter.

"We don't have it. But we could call directory assistance…"

She balked. "It was three months ago when we made the arrangement. I don't remember his name."

We stood there looking at each other.

It was still 10:50.

Dad wandered over and asked what the problem was. I told him, and he gave me his *when-will-you-stop-fucking-up* look. He went over to mom to spread the news.

It was still 10:50.

Liliana and I started making phone calls, trying to reach someone back in Svatý Hubert so they could rifle our documents and find the translator's phone number. The phone rang and rang.

It was still 10:50.

Einstein and his stupid relativity; the next 30 minutes of waiting were a geological epoch.

Jake and I were standing in the parking lot chewing tobacco, so we noticed right away when the white car appeared on the road that serpentines through the hills on its way down to Krakovec. It was still miles off, but we could see it moving fast through the fields. We watched it the whole way in with a sort of forlorn hope.

The car screeched to a halt just in front of us, double-parking a couple cars, and a man jumped out.

I turned to Jake. "If that's the translator, hit him in the gut for me, willya?"

The thin, bespectacled man stopped short and looked between us. He gave a nervous chuckle.

"Are you the translator," asked Jake, moving towards him menacingly.

"Yes," he said, holding his hands in front of his chest, "and I'm so sorry, but there was an incident on the motorway and traffic was blocked in for the hour!"

*The old traffic excuse.*

Still, he was the translator, he was ingratiating, and we hustled down to the castle green to relieve everyone.

Once down below, the assistant arranged us into place for the wedding march and then ran inside to let the mayor know we were coming in.

I was paired with mom, behind me was dad and Liliana's mom, then the witnesses, then various family members and friends. The procession numbered at least 35 of us.

I was standing with mom at the foot of the high wooden bridge, the railings lined with white ribbons and flowers. At the far end was the castle's main entrance, its gates thrown wide apart. Along the only wall I could see were people I didn't know.

I looked at mom and took a deep breath.

"You'll be fine," she said.

The assistant motioned us to follow her and time shifted into overdrive.

We crossed the bridge and entered the gate. As we did so, the open courtyard came into view and my eyes went wide. There were perhaps 30 onlookers, some I knew, most I didn't. The violin and cello musicians were playing from their perch on the stairs above and behind us. There were benches in the middle of the courtyard and three walls of the ancient fortress rose up five stories high. The fourth wall, to our left, wasn't there, revealing a pine forest across the valley. The sun was shining but its heat was tempered by high, streaky clouds.

As arranged, mom walked me up to the mayor's table. He was standing behind it proudly in his baby-blue suit, the bronze Mayor's Medallion suspended by a red and white ribbon around his neck. On the white table was a flower centerpiece and candles. After seating Liliana's mother, dad came to collect mom. He shook my hand and winked, and mom pecked me on the cheek before they went to sit down. Behind me was Jake. We looked at each other and he whispered that I had a booger.

When everyone was sitting, the musicians paused before taking up a different tune. It wasn't "Here Comes the Bride," but rather a quiet, harmonious song that brought everyone to their feet.

Time slammed on its brakes as Liliana's father escorted her in. She looked fantastic, glowing. I started to walk towards her but Jake held me back.

"Not yet, dude," he whispered.

Finally she was standing at the designated spot and I walked back to collect her.

Her father shook my hand and in the only English I ever heard him utter, said, "Be good to she, Elijah."

"I will."

And then he handed her over.

Looking at her radiance, I was overcome with love and kissed her, drawing a chorus of disapproving "Heys" from the congregation as we walked up to the mayor's table.

A wall of 10 cameramen suddenly materialized. Liliana and I looked at each other in puzzlement as the flashes went off and each photographer tried to get our attention. It was a wall of paparazzi, and we were grateful when they finally stopped and faded away.

The mayor started our service by voicing his incredulity at the weather, (it truly was divine) and telling an anecdote about being caught in the rain (pause for English translation). Then he tied it in nicely to the service, wishing us that if ever, in our marriage, we are caught in the rain without an umbrella, our love would see us through (pause for translation).

The service was straightforward and standardized, aside from the poems that our friends read. Colin read, in English, the e.e. cummings poem, "Somewhere I Have Never Traveled," while Liliana's witness read a lovely poem in Czech.

A minute later, after exchanging vows and rings, we turned and faced the congregation as Mr. Counts and Mrs. Countsova. There was applause and then we kissed again, this time longer, until Liliana's mother yelled, "Enough! Enough!"

Our parents were invited up to share in a first toast, and the coolness of the white wine was a relief. After we finished it and placed our glasses down, our parents were the first to congratulate us, and man did the tears begin to flow! Even dad got in on the act. It was a regular love-fest, and it continued until every one of the people present worked their way up to hug and congratulate us in person. (This portion took longer than the service itself!)

The emotional release of being finished with the ceremony was tremendous, and after all of the milling around, the group photos, the family photos, the men and Liliana photos, the women and Elijah photos and all the rest of the photos, I sat down alone on a bench and looked around.

I sighed.

The castle was truly wondrous, welcoming, and it had a certain energy about it that I couldn't put my finger on. Liliana came over a moment later and sat next to me. The first thing she said was, "Elijah, don't you feel something wonderful here? Like a presence or something?"

I looked at her and smiled. "I do. Fantastic, isn't it?"

"Yeah…" she said. She was crying again.

"Come here, Mrs. Countsova!" I said, and held her to my chest.

We kissed again and with closed eyes listened to the music until someone came and demanded our attention.

When we arrived at 13:30 at the hotel, it had started raining again. The staff were all waiting at the front door and the manager scared the hell out of me when she took a plate from behind her back and smashed it at our feet. The pieces went flying everywhere, and after I landed back on the ground, someone thrust a broom into my hands and a dustpan into Liliana's. (I later learned that cleaning up together is supposed to signify cooperation in the relationship.) Midway through the chore, someone kicked the dustpan, knocking the shards everywhere and forcing us start over again. *Fun-ny.*

After we cleaned up to the crowd's satisfaction, the hotel manager brought us a platter with two shot glasses. I downed mine, but Liliana sipped at hers. It was vodka. At least, mine was. Hers was water. Tradition says that the one who gets the vodka will wear the pants in the family, but time will tell on that one.

We led everyone into the dining hall, pleased to find the dead animal heads gone, and sat down at the head of the U-shaped table. Last-minute seating problems arose and were dealt with.

The toasts followed soon thereafter, with my father giving a great tear-jerker, followed by Liliana's mom. Then it was Jake, who had written a three-page tome. (A friend of the family translated everything, as the official translator had returned to Prague.)

Right after Jake's speech, Liliana went to the bathroom, making my spider-sense twitter, so I got up and followed after her. In the hallway I discovered that a group of men had her surrounded, intending to abscond. I muscled in and brought her back to the banquet hall to the cheers of the party.

The meal was probably delicious, but I don't remember eating. Afterwards, people began to drift about, some going outside but having to stay under the porch because of the heavy rains that had returned. Some went into the pub, and others into the dancehall where there was a live band playing traditional Czech music.

I was keeping a close eye on Liliana because every time I met the eyes of one of her men friends, they'd try to distract me – call me over for a shot, try to lure me outside for a one-on-one talk, you name it.

Then my mom even got into the act.

She took me into the bar and said "So, uh… how about a drink?"

In all the time I'd known her, she had never drank before 6 p.m. I squinted at her. "What?"

"A drink."

"Have you gone over to their side, mom?"

She got an ornery smile and said, "What do you mean? Can't a mother talk to her son on his wedding day?"

I turned and started off, but she grasped my hand.

"Wait a second, what about the drink?" She was smirking even larger now.

I jerked my hand away and ran into the parking lot, pouring rain, and saw tail lights going up the hill.

*Well, thank you, mom.*

Back under the roof I was all sour until Liliana's father came over and told me he knew where they were going and not to worry. It wasn't such a big deal. He invited me back for a drink and along with mom (I forced it on her as punishment) we did a shot together before I got a driver and went to fetch Liliana.

By the time we got to the designated pub, the group were all gathered around a table littered with empties. A chorus went up when I entered the room.

Liliana seemed happy, which eased my bitterness at the situation, but when they all started bragging about how they'd outwitted me, how even my mom knew I was a patsy, I got a little red.

A few minutes later, when eyes were turned to something on TV, I shady-pocketed someone's car keys lying on the table, then asked Liliana to dance. There wasn't much space and she was confused, but she agreed anyway. As we swooped around, I whispered my plan to her. Her eyes lit up.

"You're going to kidnap me back?"

"That's right, baby. Come on."

We calmly walked out the door and then ran through the rain to the car they'd come in. The doors were unlocked and we jumped in and started it. As I backed out, the car's owner ran out of the pub, shaking his fist at us. I beeped and Liliana waved at him as we drove away.

Not only had I gotten my girl back, I also got out of paying for their drinks, the rascals!

With the kidnapping out of the way I was finally able to relax, and the rest of the day took on a pleasant, laid-back ambience. The six kidnappers returned and piled out of the one car, loudly complaining to anyone who would listen about my breach of etiquette. As we good-naturedly argued the point, the rain began trickling off. Ten minutes later, late-afternoon sunshine burst through.

The light was perfect for photos, so Liliana and I went back to the castle with our photographer friend for some special pics. The castle groundskeeper had lent us the keys and we let ourselves in (We let ourselves into a castle… how cool is that?). It was quiet in the afternoon sun, less alive than it had been before, and we walked through the grounds in search of picturesque nooks where Liliana and I would hold each other for the camera, posing in our private love castle.

It was so peaceful, so moving, that even our photographer said he felt something there. Once, he said, his hair had stood on end when he'd gone down a set of stairs to get a different perspective. (We had wondered why he hustled back up so quickly.)

After our photo shoot the photographer headed back to the car, and Liliana and I wandered around, finally hugging in the middle of the courtyard for one last time. I told her about how I had prayed that morning and was 100% convinced that my prayers had been answered.

She looked at me skeptically, but after seeing how serious I was, she lightened up and said, "Well, it's wonderful that your prayers work… but maybe marrying here on Jan Hus Day was also helpful…"

I smiled at her. "Maybe…"

After dancing the night away to Czech music, not an American pop song in sight, I hit the wall. I was completely exhausted, dead on my dancing feet, and demanded that Liliana take me to bed. She didn't want to leave the guests so early – it was only 23:00 or so – but I dragged her away, saying that it was our day, too.

We snuck away and once in our room opened a bottle of champagne, chatting about the big day. After undressing, Liliana went first in the shower. We spoke through the curtain and then switched places. I hustled through because I was excited about wedding night activities, but when I came into the bedroom, I found Liliana sound asleep.

I ~~shook her like mad~~ gently rocked her to see if I could wake her, but no dice. She was out. I tucked her in, had a glass of champagne and then brushed my teeth. My eyes were droopy in the mirror.

When I snuggled into the covers it took me no time, despite Liliana's little bear cub snores, to fade off.

*As adult Elijah, I was in the yard of my childhood home when Gramma approached me. She was wearing a white velvet dress and her hair was golden.*

*We walked over to where my Jeep was parked in the driveway and she opened the door for me. There were some oriental figures in the back seat. Wooden, carved figures that fit into each other to form a seamless and coherent whole.*

*I leaned into the back seat. The oriental figures were inside a gym bag and I zipped it up and removed it from the car. I handed the bag to Gramma.*

*She took it from me and said, "You don't need these anymore."*

*Carrying the bag, she took it into the house and returned a moment later. I helped her up into the driver's seat and then got in myself. She started the Jeep and drove down the hill.*

*"Did you see how stupid I acted about Liliana and that guy," I asked.*

*"Oh, you don't have to worry about your jealousy anymore," she said. "You've paid your dues. That's why you're here."*

*I asked her if it were really true that I had paid my dues, because I didn't feel that way at all.*

*She replied that I had been working on myself and continuing in the right direction. "In this way you've paid your dues."*

*As she turned left at an intersection to go up a small hill, I reached out to hold her hand.*

*I intended to say, "Gramma, I love you so much."*

*But what I actually said was, "Gramma, I love Him so much."*

*"Yes," she said, "I know."*

*Suddenly she was gone and in front of me was a big, hand-written letter, taking up all of my vision. I was unable to read it all because some words were more pronounced and visible than others. Some were gray and unreadable, while perhaps every fifth word was black and in great contrast to those around it. These words formed three sentences.*

*The first sentence was, "BEWARE THE DEVIL."*

*The next sentence was, "OUR PURPOSE IS TO LOVE."*

*The last one was harder to make out, but it said, "COMMUNICATE THIS."*

*I realized that I was reading a message from God.*

*Grasping the urgency of its messages, rejoicing in its power, I tried to read more of the letter, but instead I woke up to the unmistakable feeling of something physically leaving my ear.*

Opening my eyes and looking up, fully awake, I saw what I believe with every ounce of my being to have been an angel.

It was a small, golden being, floating in the air above Liliana. It was centered in a glowing aurora, the type one would see after staring into a very bright light. But

I had just woken up – there was no light in the darkness of our room and no reason I would see such a glow.

After hovering above us for some time, the angel swooped into the middle of the room and disappeared.

I looked around in bewilderment.

The glow was gone and the room was dark again.

I was already crying, having recognized that I had been visited. No longer tired, I was simply invigorated. I sat up and reviewed the dream to cement its details into memory. As I went through it, at each significant portion of the dream I attempted to draw conclusions.

When Gramma took away the oriental figures, I inferred this to mean that oriental religions weren't for me. I said to myself, "Mine is the Christian God. Christianity is my religion."

At this thought, a solid wave of shivering ecstasy enveloped me. It went on for no less than five seconds and I knew I had made the right inference.

When considering what Gramma told me about not worrying anymore, I said to myself, "My sins are forgiven."

A second wave of ecstasy gripped me and took me away. It was more forceful than the first, and I was filled with a sense of absolute grace.

After the feeling abated, I came to realize that we are here to love. I envisioned loving and respecting even those I dislike and I was rocked by wave after wave of rapture, the ecstasy racing through my entire being.

In the middle of this rapture, the last bit became clear to me – it was my job to spread the message that everything we do in our lives affects our spirits; that the reason we are here is to love one another, and that we are all filled with a holiness that few are lucky enough to comprehend.

Most importantly, it became clear that it was my job to spread the message that *Every Thing Counts.*

This time the waves were the most dramatic of all. A deluge of energy gripped me and I cried and laughed aloud at the simplicity and singularity of the message. The feeling of sublimity coursed through me and eventually overwhelmed me to exhaustion.

When time finally started again, I closed my eyes and fell into bliss.

†

# Book II

# The Akashic Reader

**“Don’t ever think that your life isn’t written in the Book of Life! I found it! I have seen it! It is being written; YOU are the writer!”**

Edgar Cayce, 1933

# Foreword

The idiom *I saw my life pass before my eyes* is not limited to the English language.

Danish, Ukrainian, Spanish, German, Swedish, Russian, Czech, Korean, French and Arabic are but some of the others that also have the expression, or at least a phrase carrying a similar concept.

Why does this phrase appear so regularly across such vastly different cultures? Could it be a universal experience to see a replay of *this* life at the moment one passes into the next?

And if so, where does this replay come from? Where does it go?

The premise advanced here is that a person's life flashing before their eyes is the "uploading" of their life experiences to the Akashic Records.

And what exactly might *that* be, you ask.

The Akashic Records are said to be a type of universal filing system that stores all thoughts, words and actions on the Akasha – "Akasha" being a Sanskrit word meaning "sky, space, or ether". Akasha is used to speak about a non-physical substance, a sort of dark matter that fills the universe but which cannot be seen; it is the medium upon which the Akashic Records are said to be recorded.

Exactly how this functions, of course, is beyond our understanding.

What helps ease one's natural skepticism of such a phenomenon is that the Akashic Records are referred to in various religions, for example Buddhism and Hinduism, and receive pertinent coverage in Christianity as well, albeit under a different name, i.e., the Book of Life that Saint Peter is said to hold at the Pearly Gates – the one he is said to use for reference on Judgment Day.

Other religions or peoples said to have been able to access the Akashic Records include the Druids, the Mayans, the Persians, the Hebrews, the Chinese, the Hawaiians, the Greeks, the Tibetans and the Egyptians.

Some believe it is the Akashic Records which make clairvoyance possible.

Others believe that the Akashic Records can help a person perform extraordinary mental feats.

Still others believe that with practice, the Akashic Records can be accessed through meditation, hypnosis, or while dreaming.

The Castle Church, Lutherstadt-Wittenberg, Germany

**Chapter 1**

"Aren't you coming to bed?" Liliana was already in her new, pink pajamas at 8:30 p.m.

I looked up at her from my dad's luxuriously padded brown easy chair.

"I'm not tired yet, sweety. I think I'll stay up a bit longer."

She padded over with droopy eyes and flopped across my lap, lying her head on my shoulder. Her shower freshness enveloped me.

"Are you happy to be watching TV in English," she asked.

"Yeah! It's fantastic... they have the Discovery Channel, National Geographic, ESPN 1 *and* 2..."

"And what..." her question morphed into a wide yawn, then back into a question again, "...are you watching now?"

"Married with Children."

"Is it good?" Her voice trailed off at the end of the question.

"Eh...not really. But there's a football game that starts in a bit."

She didn't respond, and I felt she was asleep. It was nice holding her all cuddled up, but I got fidgety after a few minutes and wiggled around to wake her. She stirred but didn't open her eyes.

"Come on baby," I said. "Up to bed with you..."

She clenched her eyes shut and growled.

I laughed and jiggled her around. "Come on..."

She reluctantly got up and I followed after as she plodded out the door and upstairs. Mom and dad were watching TV in the upstairs living room and when mom saw us she said, "Liliana, you look *so* tired..."

Liliana looked at herself in the large wall mirror and chuckled. "I really do... oh, that's such a long flight..."

Dad looked at me and said, "You don't seem that tired, though."

He was right. I was tired, but not like Liliana was.

Liliana went over and kissed them both goodnight. "Thanks again for having us."

Mom tutted her. "Oh, you don't have to thank us for that. We're just happy you're home... though it would have been nice if you were here for Christmas..."

Ignoring mom's subtle dig (we had spent Christmas in Svatý Hubert again and had flown back on the 26$^{th}$) I walked Liliana back to my old bedroom. The cozy feeling of childhood caressed me as I sensed the wall photos and felt the familiar texture of mom's carpeting under my bare feet.

Our new double bed – mom and dad had bought it as a Christmas gift – was already turned down and Liliana collapsed into it, struggling her way under the covers.

Giggling, I sat next to her and kissed her forehead. She was almost asleep.

"Good night, baby," she mumbled.

I kissed her again and wished her good night.

I watched her sleep for a minute or so before deciding there was no way she'd catch me. She wasn't getting up for a good, long while. I turned off the light and closed the door behind me. I was at once excited and guilty-feeling. My upper voice was telling me not to do it, that I didn't need it, that I had given it up, but my lower voice had decided as soon as we had purchased the plane tickets home. And now that it was so near, my anticipation had rendered any objections moot. The compulsion was simply greater than the logical refutations.

I went into the kitchen to get a Yuengling out of the refrigerator, in the process chatting to mom and dad about the flight and how I needed the beer to knock me out.

"There's more in the garage," said dad. He wasn't a big beer drinker himself, but he always had a case waiting for us.

After some more light banter, I went downstairs and closed the door to the family room. I was still nervous that I might get caught, and drank the beer to give Liliana time to really be asleep.

The college football game started – two teams I'd heard of but hadn't seen play that year – and it was fascinating to see and remember the level of violence of the game. I wondered whether the heavy padding that the players wore added to or detracted from their aggression.

I went over to grandpa's old roll-top desk and opened up the bottom drawer. I had purchased the tobacco while Liliana was in the airport bathroom and had almost swallowed my tongue when the clerk told me it cost $5 for one can – it used to cost 1/5 of that. Later, when we'd first got home, I stashed the snuff in the desk, and the thought of it had preoccupied me the whole day.

I took the can out and read the warning on the label – "This product can cause gum disease and tooth loss." Yum.

I peeled the label and opened it up. Sniffing it, I remembered that it smells hideous – sort of like salty cat pee. I took a big pinch and put it in, arranging it with my tongue. It felt like I had fire between my cheek and gum. My eyes started to water and I spit, knowing it couldn't burn like that for long. I switched it to the other side of my mouth, hoping that it would burn less, but it burned more.

The violence on the television continued as I began to feel the surge of nicotine. I actually got dizzy from it, and mused that this is what all tobacco users are after – that initial rush from the nicotine as it enters the system. Unfortunately, habitual users rarely feel it – just as with any habit, the more one does it, the more tolerance one builds. Eventually the habit loses its luster, and all that's left is the addiction and the endless searching for that first-hit rush that will never come back.

But I did have it back. Months of non-usage had ensured it. The burning eventually dwindled to an acceptable level and I settled back in the chair to enjoy the game.

A few minutes later mom came in the room and said, "Eli, I just…" She caught her breath. "Are you chewing? I thought you quit!"

I felt like a busted teenager. I had to spit into the beer bottle before I could even answer her.

"I did quit."

"Does Liliana know you're chewing?"

"No, and she won't find out, will she?"

Mom smirked at me. It was obvious that she didn't particularly like the secret, but that she loved being in on it.

I smiled my bulging-lip smile and mom shook her head. "That's such an ugly habit."

"I know." <spit> "I'm glad they don't sell this stuff in Europe."

"They don't?"

"Heck no, I'd be a chewin' fool if they did." <spit> "As it is, I have to smoke every now and then to deal with the monkey."

"Don't smoke, Elijah. It's a terrible habit. I wish I'd never started."

"I know, I know." <spit> "Hey… what did you start to say before? When you came in?"

"Oh… I just wanted to know if you were hungry…"

"No, I'm fine." <spit> "They fed us on the plane."

"How *was* the flight? Bumpy?"

"No, it was fine.

"Well, we're glad you're back, even though it's only for two weeks."

"It's good to be back, mom."

"Dad says goodnight." She kissed me on the cheek before going upstairs.

I was left alone again with the chew and the football until I discovered the soft porn channel.

And just like that it started.

One foot in the door is all it took for the monkey to pry his way back into my life by pretending to be all buddy-buddy. Thereafter, for the duration of our holiday I sneaked around wondering where I could score my next chew. When we were out for the day, I had to plan ahead, hiding it somewhere in my jacket or bag and hoping I'd find time for it. But mostly I had to wait until we got home, when I'd run into the bathroom.

"You sure have to *go* a lot," Liliana said halfway through the trip.

"Oh, I'm just regular," I said.

So there's another mark against me – I was sneaking around behind Liliana's back. I justified it by thinking I wasn't really harming her, but in my upper mind I knew that's exactly what I was doing. If one believes statistics, every cigarette takes seven minutes off of one's life – surely that applies to snuff as well. And every minute I took off of my life was a minute that Liliana might have to spend by herself.

"Maybe she'll be ready for you to kick off," interjected the monkey from where he sat in the corner. I eyed him threateningly but he wasn't the scared, intimidated monkey he used to be. He was getting more robust by the day, and eyed me right back.

☯

Jake and his new girlfriend Sherry popped by a couple days later. He looked the same – a little pudgier perhaps, but his dark Italian looks and his intense blue eyes were still as striking as ever. He had a big grin as he came up the stairs.

"Well, well," he bellowed. "Mr. And Mrs. World Traveler!"

"How's my Jeep," I asked, trying to sound tough.

"*My* Jeep," he said, making a big show of ignoring my outstretched arms and going to Liliana first.

I bent down to hug Sherry. Five feet tall but athletically-built, she had a very strong presence about her.

"How are you, Sherry?"

"Awesome to see you guys, Elijah!"

"Yeah," Jake piped in, "*totally awesome*!"

Sherry poked him in the ribs and his wince was obviously no act.

Liliana and I both giggled at them.

As Jake and I hugged hello, he turned to Sherry and in a deep voice said, "This is a masculine hug, ok?"

"Oh, I know you have a crush on Elijah," she said, winking at Liliana.

After some chit-chat with mom and dad, who were on their way out so we could entertain for the evening, we all parked on the living room couches. Drinks and snacks were consumed, pictures exchanged, Christmas gifts described, and after awhile, Jake wondered if I could tell Sherry about my God dream (he'd been freaked by it). Liliana had freaked as well, though she seemed to believe it was a message much more than Jake did – he thought it was some sort of alcohol poisoning.

Anyway, I launched into it, happy for a fresh audience.

After I finished, Sherry whistled and said, "Wow. What do you think it all meant?"

I told her about how I lay awake afterwards and drew conclusions about it – how, after I would reach a proper conclusion, a powerful wave of energy would come over me, which I felt was a type of ecstatic rapture – and how I laughed and cried with joy over what I had been shown. In fact, I was almost crying again at the re-telling.

When I finished, Jake said to her, “Crazy, isn’t it?”

Sherry shook her head. “What does one *do* with that information?”

They all looked at me. I sighed and said, “I’m not sure, but I’m thinking of-”

Just then, the downstairs doorway opened and dad yelled up, “Ok, get your clothes back on!”

We all exchanged looks, and as mom and dad came upstairs we changed the subject.

Later on, Jake and I snuck downstairs for a chew.

I woke up the next morning and felt utterly compelled to write down an odd dream I’d had, so I hustled downstairs to the family room for some private time. I had written two sentences when dad came in. It was 09:36.

“About time you got up. You ready to go? I wanted to leave at 10, but it doesn’t look like that’s gonna happen.”

The night before we had talked about going shopping. The discussion ended with mom, Liliana and me all thinking we were going out to lunch first, and then shopping afterwards.

Blinking at him, I tried to figure out where he was coming from. He probably had five cups of coffee in him already.

“I thought we were going for lunch first…”

“I didn’t say lunch, your mother did. Anyway, before we leave, I have to clean out the back of the truck. When you gonna be ready?”

I slumped back into the couch. My compulsion to write was as strong as ever, but it was obvious that it would be squelched.

“When do *you* wanna go, dad?”

He didn’t even look at his watch. “An hour?”

“Ok,” I said, and threw myself back to writing. I got maybe ¼ of what I needed onto the page before time demands got the best of me. The rest was left to fester.

I’ve never been a great skier and in fact dislike the cold, but Liliana was keen on seeing something new, so off we went to Seven Springs, a resort in Southwestern PA. We found a decent hotel a few miles away from the mountain, stowed our bags inside, and hit a rental facility. The kids running the shop were youngish and I let them talk me into renting a snowboard instead of skis.

"It's *way* cooler," they enthused.

Liliana decided to stay with skis and off we went.

The first thing I learned on the slopes is that for beginners, snowboarding is no darned fun. I was on my butt constantly, and the subsequent writhing around like a turtle trying to right itself not only frustrated me, it also gave Liliana the giggles. Those first hours were testing.

But after we had a lunch break, something clicked. Whereas before I would fall constantly, I was now able to negotiate the beginners slope with no problem. After two times in a row without incident, Liliana returned (she had gone off by herself) and suggested we take a longer run together.

Problem: I had thus far only used a t-bar to get up the hill, and hadn't even remotely mastered that. So the one-legged shuffle with a snowboard attached to the other leg turned out to be simply beyond me, and the chair lift had to be stopped twice as I bit the snow, face first, as I tried to get on. The first time I fell, one of the benches swung over me before the attendant was able to stop the thing, and it swept up Liliana before she could get out of the way; she had to ride the lift ahead of me by herself.

The second time I fell I was actually knocked over by the chair, and as I lay on the ground the attendant came over and helped me take off the snowboard.

As I brushed off the snow and tried to laugh along with everyone, the attendant handed me the snowboard and said, "Dude, just carry it from now on, ok?"

"Absolutely. I wish I knew that before."

"Me too," he shot back.

I sat down and after the lift had been started, I waved to a laughing Liliana, who had turned in her seat to watch the spectacle. She yelled something that I couldn't hear, and then eventually turned back around.

Dangling above a thousand brightly-clad and quickly-moving people, I breathed deep and was carried upwards into a silent, snowy world of wind, trees and hillside. Every so often some brave souls would ski through the trees and rocks below us, but otherwise the silence was glorious. That ride alone made me glad we had come.

Coming out of the forest and gliding silently above the skiers, I watched the people in front of me unload, and decided that when my turn came I would get off and run to the right. But seeing Liliana ski off to the left made me change my plan and I readied myself, lifting the safety bar out of the way.

I got off the chair, moved to the left towards Liliana and then felt a sickening thud on the back of my head.

*You're here soon.*
What? Where am I?
*But I don't think you're ready.*
Ready for what?
*You have to go back.*
Back where? What is this?
*Soon...*

When I opened my eyes, the light was incredible. It was so intense that I scrunched my eyes back together, and that's when the pain commenced. I felt a hand on my head and opened an eye. The light was still blinding, but right in the middle was a lovely angel calling my name. Calling my name and smiling, beckoning to me. I smiled back and then the pain stabbed me and when I looked up at the angel again I realized it was Liliana and I wondered where she got the wings.

Then she was gone again.

"You gave us quite a scare, young man."

"Where am I?"

"Maybe you can tell *me* that?"

"Uh... the moon?"

The doctor's eyes widened and he said, "Nnnnoooo... can you-"

"I'm joking, doc. But I don't know where I am. In a room, yes. But where, I don't know."

"We're in the ski area's clinic, and *you* have a nasty bump on your head."

I tried to get up but he cautioned me against it.

I sighed and lay down. "Do you know where my girl is?"

"She's waiting for you outside."

"Ok."

"Can she drive?"

"Yeah... "

"Because it would be a bad idea for you to."

The doctor then called in Liliana and after I assured her I was fine, they spoke about me like I wasn't there. It was agreed that I was to be taken to bed and left there for awhile, but not be allowed to sleep for at least six hours.

They wheeled me out to the car in a wheelchair and I found that I enjoyed it immensely. I also enjoyed the drive to the hotel room, the hot shower that left me feeling dizzy, and lying on the bed. I was in excellent spirits, though woozy. Even the afternoon television was cool. Still, I was deadly tired and wanted to sleep right after the pizza man came, but Liliana was vigilant with me.

Finally the six hours were up and I was allowed to drift off. But you know, every time I'd fall asleep, I'd wake right back up. My wiring seemed a bit off and I could only lay there in bed and wonder about things.

I must have fallen asleep though, because when I opened my eyes I noticed that Liliana wasn't in bed. Then I heard the shower and tried to get up. My head still hurt, but I was able to stand without problem. Walking, no problem.

Scaring Liliana in the shower, no problem.

Two days before we were to head back to Europe, I went to St. Mary's, the church where I had made my first and only confession. First confession because I had been just eight, and only confession because it had resulted in a spanking.

The confession itself took place in a small, dimly-lit room, and the priest could either sit behind a screen to provide the sinner with anonymity, or in a chair directly opposite. (Aside: I've always wondered how a priest can resist judging the people who reveal to him the vile and heinous things they've done. When and if the priest sees the sinner on the street, wouldn't the first thing to pop in his mind be the sins that had been confessed? How could one get past that?)

But back to my first and last confession, which was done face-to-face: Before it started, I was told all my sins would be forgiven, so I naively unloaded on the priest about how my friends and I had accidentally set fire to the woods behind our house – an act that I had never before admitted but had felt deeply guilty over – as well as some minor things like swearing. After confessing, I got a forgiving and educational lecture from the priest, plus a bunch of Hail Marys.

But since I had been sitting on my mother's lap as I confessed, she – I suppose due to a lack of training in such things – neither forgot nor forgave.

Indeed, on the drive home, the lecturing began almost immediately, lasted all the way to our house, continued well past the time when my father got home, and in the end I got a spanking.

So much for my desire to confess.

But now as adult Elijah, my newfound faith was driving me back towards the church, and since priests in Prague didn't speak English, I found myself in PA, standing in line for confession in the newly-built wing of St. Mary's.

Far, far from the splendor of a European cathedral, Our Lady of Fatima appeared prefabricated, with plain white walls, a low ceiling and extremely wide, unpadded pews arranged on a slant, like a middle-school auditorium. There was no real altar aside from a generic wooden lectern and a large wooden crucifix on the wall behind it. Beside the altar were the confessionals.

Standing in the short line to confess, I tried to focus on what I could tell the priest I'd done in the previous 20-some years. No question, pornography was at the top of the list. Cursing was up there, too. Mustn't forget adultery. Didn't listen to my parents. Cheated here and there. Stole some stuff. Lied a bunch.

*Holy hell*, I thought, unsure I wanted to go through with it. *What if he condemns me? Can priests do that? If they can absolve you of your sins, can they refuse to absolve you as well? I could end up doing penance forever...*

After the previous ~~filthy sinner~~ person exited, I entered the confessional and knelt down. When the peephole slid back, I said, "Forgive me father, for I have sinned. It's been 20 years since my last confession."

"My goodness. Why so long, my son?"

"Uh... my parents, I suppose."

Silence.

"Yeah... so, I guess my largest problem has been pornography. I... er... used it very often before I got married."

"And now?"

I hesitated. "Sometimes."

"Go on..."

"I can remember times when I've cheated. Or stolen. I've lied a bunch. And I slept with a married woman once, though I didn't know it at the time. She actually tricked me into it and I ended the affair as soon as she told me. Does that count as a sin?"

"All adultery is a sin, my son."

"Hmm... I also slept with two women at once."

"Uh-huh."

"And sometimes I get impatient. Or aggressive, like when driving sometimes."

"Have you ever hit someone?"

"No."

I couldn't think of anything else to say.

"Is that all?"

"Uh... yes, father."

After a short pause, he asked me what kind of pornography I looked at.

"Uh… Sorry?"

"Anything…" he pressed on, "out of the ordinary?"

"Oh. Uh. No, just women. Sometimes men and women together."

"Well," I overheard him mutter, "at least that. Tell me, son, do you pray?"

"Yes, father. Every day."

"*Really?*"

Guess he hadn't been expecting that one.

"Uh… yeah. I've had some experiences that I'm trying to make sense of…"

"I see. What… *kind* of experiences?"

"I once had… I don't know, I guess it was a visitation. And I had two dreams where God seemed to be speaking to me, to be giving me directions."

He looked at me directly through the peephole – his dark eyes sort of bulging from his eyeglasses – and asked, "And have you followed these directions?"

I sighed. "Mostly. But they require me to be a much better person than I seem able to be. I struggle to do better, but I often slip backwards."

"We all slip from time to time, my son. The trick is to lessen the degree to which we slip."

I thought about that for a moment and then asked, "Do you sin, father?"

A pause.

"Yes."

"And do you confess?"

"Yes. But I try to live so that each time I confess I have less and less to say. This is what God wants us to do. This is how God wants us to *live…*"

I didn't say anything.

The priest seemed finished with me and said, "As penance, say 20 Our Father's, and 25 Hail Mary's. Do you understand?"

"Yes, father. Thank you."

After his blessing, I stood up, opened the door and was surprised to see no one waiting in line – I guess I had taken too long. But I was even more surprised when the priest's door swung open behind me. He had a concerned look on his face and a piece of paper in his hands.

"If you ever need to speak to someone about your… signs… please feel free to contact me." He smiled and handed me the paper.

"And if they are positive, *follow* the signs," he said forcefully. "Not many people receive them."

He wished me luck and then slipped back into his confession box, leaving me there holding the piece of paper.

As the plane was taxiing out to a runway at JFK, the captain of the Czech Airlines red-eye to Prague gave the following pre-flight announcement: "Ladies and gentlemen, this is your captain speaking. I'm sorry to tell this, but the forecast for the flight is bad."

The passengers all traded looks, and one could feel the mood of the cabin darken.

The captain continued: "We expect light to moderate turbulence the whole way. This is normal for this time of the year, and not a problem for safety. So... sit back and... try to relax."

Liliana and I looked at each other through our droopy eyes. We had taken Dramamine and it was starting to work already.

"I love you, sweety," I said.

"I love you, too."

Holding Liliana's hand, I closed my eyes and began my ritual of praying before, during, and after takeoff. My problems with flying are strong, and have entirely to do with control. I simply hate not being in control of my destiny. Of course one can argue that ultimately I *am* in control because I exercised choice when I bought the ticket. But once in the air, this is an argument I find hard to swallow.

With eyes closed and holding tight to Liliana's hand, I prayed for many things, chief among them that the pilot and the plane have the strength necessary to spirit us to our destination. Second, that I would have the strength to accept God's will should he decide to take us. Third, to help us find our way to His bosom should He decide to take us.

Praying thusly always has a calming effect on me, and that I'd been absolved of my sins so recently (sounds funny, but that's how I viewed it) also made me feel somewhat light and calm. I think I even managed to fall asleep for awhile as we rose to cruising altitude.

Then the bumps started.

We were sitting amidships, Liliana by the window, and she nudged me and pointed to the right wing tip. It was flickering up and down like a cobra's tongue, and calm or not, I simply could not look at it. Later, when the drink service started, the staff were short-tempered, even by the relative Bolshevism of Czech service standards. That much of what they were serving got spilled did not help anyone.

The "light to moderate" turbulence the captain had warned us about was relentless. Though there were calm moments during which one could feel the tension of the passengers ease, these were more than offset by the random thuds and losses of altitude that the plane was going through.

Prior to halfway through the flight, still feeling hopeless, a woman became so ill that she had to be laid out in the aisle. Though I'd always thought it was a cliché, the announcement came: "Is there a doctor on board?"

But there was no doctor. The best they could do was pump oxygen into her and get her lightheaded enough to forget she was in a rattling deathtrap somewhere over the Atlantic.

I could have used some of the oxygen myself, because while the Dramamine was effective for my gut, I still couldn't sleep. As usual, Liliana slept easily. She once told me that she gets on a plane knowing she might not make it safely off, and that she's ok with that. She just surrenders, she says.

So I sat there and tried to numbly surrender to all the thrashing.

Which didn't work – I was nervous and wanted a chew terribly. The monkey cursed and tormented me for not bringing any with us.

Despite being exhausted, I didn't sleep a wink. My stomach was jostled, my nerves jangled, and my neck jarred from the constant thrashing of that wild bull of a plane.

But then, when we finally drew near Prague, something wonderful happened.

The pilot apparently had had enough of the turbulence as well, because we powered up and for the last 30 minutes of the flight the plane skimmed just above a blanket of clouds. Just like that, the turbulence disappeared and we were greeted by the rising sun, which had turned the horizon into a deep, pumpkin orange, topped by a brilliant band of blue that finally blended into a wondrous violet that stretched above into the dark, star-filled sky.

It was the light at the end of the tunnel.

*I was walking along a small street in Prague and noticed a store window displaying tobacco products. Walking closer, I was overjoyed to find that they sold Copenhagen, so I went inside. A good-looking shop girl who I recognized came over to me and began to unfasten my belt. I have been waiting for you, she said, flitting her tongue at me. I stumbled back and she looked at me all annoyed. I think I just want the tobacco, I said. She made a face and said suit yourself. She stepped behind the glass counter and brought out a roll of ten cans of Copenhagen. The boss sent it just for you, she said. I looked at the wrapping. It was a jumble of pornographic images.*

**Chapter 2**

A modern-day fairy tale: A rich American man seeking a beautiful girl, a good housekeeper and an obedient wife to produce his children, snatches up a small village beauty from Central Europe, much to the consternation of her family and friends. The couple moves to America and lives out the American Dream. On their infrequent visits back to her village, the girl dresses fashionably and shows pictures to her loved ones that demonstrate a standard of living which they can only dream about. In her absence, the girl's friends and family speak about her often, but the most frequently-occurring theme is one of slight dissatisfaction: Where is the justice in her having so much and they so little?

Sound about right?

Well, forget it.

Liliana, the girl from the Czech Republic, did indeed marry an American a few years her senior. But the similarities end there. Instead of being the rich American man, I was the poor one, with a teaching job that ran only 6 months out of the year, and poorly paid at that. (Not that I'm complaining, mind you. Corporate America can go pound salt).

Liliana, on the other hand, after receiving her doctorate in economics (summa cum laude) from the Czech Agriculture University, was granted an interview for a prestigious European Union fellowship program that, if secured, would ensure that the first step along her career path was a stellar one. It was this interview that led us to Germany, to the town where Martin Luther was born.

Our first look at Lutherstadt Wittenberg came through the slightly smeared windshield of Liliana's 1989 metallic blue Fiesta. Though it was overcast, the two towers that form the east and west borders of Wittenberg's Old Town were clearly visible and seemed to be the only buildings in the tree-dominated town.

Off to the west we could make out what seemed to be a cloud-production plant – one could not tell where the steam it was churning out ended and the clouds began.

As we crossed the long bridge over the river Elbe, the towers' features sharpened and a few buildings came in to view through the February trees – low buildings with red tiled roofs. Only the towers loomed large over the town. To the west, the lone tower was topped with a corroded brass dome, providing a blue relief to the thorny gothic spires that adorned it like a crown. A kilometer to the east were two square towers tipped with roundish cupolas.

"Those must be the cathedrals," said Liliana.

"Which one did Luther preach in," I asked from behind the steering wheel.

"Probably both." She was studying the map again.

My mind started to wander. *That thesis thing. Wonder if the door is still there.*

"How did Luther die," I asked.

She looked up through the windshield and squinted. "Turn right here. I don't know how he died, but I know he was married."

"*Married*? I thought he was a priest!"

"He was, but he quit and married an ex-nun. Left here."

"Ex-nun? What, you can just quit if you want?"

'They did."

By this time we were in the town proper, and soon located the institute where Liliana's interview would be. It was a three-story corner building that was clearly ancient, but had been recently renovated. The walls were grayish-white with plain but tall windows, and the entrance was on the corner.

After parking nearby I looked over at her and asked, "So? How do you feel?"

"Not so good." She had a worried look.

"Why? What's wrong?"

"It's my first interview! And it's in German! They'll think I'm stupid!"

"Liliana, they invited you for the interview because they know what kind of work you do. And if you don't get the job, you don't get the job. Wittenberg isn't the only place in the world."

"Where will you take me if I don't get the job?"

"Anywhere you want."

"Africa?"

"Uh..."

"You said anywhere!"

"Ok. Africa."

She smiled triumphantly and we got out of the car. Going inside together, Liliana checked in at the receptionist's desk, and then walked me back outside.

"Give me luck," she said.

"I wish you great luck, Liliana. I know you'll get it – who better?"

"Yeah..."

"Just be your great self."

"Yeah..."

We hugged tight and then I opened the door for her. She went in and looked back at me all sad because she had to do big-girl stuff while I went off exploring.

I gave her the thumbs up and she turned and walked into the waiting room.

Standing on the corner, I looked both ways down the street and decided to go left. After a few steps I turned around, heading to the right after all.

Invariably, institutions have a great inertia about them, and even though the Agricultural Institute for Transition Economies offered Liliana the job, a waiting process ensued that was attributable, in some cryptic Catch-22 way, to her lack of a residency permit, and due to that, her lack of a work permit. Of course neither could be granted without the other, and since my residency status depended on hers, we were sufficiently confounded by the situation that we just let the institute handle it. They assured us the paperwork would be sorted eventually, and a tentative starting date was set for a month hence.

Liliana was positively rapturous about having landed the job, and we spent the intervening month in Svatý Hubert enjoying the certainty of future employment and new cultural experiences for the upcoming few years.

However, when informed of our move, Liliana's mother reacted ambivalently. Germany is Germany after all, and Germans are, after all, Germans. It was during this time that I began to understand that the collective Czech memory of World War II is long and far less abstract than my own. Indeed, Liliana's mother and father both lived through that time; they knew what it was like during the war and to this day harbor an instinctual distrust for their neighbors.

For myself, I no longer solely pictured Germans as the people who did all that horrible stuff during WWII. Instead, I saw them as a peaceful EU country, a NATO ally, members of the UN. The rest is history – not to be forgotten, but not to be dwelled upon, either. Still, I had the luxury of distance from the issue, and my Czech mother-in-law's view on the matter made me realize that time can only heal so much. The rest has to be actively and constructively pursued – by both sides.

The surprise supporter of the move to Germany was Liliana's father; he had often tutted Liliana's studies, saying that a woman's place was in the home, that she should be cooking instead of studying, and so on. But now that she had gotten the job, her dad was quick to tell everyone how he had supported her studies and how he had always known Liliana would succeed in life. This flurry of compliments actually helped Liliana a great deal in her relationship with him, because prior to that, she had let her father's criticism bother her to an unhealthy degree. But with his sudden overpraising, she realized that criticism or praise can be treated similarly – as mere words. Of course it's nice to hear that one's father is proud, but if the words ring hollow, what good are they worth?

Anyway, we arrived in Wittenberg a day before Liliana was to begin work and moved in to our residential hotel. We had taken it at the recommendation of the institute, but were disappointed from the start. Yes, it was clean and adequate, but the sumptuousness of the lobby had absolutely nothing in common with the dark, dreary rooms, and we immediately began scouring the town for a new place. In fact, it was after having visited a potential (too small) apartment that we happened by a language school – Easy Language School – and decided to pop in to ask about teaching work for me. The receptionist, an attractive brunette with a vaguely American accent, greeted us from behind her high counter and encouraged me to come back the next day to speak with the school's owner.

I arrived early the next afternoon for the scheduled meeting and was directed to the well-appointed, faux-Scandinavian furnished waiting room. There were outdated English periodicals scattered around and after I looked over my cheat-sheets for the last time, I picked up a *Newsweek* and began reading about how the American president was exercising his unique brand of diplomacy.

A few minutes later, a lean man with a bushy mustache, curly brown hair, and heavy black circles under his eyes bustled in. David introduced himself and I immediately recognized his east coast accent. He asked if I was new in town.

"Yes, we've been here in Wittenberg just a few days."

"Well, here," he said, "take this. It's all about the town. I'll be with you in just a second."

He handed me a stapled, photocopied brochure about Wittenberg, written in English. It looked as if it had been copied a hundred times and one could *just* make out the photo on the front – it was the famous door where Martin Luther had nailed his 95 Theses.

"Wow! Thank you," I gushed. I was grateful to have an English text about the town because my German skills were virtually non-existent.

I opened up the brochure and read with great interest for a few moments before my mobile phone rang. It was Liliana, who told me we had an appointment to look at an apartment right after my interview – could I write down the address?

I fished for a pen, then wrote the address on the guide to Wittenberg. The apartment was just around the corner from the school, she said.

I put the phone back into my bag and David came over, smiling and ready for the interview. His smile faded, however, when he noticed I had written on the brochure. He pointed at the photocopy in my hands. "Did you write on that?"

"Uh... yeah," I responded. "You gave it to me, didn't you?"

He sighed deeply, then frowned and turned to the receptionist. "Do we have another copy of that?"

She was also frowning. “I’ll look.”

I apologized profusely, but any attempt at reconciliation was brushed aside.

“Forget about it,” was all David said as he led me into one of the teaching rooms. We sat directly across from one another as he looked at my resume. It was a long time before he said anything.

“Classified Advertising Account Executive,” he read aloud.

“Yeah, that was out in Los Angeles,” I volunteered.

“I see that,” he answered flatly.

Oh, this is just lovely, I thought. I ruined his day by taking that crappy flyer and now he’s all negativity on me. Perfect.

David suddenly looked up said, “Ok, Elijah. Let me tell you a little bit about us before we start talking about you.”

He then commenced to speak for the next 20 minutes.

When he eventually did ask a question, the secretary interrupted during my answer, which led to a stilted answer on my part.

The awkwardness of that moment was a common feature of the next half-hour, and I was relieved when the interview finally drew to a close. I was putting on my jacket to get the heck out of there when David somehow caught a glimpse of what I had written on the brochure.

“Schatzungstrasse 15? We have a client in that building.”

“Oh yeah?”

“Hmm. It’d be interesting to teach in the same building you live in, wouldn’t it?”

“Sure would,” I answered. “What a great commute.”

I picked up the brochure and rolled it in my hands, noticing David wince as I did so.

“Ok, thanks again for your time,” I said.

“We’ll be in touch,” said David.

I walked out the door and puffed out my cheeks in the February cold. I fully expected to never work at ELS, and anyway, I was relieved I wouldn’t have to deal with the overbearing David anymore. I hurried off to meet Liliana so we could check out the apartment.

A common misconception of the expatriate lifestyle is that it’s all hugs and Sunday brunch – that it’s filled with fabulous people, exciting places, and scrumptious culinary delights.

Naturally, this is not ~~always~~ the case.

Consider: No matter the country under discussion, small town people (Wittenberg has a population of 50,000) tend to be of a conservative character. And since the average landlord doesn’t exactly have Harvard on their resume, they tended to be even more… conservative than the rest of society. Time and again during our apartment search, we had the pleasure of being treated in one of two ways: As rich and strange, to be taken advantage of, or as poor and strange, to be treated with contempt.

Even mundane details such as the abbreviations in the real estate classified ads (NK, Wfl., KM, WB-Schein, EFH) were decidedly challenging. These things are not in dictionaries, and even Liliana, with years of German language usage behind her, was puzzled.

Additionally, and as any expatriate will tell you, foreign currency, customs, values and laws are but a few of the obvious challenges to living abroad, all of which require a great deal of flexibility and patience – two things which are not always easy to come by.

So I was extremely lucky to have Liliana's help when dealing with these challenges. Yes, her work was the reason we had landed in Germany in the first place, and a certain measure of responsibility therefore fell on her shoulders. That she spoke fluent German was also a big reason. Still, I sincerely doubt I would have been as patient as she was with my ceaseless *What did they says?* when dealing with prejudiced landlords, hesitant bureaucrats, and backward store clerks.

And in two foreign languages to boot.

*The sycamore tree was ancient and exuded a feeling of love and wisdom as I climbed its leafless branches. I chose one of the larger trunks to ascend. The trunk became more difficult to navigate the higher I got, until I was swinging pendulously back and forth, holding on for dear life.*

*By remaining still and calm I willed the swinging to cease, and the tree somehow formed, from its more supple branches, a welcoming throne for me to sit upon. But a feeling of panic filled me when I sat down, for suddenly the throne pitched forward and I found myself staring face-down at the ground hundreds of feet below.*

*I intuited that my faith was being tested and I knew that the answer was to completely submit to the will of the tree and to trust it to keep me from harm.*

*The branched throne then morphed around me, cradling me. I held my arms outward and felt a blissful emptiness enter me.*

## Chapter 3

The morning temperature was lower than it had been the night before and the branches were bowed with a thick, icy coating. The mist, having lost much of its romance from being mixed with the heavy smell of coal smoke, was forecast to linger.

My morning run complete, I took the wide stairs of our new building two at a time. I was looking forward to being back in our apartment after accompanying Liliana to work and then running home. The place was just starting to feel homey – the books were coming out of the boxes, the plants were starting to find their nooks, and even though it was in slight disarray, the apartment was still welcoming.

Located on the third floor of a corner house built in the middle of the $19^{th}$ century, the place wasn't big, but it was open and lined with ceiling-height windows. The star of the space was the corner rotunda, reached by ascending three wide stairs in the living room. The rotunda itself had a beautiful ceiling medallion juxtaposed with an exposed electrical wire, and five tall but narrow windows.

Out of the south-facing rotunda window, one could see the brown brick tower of St. Phillip's church just half a block away. The weathervane on the church spire read 1835 (the year of The Great Moon Hoax) and there was a deserted feeling to it even before our landlord told us the tower had caught fire years before.

I was watching people and chugging water when down on the sidewalk across the street appeared the old nurse I had come to recognize. It was only the third time I'd seen her, but her figure was already cemented in my mind. She was a short woman, about 5 feet tall, and she walked with a slight limp. She wore a long, black rain jacket hunched close around her. The *coup de grâce* of her outfit, a white nurses' cap, was pinned impossibly far back on her head. She walked slowly and with dignity – probably, I supposed, on her way home from the night shift.

As I watched her from the window three stories up, I thought I noticed her walking slower than normal. But still, her dignity never seemed to abandon her, even as she collapsed into an unmoving heap on the sidewalk.

I turned and darted for the hallway, Fred Flinstoning on the slippery hardwood floors. After I put on my shoes, I grabbed a blanket from the bed and ran out the door without taking the keys. I ran down the wide staircase, stumbling past the adult education company that took up the bottom two floors of the house. Outside now, I jostled into a crowd of middle-aged students on break from their courses. I bumped and ran through them, causing them to grumble in German. Some of them spoke in English because they recognized me.

I ran across the cobbled street and around a decrepit Renault with flat tires and there she was. She was lying on the ground and her lips were blue. She wasn't breathing and she lay flat on her back. I lay the blanket on the ground beside her, checking her airway for blockages – nothing. But she wasn't breathing. I moved her onto the blanket, half covering her up. I checked her neck for a pulse and there was none.

*No pulse and no breathing. No blockage but no breathing. Shit. Keep her on her back. Mouth-to-mouth. Hand under neck, pinch nose, deep breath, blow. Deep breath, blow. Deep breath, blow. Find the breastbone, find it, find it. Shit. Calm down. Calm... hands together – not too hard – push... what was it? Fifteen? Thirteen? Yeah. Thirteen and three breaths... eleven... twelve... ok... deep breath and blow... deep breath blow... deep breath blow come on nurse, you can breathe... pulse... Is that a pulse? Wait for it, be sure...no, no pulse... no breathing no pulse... find the breast bone again... gently... push it, push it... eleven... twelve... ok, deep breath, blow... deep breath – shit!*

The woman started coughing into my mouth and brought up a big piece of lung – she weakly choked on it and I had to remove it. She continued on with a phlegmy hacking and nasty though it was, to me it sounded like a symphony of life… I put my hand behind her head to cushion it from the stones and found I was jittery.

I needed help. Across the street, the students probably hadn't seen the action, so I yelled at them.

"Help! Help me! We need a doctor!"

Nothing.

Lying her head back on the stone, I stood up on weak, rubbery legs and yelled at them again. Most of them just looked at me, but then a man in a German army jacket ran into the building. Some of them crossed the street to see what was happening. They all spoke German and asked questions that I couldn't understand.

"It's her heart," I blurted out.

After some time the sirens commenced and became louder, and then there was the ambulance and the paramedics. They came hustling over asking many questions. Shaking from the adrenaline, I could only describe the situation in English, and someone translated. I soon found I couldn't speak, and tears came to my eyes as the shock of the situation got to me.

After seeing the woman into the back of the ambulance and watching it roll away, I turned and went across the street. There was a lot of commotion and back-patting from the ten or so students, but it barely registered. Upstairs, the door to our apartment was wide open and I went inside. I felt a strange elation and was unable to sit. I wandered around the apartment, ending up in the rotunda.

I replayed the whole thing in my mind to cement the details and found I was crying hot, strange tears of jubilation.

*The saving of another's life.*

As a lifeguard years before, I had never actually saved a swimmer, and Wittenberg, Germany, was the last place I ever expected to make a save.

I wondered about her a long time before I called Liliana.

After the save, I began to actively seek opportunities to help others: Walking by parallel parkers, I would stand behind them to show how much space they had left. I smiled more at people. I held doors open more often. I always gave up my seat on the tram. These little things made me feel as if I were being of help, but I found it just wasn't good enough. I wanted to do more. In fact, I felt I was wasting my time if I wasn't out looking for ways to do something beneficial.

Liliana thought it was wonderful that I wanted to help others, but that I might be going a bit overboard with my frenetics.

I myself thought – though I didn't mention it – that it might have something to do with the surfeit of nervous energy I had at my disposal courtesy of nicotine withdrawal.

*A man in an angry-faced gladiator helmet was facing me in the middle of an immense arena. Affixed to the end of his long staff was a chain that he swung over his head. I was defenseless. He approached me and easily wrapped the chain around my legs and yanked me into the air. He held me suspended above the ground and yelled at me.*

*"Get rid of it," he demanded. "Get rid of it!"*

*A moment later I felt myself vomit and only then did the chain lessen its hold. I was dumped unceremoniously to the ground.*

**Chapter 4**

After six months of marriage, I was still blissfully in love – nervous when Liliana wasn't around and tight in the chest when she was. Sometimes when we were to meet in the town, my heart would actually skip a beat when I saw her materialize from a crowd. Being blessed with a kind, good-natured and beautiful wife is certainly a gift beyond measure.

Plus, Liliana was fascinating as well. Growing up under socialism and then seeing it lifted in 1989 – the very time she was coming to be aware of the world around her – had given her experiences that I could only marvel at.

For example, one night at around 9 p.m. we were sitting at the kitchen table drinking Czech beer when I asked her to tell me a secret about the Czech mentality. She couldn't think of one and wanted me to provide an example that might inspire her.

So I told her that in addition to the National Anthem being played before every organized sporting event in the United States, American public schoolchildren are required to say the Pledge of Allegiance at the beginning of each school day.

This reminded her about a story about the Pioneers (pronounced *pee-on-eers*), the socialist equivalent of the American Boy and Girl Scouts. The Pioneers camped, held competitions, provided camaraderie, and essentially kept the youth fit for the inevitable day when the capitalist hordes invaded. Anyway, Liliana happened to be a Pioneer when she was younger, and told me of a competition she had taken part in around the Křivoklát Castle. A number of different schools had entered teams in a type of orienteering competition, and they also had to perform various first aid tasks at checkpoints throughout the hilly terrain.

She mentioned that she had to wear a gas mask as well, which prompted me to exclaim, "Wow! Did it have a canister on each side of the mouth?"

"No, it had only one, right in the center of the mouth."

"Was it difficult to breathe through them?"

"A bit, because you were breathing through the filter. Mostly it smelled bad because you got the mask from another colleague and you had to disinfecticate the rubber. Some of the people got sick from wearing them."

"What about the eyes," I asked, "did it have two pieces of glass or one?" I held both hands in circles over my eyes.

"It had two."

And then an interesting thing happened. My perspective instantly switched, and I jumped ahead in time and saw how ridiculous those gas masks would look to people 500 years from now. It would be like seeing one of those iron chastity belts that women had to wear during the middle ages. My thought process led me to the conclusion that we humans, as a race, are very, very young. We may have been around for 2.5 million years or so, but we've only just begun to lurch towards advanced civilization. Furthermore, when considering the age of the universe (scientists reckon it to be somewhere between 11.2 billion and 20 billion years) it must be concluded that we are infantile.

These thoughts prompted me to say, "Humans are so primitive, it's unbelievable."

Liliana seemed angered. "I wouldn't call us primitive. I think that normal people-"

"Wait a moment," I interrupted. "What is normal?"

I had learned that sometimes Liliana and I mixed words up – an inevitability when dealing with a foreign language.

She took a drink of beer from her tall glass and said, "Normal is a person with high school education, watching television, going to work, having an apartment or a house, and having a family."

"Ok," I said, "so by primitive I mean that high school education is nothing. A person in the future will be much more educated than we are now and will waste much less time on simple things than we now do. Keeping house is a giant waste of time; cleaning, washing, cooking, dishes, laundry, all of those things take up time and are just a little bit wasteful in my opinion. Watching television is a waste of time. Having a family, ok, very important. Necessary and good work. But mostly, on average, a normal person wastes an awful lot of time on-"

Liliana's eyes flashed. "You spend half our trip to America watching football and you talk about people wasting time watching TV!?"

"That's not the point," I said, "and besides I hardly watch any television over here."

"Because you don't understand German."

"Still. The point is that if you look at us as humans, we use perhaps 10% of our brain – let's even say 20% for argument's sake, ok? Well, 20% is nothing. Look back 10,000 years ago at man… back then, we were just concerned about food, shelter, and survival. That's primitive, right?"

"Yes, that's primitive. But this is how mankind should have evolved. This is the natural progression of things, and if you look at it historically, we have progressed just as we should, and I don't think that-"

"Liliana, I agree with you that we are progressing as we should. But again, we're young, and what I'm talking about is if a man from 500 years in the future looks at what we today accept as normal, he's going to find us primitive and just a bit silly. Furthermore, with the abilities of our brain, of which we use like 20%-"

"Don't use that 20% argument again," she said. "I don't want to think about somebody programming me to use the other 80%, making a homogenous society."

"I'm not talking about programming at all. I'm just saying that we don't use our potential, and that's what I mean about being primitive."

"If you're talking about primitive in that we still fight about nationality, race, money, territory and so on, I agree with you. We're primitive."

"And don't you think that war in general – fighting even – is a primitive trait?"

"Because it's linked to survival, and survival is very basic, yes, it is a primitive thing."

"This is what I'm saying. We're not using our potential, we're at the very beginning of our development, and we have a lot left to learn, especially considering the fact that we use so little of our brains."

Liliana finished her beer and with droopy eyes said, "I need to go to bed…"

"Ok, but just one more thing: Are you the best Liliana that you can be?"

She regarded me for a moment. "No..."

"And I'm nowhere near the best Elijah that I can be. And this is what I'm talking about; people – both individually and as a race – are not yet living up to their potential. But I think in the future, all of our accumulated knowledge will have added up to the point that normal people will know a great deal more than we know now. I mean, the education we receive now about history and stupid wars and political intrigues will hopefully give way to learning about the truly important things like health and our bodies, or travel without pollution, or sustainable things or just how to live better and in harmony with the universe and… ok, you're tired. I'll stop."

We got ready for bed after that, but the discussion itself, for me, had been keenly interesting. I just loved talking about that stuff, and was overjoyed to have a partner who was willing to indulge me.

*I was walking next to the river nearby our cabin when a woman I didn't know but whom I recognized as terribly powerful appeared on the path ahead of me. She had with her a bear-sized German Shepherd and by its posture I could tell it was about to attack me. Suddenly, out of the forest to the left came three men who surrounded the woman and dog and began to shoot. The woman crumpled, but the dog was only wounded and continued after me.*

*I had a gun and pulled the trigger, but it wouldn't fire. The dog was nearly to me now, his fangs bared for a lethal bite, and at last my gun fired into its open mouth. It fell at my feet.*

*The three men came over to me. I knew they were my allies, but I didn't recognize them. They told me I had better go before the woman woke up.*

*I ran up onto the road, and some distance away the actor Michael Caine was standing next to a car. He met me and walked me to the vehicle, advising me to get out of there. He was some sort of guardian angel.*

*I got behind the wheel of the car and took off, but the steering didn't work correctly and I was weaving all over the place and having to stop and turn around. It was very chaotic.*

*As I finally got going, the powerful woman ran onto road the beside me. I floored it and escaped in the nick of time, but I could feel that she was going to follow me.*

*I drove to the next town, an Oceanside resort, and found a hotel, checking in under an assumed name. For a time I spent my days reading in an enormous private library I had discovered. But one day on the street, the powerful woman spotted me at the same time I saw her. I hustled away as she followed me through the crowd.*

*I walked up a hill to an amazing structure, perhaps a mosque, with many small jewels and decorative ornaments everywhere on its facade. I touched it with reverence before crossing the street towards the sanctuary of the immense, Gothic cathedral.*

*Standing in the middle of the road blocking my path was the powerful woman.*

**Chapter 5**

Liliana's eyes narrowed as she lowered her wine glass.

"So you think being religious is the only way to be a better person?"

"Right," I said. "That's what I mean."

The same old discussion; this time it came during a dinner we'd prepared to celebrate the end of her first month on the job.

"And do you still have a problem that I'm not religious," she asked.

I hesitated. "I've never had that problem. It's your choice, and I can't force you into anything. I'm a believer because of what I've seen. But I also recognize that I have to study religious texts because I'm not as inherently nice as-"

"You're nice!"

"Yeah," I said, "but I behave stupidly sometimes. Like last week – I didn't tell you this one."

I scratched my head, the overgrown brown hair falling out of place as I did so. Liliana reached over to smooth it.

"Anyway, I was parking in front of the building, and our neighbor who parks his BMW on the sidewalk and thinks he owns the world drove up. I guess I was in his way, because he leaned on the horn."

"Were you in his way?"

"A little, but the point is his manners. Why didn't he pull up beside me and nicely ask me to move? So anyways, I moved out of the way for him, he parked, and then I blocked him in with our car."

"You blocked him in?"

"Sure. I was there first."

"What did he do?"

"Got all German on me."

"What did *you* do?"

"Tried to yell back at him in German until he looked at me like I was an idiot, then I switched to yelling at him in English. The cursing came out smoother like that."

"You cursed at him?"

"That's my point – I got all fired up and cursed at him and we walked away with this whole poisoned relationship. I left the car there to prove my point, but was totally obsessed with it until I went to move it an hour later. It was definitely not the embodiment of 'love thy neighbor'."

"Why didn't you just park somewhere else?"

I shrugged. "Anger. Stupidity."

"So that's why he didn't speak to me yesterday."

"Probably... oh, and then this afternoon some smartass put a lock on the back wheel of my bicycle."

"Where?"

"Here inside the building."

She shook her head. "How did you get it off?"

"I cut off some spokes. But I bet it was that guy who did it."

"Karma," she said.

I paused. "*Exactly.* You see what I get for being so nice…"

She half-frowned, half-smiled at my sarcasm. "But you're not normally like that. This is the first nasty thing you've done in a long time."

Taking a drink of the red wine, I was happy the conversation was turning away from my opinion of her spirituality and I chided myself for bringing it up in the first place.

"Hey," I said, "speaking of nasty, how was work?"

"My work is *not* nasty."

"It's nasty when you work until 8 p.m."

"We knew it would be like this when I got the fellowship. Anyway, it's just for the two years and then we do something else. Maybe we'll move back to Prague…"

"Don't tease me."

To be frank, moving from the majesty of Prague to the provinciality of Wittenberg was not entirely fulfilling. This is not to take anything away from Wittenberg, which is a pleasant, green and occasionally festive town with an historically-important heritage.

But once you've lived in Prague, your scale of comparison is thrown all awry. Indeed, how to compare to the immensity and grandeur of Prague Castle? How to compare with the majesty and architectural wonder of Old Town Square? How to compare to the vibrancy of the Charles Bridge? In sum, how can one compare to a life – in word and in deed – that is truly Bohemian?

What I especially missed was St. Vitus' Cathedral. The feel of that place was completely… *proper* for me. I could go in there any day of the week during a reasonable span of hours, sit on the pews and read the Bible or some other philosophical text, and just feel as if I belonged to something bigger than myself.

The Wittenberg churches – for me at least – weren't like that at all. St. Mary's, for example, is a Gothic church dating from 1400, and has some fascinating paintings detailing Luther's Reformation, but is otherwise plain, and in keeping with the spirit of the Reformation, quite austere. I went there once, felt oppressed, and only returned if accompanying visitors.

Then there is the Castle Church, which is home to a very famous door – the one upon which Luther pinned his 95 theses. The bronze door currently in place is cast with these theses in Latin and is certainly an impressive sight. The Castle Church's interior is also striking; the vaulted roof is adorned with colorful floral and arboreal designs, and the supporting pillars, likewise ornamented, provide the space with a feeling of natural connectedness – as if the pillars were actually trees, and the ceiling a forest canopy. Moving downwards, a high walkway along the walls is adorned with sculpted coats-of-arms and colorful mosaics. Further, the pulpit is a late-Gothic wonder of carved wood, and the altar marvelous beyond description. In short, it's a beautiful space.

I very much liked the Castle Church, but with apologies to all of the pastors who undergo their theological studies there, I never felt as if it were all that holy. Yes, I felt it was a calm place worthy of contemplation, but the feeling was always much more akin to the way one feels while in a museum; in the Castle Church, there are perhaps a dozen statues of notable personalities from the Reformation, many stained-glass windows portraying other personas, two huge paintings of Luther and Melanchthon, and the back wall of the church bears the German translation of Luther's original 95 theses. All these things are impressive to say the least. However, I always felt the Castle Church was more a place to admire in a historical sense, not as a place of worship.

So it was lucky that I stumbled upon the Evangelical Christ Church on one of my bike rides on the outskirts of town. There, I was immediately struck by that mysterious feeling one only feels in holy places, be it naturally-occurring or man-made.

I liked it there because the air was heavy with incense.

I liked it there because the organ player would often practice during my visits.

I liked it there because the details of the colorful woodwork never failed to captivate me.

And I liked it there because the pastor, after learning I was a teacher, chatted with me in English from time to time. Thus, it was the Evangelical Christ Church that I visited to continue my Bible studies, and I felt I was moving in the right direction.

*A group of people were in Gramma's house watching a wonderful cosmic event on television – it was all colorful supernovas and nebulae merging and pulling on one another. The people were all very good friends and I felt at ease and privileged to be there.*

*Suddenly, Darth Vader appeared outside of the front picture window in a floating chariot. Translocating inside and among us, he attempted to influence the cosmic event by using his light-saber on the top portion of the screen.*

*I realized I had the power to prevent him from influencing the event and I used my will to stop him. Thwarted, he returned to his hovering chariot just outside the picture window.*

*After a time, Darth Vader was overcome by the positivity that he had witnessed through the picture window and took off his helmet. He was a changed man – he had chosen to return to the light. We welcomed him back inside, where he sat with his knees drawn up to his chin, weeping.*

*We continued to watch the cosmic event.*

## Chapter 6

Shockingly, Easy Language School called to offer me a job and in my confusion I immediately agreed to it. So the next day I turned up before my new class was to begin and David showed me around. There wasn't so much to show, actually. In addition to the reception area, there was a teaching room with a locked bookcase, a photocopy machine, a small kitchenette and a toilet.

David described the system for me: Each time copies were made, a form which lived overtop the copy machine had to be filled out specifying who the copies were for and what materials were being copied. The machine had to be opened up and the number on the counter recorded. A signature had to be provided. The key for the bookcase lived with the receptionist. The books were at all times to be kept locked up, and if the teachers wanted to borrow materials, meticulous records were kept. Teachers could have a cup of coffee if there was coffee already made, but they could not make the coffee themselves. The students could have a cup of coffee for 50 cents, or could purchase a bottle of water for 1 Euro. Students also had to pay for all photocopied materials they received.

Clearly, this was no laid-back office. Still, after moving in to our new apartment at Schatzungstrasse 15, the school was only two blocks away, and because of the convenience factor, I decided to take as many classes as they wanted to give me.

Private language schools in Europe can be great places to work. A good school offers courses in a variety of languages taught by native speakers, and as such, the schools tend to be hubs of multiculturalism where a wide spectrum of perspectives are focused through a small lens.

In addition to being an oasis for meeting other foreigners living abroad, the students of said schools tend to be educated adults, and that they must pay market prices for their instructors' knowledge makes them rather motivated. Discipline is therefore rarely a problem, and homework tends to be completed on time and in full.

Furthermore, in addition to teaching in the school itself, sometimes businesses hire language teachers to visit their premises and conduct classes on-site. This is actually the more interesting part of teaching English as a second language, because in this way a teacher is able to learn much about the town in which he or she happens to be living.

For example, one of the classes which ELS assigned me was at a travel agency across town. Travel agents tend to be gregarious people and these students were no exception, so teaching them English was a pleasure.

A second group of students that I began teaching after a spell were housed in the Martin Luther House, a museum dealing with Luther, Wittenberg University, and the history of the Reformation. The staff members there were inundated with English-speaking visitors, and while the cashier spoke the handful of phrases necessary for selling tickets, the rest of the staff needed help. It was also hoped that someone might once be able to conduct tours or record an audio guide in English.

There were five students in all at the Martin Luther House, but based on attendance, only three of them were serious about learning. The first was the central secretary, Helga, who was in her plump early-50s, was nice as pie, but was not terribly bright. Helga had several nervous ticks, including blinking spasms and head wiggles – though thank goodness never at the same time – and she was totally unconfident in her English. Because of this, her lack of fluency was especially tedious for the others – notably Mathias.

Confident to the point of arrogance, Mathias seemed to believe everyone around him was interested in every word he uttered. But aside from this, like everyone else he had his redeeming qualities: He was a quick study and occasionally would stumble upon a topic that the whole class found genuinely interesting. It was on those days that class proceeded smoothest.

What helped me immensely in dealing with Mathias' ego actually happened outside of class. On my way to teach at the institute – it was my fifth or sixth week there – a BMW that was parallel parking caught my attention. The driver was scraping the wheels and tires along the curb, producing a high-pitched and ugly combination of screeching and scratching. I felt sorry for the driver, but then as I walked by I caught a glimpse of him – it was Mathias.

The last of my regular students was Luther House's marketing specialist, Angelica, who was youngish and quite pretty in a pants suit and turtleneck kind of way. Sharp as a tack and eager to learn, Angelica was the one who asked the questions I generally couldn't answer. One that I clearly remember was, "Elijah, why is it that an intransitive verb cannot be made passive?" To this question (and many others) I was forced to reply, "Great question Angelica, but it's a bit too complicated for me to explain quickly. Can I address it at the beginning of class next week?"

I never had to search for lesson ideas with Angelica around.

I enjoyed biking to work for its fitness aspects, but even more so because it allowed me to acquaint myself with Wittenberg's various districts. Since we lived in an outlying residential quarter, the ride to the center took about 15 minutes and after awhile I whittled that down to ten minutes of riding exclusively on smooth, car-free bike paths.

The town center of Wittenberg is really fine – filled with green parks and duck-filled ponds on the outside and lovely medieval architecture and shops galore on the inside. And this is to say nothing of the constant comings and goings on the narrow cobbled streets of the historic center.

Which brings me to an aspect of European living that should not be overlooked: When a town or city has a certain character or charisma about it, be it due to rich cultural offerings, a geographic blessing, or an impressive architectural heritage, people are understandably drawn to that. So it was with Prague, which during the summer months was simply a beehive of tourists (though probably far less organized).

At any rate, after some weeks of elbowing through these crowds during my first Prague summer, I realized that by simply expanding my own knowledge of the town – going into outlying districts – I could discover enchanting and peaceful spaces where I could enjoy the Spirit of Prague without having to suffer the throngs of easyJetters in town for a beery weekend.

And while it is no Prague in several senses of the word, Wittenberg, because of its being the birthplace of the Protestant Movement, enjoys its share of tourists to be avoided. Take my favorite Biergarten, for example. Situated in the rear courtyard of the castle, and with a wondrous rear view of the Castle Church and tower, I could read in the afternoon sun for hours and see no more than, say, 50 tourists. Why so few? Because the passage to the rear courtyard wasn't – thank goodness – well signed. No neon arrows pointing in that direction meant that the less courageous simply poked their noses in and continued on their way.

There were other places that I came to enjoy for their solitude or for the presence of some wonder upon which to feast the eyes. Many times I would ride out to the riverside and watch the sunrise or sunset. Or I would bike out of town and sit at the edge of a grassy field and watch the horses and sheep graze. And if I were really feeling ambitious, I would ride down to Wörlitz gardens.

There were just three apartments in our whole building, all of them on the top floor. The adult education organization called CESA took up the first two floors, and quite a few men attended classes there. When moving in, I had passed them up time and again at the entrance of the building. They took frequent 15 minute breaks, and watched me carry in all of our suitcases and furniture (with Liliana working, I was the moving company).

Recognizing me as a foreigner, sometimes the students would speak to me in English, but mostly they would talk among themselves in German; still, I felt their eyes on me constantly. Anyway, it came as a bit of a surprise that during the early spring I found myself teaching classes at CESA, which meant that I worked in my own building: The commute was 30 seconds, I drank my own coffee (I had begun drinking decaf as a cleansing measure), and I could take lunch in my own home. The class I was assigned to teach was a group of 15 unemployed men, and on the first day of "Everyday English", I recognized most of them.

The first question asked of me was, "Where are you from? America?" The questioner was huge – almost seven feet tall – and barrel-chested.

"You got it," I replied.

"You got it," he said in a high, mocking voice. And that was the start of it. This guy – about 45 or so – had never outgrown the belligerence he'd apparently acquired along with his size. He was the class clown and the one who tried the hardest to be cool. He didn't like his English being corrected, and he hated when the class didn't pay him enough attention. Because of all these factors, I rarely called on him to speak, which he further resented.

When the classes finished after two ardous weeks, I was relieved that I wouldn't have to deal with the guy anymore. But still, he continued taking classes in my building and we ran into each other from time to time. And every time we saw each other, he'd have something to say about me being American.

"Hey, it's Mr. A-*merica,*" or "What does Mr. A-*merica* have? Oh, it looks like A-*merican* food," or "We like your A-*merican* car."

And so on.

At first, I good-naturedly took it, and sometimes joked back. But after this kind of interaction twice a week for about a month, I began to tire of it and finally took the offensive.

The next time I saw the man, he was loitering in front of our building with a bunch of his classmates. We made eye contact and before he had a chance to say anything, I called out, "Hey, Mr. *Unemployed*!"

He hesitated for a second, clearly taken aback, and then said a short, "Hello, Mr. America."

I walked through the group of silent students and up to my apartment feeling full of myself. Later that afternoon, as I walked through a crowd of the men taking a break downstairs, the bully said, loud enough for all to hear, "Hello, my friend."

I blinked and said hello, and continued on my walk over to ELS to sign out a book. During the walk I mused on my sudden success in dealing with the guy, and reckoned that my only remaining challenge was to figure out how to handle David, because in plain terms, he was no damned fun to be around.

In addition to being a control freak – he was full of endless explanations and qualifications of why things had to be done in his particular way – David was also an energy-taker.

Here's how he operated: You'd walk into the school feeling happy. You just came, say, from a wildly successful class. David, behind the counter, would ask you how class went. Great, you'd reply. Great how, he'd ask. You'd provide a short report on the class and in the middle of it he would decide the materials you had used were improper. He had something that had proven invaluable, he would say. He'd want to show you the materials in question. Thc search would take awhile. You were expected to wait for him. You'd try to sneak away while he was searching so you could fill in your paperwork, but he would sense you sneaking off and say no matter, he'd find it later and put it in your mailbox. Then he might digress and ask you a personal question about, say, the lottery you had recently won. Yes, you'd reply, I'm now a millionaire. Oh yes, David would say, I remember the first time I hit the lottery. Wonderful feeling, isn't it?

Yes, isn't it, you reply, and tell him that with the winnings you're going to fly to the moon. Oh, he says, you simply must visit the Sea of Tranquility. Wonderful views from there.

And so on, until you leave the school feeling mildly depressed, not only because you have just wasted an hour of your day, but also because you realize that David is an energy-taker and that you have just provided him with a healthy fix of the stuff.

Similar to many other days, the first thing out of David's mouth when I walked through ESL's door was, "I'm having trouble getting a hold of you."

"Is that right?"

"Don't you check your email?"

"Sure."

"Did you get my email yesterday?"

"Yeah…"

"So why didn't you come in?"

"I didn't have time. Anyway, I'm here now, so what would you like to discuss?"

"Let's go in the classroom." He gestured for me to walk in front of him and I plopped into a chair.

He shut the door and sat down across from me. I did a mental search for reasons to be concerned, but couldn't come up with any.

"So what's up," I asked.

He drew a circle on the table with his fingers.

"Elijah, you've been here what… four months now?"

"Yeah, around that…"

"Well, you've probably noticed that the teachers go out for drinks every so often…"

"Yeah," I answered, "they've asked me along once or twice."

He pointed at me abruptly and said, "That's-" and then, retracting his finger, continued, "That's the point. The teachers are a social bunch, but they never ask *me* to come along."

I blinked at him and thought, *That's because you're the main topic of conversation.*

"Well," I said, "have you asked to join them?"

"Yes. I have."

"And?"

"And I go, and I end up thinking everyone had a good time, but then I'm not asked along the next week."

"Do you express interest in going again?"

"Sometimes. But why do I have to beg all the time? Anyway, you know how it is being an expatriate – it's lonely sometimes."

I myself had always welcomed the solitude, and remained quiet.

He sighed again. "The reason I'm telling you this is that I was hoping we could do some things together. I'm not that big on pubs and I know you like to jog… so maybe we could run together sometime…"

I made a slight wince. "Er…I don't know… what about soccer?"

"I've never played."

"Basketball?"

"Bad knees."

'Tennis?"

"Uh-uh."

It was my turn to sigh. "Ok, jogging it is."

He smiled and said, "Great. Next Monday?"

I forced a smile and said that would be fine. We concluded our meeting and I left right afterwards, pondering my unsavory situation during the walk home. It was only when I got through the front door that I remembered I had gone to ELS to collect a book.

Which I'd forgotten.

"Well, why did you agree to run with him, then?"

It was an overcast evening and I was whining to Liliana as I walked her home from work.

"Because I didn't want to hurt his feelings. He looked so *little* when he asked me to do something together."

We walked a moment in silence before she said, "I think it's nice of you. And you don't know… maybe you get along fine out of the school."

*Sigh.*

"But he's such a *pain.* I can't go into the office without him hovering over my shoulder, micro-managing everything I do."

I started gesturing a lot at this point. "And you know what? Teaching English ain't rocket science. It doesn't need to be charted, quantified and tracked in triplicate."

I took a breath as Liliana giggled at me.

"And as far as the argument that a business requires such painstaking documentation, I don't buy it. A business entity reflects the personality of its principal manager or owner, and this one is no exception. It's a pain to work at ELS because the *boss* is a pain. And now I have to introduce pain into my personal life in the form of *David.*"

Liliana stopped walking and looked at me. "Hey. What about your big 'minimize the negative' idea? Isn't this a perfect situation to apply it?"

I sighed heavily.

"*Yes.* But-"

"I think you should view it as an opportunity to help. You're always saying how you want to help people, and this is a chance to help someone that you know. He is asking for help and you are able to help him."

Her logic was irritating.

"Fine. But I would *never* seek out his company. You know, normal friendships are give and take. It's an energetic trade-off that leaves both parties feeling better at having spent time together. But David – he's an energy sponge, and the reason he's asked me to hang out is because he recognizes my energy. He wants some and he'll just end up *taking and taking.* It's like that girl you knew in your PhD program – the arrogant one with the black hair?"

"Ooooh, she was unpleasant."

"She was. And her way of taking energy was to make everyone around her feel like they weren't good enough."

Liliana took up the baton. "I remember her big trick was not listening when you spoke to her… one could always see she was thinking of what she was going to say next, not listening to you. Another trick was to not look at you when she spoke. She would ignore all but the important person in the group."

I smiled. "I wish David would ignore *me.*"

Liliana giggled as I continued. "And anyway, why do *I* have to be so nice all the time? Why can't I be mean and say NO to David and tell him he's a big pain in the butt?"

"Because he is your boss?"

I looked over at her. "But wouldn't telling him about his personality defects *help* him in the long run?"

"Oh, yes. And it's your work to change your boss' personality."

We had arrived home, and as Liliana checked our postbox I let out a grunt.

"This sucks."

*I was flying over the seaside. I had my arms spread and this somehow provided me with a semblance of stability, though it took a great deal of concentration to maintain it.*

*The waves were encouraged by terrible winds and were as high as buildings. They were a danger to the whole coast, and sometimes came rolling in so high as to threaten me as I continued my flight up the coastline.*

*My flying height was just out of their reach, but I somehow knew it wouldn't last for long.*

**Chapter 7**

"Why don't you wear Adidas instead of Nikes? They last longer."

"You should hold your hands looser when you jog."

"Can we go faster?"

The entire circuit David and I jogged would be filled with such questions and comments, and by the time we would finish, I was invariably an irritable wreck. The fabled runner's high was nowhere to be found, and to boot, David had convinced me to jog three times per week. On the one hand, I was ok with the idea of exercising so much because I thought being more fit would help boost my energy levels and thus assist me in the spiritual area. But good gravy was David abrasive!

And it wasn't only about jogging that he was such a pain. He would ask about how often Liliana and I made love, whether we found it difficult being an intercultural pair, how often we argued, and so on. But most of his questions went unanswered because he pressed my buttons just way too hard.

Liliana counseled me to stop seeing him so often, but I couldn't find the gumption to do it, especially after he revealed that he and his German wife were having problems. We were walking around the jogging path to warm down when it came out.

"You know, Katrin and I used to understand each other so well. We'd talk for hours about the simplest things. But since we started working together at the school, all we talk about is work, work, work."

"And she's been traveling a lot, too, hasn't she?"

"That's another thing. She's been on the road for like 2 of the last 4 weeks, and truthfully…"

He stopped walking and turned to me.

"Don't tell anyone this, but she told me…" A look of disgust crossed his face. "She told me she's seeing someone."

"What?"

"She's…"

He couldn't continue talking. It was the first time I'd seen him become emotional. We resumed walking and after a bit he continued.

"She said she wants a divorce."

"Oh, man. I'm so sorry…"

"And if I agree, then it's goodbye Katrin, goodbye ELS, goodbye my whole life here! We've been together over ten years, and pow!"

"Maybe it's just a one-time thing," I said. "Maybe she just needs to get it out of her system?"

"*Shit*… I doubt it."

We sat down on a park bench and I said, "Maybe it's time to move on, then. I mean, you can't just let yourself continue to be hurt by someone – especially your wife."

He shook his head at me. "Ten years we've been together! And I'm not *ready* to give up. Why should I?"

We sat quietly for a moment as a slow-walking couple passed, then I asked, "How long have you known about it?"

He leaned his head back, sighed, and said, "Six months."

"Holy cow. David, how can you live like that?"

"I love her."

"Fine. But she's scr-..."

I'd almost said 'screwing someone else'. David heard me stifle the word and stood up.

"Listen," he said, "I'm sorry to lay all this on you – I just had to tell someone, and you're the best friend I have..."

"No problem... I'm really sorry, man."

"Thanks."

I watched him walk off and felt terrible for the guy. I mean, here he was living in a foreign country, married to a German girl who was cheating on him, and his best friend and confidant – me – didn't even like him much.

I sat on the bench in the crisp, early spring sunlight for a spell wondering about David's situation, and then walked through town to pick up Liliana from her institute. I was still sweaty when I arrived, and stood outside in the sunshine waiting for her.

A few of her foreign colleagues came out and I traded pleasantries with them before Liliana emerged. We kissed hello and I asked how her day was.

She threaded her fingers through mine and said, "Oh, ok."

We started walking and she put her arm through mine. "Tell me – what would you do with a week of freedom?"

"What do you mean?"

"I mean, if you were alone for a week, what would you do?"

"Get drunk. Sleep all day."

"You would not!"

"No, I don't know. Maybe take a trip. Why?"

"Because I have a work trip next week."

"Great! Where are we going?"

"Bratislava – but you cannot come because we will travel by car, and it's full."

"Oh, man! You're going without me?"

"I don't want to, but it's for work."

I took my hand from hers and folded my arms, playing hurt.

"Don't make me feel bad," she said. "I don't want to go, but it is important for my project."

She looked at me a moment and then said, "We will meet people from the Czech University there, too."

I looked over at her. "Oh yeah? Who?"

"Oh, my old boss… Lubica… Vlada …"

"*Vlada* will be there?"

"Yes. He is a representative from the Czech University."

"Oh, that's lovely. So *you'll* be the drunk one."

"What?"

"*You'll* be the one drunk every night – you and Vlada."

"I will not. We'll be working, and maybe go out for dinner."

I saw red. "Who – you and Vlada?"

"No! What's wrong with you? I mean the group."

"Yeah, right. Like when I was in the States, it was all you and Vlada every night!"

"We're *friends*."

I couldn't think of anything nice to say, so I shut up and we walked home with a wall of tension between us. Later I would come to realize that I was being overly-sensitive, most likely due to David's revelation, but I still didn't like Vlada being in Bratislava as well.

The next two days – the weekend – were not very fun. Liliana had to prepare for her trip and whenever we were together, instead of enjoying our time, I pouted like a hurt little baby. Only after she left on Monday did I realize how stupidly I had acted – that I had basically wasted two days with negativity. Liliana was a grownup, after all. And a grownup who loved me at that.

Which is easy to tell yourself during the daytime, but try it when you can't sleep at night.

*In a castle overlooking the sea, I was walking along a row of picnic tables that had identification cards and passports lying on them. Picking them up, I saw that some of the cards were valid but without photos and I realized I had stumbled onto a system for making false identifications.*

*I hurriedly collected all the ID cards – it was a sizeable stack – and was walking away with the intention of turning them in to the authorities, when out of a large stairway (similar to an underground subway entrance) a huge group of men emerged, dressed in black ninja-type outfits, wearing red headbands and carrying rifles.*

*They came directly to me and the leader said, "Good, you have my identifications. Here is the money."*

*He gave me a duffel bag and held out his hand for the identifications. I looked inside the duffel bag and inside was a nest of snakes.*

**Chapter 8**

Marketa, a former colleague of Liliana's from the Czech Agriculture University, had called a few weeks before saying that she was coming to Wittenberg for a weekend yoga course and that she wanted to meet up. Liliana had planned on spending a lot of time with her, maybe even joining the yoga course herself, but now she would be away for business. To make up for it, Liliana told Marketa that she could stay in our living room. Marketa gratefully accepted and I was not at all thrilled.

Thus faced with the prospect of entertaining for a long weekend, I decided to drive down to a village in Thuringia where the Christian mystic Meister Eckhart was born – maybe I could learn a thing or two down there. But before I could hit the road, I had to drop off our keys at the only place in town that Marketa had directions to – the yoga school. It was a couple blocks away from us, no problem to find, and after I parked in front of Melanchthonstrasse 33, the building was so arresting that I had to stand in front of it for awhile to take it all in.

A two-story Queen Anne villa of blonde brick, Melanchthonstrasse 33 was a motley crew of architectural styles that somehow pulled itself together into a thing of beauty: In addition to its Victorian façade and pavilion roof, it had a square Roman tower on the left side with a glassed-in lookout room and flattish roof, on top of which was a golden weathervane indicating the year 1877. On the right side of the building, set somewhat back from the street, was another tower – this one round and speckled by stout, stained-glass windows with pointy gothic arches. The round tower looked like it contained a stairwell, and was topped with a black slate witch's hat.

After the novelty of the place wore off, I shook my head and followed the walkway toward the roughly-hewn, dark wooden door of the round tower. As I wondered how to knock loud enough to be heard without breaking my hand, the door squeaked open and a buxom, brown-haired woman, no younger than 40, poked her head out.

I was about to speak when she said, "My goodness! Aren't *you* a chubby one?"

"Huh?"

With a mischievous twinkle in her dark eyes, she opened the door wider. She was wearing a loose saffron robe and sandals, and followed up the chubby statement with, "You probably drink beer, don't you?"

"Uh… what," I asked, trying to get up to speed.

"Beer. Do you drink it?" She placed her hands on her hips.

"…Yeah..."

"You see? Not a hard question… my point is that beer can make one chubby. Like you. Now, why don't you come upstairs and try some tea instead?"

"Uh… no. Thanks… I just need to drop off these keys."

"Ah, so you're Marketa's American friend. *That* explains your weight. Still, you must come up for some tea," she said, and was back through the doorway before I could respond. "And please close the door."

*That explains your weight, my ass,* I thought, frowning as I followed her inside. When I closed the huge wooden door, I couldn't believe how light it was. It glided easily and clicked smartly into place.

It was quite dark inside.

"Uh… hello?"

"Up the stairs," she answered in her faintly amused voice. "All the way up."

Suddenly a fatass, I noticed that the wooden spiral stairs creaked under my weight as I trudged reluctantly upwards. After a few steps, the red-, green-, and blue-colored light from the windows illuminated the way, making the place feel solemn.

When I reached the top, directly across from me was a carved mahogany-colored doorway that led into a vast, bright, high-ceilinged hall. Running my hands over the intricate patterns of the doorway, I peered inside. Above, it was supported by immense, dark wooden trusses. Further down, the walls were covered by rough white plaster.

The bright hardwood floors were scattered with inviting rugs and pillows, and the woman was already sitting on one of these in the corner to my right. Between her and another sitting pillow was a low, dark wooden table with dozens of multi-shaped crystals of various colors laying on it. She indicated that I should sit down opposite her.

I had planned on being halfway to Thuringia by now, but I still sat down.

She observed me as I tried to get comfortable.

"So you're chubby *and* nervous."

I tell you, I actually saw red. I saw red and raised my voice, "*Hey! Enough*, all right? I'm just here to drop off a key, not be insulted by some..." I searched for some non-insulting words, but couldn't find them.

"And we really have to do something about the anger," she said.

I stared at her for a moment before letting out a huge sigh. I looked away and shook my head. When I looked back at her, she regarded me with her little smirk for a few moments before she offered me the tea that was sitting near my right hand. I asked what kind it was.

"Green."

I took a slurp, made a face, and then began to rifle through my bag for the keys. I certainly had better things to do than be insulted and drink nasty-tasting tea.

"Elijah, do you like crystals?"

I looked up at her. "How did you know my name?"

"Marketa told me. My name is Beatrice, by the way."

I looked back down into the bag. "They're ok."

"Then, why don't you choose one?"

"What do you mean, 'choose one'?"

I found the keys and looked up to see her sweep her arm across the table. She had long, sinewy fingers, and her hands were covered with intricate designs that I later learned were of Henna.

"Look at them," she said. "Consider them. Choose one."

"Why would I do that?"

"A game."

*How about you shut the fuck up,* I thought. *How's that for a game?*

She caught my eye then, and I cannot adequately convey how disconcerting it was to watch her mouth remain motionless but to nonetheless hear her voice in my thoughts.

*Now, now,* she "said".

I felt as if someone hit me in the stomach. I physically quaked and my flight or flight reflex demanded that I put distance between us. I struggled to stand up, in the process tripping over the pillow I had been sitting on. I toppled onto my back and when I finally, indignantly, found my feet, Beatrice was wearing a smug smile. I absolutely despised her. Feared her.

"How did you do that," I demanded.

*Do what?*

That smile.

"Listen, I'm about a second from wiping that smug fucking smile off your face, so-"

"Ok, ok. Calm down... We can talk this way, too."

She was speaking normally again.

"How did you do that?"

We both noticed that the finger I was pointing at her was trembling.

"Perhaps someday I will tell you. But for now, please sit down. Relax." She swept her hands across the crystals again and beckoned me back.

"Relax. That's funny. Yeah, I'll just do that."

I was struggling to maintain a grip and she wanted me to relax. Had she just spoken telepathically?

"Did you just speak telepathically?"

A small smile played across her full lips. "Yes. But only because *you* are also able."

"Able? Able to what?"

"To hear it."

"So are you psychic or what?"

"Oh… sometimes. One has to be in a certain state of mind to accomplish these things, and today is a good day for me. That's how I knew you were coming, by the way. And why I answered the door before you knocked."

"And how you read my mind."

"*And* how I read your mind – though it didn't take much effort to pick up your anger – I can also project sometimes, and very seldom I can… read things."

"Wait – project? Project what?"

"Myself."

I scrunched my eyes closed and said, "Project yourself?"

Looking at her again, I asked, "Project yourself where?"

"You know of what I speak…"

She gave me a searching look, and I had absolutely no clue what she was after.

"Your dream, Elijah? The letter from God that was so difficult to read?"

I felt another jolt. My rational, reactionary mind just couldn't fathom all this, and canceled out my natural curiosity – as usual – with aggression.

"How the hell do you know about my dream?"

She gave me a hard look and said, "It's difficult to explain, but in your terms, I saw you there. I saw you being given a letter, because I was involved in a reading myself."

"Reading of what? My letter?"

"No. It doesn't work like that. I was reading another portion of the Records."

She spoke "the records" very solemnly.

"The what," I asked, already feeling vaguely like I knew what she was talking about.

Portions of the God dream had come back when she mentioned it. I remembered that although I had been focusing on the letter, there was more space surrounding it, that the letter seemed to be floating among many other documents – not really books or parchment, but not entirely unlike them, either.

I shook my head in rejection. "This is… just too strange."

"Not many people understand the Akashic Records as a concept, Elijah. Not many want to. They don't even like to name them. But they can be a source of great help if you can access them. And especially if you use them wisely."

"Access them?"

"Yes. Through meditation. Or in your case, dreams. I know some who do it through hypnosis."

*What a crackpot,* I thought.

She lifted her thick eyebrow and I knew she'd heard me again.

"Uh… can you control your dreams," I asked.

She sighed. "That's not really the proper term for it. I can, let's say… *influence* my dreams, but not always. It's a very sporadic phenomenon and it's like everything else we humans put our hands on – if we're not careful, we foul it up."

I laughed a little harder than the small joke merited, but I couldn't help myself. "I'm sure of that," I said.

"Do you want to know more," she ventured.

"Yeah, I do. Why did you call me fat when we met?"

"Anger," she said, "is a wonderful cleanser of the mind. Although it is true that *when* we are angry it is hard to focus, afterwards, when our mind settles, we forget nearly everything, and we are more open. This is why I angered you. I am sorry, but it was the only way."

"Uh-huh."

"Would you like to know more about all this?"

I took a deep breath and looked at her.

She took this as a yes and began to speak.

"You should understand this isn't just a bunch of nonsense that I am personally making up. What I'm about to tell you is real, just as real as we are sitting here. I am not the first, nor will I be the last to be able to do what I do. Now. You experienced something startling in the dream I saw you in, didn't you? Something that touched you deeply?"

I nodded. "I think it was a letter from God."

She nodded back. "And right you are."

A pregnant pause.

"How do you know that?"

"Because the Akashic Records are *of* God. That is, they're a part of God because they're a part of the universe. And as a part of the Akashic Records were revealed to you, you may safely say that it was a letter *of* God, though I bet his handwriting was awful hard for you to read…"

She gave me an expectant look.

I nodded. "I could barely read it. It was all cloudy and oblique and when I looked at it directly, it just got more blurry."

She nodded.

"This a common experience with the Akashic Records. Later, if you are able to return to them, you will learn how to better clarify what you are presented. It's not easy, but once learned, it will open up vast worlds of meaning that you had no idea ever existed."

"The Akashic Records," she continued, "are both of this world and not of this world. It is very difficult to explain exactly, but simply put, they are a type of recording device. Think of it this way: Imagine there is a camera slightly behind you that films your every move throughout your whole life. But the camera's microphone doesn't only record sound – it records your thoughts as well."

She smiled. "Just imagine what such a camera and microphone would record…"

I blinked. "You're saying that my life is on candid camera?"

She didn't get the joke and continued with her explanation.

"What I'm saying is that all our deeds, thoughts and intentions are being recorded on the Akasha, and that you were shown a file from the Akashic Records in your dream."

"Uh-huh. And every person in the world who's ever lived has had a similar file?"

She rocked back and forth and said, "Not exactly. You see, we are all spiritual beings. We are spiritual beings who happen to be – temporarily – in a physical form. But when *this* physical body wears out, we will continue on our journey. Perhaps we will have learned all we need to learn and will unite with the Great Spirit. Or perhaps we have more lessons to embody and will come back for further lives. This is what the Akashic Records are all about – they are a document that records how our spiritual self is progressing."

I squinted at her. "You're talking about reincarnation?"

"That's one term for it."

My concentration, which had been so keen when she began her explanation, was suddenly and thoroughly depleted. Now she was babbling about reincarnation.

"Uh-huh," I responded. I looked around the room. I wanted to change the subject. "So… what do you use this room for?"

She regarded me for a moment before responding.

"Yoga. Other activities."

"Hmm. Well… you've certainly given me a lot to think about. I appreciate it. But I've really got to get going."

She waved her hand dismissively. "Of course. Of course… but you'll come back again for tea sometime, won't you?"

I intended to never return to that nutcase's house.

Never, ever.

"Sure I will."

*I was climbing down a cliff with my father, who was leading the way and giving me pointers about how to navigate the rocky terrain. Far below us was a deep lake. It seemed to be an old, open mine that after abandonment had filled with rain water.*

*The cliff had been navigated before, and others had left a mostly-forgotten path with footholds and exposed roots from the sparse trees. It was tricky going, with many rocks giving way and tumbling into the water below.*

*When we came to a particularly difficult area that wound through some scrub brush, I paused and looked downward at the water. It was green and inviting and only then did I realize it was a hot, sunny day. I was looking at the edge of the water carefully, because if I was unable to navigate the next portion of the descent, I would fall into it. I saw that just under the water, extending in both directions, ran what looked like an irregular, rocky ledge. About five feet out from this, the water turned unfathomably deep.*

*Dad saw my hesitancy and said that I didn't have to worry, that I could manage the difficult maneuver. And anyway, he said, falling into the water was really only falling into myself.*

*He saw that I didn't understand what he meant, so he just continued encouraging me. I continued downward and succeeded with the tricky maneuver.*

*Just yards above the water now, I thought that by grabbing the top of a young, flexible tree, I would be able to ride it down to the water, where dad was already standing ankle-deep near the edge.*

*I caught hold of the tree and as I rode it down I realized it was going to hit my father. He knew it, too – he'd been expecting it – and just before the tree scraped his legs, I saw his bemused smile as he shook his head at me.*

*I landed on the water's edge and apologized for hitting him, but he smiled at me indulgently and reassured me.*

## Chapter 9

In my ongoing ignorance of the German language, I was unable to track down any traces of the Thuringian village where the Christian mystic Meister Eckhart was born. It wasn't on the map any longer, and the people that I asked for directions either had no idea where it was, or knew *exactly* where it was and I couldn't understand their directions.

So instead of learning about Eckhart's work, I spent my time wandering the rolling hills, visiting castles, drinking beer, and thinking about my meeting with that crazy lady. I was vaguely intrigued by the idea behind the Akashic Records, but was still completely and totally skeptical. What bothered me the most was this: Had she really said that *I* have the ability to visit the Akashic Records?

My memory told me she had.

So on my third day in Thuringia, on a rocky outlook I had hiked hours to arrive at, I decided to try a little experiment. I would try to find my way to the Akashic Records.

I sat cross-legged on a flat space and breathed my way to calmness before I began to pray.

*Dear God, Jesus and Mary, please accompany me to the gates of the Akashic Records so that I may help my brothers and sisters with the knowledge stored there.*

I waited.

Nothing happened, so I tried again.

*Dear God, Vishnu, Mohammed and Allah, please accompany me to the gates of the Akashic Records so that I may help my brothers and sisters and all mankind with the knowledge stored there.*

I waited.

And then I heard: *Because you have sought us out, we shall reward you with a key to the gates of the Akasha. You will be assigned an identity card and should you return any of the materials late, you will be penalized one human lifetime of servitude per each calendar day.*

Ok, ok. Obviously I didn't hear anything. And honestly, I didn't seriously try to access the Akashic Records in the first place because I still didn't buy it. Despite the allure of such an idea, it still sounded a touch too New-Agey for me. But on the other hand, the possible wisdom offered through such a medium *was* seductive.

I mean, imagine being able to read your life-story in an objective sense, without the selective filters of memory and self-love getting in the way. Imagine being able to see what the universe thinks about how *you* are spending your time on this earth.

I wondered about how my own life would look to the universe... and simply shuddered at the thought.

Me, a selfish, half-assed back-slider, and some crackpot lady tells me I'm able to read a message that God Himself presented to me via the *Akashic Records*?

Please.

*Liliana and I were dressed in black robes and were walking together through the bustling marketplace of a medieval European town. We felt unsettled by the boisterousness of the vendors, as well as the screeches and calls of the various animals. We eventually made our way to the edge of the square.*

*We came to a large wooden doorway adorned with black iron hinges and a pull ring, and as I reached out to open the door, I noticed that I was wearing a very ornate gold ring. I suddenly realized the reason for our feeling unsettled – we were being hunted for the ring.*

*The wooden doorway opened into a long, dark passageway and as we hurried through, the shadow of a figure appeared behind us at the passage entrance. He was outlined there until the door shut behind him and then we saw nothing. We hurried ahead and emerged into another square filled with bustling market activities.*

*I immediately spotted four figures in the crowd who I knew were after the ring. They began to encircle us and a fifth robed figure – this one riding a sort of flying carpet – quickly descended upon us. As he swooped near us, though, we were able to unseat him and take control of his flying carpet. We got on and flew above the gasping, gaping crowds to safety.*

*But the carpet had a will of its own and wouldn't respond to our attempts to steer. Instead, the thing took us higher and higher – the height holding us captive – until we reached and rounded a distant mountain peak.*

*On the other side of the mountain range was a vast ocean, and far out, impossibly far out - though we were moving so fast we would be upon it quickly - was a glowing purple luminescence under the water which was acting as a tractor beam.*

*Helplessness overcame us and Liliana and I looked at each other in resignation.*

## Chapter 10

Just for kicks, I decided to research the Akashic Records on the Internet. Expecting a whole lot of nothing, I Googled the words and to my dismay came up with over 280,000 hits! My skepticism, it must be said, took a blow. At the top of the list was a link titled, "Akashic Records – Edgar Cayce". The name was vaguely familiar and I clicked on it. The page I was taken to was well-designed and colorful, but looked like it was selling something. I clicked onto the link, "Who is Edgar Cayce?"

What I read went something like this: "Edgar Cayce was a bona fine mystic. Born in the late 19th century, Cayce was a poor student and showed little promise until one day he fell asleep on one of his books. When he later woke up, to both his and his stern father's dismay, he was able to answer any question from the book that his father put to him – even regarding chapters he hadn't yet read. This was the first indication that Cayce was gifted. Some time later, Edgar was playing a game of baseball when the ball somehow hit him in the spine. When he returned home behaving strangely, he insisted on going to sleep. Once unconscious, he *dictated* to his parents the recipe for a cure that would help him overcome his injuries. His parents followed the instructions and the next day Edgar was cured, but woke up with no memory of dictating the cure. By and by, Edgar grew into a very down-to-earth and simple man who worked in a bookstore, where he met his future wife. Edgar's gift lay dormant for some time, until he came down with a throat problem and was able to heal himself, again by falling into a sleep-related trance and dictating the treatment to a bystander. That episode was the start of a 40-year period in which Cayce, by falling into his sleep-trance, was able to help thousands of people – both in person as well as remotely – with various methods of healing, both physical and spiritual. He said he did this by accessing and reading the Akashic Records."

Which is all interesting enough: But amazingly, each of his "readings" were documented.

Fascinated, I followed another link from the Googled list. This one said that Cayce delivered Akashic readings to Thomas Edison, Harry Houdini, George Gershwin, and even Marilyn Monroe! Dozens of other links described the Akashic Records, and the information mirrored what Beatrice had told me. Thus helped along by these outside sources, I grudgingly began to ~~believe her~~ distrust her less.

Another link I visited even had instructions for actually accessing the Akashic Records, and I downloaded and printed out the .pdf file. I broadened my search to include reincarnation, and later accessed a comparative religions website where I read about Hindu, Buddhist and Taoist beliefs on reincarnation before I finally ended up at a website called the Universal Love Church.

The words at the top of the page read, "Become a legally-ordained minister today. Conduct weddings, funerals and other clergy services."

My ears pricked up.

The Universal Love Church Mission Statement read: "To do only what is right".

Which sounded ok to me; on a whim, I decided to join up. It was a simple process, becoming a minister for the Universal Love Church, and within five minutes I had downloaded my shiny new certificate.

I was now a Reverend.

Reverend Elijah Counts.

And though it sounds idiotic, I was *completely* elated.

Of course, Liliana thought I was being ridiculous.

"Real ministers have to study for years," she said, "and you think you can be one just because you get a certificate from the Internet?"

She had just arrived home from work and we were standing in the hallway.

"Hey," I said, "Relax. I'm really excited about it."

"But it's not real."

"Oh, I see. You can look into my heart and tell me it's not real. You can tell I'm not good enough to be a minister."

"You're *not* a minister."

"That's not what my church says."

"Your *church*? Elijah, it's an Internet site!"

"That's just a part of it. They have a physical presence in California."

She breathed deep and walked into the bathroom.

After a second she poked her head out the door and looked at me.

"Did it cost anything?"

I shook my head.

As she closed the door behind her, I thought I heard her mutter, "You're lucky."

*I was flying through Wittenberg – primarily through the narrow streets of Old Town – and was able to easily keep myself aloft. I was enjoying myself a great deal.*

*I spotted Jake standing in front of my house and I landed to pick him up. I took off into the air with him holding onto my shoulders. With great difficulty, I flew to the roof of the house across the street. Upon landing, I expressed how hard it was to carry him, and he began to lecture me on how I could fly better. I listened to him as we took off from the roof, but in heeding his advice, I progressively lost my ability to fly and we ended up landing where we had started.*

## Chapter 11

How much time have you spent considering the possibility of an afterlife?

And by "considering an afterlife", I don't mean in the abstract way we've been taught to by our various religions, but instead to consider it concretely, as in: Assuming there is one, what will the afterlife *be* like? Will we be able to hang out with those who have gone before us? Will we have houses? Will we have to cut our nails? Eat? That sort of thing.

It's my feeling that most people haven't actively considered such ideas, because doing so requires the mind to first wrap itself around an extremely unsavory prospect – the prospect of our *self* not being around anymore.

Well, guess what? This unsavory prospect will indeed happen, and that sinking feeling you're experiencing is a warning, because the bodies we live in just aren't designed for the long-term. Nor do we take care of ourselves like we should. We ingest too much booze and caffeine, eat junk food and other nasties, don't get enough exercise – or overdo it when we do – and most likely don't sleep enough, either.

We fill our heads with junk as well. For while television can be a very useful medium, it nevertheless has the potential to incapacitate. Witness the worker returning home, eating, and then sitting in front of the television, indulging in evening after evening of downtime.

Witness children spending sunny afternoons indoors in front of re-runs and cartoons.

Witness the nightly news, filled with destruction, strife and dour forecasts.

The problem is, eventually these things come to fill our thoughts at the expense of the mysterious ways of the world. Or of the universe – or of the soul.

But I don't mean to criticize. We can't all philosophize our days away. The System doesn't need it, want it, or allow it. So instead of dealing with silly *ideas* in our free time, most of us deal with the mundane stuff of life – errands, shopping, cleaning, putting things into order, entertaining each other and so on.

But is this *really* how it should be?

Consider: How much *inherent* value is there in shopping?

Or putting things into order?

Cleaning… well, ok. That's a necessity.

But the point is, we tend to keep our considerations inside our respective circles of influence (family circles, circles of friends, and so on). Thus, what these circles tend to think about, *we* tend to think about, and most of us don't venture – in an intellectual sense – any further than that.

Is this because we are not intelligent enough to do so?

I refuse to believe it.

Rather, I think we have too many distractions to consider a concept as abstract as the afterlife, because it really doesn't seem to affect us anyway. For if there *is* an afterlife, we'll only know it for sure *after* we arrive there, right? So why waste time on it?

Indeed, why waste time at all?

But that is precisely what we do when we watch television or go shopping all day for new clothes, or go boozin' at the local bar, or surf the Internet for porn.

We are all horrid time-wasters and we do this because we just don't grasp the simple truth that life is terribly short and that we will be gone from this earth before we have had a chance to fulfill a fraction of what we could have.

And I am as guilty of it as anyone.

My ongoing studies revealed that a great many people throughout history were aware of the Akashic Records (the ancients were apparently more attuned to the mystic ways of the universe than, say, a Clevelander). Indeed, some peoples were even purported to *access* the Akashic Records.

For example, the Mayans are said to have amassed a great "Hall of Records" (as yet un-recovered) which is rumored to be a partial collection of what mystics were able to remember from their visits to the Akashic Records. (A relevant linguistic aside: The Mayans, in denoting the inter-connectivity of the past, present, and future, used just one word to refer to all of them. Roughly translated, the word means, "it came to pass that").

And the ancient Persians *must* have believed in the Akashic Records (though they didn't name them as such). On what other basis could Rashnu, the Divine Angel of Justice, have been able to judge whether the dead could cross the Chinvat Bridge and dwell in the Land of the Blessed?

Or take the Babylonians. They believed that Belit-Sheri kept records of human activities so she could advise the Queen of the Dead regarding a soul's ultimate judgment.

The Judaic belief has their Book of Life, upon which is written the names of the righteous.

Then there are the Egyptians, who believed that the patron of scribes and inventor of writing, Djeheuty (often pictured with a pen and palette) was present at the deads' final judgment (the Greeks took over this belief and renamed the deity Thoth).

As for the Chinese, the San-guan, or "Three Rulers" of Taoism are all said to keep registers upon which they record the good and evil that people do.

The coincidental nature of all these theosophical ideas spurred me to conclude that throughout history, travelers either transferred these ideas from culture to culture, or buried deep within all of us lies the belief that any judgment rendered on the day of reckoning simply must be based upon some set of external criteria.

And yes, ten years prior (or even one year, for that matter) I would have dismissed all of this out of hand. But what began for me as far-fetched and flakey, through weeks of reflection, commenced to take on a more compelling character. Indeed, it all began to make sense in a way that one might feel when one is building a jigsaw puzzle and a seemingly unremarkable piece is inserted, and then *bam*, in a flash of insight, you recognize the pattern behind it all. (The pattern itself had always been there – only your *perception* of it changed.)

The point is that I began to feel compelled to learn as much as I could about the Akashic Records. I doubt I could have avoided it had I wanted to.

*I was on the edge of town in Wittenberg, walking along a bike path when I came to a detour. I had to cross the street, and there I noticed a temporary office trailer like the ones they use on construction sites. I walked up the metal stairs and entered into the relative darkness of the space.*

*Inside, carrying out some sort of alchemy experiment was Mattias, my student from the Martin Luther House.*

*I asked him what he was doing and he looked at me very intently and said, "Schopenhauer, Elijah. You need to dig on Schopenhauer, my man!"*

## Chapter 12

Below are the instructions I used for accessing the Akashic Records for the first time. I recorded them onto a cassette and played them back one morning after Liliana had gone to the office. After pressing the play button, I sat down in my favorite chair – a Spartan but comfortable IKEA number – and placed the cordless headphones over my ears. My voicc sounded strange – far less bass in it than normal – but I gradually got used to it, and the words washed over me…

"Breathe deep a few times to relax. You are going to enter a very shallow and pleasant hypnotic state.

…

Take another deep breath and as you release it, let go of any tension you might have.

…

Take another breath and slowly release. No tension. No stress. Just peaceful relaxation.

…

You are becoming more relaxed.

…

More relaxed as you breathe deeply… and close your eyes.

…

Breathe deeply…

…

And feel yourself coming to a very peaceful, very relaxed state of mind.

…

You can hear what is happening around you but it is not important. What is important is your journey.

…

As each part of your body is mentioned, spend a moment relaxing it.

…

Begin with your feet…

…

Your legs…

…

Writsts… and arms…

…

Shoulders…

…

And neck…

…

You are deeply relaxed.

…

Picture yourself walking along a passageway…

…

What does it look like?

…

You continue along until you see an entrance...

…

What does it look like?

…

Once you are close to the entrance, you notice the door slowly swing open. It is bright there, and inside is a large, open space.

…

You feel at ease. There is wisdom and peace inside.

…

You walk inside...

…

What do you see?

…

Look around and note the details. Are there things you want to remember?

…

Remember where you are and why you have come…

…

Do you have any questions? Ask them and try to remember the answers you are given…

…

<extended silence>

…

It is time to come back now.

…

Gratefully acknowledge your visit and any information you have been given.

…

Take another look around and try to remember where you are.

…

Breathe deeply… You are becoming more aware of your physical surroundings.

…

You feel your chest and torso expand with every breath.

…

Breathing deeper now, you start to move your fingers.

…

Now with open hands, move your wrists…

…

You are more alert now, but you remember what you have been told.

...

Take one more deep breath...

...

...and open your eyes.

...

I blinked rapidly and looked around the apartment.

I noticed that the tape continued to play with no sound coming out, so I got up and turned it off, placing the headphones next to the stereo.

I stretched my hands over my head and yawned, then went to the toilet.

The experiment hadn't worked.

I hadn't gone anywhere but my own mind, and though I was indeed relaxed, I just didn't think I could get myself into a trance by listening to my own voice. As I washed my hands, I laughed aloud at my ridiculousness.

Giggly, I went into the kitchen to get a cup of coffee and as I poured it, a long memory suddenly stifled my laughter. It wasn't a flitting butterfly of a memory, but rather a harried, horn-blowing, tailgating string of events, and I got caught up in its flow from beginning to end. I stood there staring at the coffee pot as the images presented themselves: Ten years prior, I was living with Jake in his Pittsburgh pad, crashing on his couch and killing both time and brain cells. After a series of no-future jobs, I decided to return to school at Penn State. I was familiar with Happy Valley from undergraduate time, and I really appreciated its location in the Appalachians, which was close enough to home for weekends, but far enough away that the parents weren't going to pop in unannounced.

I applied to and was accepted by the Communications Department, but that was only the first step. The problem, of course, was money. I didn't have any and wasn't keen on taking out more student loans. The thing to do then, was to set up an appointment with Dr. Mathis, the departmental head. He was the man who handed out graduate assistantships and the man I had to dazzle if I wanted one. (A graduate assistantship provides a tuition waiver and a modest stipend in return for half-time employment within the department.)

I finally pinned Dr. Mathis down to a time, and from the outset of our meeting he seemed to take a liking to me. Still, it was obvious to both of us that my experience was of no use to him. He was looking for lab rats, where I was more of a media practitioner. Long story short, I didn't get the graduate assistantship that year and instead Jake and I moved into a bigger apartment.

During that time I hustled around town doing part-time jobs as a lifeguard, barman, aqua-aerobics instructor (the old ladies *loved* me) and landscaper. It was an interesting time and I learned a lot from many different people, but I still wanted to go back to university. So during the summer when the time came for Dr. Mathis to decide upon graduate assistants again, I called every week looking for news. Finally the decision was made – I was again passed over.

I was beyond disappointed. I was kicked-in-the-gonads dizzy from the blow and felt that life was in the process of slipping away from me. I had placed all my eggs in that one basket, and that they had failed to hatch and were giving off the whiff of defeat was simply tragic.

During the phone conversation when Dr. Mathis told me the bitter news, we spoke a touch longer than necessary about personal matters, and then he hesitated for a moment. When he resumed, he said, "Elijah, I'm going to put you through to a fella in the PR office named Mike Flannery. I know they have a grad assistantship position over there and I think that you'd be better suited for a job in PR than in this department. Hold on, and I'll put you through…"

Well, put me through he did, and over the next few weeks I was able to convince first Mr. Flannery, and then the whole PR department through a terrifying panel interview that I was the man they were looking for. I was given the job and went on to spend two more rewarding years at Penn State. I learned a lot, got pushed into places I'd never have reached on my own, and somewhere along the way I became hugely impressed with the worldview of my international student classmates: Their outlooks were both intriguing and intimidating, and I endeavored to spend as much time with them as possible.

Along towards the end of my studies – I guess it was about two weeks before graduation – I got a phone call from Rose, Dr. Mathis' very efficient and kind secretary, who said Dr. Mathis wanted to put me into contact with Ted Simmons, a recruiter from the State Government of Pennsylvania who was in town and was on the lookout for a mass communications specialist.

So I phoned Mr. Simmons at the Nittany Inn and we set up an interview for the following day. The "interview" was actually more like walking through an open door. It turned out that Mr. Simmons and Dr. Mathis were old friends and I was hired on the spot, with the promise of receiving more money than I ever thought I would make.

I moved to Harrisburg, a beautiful community in which to live, but the work (rather, my state-ordained lack of it) led me to short a circuit – probably the very one that makes all of America get up and go to work because of the money. This short-circuit led me to eventually chuck it all, move to Prague, get married to a Czech woman and then follow her to Germany…

In remembering all of this, I came to realize that Dr. Mathis did not have to put me through to Mike Flannery that day. In fact, Dr. Mathis' duty was actually done when he told me I wasn't being awarded an assistantship in his department. But still, his character or instinct or beliefs or whatever, gave him the idea to put me in touch with this Mike Flannery.

And from that *tiny little decision*, the thread of my life had led me to the incredibly fulfilling point of having been awarded a master's degree, living abroad and being married to a disarmingly lovely woman. And while it is true that Dr. Mathis didn't exactly put me where I was, his transferring me to Mike Flannery that day certainly had a very big influence on it.

Thinking about this as I stood over my no-longer steaming coffee, I realized that I was hugely indebted to Dr. Mathis. So after thinking about what I might say to him, I got on the Internet and looked up his office telephone number. It wasn't there and I reckoned he had retired in the intervening years, so I searched for his home number and there it was in the white pages.

Later that day, allowing for the time difference, I called Dr. Mathis. He was surprised to hear from an old student, and though the conversation was cordial, I could tell he didn't really remember who I was.

But when he heard my earnest gratitude for the overwhelmingly positive impact he'd had on my life, and that in my opinion I was probably just one of the scores of grateful students he'd done the same for during his long career, he got choked up. (As, I admit, did I.)

At the end of the conversation, as we were hanging up, Dr. Mathis told me that I had made an old man very happy, and that my call had been like a voice from Heaven.

Which made me think my attempt to reach the Akashic Records had been good for something after all.

*I was exploring a back street in Berlin when I came to a courtyard. On both sides were high, red-brick walls, about six stories high. At the far end of the courtyard was a building with no windows, but which had one glass door. The middle of the courtyard was grassy and peaceful. Music was floating down from the building on the left and I got the sense that it was a part of a campus.*

*I wanted to enter the glass door at the far end of the courtyard, but as I got near it, I noticed that it was a service entrance and sure to be locked. As I stood outside wondering how I would open the door, a worker came out and I scooted past him to catch the door before it closed. Once inside, I found myself on the ground floor of a large, brightly lit library that was many stories high.*

*Wandering through, the first batch of books I came to were a gilded set of encyclopedias, very old, and in very good condition. I perused them and decided to come back to them later...*

*I continued down the corridor and came to a classroom, a physics or earth sciences classroom, and I discovered a large book lying open on a table. I started to read it, but a professor came over and started to hassle me. I tried to ignore him, but it was no use. I couldn't read the book any longer and eventually woke up disappointed.*

## Chapter 13

On a brilliant early-spring Saturday, I set out for Wörlitz, a huge landscaped park that was first laid out in the 1700s. Liliana felt like nesting and I was pleased to have some quality time with my bike. Once out on the road, the cool air and hazy sunshine made me feel I could go all day.

The shortest route from Wittenberg to Wörlitz Park requires a ferry crossing and as I stood waiting for it to return from the other side of the swirling Elbe, I marveled at how some communities have resisted modernity for so long. Not to judge; if they don't want to bear the monetary and cultural costs of a bridge, why should they?

Once on the other side of the harried brown Elbe, a rocky, cobbled road commenced and I feared I would have to spend the next five hours jostling my way to Wörlitz. But luckily, the bit of progress the region was willing to embrace were proper bicycle paths. Once these started, it was smooth sailing for the 6 km to the park.

I locked my bike and entered Wörlitz Park from the north. What immediately struck me was the careful balance that the park maintains between the cultivated and the unkempt. There are many spaces, such as the Floratempel, which are so fantastically landscaped with flowers and bushes that one feels privileged to be there, and halfway expects a king's court to round the corner at any moment. But then one walks through a wood, where on each side there are only trees and shrubs and one feels isolated – as if in the forest proper.

These periods of alternating isolation and cultivation did something to me – kind of woke me up, I guess. I felt extremely alert and was noticing the tiniest details around me. The cat sneaking through the forest may have froze as I walked by, but I spotted him with no problem. The spider web that I normally would have walked into face-first was easily avoided. I discerned the various sounds that the wind made. I even noticed individual bird songs, where I would normally lump them all together as a sort of background noise.

I continued walking until I came upon two sunlit columns, each about 8 feet tall, made of reddish-brown and roughly-surfaced stone. Placing myself between the columns, I was cheerily pleased to find that they anchored a rusty chain-link bridge sagging over a grassy-banked canal. Sturdy wooden planks were laid atop of and then fastened to the chains. I stepped onto the first plank and was surprised at the wave of ricocheting energy that shot back through the chains. I plodded further, riding these waves across the bucking bridge. Once on the other side, I followed the path down into an area of shade trees and musty tunnels that burrowed into a rocky, shrub-covered hillside.

The first tunnel was so dark I couldn't see inside, so I took a flash photo to illuminate it. When the strobe revealed no creepies, I ducked in, walking hunched over to avoid concussing myself. Inside the blackness, I took another picture and it revealed a second tunnel ahead and to my left. After I turned into this one, dim, filtered light allowed me to navigate without incident, and I emerged at the edge of a round grotto surrounded by a high circular wall of roughly cut rocks. Overhead were many shade trees, and the air was cool in the shadows.

Opposite the opening I had come through was an altar of some sort, with a small stone bench and a slab of smooth rock set into the wall. I noticed some words chiseled into the rock, and as I walked over to read them, high ferns brushed my legs. I could no longer hear the birds' singing.

The words in the stone formed a poem in German:

| | |
|---|---|
| Einsamkeit und Stille | Solitude and silence |
| fuereht zu Gott | lead to God |
| wie einiges Unglück | like some misfortune |
| zum Guten fuereht | leads to the good. |

Though my German was still terrible and I didn't yet understand the words completely, I instinctively felt the deep peacefulness of the grotto itself. The moist freshness of the air, the canopy of the trees and the unforced order of the walls combined to make the space soothing, though somehow mysterious.

Standing there trying to comprehend the poem, I felt a sudden cold wind and a chill ran up my spine. I whirled around, fully expecting to see someone there, but found nothing. I turned completely about, feeling an unnerving presence just beyond my sight, and ended up facing the smooth stone again. Dimly, I noticed a circle of blurriness in the middle of the stony text. I blinked to clear it away, but instead of retreating it began to expand, quickly engulfing the text until the whole of the message was blurred. I rubbed by eyes with my fists and was relieved that the blurred circle began to clear. But the lettering had changed, and a different message was now written in the stone.

Battling the fight or flight instinct which was urging me to run back through the spooky caves and not stop until I was far away, I took a step forward and squinted my eyes.

I couldn't read the message, for though the writing seemed to be English, it was nonetheless partially obscured by the blurriness that had created it, and the more I looked, the less I could intuit of it. The message was frustratingly close, but I couldn't decipher it.

Just then a dove distracted me. She winged down to my left, landed near my feet, and after walking up close to the stone, commenced to coo. I watched her with surprising comfort – as if having another living thing present grounded me in reality. Then I noticed that above her head, the blurred message seemed to be clear. I looked directly at the words, only to see them blur again.

Confused, I turned back to the dove, and when I did so, it seemed that out of the corner of my eyes the text became clear. Looking quickly back at the text only to be unable to read it was a tiresome game, but I couldn't help myself. Finally I realized that by looking at the dove but concentrating my peripheral vision on the text, the words became legible.

I went back and forth between the dove and the text until the bird flew, taking my patience along with it. I stared at the blurred stone again until my eyes crossed – and in the process, the message came into focus! The secret was to not look *at* the message, but rather to look *past* it. Now the full message came into view and I was able to read it for the first time. There were three sentences, and I recognized them simultaneously.

*"BEWARE THE DEVIL."*

*"OUR PURPOSE IS TO LOVE."*

*"COMMUNICATE THIS."*

It was the same message I had been shown in my dream.

Upon this realization, a shockwave of energy coursed through me, so powerful that I slumped onto my knees, clenching my eyes shut as a rapture gripped me. I don't know how long it went on, but after it finally left me, I convulsed from its power and began praying for... truthfully, I don't remember what I prayed for. Survival and protection, most likely.

I don't know how long I was on the ground, but I do remember feeling it hadn't been nearly long enough before I opened my tear-filled eyes because I sensed a nearby figure. Blinking rapidly, I saw a woman in flowing, yellow robes.

She spoke words I couldn't understand and gestured at the stone wall. Dumbly following her gesture, I saw that the wall had returned to its original form again. I warily looked back to the woman and said, "I... I don't understand."

*Can you stand?*

I realized I was still on the ground and made to get up. I must have stumbled a little bit, because the woman moved towards me, extending her hand as if to help. I instinctively reached out for her, but grasped a handful of nothingness and fell back onto all fours. Startled and beginning to weird out, I looked back up at the woman and suddenly recognized her as Beatrice, the crackpot Akashic Records lady.

"What...what are you..." I stammered.

She held up a reassuring hand and "said", *I was... in the neighborhood... and I heard you.*

"In the *neighborhood*? How are you-"

*I'm sorry, I cannot continue this projection. But don't worry about it coming back.*

She gestured at the stone altar.

*It doesn't seem to be working this way.*

Her radiance began to fade and a moment later I was again the only person left in the calmness of the grotto. The birdsong started again and I stood and walked over to the stone slab on the wall. I ran my fingertips over the poem carved there – it was *definitely* set in stone.

As I had my hand upon the wall, an older woman entered the grotto and nervously eyed me. By the time the rest of her group trailed in, there were at least 10 people, and the sense of presence that had been so prevalent just moments before was rendered impotent.

I hurried back through the caves and over the rickety bouncing bridge wondering about the lady's admonishments.

*What wasn't coming back?*

When I arrived home that afternoon, Liliana wasn't around so I showered and sat on the living room rug to stretch. Though it was still hard to fully grasp, my mind was racing with the implications of what I had experienced and try as I might, I could *not* slow my thoughts.

Just a few minutes later I heard Liliana open the front door and call my name. I jumped up to help with the grocery bags that I could hear her struggling with, and as soon as she saw me her eyes got big and she asked, "What happened to you?"

"What do you mean?"

"I mean, what happened? You seem strange."

I shook my head, kissed her, and relieved her of two bags. "Thanks for the compliment, but it's a long story. Let's get settled and then I'll tell you."

She looked suspicious but relented, and as we unloaded the bags in the kitchen I gave her a quick rundown of how lovely Wörlitz Park is and how long the bike ride there took. "And the yoga woman – Beatrice – was there as well," I finished.

"The one who held the keys for us? Did you speak to her?"

I said, "Yeah, we spoke a little. But she didn't have much to say."

"Did she recognize you?"

"Oh, yeah."

Liliana looked at me hard and finally said, "Now what happened?"

Walking over to the fridge, I sighed and said, "I think we're going to need a drink. Would you like some beer?"

"Ok..."

I opened up the Pilsner Urquells and sat down at the kitchen table. Liliana was listening attentively as I poured.

"I didn't tell you everything about dropping off the keys at the yoga lady's place…"

After Liliana's underwhelming reaction to my becoming a Reverend of the Universal Love Church, I was convinced that she would dismiss my latest experience out of hand. But to my surprise she listened patiently throughout the story and even asked questions to clarify the trickier points, of which there were certainly quite a few.

After I finished, she considered me awhile as I drank the beer and then she said, "So besides speaking in your head before, you think you saw the yoga lady as a ghost today?"

I nodded.

"And you think you saw the same message from God again today?"

"Definitely."

"And you think you can go to the Akeshrik-"

"Akashic. Akashic Records... and I don't know if I can go there or not. I tried it once and nothing happened, but I don't know."

She shook her head. "And do you have any idea why it's *you* having these experiences?"

"No."

Looking out the window, she spoke as if to herself. "I am having a hard time believing what you are telling me, but you certainly seem to believe them yourself." She turned back to me and continued. "So I am not going to tell you that you are crazy or having psycho troubles. But I do think we should visit Beatrice and ask her about these things."

"You'll come with me?"

"Yes, to be sure that nothing strange happens."

"We'll be very lucky if nothing strange happens," I said.

"And if you got this message from God again, maybe you are really supposed to help other people somehow… Which cannot be bad, can it?"

"Yeah…"

"Now, show me these internet sites…"

*I was bandaged from head to toe, strapped to a gurney, and was being trundled through a jungle forest by several allies. I saw their concerned faces from behind my bandages.*

*Closing my eyes and leaving my damaged body behind, my dream perspective switched and I was now one step above the action, an observer.*

*We drew nearer to an overgrown, forgotten temple and ascended the steps. I willed the wide stone gathering place to be cleared, and the vines and trees disappeared only to reveal the black stones of the ancient temple.*

*A moment later, bright sunlight pierced the jungle canopy to illuminate the rocks; they were covered with messages written in a language not of this earth. Each of the stones contained a single message, and I instinctively proceeded to the one which was required.*

*"Elijah Counts" was written in the rock.*

*I read aloud the message underneath my name and watched in wonder as my body shed its bandages until it was standing up and luminously healthy. At the same time, I – the observer – was drawn closer and ultimately back into my body.*

*I felt a fervent brilliance of being and woke up with a shudder.*

## Chapter 14

Because I am able to remember most of my dreams – the result of being a light sleeper, I suppose – I have always recorded them. I also frequently discuss my dreams with friends and family, hoping to interpret and apply them to my life. The dreams themselves are invariably self-disclosing, but some of my family's dreams are also quite telling: Dad once dreamed he was honored by a parade celebrating him as Man of the Year; mom often dreams about having to go to the toilet only to wake up and discover that she really does have to; sis once dreamed that she and Bill Clinton were jamming on saxophone together.

But there are many aspects of dreaming that I just don't understand. Where does it occur, for example? And for what purpose? I am not the first to wonder about this, of course. Dreams and their study have occupied humans for a long time. Oneiromancy is an ancient word that refers to divining meanings from dreams, and in many religion and cultures, dreams are often seen as portents of doom and gloom or good times ahead, or any old thing in between.

Most schools of thought believe that dreaming takes place in the dreamer's subconscious – but the reason *why* is harder to place. Sigmund Freud, for example, believed that dreams were a form of wish-fulfillment, but that the symbolism was very intricate. Thus, if one dreamt about, say, buying a new car, the dream wasn't actually about a car but rather about freedom and the male genitalia as represented by the car. If a male entered a cave in a dream, well, that was the desire to make love. A tower in a dream meant a penis; a bowl meant a vagina. A ball? The male genitalia. Milk? A female breast. And so on and so forth, in a similar vein.

Carl Jung agreed with Freud about certain things – certainly that the placement of dreams was within the subconscious – but Jung also believed that Freud's over-reliance on the sexual aspect of the human condition clouded his judgment on certain issues. For instance, Freud spent little time exploring the possible connection between dreaming and mysticism, whereas Jung spent most of his time on precisely that.

Jung, in fact, is credited with coining the term "collective unconscious", which he believes is humanity's unconscious collection of memories, containing many archetypes such as the trickster, the divine couple, the hero and so forth, which appear very similarly across cultures, as well as in humanity's great narratives. Examples of this can be found in works such as The Iliad, the Odyssey, Beowulf, Cantar de Mio Cid, as well as the eastern stories of Ramayana, the Epic of King Gesar, Gilgamesh, or Shahnama.

To move in a slightly different direction, two modern researchers by the name of Francis Crick (famous for discovering, with James Watson, the DNA double-helix) and Graeme Mitchison posited that dreams act as a filter for removing the trivial bits of one's life in order to efficiently store the more important aspects.

Other schools of thought place the dreaming arena beyond the human context and reckon that it takes place somewhere in the universe at large. Some followers of Islam, for example, believe that in dreams, the soul may detach from the body and consider the universe to the degree which that soul's purity allows. Thus, a person with a "pure soul" would enjoy a greater degree of communion with the universe during sleep than a person possessing a "less pure soul".

And then there are the physical aspects of dreaming.

My nephew, for example, often sleepwalks and can maneuver through doors, up and down stairs, operate faucets and other appliances, you name it. My sister once found him outside in the yard – barefooted – in January.

Liliana sometimes has waking dreams as well – once or twice I have woken up to see her standing on the bed, trying to "open" the painting on the wall as if it were some sort of gateway. Sometimes I'll even hear her laughing in her sleep, or she'll talk out loud. I try not to listen, as I feel it's almost like spying on her, but sometimes I can't help myself and I'll ask her questions like "Where are you," or "What are you doing?"

Sometimes she'll answer freaky stuff like "under the leaf of a cloud," but more frequently she'll giggle and go back to sleep.

For myself, the nature of my dreams has taken some strange turns. In college I dreamt of three things, mainly – girls, girls, and girls. But ever since Prague and the Germans, my dreams had begun to present me with some captivating topics: Alternate realities, soul issues, spirits – both good and evil – as well as more out there topics.

Which is interesting and all that… but the question I struggled with was *why*. And why me?

*I was visiting a high, spooky cathedral that had no stained glass windows – it was made only of reddish stone and was cave-like. There was a sense of foreboding as I walked through the middle aisle towards the altar. Up on the second level walkway to my right were a group of friends who were watching me. I came upon a pile of money in the aisle and kicked at a coin. The clinking noise attracted the attention of the spirit who had left it there – she was flying around in the rafters – and she fixed her gaze on me. My friends yelled at me to leave the money alone, that it was the spirit's money, and that she'd left it as an offering for her soul. I walked closer to the altar.*

**Chapter 15**

Sunday afternoon when I called Beatrice to set up a meeting, the first thing she said was, "I've been expecting your call."

Feeling ornery, I said, "Uh-huh. And why do you think I'm calling?"

There was a pause before she answered. "Your wife is unconvinced – as are you – about what is happening. Perhaps you seek clarity."

"Huh. So… do you have time to meet this week?"

"Certainly – you can come over right now if you'd like."

I covered the mouthpiece and spoke to Liliana. "She wants us to come over."

Her eyebrows shot up and she mouthed the question, "Now".

I nodded at her and she rolled her eyes.

"Give us an hour," I said.

When we reached Beatrice's building, Liliana stood there in open-mouthed admiration before blurting out, "What a building!" She pointed out some intricate details in the latticework that I hadn't noticed, and commented on the strange combination of styles before she allowed me to lead her to the heavy door of the tower. Beatrice had told me on the phone to just walk in, and I pretended to struggle with the heavy door before motioning for Liliana to enter.

"You first," she said, so I walked in ahead of her.

"But you close the door," I told her.

She gave me a mock-exasperated look until she put her weight into the door and found how easy it was to move. After the door clicked into place, she looked toward the stairs and commented on the age of the place, and when she saw the sunlight streaming through the stained glass she literally cooed at the beauty of it. As we walked up the wooden spiral stairs with primary colors splayed against the walls, I had to admit it really was lovely.

At the top of the stairs I walked to the only doorway that I knew. "This is the huge hall I was telling you about," I said. I tried to open the door but it was locked.

We looked to our right, and perhaps ten steps away there was a dark wooden door covered with symmetric carved squares. It stood ajar and inside the semi-darkened room we could make out some bookcases lining the opposite wall.

"Beatrice?"

There was no reply. "Let's look in there," I suggested.

She nodded, took my hand, and we walked up the hallway together. When we reached the door, I knocked and poked my head in. The Nag Champa incense was heavy and sweet, and breathing it in took some effort.

"Beatrice?"

I had swung the door open and started inside when from behind us we heard a voice command, "Don't go in there!"

We both jumped and when we turned around there stood Beatrice, in front of the now-open doorway that led to the large hall. She was bathed in the light coming from the airy room and said, in a much kinder voice, "I'm sorry, but you cannot go in there."

Liliana and I both exhaled and I said, "Beatrice, this is-"

"So nice to meet you, Liliana," replied Beatrice, and beckoned Liliana to approach her.

We both walked towards her and Liliana said, "Thank you for inviting us."

When they shook, Beatrice put her left hand over Liliana's right and held it for a moment, bowing her head slightly before looking upward into Liliana's eyes.

"It is wonderful that you could come," she said. "We have much to discuss."

Turning to me, she said hello and motioned us into the hall.

Once inside, Liliana did a pirouette to take in the view and ended facing us. "What a room," she said.

Smiling, Beatrice nodded and motioned us towards the corner. Liliana was still looking at the ceiling when Beatrice and I sat down, so she didn't see Beatrice, in her loose robe, lean over a little… too far. After she sat down, she looked at me meaningfully but restrained herself well before Liliana rejoined us.

Liliana and I occupied two thick cushions in front of the crystal-covered table – she sat on her knees and I was cross-legged. I casually picked up the nearest crystal, a rust-colored, metallic piece, and passed it from hand to hand.

Looking amused, Beatrice asked, "Do you know what you are holding?"

"Uh… a crystal?"

"That is a meteorite crystal," she said, as if that summed it all up completely.

Liliana looked at the crystal in my hands and asked what that meant.

"Meteorites are a sacred stone," said Beatrice. "They symbolize the energy of other worlds." She paused to look at me. "And they help us when we seek information from these other worlds. So you see, the crystals, as ever, speak to us."

I looked down at the crystal and wondered how a rock might speak. When I looked back at Beatrice, she had turned to Liliana.

"And you, Liliana, would you like to choose a crystal?"

Liliana laughed nervously and said no, she really shouldn't. But Beatrice insisted until eventually, after considering the 50 or so crystals of every color and shape, Liliana settled on a frosty white rock the size of a fist. Holding it up, she said, "This one feels nice."

"And that," said Beatrice, "is a Moonstone..." she smiled knowingly and continued, "...which is a sacred stone in India. It is said to soothe and heal emotions while aiding in spiritual growth."

Then she looked between Liliana and I for a moment and said, "Consider them gifts."

We declined for a few moments before Beatrice held up her hands and said, "Please. I do not wish to argue. Keep them. And let us move on to other issues... Elijah, did you smell the incense in the other room?"

I nodded. "It was heavy."

"Yes. This is to help one concentrate on breathing – in so doing it creates an atmosphere conducive to meditation. Nag Champa is a sacred incense, blessed by Sri Sathya Sai. But perhaps you know him better as Satya Sai Baba?"

I looked at Liliana and we both shrugged.

"Sri Sathya Sai," said Beatrice, "is a godman who lives in India. He is regarded by many to be an incarnation of Shirdi Sai Baba, an Indian holy man of the 19th and 20th centuries. And though I have never met him, I regard Sri Sathya Sai as one of the holiest men alive."

During her expectant pause, I asked, "Why is that?"

"Because he is a reconciler – a uniter, even." She sighed. "So many heads of today's religions – Catholic, Jewish, Orthodox, Islam, it doesn't matter – they hold so steadfastly to *their* version of religious reality that they overlook the essential truths that form other religions' respective foundations. And in so doing, they shield their followers from these beneficial truths. But for me, there are two exceptions to this rule. The first is Satya Sai Baba, and the second is Tenzin Gyatso, the-"

"Who?"

"Tenzin Gyatso... The Dalai Lama."

"Ah."

"For me," she continued, "the Dalai Lama is another wonderful example of a spiritual leader. He does not tell people what they should and shouldn't do. He does not try to convert them. He merely tries to reach out to people – Buddhists as well as non-Buddhists – and tell them that living a more holy life is within everybody's reach. He does not teach utopia or unattainable things. He-"

"I'm sorry to interrupt," said Liliana, "but I recently read a book written by the Dalai Lama, and it was wonderful – very helpful."

"You see," Beatrice continued, "this is what I mean. Indeed, one only has to look at the titles of his books to realize that they are written from a heart that is filled with love. My favorite book from the Dalai Lama is called *Beyond Dogma* – a lovely title, no? A title that provides so much basic instruction in just two little words."

She paused and then said, "If only we could all embody something like that... but back to Sri Sathya Sai – he is an Indian holy man who claims to be God, but-"

My eyebrows shot up. "He claims to be a God?"

"Not just *a* god – God incarnate. But let me finish... Sri Sathya Sai claims to be God, but he also acknowledges that we are *all* divine and we are *all* God. He claims only that it is his privilege to be aware that he is divine, while the rest of us remain largely ignorant of it. Which, if you think about it, makes a great deal of sense. Also, and this is the reason why I value his guidance so much – he believes that *all* of the world's great religions contain the truth. In fact, his crest symbolizes the integrity of five great religions – Islam, Hinduism, Christianity, Sikhism and Buddhism."

"He's a follower of all those religions," asked Liliana.

"Actually, he claims to follow none of them – he merely indicates that each of them contain a valid and useful pathway to salvation... that if one is of pure heart and follows a valid set of truths in one's quest, then it does not matter which road one takes. What matters is that the destination is the same – purity of body and soul."

With these last pronouncements, Liliana's nodding agreement intensified. Perhaps she was becoming more convinced that Beatrice was bona fide. I know I certainly was. Beatrice must have felt this, for she smiled lightly before continuing.

"That was the long way around the schoolyard. But now let us come to the reason you are here.... Elijah is in a… challenging place. Liliana, you are aware of what happened in the park?"

"Yes. But it seems strange that you two have such abilities. You both seem so… normal..."

"Yes, these powers can seem strange. In fact, I'm confused over Elijah's seeming powers myself – because in looking at his chakras, I see significant blockages that would normally prevent anyone from accessing the Akashic Records, and yet I have been a witness – twice now – to Elijah's exposure. I cannot fathom it."

The mention of chakras made Liliana and I exchange glances.

"I... don't know about chakras," started Liliana, "but I do know that Elijah seems to want to help others... is that maybe the important part?"

Beatrice looked at Liliana long and hard, until I finally asked if anything was the matter.

Turning quickly to face me, as if surprised that another person was so near, Beatrice said that she now understood my accessing powers. "Liliana's fourth chakra is remarkably pure," she explained. "I think it is from this that you are able to draw inspiration and energy for your abilities."

Liliana looked at me and then back to Beatrice. "I'm confused on so many levels I don't know where to begin... but could you please tell me what a *chakra* is?"

"Of course," replied Beatrice. "I'm sorry... a chakra is basically a representation of one's energy centers – each chakra is located over one of the spine's seven nerve ganglia – and each one represents a different portion of one's energetic makeup. I won't bore you with descriptions of all seven of them – I can lend you a book if you wish – but each of the seven chakras need to be free of blockages if one is to attain the highest level of mentality, that is, illumination. Not many people attain this, and virtually none *maintain* it."

"And you said my... fourth charka… was helping Elijah?"

"Yes... the fourth chakra is called the heart chakra. It is related to love and compassion, and can provide one with a sense of unity, integration, and peace. People such as yourself are able to help those around you become... shall we say, better... than they normally are. I think this is the case with you and Elijah, who, though he is able to periodically embody the higher states, seems to have blockages in chakra two, which deals with self-gratification."

Beatrice looked at me hard as she pronounced this, then lightened her gaze and turned back to Liliana.

"Which is probably good for your sex life, isn't it?"

Liliana kind of flinched, then blushed, then said, "I... think we're doing fine." She reflexively moved her hand over to hold mine and we smiled at each other.

"Fine," smiled Beatrice.

I switched the crystal into my right and held Liliana's hand with my left.

"She wasn't anything like I was expecting... she's much prettier somehow," Liliana said.

"She does have a presence about her, doesn't she?"

"For so small a person to have such a command over things, she must be very smart... or very aware..."

"Yeah," I said, "but I still don't believe what she told me about not being able to access the Akashic Records through meditation. I still think that if I work hard enough that I'll be able to do it."

"But she says you would have better luck with your dreaming... and you've always been able to remember your dreams very well, so why not try to concentrate there?"

"Because like she said, it's the most difficult way to access... when were *you* able to control your dreams the last time?"

"But my dreams are not the issue. You're the one who has always placed importance in your dreams and I think it is a natural extension. Maybe you can learn to manipulate them from that book she mentioned."

I shook my head. "I read that Castaneda book before we met, and I tried to do some of the things it mentions. The first thing it tells you is to try and look at your hands in your dreams, which seems like a simple thing, but because your mind is on a whole different level, it's terribly difficult. Anyway, when I was reading the book and trying to play around with the techniques, I started to have just the blackest nightmares."

"What about?"

"I don't remember specifically, but I wasn't able to sleep well for weeks because any dream I had was filled with black, empty images." I shuddered at the thought of it.

"Did you stop reading the book?"

"Right after the nightmares began."

As we neared our building, Liliana said, "Well, I think Beatrice is trying to help you. Perhaps you should listen to her and borrow that book about the chakras… but you're *not* burning that incense in our apartment."

*I walked into an airy white hall. Against the far wall, a robed woman was sitting on the edge of a thick cushion. She beckoned and I walked across the room and knelt in front of her.*

## Chapter 16

I sat on the couch with my legs crossed and closed my eyes. The sweet, heavy musk of the incense permeated the room. It was just after Liliana left in the morning and I was feeling fresh from a cup of tea. In the two weeks since we'd seen Beatrice, I had stopped drinking alcohol and caffeine in an attempt to build up my energy levels; there had been terrible headaches getting off the caffeine.

From behind closed eyelids, the apartment was noisy. Trams thundered by two blocks away. Cars were driving by on the cobblestones. A high-revving scooter. Territorial dogs. Chattering birds. Unidentifiable clacks and rattles.

The incense was heavy.

I placed my attention on the floor and tried to picture the carpeting. The blackness behind my eyelids was a miasma of colors and patterns, indistinct. In my mind I pictured the carpet – tri-colored earth-tones. Raw, rough wool. Lint here and there from not vacuuming.

I moved my attention to the wall behind it. There were two paintings. One that Liliana had made of a flowering bush with an abstract background. Greens and pinks and whites. The other was an abstract that I had done myself. A rainbow-smattered background, oil overtopped by acrylics. The corner of Liliana's painting was chipping off from where it had been dropped.

A barking dog somewhere brought my attention back to me. The strange colors of my eyelids were swirling, chaotic. I listened to my rhythmic breathing.

A yelling woman.

Deep breathing of sweet heavy muskiness.

I saw the paintings again before moving through the living room and into the hallway, where the sunlight was weak.

The kitchen's brightness was like a beacon.

A knock on the neighbors' door. The back of our front door, smooth tan wood. No peephole and a gold handle.

Behind me, the kitchen's brightness draws me to it. Along the wall I see the antique brass fixtures on the white wooden frames, the windows so clear as to be without glass. They are high, stretching nearly to the ceiling. In the near window I see the outline of the plants we keep there. They're not green, but golden, vibrantly golden and I cannot look at them. That whole side of the room is illuminated.

I ignore the sound of a car beeping.

The kitchen table is below me. The green and blue plaid tablecloth. The six white dice I had rolled and turned my back on before meditating.

I see two of them nearby each other. The ebony dots shine a two and a three. The other four dice are scattered. I can't find them. I find one almost at the edge of the table. I look at it a long time but can't divine the number.

I look out the clear window and draw close to it. Outside the window is a gigantic sycamore tree, its maple-shaped leaves an indistinct color. Red, perhaps? The bark is elephant grey, smooth and cracking in places. I look down at the trunk where the dog is urinating. It's a neighbor's beagle on its extendible leash. It looks up at me and begins to bark furiously.

I opened my eyes at the sound of the barking dog. Standing and stretching, I walked into the kitchen, opened up the window and sure enough, the beagle was there. The neighbor saw me poke my head out the window but didn't return my wave. On the table were the six dice, and two of them were nearby one another. One was a three. The other was a two.

I gathered up the dice again and threw them, turning away before they settled. I went back to the couch and tried to see them again, but the first experience had tired me out and I fell asleep.

*The house was deeply familiar and welcoming, save for the crumbling wooden stairway at the far end of the house. Down those stairs, the blackness of the cellar was frightening. I floated downwards, tingling with apprehension, and came upon a mirror. My reflection was beautiful and delicate, but as I lingered on it, the image melted into a grimacing red face, full of fury. Two claws formed and reached out for me. I somehow flew from its grasp and was jolted awake.*

**Chapter 17**

Shortly after my experience at Wörlitz gardens, I emailed the priest I had confessed to while we were in the States. Basically I told him about Wittenberg, as well as my experience with the stone wall and the repeat of the three lines of instructions. I also mentioned Beatrice and how she was encouraging me to learn more about and then try to access the Akashic Records.

I was hoping for some sort of calm appraisal of the situation. This is what I got:

*Dear Elijah,*

*Thank you for writing - it was very pleasant to hear from you and to learn more about Wittenberg. Though of course I don't exactly agree with the Lutheran approach to religion, it is nonetheless fascinating to contemplate the historical aspects of such a location. You are lucky in that respect.*

*It was also fascinating to hear about your spiritual experiences – I took the liberty of sharing their details with a few of my colleagues and we are all in agreement that your dream was likely a gift from the Lord. And as I told you when we met, not many people receive such signs. Again, you are lucky in that respect.*

*What I find troubling, however, is the direction that your interest in spirituality is taking. Permit me to be direct: The occult is exceedingly dangerous and should be avoided at all costs. The church has extensive experience with so-called seekers who have come into contact with such powers and have been unable to cope with them. Without exception, these well-intentioned individuals wound up regretting their dalliances. Thus, I must caution you against such activities. The occult is seductive. It takes one into the blackness, and it is there that foulness is committed and God's will is scorned. You must avoid this. I cannot stress this enough.*

*God was reaching out to you in your dream, Elijah. You need only take his hand. That is the direction I would advise.*

*May God bless you,*
*Father Peter Dodds*

As I said, I had been expecting something a little different, though after reading the letter I realized I shouldn't have: The Catholic Church has protected its secrets for centuries. Why would an appeal for advice from a spiritual seeker influence the party line?

*At twilight, I was riding in a car with my cousin Paul, who was driving. We were passing a five-story, partially abandoned wooden house. Three of the second-story windows were illuminated and Paul said that his brother was living there even though the house was haunted.*

*I asked Paul if he would consider returning there himself and he looked at me as if I were crazy.*

*Don't you remember the basement, he asked.*

*I did, and the memory came flooding over me – the basement had a set of wooden stairs that descended into the middle of a large, open space.*

*I found myself at the foot of those stairs surrounded by darkness. Without warning I was attacked by a predatory spirit and I knew I had to escape. Ever fiber of my being fought to reject the ghost, and I attempted to scream but couldn't.*

*I awoke into another dream.*

*In this dream I was lying, horrified, on our living room floor as a red, humanoid ghost approached me. I tried to scream but couldn't. I tried to get up but couldn't move.*

## Chapter 18

After I finished teaching one afternoon I stopped by Beatrice's to borrow the Chakra book she'd mentioned. There was no answer at the door, but it was unlocked so I let myself in. At the top of the stairs, I knocked on the closed doorway of the large hall and waited, shifting my briefcase to my left hand.

Beatrice half-opened the door, and from the late-afternoon sun was radiantly outlined in white, her yellow robe appearing darker against her.

She smiled and said, "Elijah. Good to see you."

I started to walk in the room but she put a hand lightly on my chest.

"I'm sorry," she said, "but I have clients right now. You are here for the book, yes?"

"Yes, but I could come back..."

"We will only be a few moments. If you like, you can wait in the library."

She took a step toward me and motioned to the door at the end of the hall.

"No, that's fine, I-"

"Really, we were just finishing up. It will only take a moment.... But I leave it up to you..."

She smiled, gave me a short nod, and closed the door.

I was halfway down the stairs when my curiosity to see the library got the better of me. I turned around and double-stepped up, then found my way back to the slightly ajar library door. It creaked open as I pushed it and I stepped inside. Despite two bright floor lamps placed in opposite corners, the room was much darker than even the hallway was, perhaps because it was nearly the same size as the big hall but had no windows. Three of the walls were covered with ceiling-high wooden bookshelves that seemed to have been there forever. The fourth wall, to my right, was covered with an oriental tapestry that depicted mountains, a placid lake, and a rural village scene.

In the opposite corner of the room there was a small door – perhaps a servant's entrance – and nearby that were two leather chairs, a couch, and a writing table strewn with office objects. Throughout the room were tables that had huge open books upon them, but the room was large enough that these things seemed insignificant. It was really quite an open space, and quite a collection.

I set my bag near the door and wandered into the room. Most of the volumes were bound and large, and the organizational scheme appeared to be by language. There were several sections that I couldn't recognize, then some in Latin, some in Arabic, and many in German. Returning to the table nearest the door, I was surprised to see that a book was open to an illustration in which a dark-skinned woman had pulled up her robe from behind, and was offering herself to a long-penised nobleman.

I turned the exquisitely-illustrated pages at random, and stopped at a picture of a woman pleasuring a man orally. The book seemed very old and I closed it to see the title – not surprisingly, it was the Kamasutra. I turned back to the last illustration and was considering it when from over my shoulder, Beatrice asked, "Do you like it?"

Red-faced from being busted, I tried to change the subject.

"Uh... yeah... the library's nice."

Walking closer, she smiled and said, "Thank you. But I mean the book."

"Oh, sure… it's interesting. How old is it?"

"Though the original version, the Vatsyayana Kamasutram, is much older, this one is from the 1800s."

"Wow. And where's it from?"

"India." She came closer and said, "What do you have there?"

I let out a nervous chuckle and moved away from her, walking toward the opposite wall. "Have you read all of these books," I asked. "Even the ones in Arabic?"

"Even the ones in Arabic," she said.

I stopped at another table that held an open book, and this one, to my complete surprise, showed a very... exposed young lady who had been tied with ropes to ensure she stay that way. My eyebrows must have shot up.

"Just so you don't get the wrong-"

"No, no. It's fine. I'm ok with-"

"So you don't get the wrong impression, I just finished the second day of my new sex-therapy course, and the couples were required to look at the various photos at each station to decide if that was something they might enjoy."

"Oh... uh… ok."

She came over to me and looked at the open girl. "Surprisingly, more women than men found this type of behavior interesting… and they especially liked..."

Beatrice leaned across me to turn the page, in the process pressing herself into my shoulder. I leaned over to give her more space, but she leaned further into me.

"Yes... here it is," she said.

The picture was of a man's oiled genitals being roughly fondled by a latex-gloved dominatrix.

"Uh…why would they like that," I asked.

"Oh, control, I suppose. Many women like to control the sexual act."

"Huh."

I looked at the picture again, then began to back away, but Beatrice put her hand against my back.

"Wait."

She brought both hands to the book and flipped through the pages.

"There's another here that I want to show you..."

Images of leather and bondage swept by until she found the one she wanted. She opened up the page and on the left was a younger, more naked version of Beatrice, tied up and being attended by two other women, also naked.

I couldn't help myself and leaned in to scrutinize the picture. She was a good-looking woman in real-life, but this picture of an ecstatic Beatrice was completely enticing.

"Wow. Is that really you?"

"Yes. And the picture was taken here... through that door."

I looked up to see her pointing to the door in the back of the room.

I didn't know what to say. I couldn't look at the picture anymore because it was too... disturbing. I couldn't really look at Beatrice yet because I was sure I'd picture her naked. So I just looked at the ground and said, "Interesting… so Beatrice, I'm sorry, but I'm in a terrible hurry... Could I just borrow that Chakra book we spoke about last week?"

"Of course, you can borrow any of my books. But are you certain that you have to go so quickly?"

I looked up and so help me, she had unloosened her robe and was stripped to the waist. She stood there proudly, shoulders back, and I tried with all my will power to look in her eyes. She showed a hint of a smile and walked slowly toward me.

"You know where this is going."

I swallowed and shook my head at her.

She kept walking towards me and said, "We can do anything we want here."

I kept shaking my head.

"You want to."

"That's not... that's not true," I managed.

She was standing in front of me now, her chest almost brushing against me. Before I knew it, she was holding me with her right hand and had begun unzipping my pants with the left.

I stumbled backwards, pushing her hands away.

She tilted her head and smiled wider. "Hard. To get?"

"No, I -"

There was a knock on the door and for the first time I noticed that it was closed. Beatrice shrugged into her robe and smiled at me. "Your book is beside the door." And then, in a booming voice, "COME IN."

A hesitant couple opened the door and poked their noses in. "Excuse me," the man said in German, "Are we disturbing you?"

Beatrice switched to German as well, and I took this as a cue to get myself the hell out of there.

The couple came in the door and after greeting them I walked by and picked up my things, including the Chakra book.

Beatrice called out to me and held up the book in which she had appeared.

"Do you want to borrow this one, too?"

I gave her a pained smile and said, "No, thank you."

The other couple appeared anxious to speak to her, but Beatrice nonetheless excused herself and walked over to me near the door.

"Elijah, you know that you cannot do this alone," she said. "You need my guidance."

"Guidance for what?"

"Accessing the records."

I looked at her for a moment and said, "Maybe."

She took a deep breath and lifted her eyebrows. "We shall see," she said, and turned back to the other couple.

My walk home was far from relaxing. I couldn't seem to grasp that someone like Beatrice – who I pictured as being a spiritually-together person – would have such torrid predilections.

*A priest was giving me directions to a house in a small town. The directions were very simple and straightforward, but I was bored and let my concentration drift.*

*Later that night I was driving a car and forgot the directions the priest had given me. Instead of taking the safe path he had described, I was driving down a dark, bumpy road.*

**Chapter 19**

Coming from class at the Martin Luther House, I walked down the main street in my big boy clothes and entered the Handel Bar to meet David.

The barman was busy opening for the day and after taking one of the dark wooden tables at the window, I walked up to the bar and ordered a cappuccino. I waited for it and paid before I sat down and opened up *Way of the Peaceful Warrior* for the 150th time.

David came in too soon after that.

"Hey, this is the second time I was in here looking for you," he said.

I looked around the deserted room.

"They just opened up."

"Yeah, well, I was already here once." He looked over at the barman and asked, "Do we have to serve ourselves or what?"

"I don't know if we *have* to, but I did."

David let out a huge sigh, got up and spoke English to the German-speaking barman.

When he returned, he asked what I was reading and I began explaining it to him. After 10 seconds I could see he wasn't listening, so I stopped talking about it and instead asked how he was doing.

"Me? Oh, fine. Could be better, I guess, but all right. Considering…"

Internally shaking my head, I took the baited hook.

"Considering what?"

He sighed again and said, "Well, Katrin kind of-"

The barman set an Irish Coffee on the table and walked off.

David looked out the window for a moment and began to mist up. "She wants me to move out."

"She wants *you* to move out?"

"The apartment's under her name."

"Oh, *man.* And then what? You live separately and work together every day?"

"She wants to buy me out of the business as well."

"What?"

He was staring out the window again and swallowed before turning to me.

"She says I could stay in the apartment until I figure out what I want to do, but I can't stand it there – especially seeing her get all dressed up to go out – it's just disgusting."

My chest got tight just thinking about it.

"But I don't want to stay there anymore. I don't even want to see her, you know?"

"I can understand… I don't really want to see her, either."

He smiled a bit and said, "You know… you're really the only person I can turn to here… and I was wondering whether I could… maybe stay at your place for a few days. I mean, I can't think straight when I'm in our apartment, and I really need to do that right now. It would only be for awhile."

I blinked at him in silence, picturing the dreadful prospect a half-second too long.

"But if it's a problem…" he trailed off.

"No. No, it's not a problem. I was just wondering where we would put you. We only have one bedroom, you know?"

"I could take the couch."

"Well, it's ok with me, but I need to ask Liliana first, ok?"

"Of course, of course."

He chugged the rest of his coffee and then laid down a coin to cover it. "Ok, I've got to get to work," he said, and stood up. "Call me, ok?"

"I'll speak to Liliana and then call you later."

"Thanks, Elijah. That's really great of you."

As he left, he gave me a look of such sincere gratitude that I was ashamed of myself for already planning to tell him no.

So naturally Liliana thought it was a good idea to help him.

We wound up telling David that he could stay however long he needed, but based on the first conversation when he had said "a few days", we thought it would be no longer than that. So when I went to pick him up and saw, stacked in his living room, the amount of things that he wanted to bring with him, I stood there slack-jawed. It was at least three carloads, and included a huge TV.

"David, how much of that are you bringing?"

He looked pained when he replied, "Katrin wants it all out. She says it only reminds her of me."

"What about putting it in your cellar?"

"It's already full."

"Do you have any friends with cellars?"

"Only friends of Katrin."

"Ok… what about self-storage?"

"There aren't any firms in town."

I nodded as I surveyed the stuff. "Then I guess we better get to work."

He agreed and we started carrying boxes, most of which contained books and other heavy items.

The living room, which had previously doubled as my workspace, basically turned into a no-go zone because David's things got scattered everywhere. He sat on the couch and watched television all day, and hardly ate or conversed (and when he did it was with all the trademark David edginess). Further, he apparently had stopped bathing.

After two weeks of this, we began to take it for granted that we would be stuck with him forever – that he was simply our burden. So it came as a surprise one afternoon when he came out of the bathroom and said, "I think I'm moving back to the States."

"Back home?"

"Yeah, I think I've had enough of Europe for awhile. Maybe I'll head back to LA. I liked the sunshine out there."

I could hardly contain my glee. "When do you think you'll go?"

"I guess after all the details have been worked out with the business... maybe another week or so... If it's a problem, I could always stay in a hotel or something..."

I wanted very badly to say *Yes, go to a hotel, you damned freeloader*, but what came out was, "You can stay as long as you want."

Of course his "week or so" turned into another two and a half, and by the time he had gone ahead and purchased a ticket back to the States, I was completely fed up with our tenant, and Liliana wasn't far behind.

Still, we cooked him a going-away dinner that was filled with long-winded discourses on his side and long gaps in conversation on ours, and by the time he was out of our life, we had been thoroughly depleted of goodwill toward man.

It's funny how these things work, because in the beginning Liliana and I enjoyed the feeling of helping someone in need. But the take, take, take aspect of David's personality was simply too taxing.

And one can argue all day long that he was depressed and down on his luck, but the simple truth is that when you give too much of yourself to someone for nothing in return, you are unable to be the person you are capable of being.

*Against the far wall, the woman was sitting on the edge of a lavishly padded couch. As I walked across the room towards her, she turned around and offered herself to me.*

## Chapter 20

About a week after David had moved out, I rolled out of bed feeling fine, not a care in the world and still happy that our tenant was gone. Liliana and I had a pleasant breakfast, I walked her to work, and then I returned to the apartment to get ready for my workday.

First thing I did was check my email. In addition to the normal amount of spam, there was a message from *Simone* that essentially read: “Mad and I are fine. By the way, we have a daughter. Do you want to meet it?”

After looking at the message for a long time, I exited the email program, stood up from the computer and went to the storage closet where the sweeper lives. I plugged in the power cord and turned the thing on. The dust bunnies tried to run away but I caught them, banishing them to the darkness. I moved through the apartment trying to bring order to ~~my mind~~ the rooms, while terribly simple and simply terrible questions assailed me.

*A baby?*

*Is it really mine?*

*How will Liliana handle this?*

*Should I even tell her?*

Each of the questions carried a slew of highly-charged emotions – fear, anger, helplessness – that were not easily cleansed away. I finished sweeping and looked at the clock – I had to get to class. Out on the street on my way to the Martin Luther House, I was so preoccupied that I crossed against a light and nearly got hit by a car for it. The driver had to swerve away to miss me, and leaned on the horn insanely as she passed by. I was scatterbrained enough before that, but being nearly run down only pushed my adrenaline level higher.

Classes were a blur, and in the late afternoon my state of mind had not improved as I waited for Liliana in front of the institute. As soon as she came out of the front doors, she saw something was wrong. She gave me a searching look before and after we kissed, but I just didn't know what to say.

*Surprise, I have a daughter with another woman!*

I didn't know where to begin, so I asked how work was.

“It was fine, but what is wrong with you?”

“Nothing.”

“Nothing. Then why are you so serious?”

I smiled, but only with my mouth. “How's this?”

“Terrible.”

I managed a chuckle and as we turned towards home, she demanded again to know what was wrong.

“I think we should either go have a drink, or go to dinner. Then I'll tell you.'

She chose to go to an Italian restaurant, and after we had sat down and placed our orders, she looked at me with raised eyebrows. "So?"

Perhaps I shouldn't have been so dramatic about the whole thing, but I had absolutely no script for telling my wife that I once had a threesome with two sisters and this had resulted in one of them getting pregnant. Not only was I completely ashamed, I was worried about her feelings as well – especially how disappointed I was about to make her. But there was no choice.

"I got an email today from an ex-girlfriend. Someone I knew in Prague before we met."

She paused for a second and then asked, "Was it that Mad girl?"

"No, but close. It was her sister."

"Wait. You went out with her sister also?"

"Mmm. Sort of."

"What does that mean?"

"It means that we didn't really go out. We just… spent some time together."

Liliana seemed to be getting the message. She chewed on her bottom lip and said, "Ok. So she's an old lover. And why are you telling me this now?"

I looked around the quiet restaurant and sighed before looking back at her.

"She wrote me that she has a baby, and…"

Liliana closed her eyes for a moment. They were full of tears when she opened them.

"You have a baby with another woman?"

"Lil, I didn't know about it until today! She just wrote me."

I offered her my napkin but she shook her head and used her own. I reached out to hold her hand. She refused it and I started misting up myself.

"I'll be back." She got up and walked to the bathroom.

When she was gone, the waiter came and set our meals down and I wondered how in the world we were going to be able to eat.

I sat there trying to find a way through the impossibility of the situation. Newly-married, getting ahead, enjoying life and – BAM – suddenly I have a child with another woman. The pain I was causing Liliana was horrendous.

A different person might have just deleted that email and forgotten about the whole situation. But not me, boy. No, I had to go and open the whole can of worms. Not only that, I had to go and pour them all over Liliana as well.

She returned to the table looking a bit more composed and we looked at each other in silence. Massaging the back of my neck with both hands, I sighed, "There's this heaviness in my chest I can't get rid of."

Liliana looked at me hard and said, "Do you love her?"

"*What*?"

She shook her head. "Please don't make me say it again."

I reached out for her across the table and said, “Liliana, there is no one else. I don’t love her, I never did, and it was a mistake being with her. I love only *you*. And I’m sooooo sorry. I didn’t want this, I didn’t plan this and I am just as confused as you are. I feel so…”

I took my hands away.

“Ashamed.”

My turn to start crying. It was a deep, sobbing cry and I was a complete mess. I got up to go to the bathroom but first gave Liliana a kiss on the forehead. “I’m so sorry,” I said.

The face in the bathroom mirror was not my own. It was years older, full of regret and sadness, and had swollen, red eyes. I wanted to hide from it.

Eventually I returned and found that Liliana had been nibbling at her food. Sitting down, I said, “Aren’t we a pair?”

Liliana smiled a bit and then asked, “So when are we going to Prague?”

“What do you mean?”

“I mean, when are we going to Prague? We’re going to visit the baby, aren’t we?”

“Uh… I hadn’t thought about it.”

“Well, what else is there to do? Ignore the fact that you have a baby?”

“I wish.”

“Stop it. We didn’t ask for this situation, but what is there to do? Maybe she’s a cute girl and we’ll get to see her. But you can’t ignore this, Elijah. You might want to – I know *I* do – but we just cannot. We are talking about a little girl here.”

I was looking at Liliana but picturing the scene of meeting Simone again – Simone with my – *our* – baby.

“And you want to come as well,” I asked.

“You are *not* going there without me.”

*I was weightless and able to control my speed and direction according to my desire. I found that I could move very fast and on its own accord my body morphed into a type of energetic compactness. I built up speed and found myself in a very dark realm. I was completely frightened as the darkness closed in on me. I tried to maneuver past the grotesque, grasping arms, but my options became limited until I was completely surrounded.*

**Chapter 21**

The phone calls and emails we'd recently exchanged had not prepared me for the reality of Jake's visit. Liliana kept asking if I was looking forward to seeing him, but because of my preoccupations, the truth is that Jake's visit seemed trivial. I was far more occupied by Beatrice's advances, my growing spiritual involvement and the prospect of seeing my new child than I was with anything else.

Still, the day eventually arrived when I drove to Berlin to pick him up.

After locating each other in the arrivals terminal (Jake let out a loud whoop that shocked everyone around him before bear-hugging me) we walked out to the car all happy to see each other and talking about his flight over. He was half-drunk and punchy from the lost night of sleep, but still curious and chatty as we navigated our way to the hostel I'd reserved for us.

The Karneval Hostel was pricey and well-located in the city center, so we expected good things from it, but upon check-in we discovered they had assigned us a double bed. The clerk informed us that switching rooms was out of the question because all the others were full, and Jake started to get snooty on her. I could see her gearing up to get nasty in return, so I spoke nicely in German to her and that seemed to take some of her edge off. Still, the whole check-in process was tense, and after we had dropped off our bags in the room, we pointedly ignored her as we walked out to go exploring.

Stepping onto Weinbergsweg, we were immediately impressed by the vibrancy of the neighborhood. Trams, dogs, bikes, cars, sidewalk restaurants, fruit stands, Turkish food sellers – all were within steps of the hostel entrance. Jake propped himself up with a takeout double espresso from an Italian specialty shop, and we commenced walking through the town, half catching up, half sightseeing.

We zigzagged our way through a residential district and ended up at Alexanderplatz, where we bought tickets to the television tower's observation deck. While waiting in line for the 203-meter elevator ride, we were informed it would take just 40 seconds, so once inside Jake timed it. It actually took 42 seconds and he groused about the delay. The operator didn't seem to find this funny.

The observation deck was crowded, but the flat cityscape opened up beautifully – the only limit to one's view being the limits of one's eyes. Potsdamer Platz was easy to pick out, the fanciful skewed circus tent of the Sony Building instantly recognizable. The Riechstag's staid permanence could be seen near the Chancellor's ultra-modern office and residence, and for the things we couldn't recognize, we were able to get our bearings from the plaques that provide geographic and historic descriptions. Jake was especially impressed to see the Tempelhof airport, which the Allies used for their Airbridge toWest Berlin when the USSR imposed a blockade in 1948.

However, Jake's caffeine level had begun to nosedive, so we sat in the café to refuel. He had a Couintreau and another espresso, and I had a beer.

"So tell me something cool about Germany that I don't know," he said.

I took a big gulp of beer and thought about it.

"All right... In Wittenberg last month there was a huge festival to celebrate Martin Luther, and among other things, they had a bumper car ride."

"Uh-huh."

"And it was *so* lame! Instead of the free-for-all you'd see in the States, people banging and smashing into each other, in Wittenberg the drivers were all going around in the same direction, nudging each other from time to time, but really, hardly bumping each other at all."

"Where's the point in that?"

"Exactly. So I thought to myself, 'I'll show them how to do it for real,' and I bought a ticket and got in a bumper car during the next break. When the music and power started, I began puttering along in the proper direction like everybody else, but about 10 seconds into it, I did a 180 and started going in the opposite direction. I immediately hit this middle-aged guy head-on, and man, did he get *red.* You could see him tense up, you know? But I was feeling all ornery, so as he was trying to get around me I hit him again, and he started yelling at me, telling me I was doing it all wrong, blah, blah, blah. So we got untangled and I did the same thing to two younger girls, who were at least more playful, but you could tell that they were a little put-off by some older guy paying them attention. So I let them go and here comes a man and his kid and I hit them full force into the right front. I forced them to the side as well. The boy's eyes were all wide, and the man just *laid into me* – "What do you think you're doing? Someone can get hurt like that!"

"So as he's yelling at me, the music dies and we coast to a stop because the power gets cut. A second later the operator comes hustling over to me. "Hey, what kind of nut are you – you could damage the equipment with such nonsense!"

"*Damage* a bumper car?"

"Dude, it was a mess! He basically kicked me off and said I couldn't come back, and as I walked off, a couple of the bumper car people jeered at me. And then, when I'd gotten outside of the car zone, the operator got on the PA to apologize for my behavior and told them *now* they'd have a proper ride…"

"Man, that's crazy."

"Completely! Anyways, I felt sort of strange afterwards… I mean, I had done it to be funny, to show people there are other approaches to the bumper car, but even such a simple thing was slapped down crazy hard. For the Wittenberg crowd, there's apparently just one way to do the bumper cars."

"Like a bunch of girls?"

"The girls were the fun ones!"

"Then like a bunch of old geezers."

"Yeah, like that. Anyway… you mind if I continue?"

"You kiddin'? I haven't heard your brand of B.S. for months!"

"Right. Anyway, as I was walking away from the loser bumper cars, someone yelled from the top of the giant Ferris wheel. They were waving their arms and having a ball, and as I stood there watching them go around, it occurred to me that in some ways, life is just like a Ferris wheel: There are times when you're at the top of the world, enjoying the unhindered views, and the big question is how do you deal with it?"

"Whaddya mean?"

"I mean, you know full well that you're going to start downwards again soon, so do you worry that you'll be at the bottom again, or do you dig on the vibe of being at the top, even if it's only for that moment? What I mean is, do you live in *that* moment, or do worry about the worse times that are sure to come?"

Jake thought about it for a second and said, "I think it's more complicated than that. During those times when you're on top, it's easy to live in the moment. You have incentive *to* live in the moment – the view's great, you feel good, you have no worries. But who wants to live in the moment when you're down at the bottom with all the carny rats? Isn't that the time to live *outside* the moment, and look forward to being at the top again?"

"That makes sense. But if you don't hang with the carny rats sometimes, how can you properly appreciate when you're up there soaring with the eagles? And if you only appreciate the time that you spend at the top, you're enjoying like, less than 1% of life. And how much sense does that make?"

"Ok, but do you really need to experience the bad to appreciate the good?"

"I don't know. Maybe some people do."

"I don't."

"Me, neither. Anyways, back at the carnival, I decided to ride the Ferris wheel."

"Dude, do you ever *work*?"

"Nope. Anyway, I got stuck in the same carriage as this young lovey-dovey couple. I was uncomfortable straight away, because obviously they weren't there for the ride. I mean, as soon as we started moving, they got at it, and by the time we reached the top, they were just about grinding on each other."

"You were staring at them, weren't you?"

"Absolutely. He was all *over* her!"

"Did you join in?"

"Funny. But you know what?"

"Turkey butt?"

"No, silly. I was watching them when we reached the top of the Ferris wheel, and I *missed* when we were at the highest point because I was watching them letch all over each other. I completely missed the reason I was on the ride in the first place."

"And you saw significance in that, did you?"

"Pay attention, smartie. Yes, the significance is that I was more concerned with what others were doing than what I myself was doing. The very opposite of the secret of life! And to boot, they were all sexed up, which is like the basest of the base! I was ogling them groping each other instead of enjoying my personal high point!"

"Luckily," said Jake, "the one difference between life and your Ferris wheel parable is that on the wheel, you get to go around more than once. I hope you learned from your mistake and enjoyed the view the next time?"

"That's just it! I enjoyed watching the couple make out, *and* I enjoyed the view. It was a great ride! At least, until they opened their eyes and saw me watching them."

"No."

"Yeah, and there was this huge balloon of bad karma floating around until the ride finished. They gave me hate-rays when they got off."

"I would, too."

"Yeah, well, instead of getting off, I gave all my tickets to the ride operators, and this time, I had the whole ride, the highs *and* the lows, all to myself. And I was able to appreciate them so much more than when those jaspers were distracting me."

"So you think other people only distract you from your highbrow spiritual thoughts, is that it?"

"No, I... Yeah, ok. Pretty much."

By the time we had walked back to the hostel, Jake was on his last legs and crashed straightaway. But it was only 6ish and I didn't feel like sitting around the room, so I went for a walk. At the front door I took a right onto the tree-lined way and walked past a clutch of bistros and eateries, the Gorky Park restaurant reminding me that I was definitely in the old East Berlin. Next came a hippyish park surrounded by thick bushes, out of which emerged a couple of guys zipping their pants up.

At the top of the hill the relatively narrow street – two tram-tracks wide – broadened to include a narrow span for bikers. The sidewalks on both sides gave pedestrians ample space for window-shopping in the artsy stores, second-hand markets, and LP joints.

I came upon a takeout booze place where you placed your order at the converted front door – you had to stoop down to see the clerk's eyes – and I ordered a cold Beck's. The kid opened the bottle for me and I stood on the street watching people go by and enjoying the freedom of drinking a beer on the streets of summertime Europe.

The first beer went down so easy that I ordered another, and by the end of that one, I was feeling fine. So fine, in fact, that a little while later when I came to the tatoo/peircing joint, I poked my head in to see what the deal was.

The store was interesting – they had a lot of Arabic water pipes, tie-dye t-shirts, funkadelic posters and so on, and while I was looking at the metallic piercing stuff in the glass cases, a young girl in a skirt – couldn't have been more than 20, tops – came over and stood beside me. She was also looking at the piercing stuff. This was not surprising, because she had multiple piercings in each ear, as well as the left nostril. After a few moments, *she* actually started speaking to *me*. And in British English to boot.

"Are you gonna get a piercing," she asked.

"Nooooo," I said. "Not me. I got a tattoo and that's enough."

"Really? Can I see it?"

I twisted my leg around to show her the calf tattoo I'd gotten in a previous life, and she squatted down, knees slightly apart. As she was checking out the tattoo, I was checking out her. She was a very dark-skinned girl and was wearing a tight crème-colored top, knee-high skirt and low boots. She looked up and busted me looking at her breasts, but we both played it off.

She nodded and smiled at me. "Nice."

I asked if she were going to get pierced.

"Yeah! I'm gonna get my tongue pierced, and I'm really excited about it."

"Your tongue? Why would you *do* that?"

Staring at me flatly, she said, "Because it's cool."

"Uh-huh."

She said she was waiting for the piercer guy to return from his break, so we stood there joking about the size of the stud she was going to get, the pain factor, and the prices (ear – €25; bellybuttons and eyebrows – €40; nipples – €50; tongue – €60; others = negotiated).

We were getting along well, but still, I was surprised when she asked me if I'd come with her when she got pierced. I hesitated, trying to picture the scene, and she hastily explained that she was only asking because she was there alone.

"Alone in Berlin?"

She smiled and said, "No. Alone in general."

Just then, the bell over the front door rang. We both turned and looked as a ponytail slacker type came into the shop. Going into the back of the shop, he opened a door and turned on the light. The piercer was in.

The girl looked back at me and raised her eyebrows. "So?"

I nodded at her and then followed her towards the back.

The room was smallish, with a mirror on the entire far wall. It had all the trappings of a doctor's examination room – a table covered with tissue paper, stirrups (!) and a tray full of invasive instruments. After some discussion, the girl and ponytail man both sat on the doctor's table, he sitting Indian-style facing her, she dangling her legs over the side. She had her head turned towards him, but was looking at me in the mirror. As the piercer put on rubber gloves, I stood across from her. She was getting nervous and asked to hold my hand. I said sure, and it was actually kind of gratifying to help an arbitrary someone in need.

"Your tongue, please," said Mr. Ponytail. He was professionally efficient.

The pink of the girl's tongue was an abrupt contrast to her dark, smooth skin, and the piercer took it between a long metal clamp with holes at the very tips – guides so the hole in her tongue would be relatively straight. The girl was calm through all of this, and wasn't disturbed until he clinically pulled her tongue far, far out with the clamp and placed the needle onto it. He was working completely outside of her mouth.

"Ok, you ready?" he asked her.

"Eh-hah."

As he pushed the needle through her tongue, she first stiffened up and then wriggled all over the place, suddenly crushing my hand. It looked like the needle was relatively easy to put through, and I was shocked that it seemed so effortless. But the girl wasn't finding it effortless. She was thrashing around as the piercer fiddled – one handed – with threading a stud onto the shaft of the thing. She was slobbering from having her mouth open for so long.

And there was blood.

A *lot* of it.

When the process was over and she could take her tongue back into her mouth, there was still the blood on the white dentist's bib she was wearing. She was smiling and happy – the blood between her teeth in a red outline – and when she proudly showed me the stud in her tongue, all I could see was the blood everywhere.

I forced a smile and said it looked great.

She said thanks and flashed that lovely smile again.

She had to stay there for a bit because of the trauma of the procedure, and I told her I'd just wait outside.

But I was revolted by the whole scene and once back into the shop I took off, actually bumping into things as I Jerry Lewised my way outta there and back to the hostel.

Jake was up and feeling thirsty when I returned, so we went downstairs to the casually hip bar in the basement. We got two beers and sat down in the cozy chairs, then I told him about the piercing episode.

When I finished he said, "Dude, why don't these things ever happen to me? You've had a threesome, your guru lady wants to jump you *and* you're picking up hotties in Berlin while I'm sleeping! What a great life!"

"Yeah, great life. Only I feel guilty about everything you just mentioned."

"Huh? What the hell for? First, you weren't married when you had the threesome – I can't wait to tell everyone back home that you had a threesome, by the way. And second, you haven't reacted to the guru lady's advances, right? The hottie up the street doesn't count because... well, I guess it does count, but then again nothing happened. You only talked to her."

"Yeah, but I still feel like I'm... I don't know, like I'm not acting married or something. Like I'm still putting out this vibe that says, *Hey, look at me, I'm available.*"

"And are you?"

"Am I what?"

"Available."

I cocked an eyebrow and asked, "You want some of this?"

Jake frowned at me in mock exasperation. "See? That's your problem. I try to get serious, you make a joke. I make a joke, you get serious. It's like you're all confused."

"Well, to answer your question, no, I'm not available. I'm just open to new stuff, and sometimes people mistake that openness for-"

"You being available?"

"I guess."

"You know, I've been talking to Sherry about this. Because in my eyes, she's too... I guess *friendly* is the word... with other men. I mean, what message does that send to them?"

"That she's friendly?"

"Yes, but men being the pigs that we are, we interpret that as *openness*, don't we? Maybe the thing is that single people act more open than married people, so when you act open, people assume you're not married."

"But why should married people act differently? I'm the same person that I was before we got married, it's just that now I have a great partner. If anything, having Liliana makes me feel *more* open than before. Now I can talk to people without fear of rejection because if a woman doesn't want to speak to me, no problem. I don't feel rejected because I wasn't making an advance in the first place. Plus, I have my lovely wife to return to... speaking of, I promised I'd phone Liliana. I'm gonna go upstairs and call her. Will you be all right here alone?"

He looked around at the scenery: The pub was becoming fuller.

"Oh, I'll be fine."

Indeed, after I came back from calling Liliana (no answer), Jake was standing at the bar talking to a couple of girls, so I joined them.

"And this," he said, "is my married friend, Elijah."

I shook hands with the girls. Martie was blonde, Jana was red-haired, and both were cute.

"Elijah is worried about being too open to new experiences," said Jake.

"Why that," asked Martie.

"Because I could get into trouble with my wife," I said.

"Where is she," asked Jana.

"At home."

"So where is the problem," asked Martie. They all laughed.

"No problem here," I said. "But let's talk about Jake. Did he tell you that he's studying to be a doctor?"

The girls' eyes widened and they looked at him appraisingly.

"What kind of doctor," asked Jana.

"An ER surgeon," he answered. "I like the action, you know."

"That's great… I'm studying to be a nurse," said Jana. "Maybe we work together once."

"Absolutely."

Jake and Jana began to pair off a bit, and Martie raised her eyebrows and asked, "Can you talk to me or would your wife be mad?"

"I guess that depends on what we talk about."

It was late by the time we got back to the room, and when I looked at the mobile phone, I noticed I had missed three phone calls.

"Oh, *man.*"

"What is it," asked Martie.

"I missed three calls from Liliana. She must be in bed by now."

Jake stood up from his luggage and said, "Ok, I'm ready."

Martie smiled at him. "Great. Good night, Elijah."

"Good night."

Jake winked as they walked out, and I closed the door behind them. Feeling guilty again for having missed Liliana's phone calls, I changed into a pair of shorts and t-shirt and had just lay down when there was a knock on the door.

Thinking it was Jake, I opened the door and was startled to see Jana there. She was also dressed in bedclothes.

"Uh… hi," I managed.

"Martie and Jake need some… time, I guess. Jake said me I could sleep here."

I blinked at her.

"I'm sorry," she said, "but I have no place to go."

"Uh... yeah. Ok."

She stepped into the room and I closed the door. When I turned around, she was looking at the double bed.

"Oh! You don't have single beds?"

I shook my head at her. "This was the only room they could give us."

She breathed out heavily. "Well, this is... awkward."

"Isn't it?"

I looked around the room and saw that the sitting chair's cushions were removable, so I took them off and lay them on the floor. My legs wouldn't be supported, but it was doable.

Jana looked at the cushions and shook her head. "I cannot take your bed."

"Don't worry about it, I can sleep anywhere. I just need a pillow and a blanket."

An hour later I was still unable to sleep. I had been debating moving up to the bed for a long time, and finally I did. There was plenty of space and we were using separate blankets as well.

*I'm not doing anything wrong,* I kept telling myself. *I'm only sleeping. I'm not doing anything wrong.*

But it still felt like I was.

"Holy hell, dude! What are you gonna do?" Jake was riding shotgun as we navigated out of Berlin.

"I don't know, but Liliana and I are-"

"Wait, wait, wait... You *told* her?"

I looked over at him. "Yeah... *that* was fun."

"What did she say?"

"It was a mess, of course. But what could I do, hide it?"

"Yes! Hide it! From what you told me, those girls forced themselves on you – though I'm not sure I believe that – and now *they* have a problem. So let *them* take care of it."

"Yeah, but we're not talking about... I don't know, a broken bicycle here. It's a human life. A little girl that wouldn't be here without me. And yes– Do I have to turn here?"

"Straight."

"Yes, it's their problem, but it's also *my* problem, even if I don't want it. Anyway, Lil and I are going to visit them down in Prague next week."

"For *what*?"

"To see the girl. See how they're doing. See if I can, I don't know, help somehow."

"Do they want child support?"

"I don't know. But me and Lil talked and we think that would be all right, as long as we get to see the baby sometimes."

"Wait. You want to get *involved* with that?"

A car cut me off and I beeped at him.

"Part of me does. Another part wants to forget it. But then I'd be expecting every phone call to be my long-lost child… and the worst would be if that call never came."

There was a long silence before Jake said, "Man, I'd just forget about it."

*Focusing on my absolutely sickening fear of not seeing them again, I tensed all of my energetic pathways and released a furious onslaught of anger. Screaming my lungs out, I shot forth from the construct and discovered that I had a type of bludgeon in my grasp. I swung it with all of my will. The construct broke apart with the force of my blow. I turned on her and swung the weapon with all the force I could muster and with the full intent of destroying her... but the blow was stopped in midair and the weapon was rendered from my grasp, disappearing into the void between us.*

**Chapter 22**

We arrived in Wittenberg in the early afternoon sunshine, and after having a piece of the cake that Liliana had prepared, we all took a stroll. The sun was still high and as we made our way through the green part of town, Liliana was a question machine about Jake and Sherry's relationship. Jake found himself sidestepping living together and marriage questions, and I was tempted to comment on his actions during the previous night in Berlin, but wondered if he, in turn, would tell on me for sleeping with a stranger.

The first touristy stop on our walk was the spot where Martin Luther had posted his 95 theses, and we were headed to the Martin Luther House itself when Jake spotted the passage leading behind the castle church.

"Hey, it looks like there's a bar back there."

I smiled at Liliana and she made a face back at me. "That's right," I said. "It's got a great view as well… Shall we?"

"Absolutely," enthused Jake, and led us through the passage and across the courtyard to the wooden tables. "I'll even buy," he said, and walked up to get the beers.

"Do you need help," asked Liliana.

"Nope. I speak German. Watch this…"

He walked up to the barman and held up three fingers. "Beer."

"*Jawohl*," answered the regular barman, waving at Liliana and me.

Jake looked over at us all proud of himself and smiled.

Liliana and I settled on a bench shaded by a chestnut tree and enjoyed the view of the castle until Jake delivered the beers.

"Hey, did that guy just say, *Ya-vol* to me, like Sergeant Schultz?"

"Yup."

"That's *so* cool. I had no idea they really used that word."

"It's used a lot in the East, but not in West Germany," offered Liliana.

"Huh. *Jawohl*."

"Here's another one you'll like," I said. "*Zum Wohl*. It's like '*cheers*'."

Jake raised his glass and said, "*Jawohl* and *Zum Wohl*." We clinked glasses and drank. Wiping his mouth with his sleeve, Jake looked around and sighed. "It sure is nice here. And what history."

"Yeah," I said, "it's fascinating."

"Do you think you'll ever move back home," he asked.

"I don't know… I really like Europe, but it hurts somewhere deep down to think that I'd never live in the States again. Like a part of me would get erased or something."

"And what about you, Liliana," Jake asked. "Would you like to move to America?"

"No, never."

Both of us turned to her with raised eyebrows.

She looked between us for a second and then burst out laughing.

"Ha! I'm just pulling your nose."

Jake looked at her and said, "Good one."

I took a drink and waited for her to stop giggling, then asked her again about living in America.

"Oh, I don't know. Maybe someday, but for now I enjoy it here."

"What about children," asked Jake.

And then he slapped his hand over his mouth. He looked at me and said. "Shit. I'm sorry."

Liliana was also looking at me.

"What? He's my best friend! I'm not going to tell him about something like that?"

She shook her head. "You telling Jake is the last of the worries. I was thinking of how much fun our trip to Prague will be."

"You're really going with him," asked Jake.

She looked at him over her sunglasses and asked, "Why would I not?"

"But won't it be... hard... to see the mother?"

"Yes. But their time was before Elijah and I were together. I am more concerned about the baby than I am about her. For example, what if the baby is ugly or retarded? I would not want children if this would be so for us."

Jake and I were considering this when Liliana blurted out, "Goodness. You two are not very funny today!"

We looked at each other again before laughing with her.

Jake took another drink and said, "I told Eli that he should have deleted the email."

"But they could find him if they wanted to."

"Maybe," he countered, "but with no email and living in a foreign country, it would be difficult..."

"But the problem would still be there! There would still be a little girl without a father and a woman with a difficult time."

"Fine, but that's *her* problem, right?"

"Are you being serious now," asked Liliana, "because I am about to be angry with you."

"Well, kind of serious... because from what Elijah told me, he basically didn't want to be with this girl. She insisted, and because of that, she got pregnant. Isn't it possible that she wanted to trap him into something? Maybe she wanted to get with an American boy so she could go to America. It wouldn't be the first time."

"Yes, it is possible she wanted him. But he is mine now!" She reached over and roughly put her arm around me.

Turning back to Jake, Liliana said, "But honest. If you were Elijah, you would not want to see your little girl? You think you would be able to live with your conscious your whole life knowing that your daughter was out there and you didn't know her?"

Jake thought for a second and said, "If I were Elijah, right now, at this stage of his life, I might contact that chick and I *might* go see the little girl. But I'm kinda suspicious of this girl's motives. Why is she contacting him now, not when she was pregnant, for example?"

"Maybe because she hoped she could do this alone, and now sees that she cannot?"

"Or," offered Jake, "because she knows that she can better guilt him into giving her money with a baby?"

"Or because she wants the girl to have a father," I added.

Jake breathed out and said, "Yeah, that's possible, but I'm still suspicious about birth control issues. You know, my wife was on the pill when we were first together. She always took it after breakfast. And since we ate together most days, I'd kinda look out for her taking it. Well, one day I'm on my way out and forget something, and when I come back in the house I hear her puking up a storm. I hustled into the bathroom to see what was up and she was standing there fine as can be, no fever or anything. I asked what was wrong, and she said it must have been the eggs or something. Fine, I say, get back in bed and rest and I'll check on you at lunch. So during the morning I remember about the pill and how it must have also come up with her breakfast, right? Come lunchtime, she's up and about, no problems, and I was happy about that, but later when I mentioned the pill probably coming up when she puked, she got all edgy. 'Oh, it was down there awhile, she said. 'It probably didn't come back up.' But it might have, I said, so why not be sure about it and take another? And she started in on how the cycle couldn't be messed up, how the days were apportioned just so, blah blah blah. And I said, well, how many more are in the cycle, and she said 17 and I said, wait, isn't that just about the whole month? And she got all cagey and argumentative, saying if I didn't want a baby with her I should just tell her, and I said it wasn't that, I just thought we were being careful, and so on. But I tell you what, I sure was more careful after *that*…"

"Man…." I said, "I'm glad you didn't have kids with her."

"My God. What a life *that* would have been."

"Imagine your kids – they probably would've been wound too tight like her."

"Or they would have been laid back like me and had a shitty life because of their overbearing mom."

"Wait a moment," said Liliana. "If she was so nasty, why were you with her in the first place?"

Jake put his head down and then half-smiled at her. "First because she was hot. Second… I guess I was always, I don't know… *intimidated* by her temper."

He got a wide grin and then said, "But enough about my *hypothetical* children, let's talk about this little kid. Have you got a photo or anything? Does it have three legs? Is it a mongoloid?"

I shook my head. "No, no photos. And even if it were a mutant-"

"*She,*" corrected Liliana.

"Right. Whether or not *she* is a mutant is irrelevant. I was a party to creating a human life and that goes beyond the other arguments."

"Yes. It is simply your responsibility," said Liliana. "Which means it is *our* responsibility."

Jake looked between us and said, "Well, I just hope this whole deal isn't too hard for you to cope with."

I scoffed. "Me too, buddy. Me too."

I had told Jake a bit about my learnings on the Akashic Records and he was more interested that I thought he would be. Not only did he want to meet Beatrice, he also wanted to learn more about the meditations I had been doing. But above all, he wanted me to try to give him a reading from the Records. That I had thus far been unsuccessful did not seem to bother him, and further, he thought that we should record the attempt with his camera. I tried to talk him out of it, but in the end I relented. Not because I was confident of success, but because of Jake's sheer enthusiasm.

I spent a few days fasting and purging, hoping that this cleansing process might be of some benefit, and then one cloudy morning after Liliana had gone to work, Jake and I set up the living room in a constellation that seemed workable: I was to lie on the couch, Jake was to sit in a nearby chair and transcribe what, if any, things of value I might say.

"Ok, I think I'm ready," I told him. I was sitting on the couch.

"All right. I'm starting the camera."

When the camera's red light came on, I said, "File number 1, attempted access for Jake Whistler."

I lay down and closed my eyes, trying to forget all the previous attempts I had made. I tried to forget where I was and what I was doing. I breathed deep and repeated my previous instructions to myself and after some time all turned dark until in the distance I "saw" a swirling and fragmented cloud.

I tried to calm myself.

I "saw" my consciousness as a cloud of colors and patterns, and wondered if I could will it smaller. With great effort, I slowly willed it smaller until it stopped swirling and twisting and began to naturally coalesce into a coherent luminescence. Upon completing this, I saw my brightness among other, less compacted forms and I concentrated on my own light.

Things began to slip and I no longer had a sense of control. There was only lightness reaching towards vacuum. Vacuum, frictionless space, and ever greater motion until space around me elongated and pulsed into strings of light, each in colors and textures beyond my vocabulary.

Suddenly I entered a black realm that terrified me completely. Not knowing what to do, I concentrated only on my lightness. As my radiance grew, hideous shadows, some of which had been lurking ever closer, began to recede.

The black realm abruptly ended and I found myself face-to-face with a being of immensity. Boundless and yet benign power radiated from her. It was obvious that she was in control and that I was there because she had permitted it. She nodded slowly at me and I felt her "touch" my luminescence. She "said" I had done well getting through the shadow realm, and that she would help me find that which I sought. I rejoiced at her praise and tried to bring forth my request, but she was already gesturing to a bound file that had appeared between us – it was opened to a page roughly midway through. Symbols floated up in front of me, and from the middle of an unreadable jumble, a message coalesced.

I read it aloud, knowing that in some faraway place, Jake would hear it.

"This human, now known as Jake Whistler, must seize the present opportunity to reconcile with his previous partner, the human now known as Laura Weaver. Only through reconciliation, through this sacrifice of self, will he be free of her again."

The immense being nodded at me.

I "heard" Jake ask, "What do you mean, 'again'?"

Jake's question broke down strands of my concentration and I began to, for lack of a better word, disintegrate. "Translating" the question seemed impossible, and it took an eternity for me to accomplish it. The old one nodded approvingly at me and a message again rose up from the book. Again, I read it aloud.

"The entities are reaching a critical stage in their development. Reconciliation will provide the most satisfactory results."

I "felt" Jake becoming agitated, and then the old one was suddenly gone. I was again in the dark realm, my compact brightness frayed and chaotic. As I streaked bodywards, completely out of control, a lunging shadow was able to grasp at my elongated frays. More than once, I "felt" it seize a piece of me only to recoil from the jolt that seared through us both. The thing's shrill voice would haunt my dreams for weeks.

As I tried to concentrate on integrity, the earth-bound glows came into view and I relaxed, falling into blackness once more.

When I awoke, I was on the floor looking up at Jake. He asked how I was.

I sighed and said, “It’s…”

I was completely exhausted and only wanted to be left alone.

“… hard to talk…”

“Why were you screaming? And then you started to go into some sort of convulsions…”

I realized I was on the floor and tried to get up, but slipped. Jake helped me lie on the couch again.

When I could, I said, “There was some… being… that was trying to stop me…”

“Stop you how?”

“It grabbed me…”

I got a terrible shudder and said that I needed to rest. The last thing I remembered was Jake worrying over me.

The clanging of a church bell woke me and I opened my eyes. I was alone in the room, and the camera was gone. I got up stiffly and walked up to the rotunda, looking down as the afternoon crowd passed by. I realized that I had a ravenous hunger and walked into the kitchen, where Jake was watching the video of our session. He stopped the tape when he saw me and said, “Back from the dead, eh?”

“How long was I asleep?”

“About three hours. Liliana called and I told her what happened – she’s worried and will be home soon.” He paused and said, “I’m worried, too.”

I sat across from him at the table and began peeling an apple. I still felt drained.

“Maybe your fasting had something to do with being so tired?”

“Hmm.”

As I ate, Jake rewound the session and said, “I think you should look at this.”

He turned the camera towards me and pressed play. The viewer was small, but it was easy to discern that above me on the couch, a figure in a yellow gown was hovering over me.

“Stop it there, Jake. That’s definitely her. Look, you can see her hair.”

Liliana was sitting on the ground close to the television, which we had connected to Jake’s camera. She was pointing at the cloudy image of the specter. No doubt about it. It was Beatrice.

“But what’s she doing there,” asked Jake.

I got up from the chair and turned on the overhead light.

"Sorry. The darkness feels a bit… uncomfortable. Play it ahead, would you? To the part where I get the convulsions."

Jake fast-forwarded until I was shaking on the couch. Then he rewound it a bit.

My televised self lay on the couch, and Beatrice was clearly hovering above me. But when the convulsions began, she shimmered out of sight.

"My goodness. Elijah, what was happening," asked Liliana.

"Well, the only negative part of the experience was when I was in the dark place and something tried to grab me. Maybe that's what we're seeing…"

"Elijah, I don't want you to do this anymore… you don't know what can happen."

"I know, sweety."

"And Jake, don't you ask him again, either."

He looked at her and said, "I won't."

Liliana affixed him with a stare.

"*What*? I won't!"

Pointing at the screen, Jake suddenly blurted out, "This is the part that freaks me out."

On the television I was lying there with Beatrice hovering over me again, but then her arms reached out menacingly and she… somehow *disappeared* into me. And that's when the convulsions began that landed me on the floor. After that, the video showed Jake coming to help me, in the process knocking the camera over and onto the floor. The video was then only of the rotunda, and was accompanied by Jake's panicky voice calling my name.

Jake was in favor of confronting Beatrice, but if she were able to… whatever it was that she did… then I didn't want to go anywhere near her. Instead, we let that part of the issue die away and the next day – Jake's last day in Germany – we mulled over the content of his reading.

First, some backstory about Jake and his ex-wife: Fresh out of high school, Jake married Laura, an intense woman with a short fuse. They lived on his parents' farm, and the deal was that Jake and Laura wouldn't pay living expenses as long as they worked there. Laura also started night classes that fall at the community college, and hearing about her classes somehow intrigued Jake. So he sat in on some classes with Laura and was shocked by the ineptitude of the teachers. When he tried to discuss this with Laura, she got defensive and said things like, "How could a farm boy know what a good teacher should be like?" As I recall from Jake, she got really nasty over it. I guess she thought Jake was being antagonistic towards her schooling.

Anyway, after visiting me a couple of weekends during my first year at Penn State, Jake got it in his head that he wanted to move up to Happy Valley and study there as well, but Laura didn't want to go. Big fights ensued, and when Jake secretly applied and got accepted a year later, they fought even more. In the end, they thought they'd try living apart for awhile, but during their separation, both found more accessible partners. They divorced shortly afterwards, and had been apart for over five years.

"So why do you think Laura's name came up now," I asked him.

He looked away, then back at me. "Because I still see her from time to time."

My eyebrows shot to the moon. "*Really*?"

He grimaced and said, "Yeah, like once, twice a month…"

"Does Sherry know?"

"Oh, sure. *That* would work."

"Where do you see her?"

"We generally go somewhere and get drunk, then go back to her place."

I leaned my head back on the couch and said, "Uh-huh… and has she changed any?"

"Hell no. She's still a cobra. And she still thinks we're good together, and I… I don't know, I guess I just like the sex."

"What about Sherry? Don't you guys…"

"Oh, she's great, but something seems missing. She's too timid. Too young, maybe."

"Then why are you with her?"

"I like her. "

"And Laura?"

"I like her, too… Kinda."

"And it doesn't seem wrong to be with both of them?"

"Of course it's wrong. But it's better than dating Rosie Palm."

"There are a lot of other women out there."

"Rosie gets jealous, though."

"I'm serious, man. It's not fair to either of them. And in fact, if you'd like my opinion I think you're being selfish. You're not sure that Sherry is enough for you, but you won't break up with her because you're not sure that Laura is enough, either. So you're hurting two people – three including yourself – because you're not courageous enough to do the right thing."

"Which is?"

"Which is to stop seeing one or the other. Or both. I can't make that decision for you, but the Records mentioned being free of Laura, not Sherry."

"Yeah..."

He shook his head and looked at me. "Are you sure that's what you read?"

I tried to picture the being again and to remember the words, but couldn't. It was another reality entirely. "I'm not sure of anything, man. But I seemed to be reading from something, and I read what I saw at the time. That's all I know."

Time was running short and we still had to swing by Liliana's institute on the way to the train station, so we got Jake's things together and drove over so she and Jake could say goodbye. The two of them had grown closer during the trip, and Liliana cried a bit when they hugged. It was good to see my two favorite people get along so well. I promised Liliana I'd pick her up later and Jake and I drove to the train station, bought his ticket, and walked to the platform.

"You gonna be all right without me to take care of you," he asked.

"That's *my* question."

"Yeah, yeah."

"Seriously. Think about our session and what it said... otherwise it's useless."

He nodded. "And you," he said, "I still think you have to kick that chick's ass."

I laughed. "She might like it."

"Ooooh. Now you're talking! When you coming home again?"

"No idea. Have a safe trip and give our love to Sherry, ok?"

"Not Laura?"

"If you must."

We laughed and then he got up onto the ICE train headed for Berlin. We waved goodbye through the window and that was Jake's visit to Wittenberg.

*I had to find a way to climb the steep hill opposite. There were few footholds and many small, loose rocks. At the top of the hill was my destination. I used a large stick to dig out footholds as I ascended. Finally I cleared the steep portion of the hill, but guarding the grassy lane beyond was a system of tangled, gnarled tree roots. Several times I became entangled, but managed to maneuver through. I continued on toward my destination.*

**Chapter 23**

In the days following Jake's departure, Liliana was convinced that I was planning to return to the Akashic Records, and no amount of discussion could convince her otherwise. For my part, there was no question. I felt a deep, instinctual fear anytime I reflected on the reading I had given Jake, and there was no way I was going back. I considered confronting Beatrice, but then I wondered how I would defend myself were she to decide to… who knows what. Or worse yet, how would I fend off a gang of her sexed-up leather goons if they wanted to chain me down in her back room and get medieval on me?

Simply put, there was a deep apprehension on nearly every level when I thought about her, and I decided to steer clear of her for good.

Thus, instead of otherworldy issues, my mind preoccupied itself with our upcoming trip to Prague; I had called Simone and in a very stilted and awkward conversation we agreed that Liliana and I would visit the following weekend.

To do *what* was the question.

In the days leading up to it, all my thoughts were wrapped up in that future moment in time. I was uncertain about seeing Simone again, uncertain about Liliana and Simone meeting, and above all I was uncertain about the baby (her name was Petra). Liliana was much, much more relaxed about it than I was, and during *my* sleepless nights, she slept like… well, like a baby.

She even made the drive down to Prague, during which my butterflies were more like flamingoes, somewhat enjoyable; the Czech radio stations reminded her of several songs that she sang and translated for me once we'd crossed the border between Germany and the Czech Republic.

We arrived in Prague in the early afternoon of a bright but windy Saturday and hassled with traffic over to Strašnice, a southeastern district of Prague. What a place, Strašnice. Nothing but crumbling, stony facades on buildings wrought (one can imagine) of Proletariat sweat. We wrong-turned our way through a maze of one-way streets that ran between the hardscrabble tenements called *paneláky*, buildings that were slapped together during socialist times, until we found Simone's building; it was over eight stories tall and was guarded by two overfilled dumpsters near the front door.

I breathed deeply before I pressed Simone's ringer. A moment later the door buzzed, and we walked in and then up the dingy stairs. There was graffiti on the walls, but the smell of home cooking was a pleasant counterpoint to the otherwise oppressive feel of the place. On the second floor landing, the door on the left was slightly ajar and we took off our shoes before knocking. A second later Simone opened it up fully. She smiled awkwardly and extended her hand to Liliana, who quickly took it, said something in Czech that I didn't understand, and kissed Simone on the cheek. Disarmed, Simone smiled and said thank you, then extended her hand to me. I hesitantly shook it and noticed that both of the girls had tears in their eyes.

Simone invited us in and shut the door behind us. We took off our jackets in the small foyer and Simone hung them, then motioned us into one of the four open doorways. Liliana went in and I was about to follow, but then I stopped and asked Simone to use the bathroom. She motioned to another door and I went in and locked it. My breathing was fast and my heart was fluttering, so I sat on the side of the exposed bathtub to collect myself. I looked around the spectacularly cluttered space and was taken aback by the low level of hygiene. Everything looked cheaply made, dirty and disused. I went over to the toilet and was afraid to touch the seat, so I flipped it up with my foot before using it. There were rust marks on all the porcelain surfaces. I washed my hands and looked at myself in the dirty mirror. I felt like puking.

Then I heard laughter from the other room.

I breathed deeply, dried my hands on my pants and went out into the foyer. I took another deep breath before turning the corner into the living room. Two things immediately stuck me. First, the clutter of the bathroom was *nothing* compared to the mess in the living room – a playpen and a couch took up most of the space, and baby stuff covered every available surface. It looked and smelled like a teenage mother's bedroom. The second thing I noticed was Liliana holding a beautiful blonde-haired baby as Simone looked on approvingly. The ladies were chatting away in Czech, the circumstances of the situation apparently pedestrian. They saw me enter the door and Liliana asked if I were all right.

"I think so. Now."

She smiled at me and said, "Isn't she beautiful?"

I walked over for a closer look, in the process stepping on a discarded towel. Simone picked it up from under my feet and threw it onto a pile, then motioned for me to come closer.

My *goodness* was Petra lovely.

She was wearing yellow pyjamas, her silky locks were done up in two pigtails tied with lavender bows, and she was entranced with Liliana's silver necklace.

Simone and Liliana bantered together in Czech for a minute before Simone reached out for the baby. Petra didn't want to let go of the necklace, but Simone distraced her with a piece of string and managed to pry her away from a teary-eyed Liliana.

Cradling Petra close for a second, Simone looked at me and said, "Would you hold her?"

I looked over at Liliana and found that I couldn't speak. I was choking up and could only manage to nod my head and hold out my hands for her.

Simone stepped towards me and held Petra out, and I took my baby daughter in my arms.

She was warm and heavy, and smelled of fresh powder. Examining her string with both hands, she didn't notice she was being held by a stranger until she dropped the thing, and then she looked up at me with complete innocence, her little eyebrows raised high.

I smiled at her and started to giggle, and then she started to giggle, and then I found I was crying, the intensity of the situation overwhelming me.

Petra got a concerned little look on her face, and then she looked over to her mom, who nodded and smiled at her.

Petra looked back at me, then reached up and grabbed my nose, making me laugh and cry all the harder, and I had to ask Simone to take her back so that I could collect myself.

"You like her," asked Simone.

"She's lovely." I looked over at Liliana and asked, "Isn't she, sweety?"

She could only nod her agreement because she was just as much of a mess as I was.

I suddenly felt all of my fears surrounding the trip melt away; all my worrying was for naught.

Not only was it easy to be around Simone and Petra, but Liliana and Simone *really* hit it off, and I had to stop their gabbing from time to time to get an update of their discussion. When Liliana was translating, Simone would pour us more tea or check on Petra, who had been put down for a nap in the other room.

Once when she was gone, Liliana told me that Simone seemed to be doing well with Petra, but was running into trouble. That's why she had decided to contact us. Taking care of the baby was difficult for a single mom, she said, and she'd had to quit nursing school and take a waitressing job to support them both. But then she had lost her waitressing job the previous month and was forced to apply for state support. The problem was that no money had yet arrived, and lots of bills were coming due. She had been asking her parents for help, but they were disappointed she had quit school and were reluctant.

"So I think she will ask for money, and I think we should help."

"And you're ok with that?"

"I am not very happy about it, but what to do? That little girl is beautiful and needs our help."

I nodded.

Simone came back into the room and sat down with a long sigh. She glanced between Liliana and me and began speaking in Czech. It was just as

Liliana had expected. Simone was asking us for help, and seemed embarrassed to be doing it.

I interrupted her in mid-sentence and said, "Simone, don't worry. We will help you, ok? It is not only your responsibility. We want Petra to grow up healthy and-"

I stopped because Simone had put her face in her hands and had started crying. I shrugged at Lilana, who moved beside Simone and put an arm around her. They spoke in Czech again, and after wiping her eyes, Simone looked up at me and said, "Thank you. Thank you so much."

We gave her what we could and told Simone that we would transfer more money when we arrived back in Germany. Funny thing; we were in very high spirits after the visit – not only was Petra a little cutie, but Simone had invited us to return anytime we liked. She even floated the idea of us taking Petra for weekends, or for extended stays in Germany. None of us had given any real consideration of what that might entail, but still... it was nice to think about.

So Liliana and I had plenty to discuss on the drive out to Svatý Hubert, where we planned to stay the night before making our way back to Wittenberg. Upon arrival, we discovered that Liliana's mom had cooked a goose, and over a heap of dumplings, her mom asked us what had taken us to Prague in the first place.

Liliana hesitated for a moment before spilling the beans, and her apprehension turned out to have been well-founded. My in-laws were hardly enthusiastic to learn that their foreign son-in-law had sired a daughter with another Czech girl, and instead of discussing it, they finished their meals in silence, then grumbled their way into the living room and glued themselves to the television.

After drying the dishes that Liliana washed, I said I was going to the garage to change the car tires; we hadn't been home since the weather broke and it was time to put on the summer treads. Liliana said she was jealous that I could escape the tension. She herself joined her parents in the living room, hoping to soothe them during the commercials.

In addition to our summer tires, the garage was where the beer was also kept, and after drinking one while playing with Doktor, I opened another and got to work on the tires. Liliana's father had an old floor jack, so I was able to change two tires at a time, and after finishing the front (as well as the second beer), I roughed up Doktor and then moved the floor jack to the rear of the car. Jacking that end was far easier, and after removing one of the tires I noticed that the exhaust pipe was hanging unnaturally, so I got on my back and scooted in to inspect it. A bolt had fallen off, so I crawled back out and rooted around the work area for another that might fit.

Doktor came over and wanted to play some more, so I chased him around until I could get the plastic bottle that he was gnawing on, and flung it out into the yard before returning to the garage. I crawled back under the car and had just threaded the replacement bolt into place when I heard a hissing. I couldn't place it at first, but then I realized the jack had begun losing pressure – it was lowering with me still underneath! In a panic, I tried to scramble out, but was unable to move quickly enough. I screamed for help as loudly as I could – and then screamed again in pain as a rotor settled on my chest. The pressure was incredible, and the last thing I remember was reaching out for the jack.

*Absolute peace and certainty.*

*I was one year old and looking up at my father; he was watching something on television that excited him and stood up quickly, causing him to lose his grip on me. I was afraid as I fell but too shocked to scream. He caught me before I hit anything, but I still cried. I didn't like him to hold me much after that.*

*Two years old and not liking to part with my stool.*

*Three years old and wanting to possess my mother.*

*Four years old, in the bushes behind the house with the Webber girls. Playing-I'll-show-you-mine-if-you-show-me-yours. I showed them mine, then they stopped the game, saying they had the same thing.*

*Five years old, a volunteer fireman dressed as Santa riding on a fire truck. When I saw him, I ran into the house screaming and crying and hid under the kitchen table with my back to the wall. I heard the screen door open and close, and was happy mom or dad were coming to comfort me. And then black shiny boots and a sea of red. Santa bent over and put his head under the table – his face a foot from mine as I screamed and tried to push myself through the wall behind me. Santa stared for five hellish seconds of sheer terror before he decided to go away.*

*Six years old, me and sis being taken fishing by our grandfather. On the way, stopping at the end of the runway to watch the planes take off.*

*Seven years old and professing love to my kindergarten teacher. The terrible pain of first rejection.*

*Eight years old and being knocked senseless by the neighbor boy.*

*Nine years old and lowering the bill of my baseball cap over my eyes, pretending I didn't see my elderly neighbors because I didn't feel like speaking to them.*

*Ten years old and setting the woods on fire. The heaviness of being made to confess to the firemen.*

*11 years old and loving to ride motorcycles with dad in the mountains.*

*12 years old and the sheer wonder of flying to visit my uncle in Montana. The mountains filling me with awe and deep respect. Beginning to understand sermons at church.*

*13 years old and wanting desperately to make love to my sister's friend. Her rebuke both a sharp disappointment and a great relief.*

*14 years old, the joy of being told by a popular girl that I was interesting to talk to. No longer caring about the sermons at church.*

*15 years old, obsessive lust over every female that was nice to me. Not caring for the taste for alcohol.*

*16 years old, obsessive lust over every female that was nice to me. Having developed the taste for alcohol, becoming well-versed in the cat-and-mouse of keeping it from my parents. The shame I was made to feel when I came home drunk that first time.*

*17 years old, obsessive lust over every female that was nice to me. The weeks of joy at Karmie accepting me for the Prom, followed by the darkness when she called it off. Priestly conversations.*

*18 years old, the glory and freedom of university. Having finally made love, no longer obsessing over every female that was nice to me. Bible reading.*

*22 years old, keying the car of the man who almost hit me as I crossed the street; shining lights of philosophical discussions culminate in the experience of enlightenment while running.*

*23 years old, sickened by the sodomy of churchmen, I turn my back on Christianity and explore Asian religions.*

*24 years old, enjoyment of first job tempered by unhealthy hatred of authority-figure boss. Plotting her downfall by planting an important document at bottom of pile on her desk.*

*25 years old, lightness of being after quitting job and rambling.*

*26 years old, burden of graduate school interspersed with instances of great insight.*

*27 years old, the joy and freedom of moving to Europe. The sadness of parent's pain. Dark pleasures. The lightness of re-discovering spirituality.*

*28 years old, realizations and awakenings.*

## Chapter 24

In every direction was limitless space, illuminated by a glow that seemed simultaneously distant and completely immediate. I was very much myself in terms of body, though perhaps less integrated, and even had sensations that were akin to thinking, feeling and seeing. When I tried to say, "Where am I," however, I found that no sound came out. I had to content myself with merely thinking things. I was weightless, and with very little effort I was able to will myself into a sort of floating motion. Soon I was able to control speed and direction according to my desire.

I found that I could move very fast and when I moved in this manner, on its own accord my body morphed into the same type of energetic compactness that I had willed myself into while giving Jake a reading. By concentrating, I was able to build speed just as I had done previously, and before I knew what was happening, I was in the dark realm that had frightened me so badly before.

An obstacle appeared ahead of me and I considered maneuvering around it. My actions mirrored my thoughts and I swung around the obstacle and continued on. Then there were more obstacles – they did not appear physical in nature, but rather as stationary areas that would diminish my energy were I to come into contact with them. I slowed down enough to negotiate my way through, and was nearly past the lot when two of them began closing in on me. I tried to speed up but was smothered in blackness. It wasn't painful in the sense that it hurt me. Rather, it was the type of pain one would feel if one's freedom was stripped in an absolute sense of the word. My bodyform had returned, and I was no longer able to will myself into the floating movement. I was no longer able to "see" anything.

I became very agitated and moved my arm to the right; my elbow immediately struck a wall. I tried to take a step forwards but my foot kicked the wall in front of me. My agitation grew until I was no longer afraid. I moved my arm harder to my right and this time my elbow smashed into the wall with great force. It took great concentration to will my arm into a "solid" object, but I was able to do it because of my anger. I struck the wall repeatedly and with great intensity until the barrier cracked and crumbled. At the first sight of "light" I was able to will my body into a malleable conduit of energy that flowed through the already-constricting hole I had made in the wall.

Once outside, the blackness attempted to entrap me again but I was able to move away with great speed to an area where there were no obstacles or barriers. As I was slowing to a halt, I noticed a point of light far in the distance. It was glowing intensely and I was fascinated by it. I noticed that it was growing larger and I remained still, forcing myself towards greater lucidity after the agitation of my imprisonment.

The glow stopped moving in the middle distance and hovered for a moment, then took on a physical shape. As it resumed moving, it became more recognizable the closer it got.

A foreign thought burst into my awareness: "So you can escape rudimentary boundaries. *Very good.*"

I had been "spoken to" like this before, and my agitation grew.

"That's right," she said. "Come to help you as promised…"

*I don't need your help.*

"Oh no? Then what are you doing here?"

*Why did you attack me?*

"I didn't."

*I saw it.*

"What you "saw" was me helping you. You would not have reached the Akashic Records were it not for me. And I promise you this: You will not reach them again without my help."

*I don't want to reach them again.*

"But you must. If you want to return to your precious Petra and Liliana, you must cure yourself."

The thought of those two entities was painful; the distance insurmountable.

"Yes. Your reason for living."

*You would help me... in return for what?*

"What I've always wanted – your energy."

*No.*

"Don't be so hasty. I don't want it all – just enough to help me onwards."

*And if I refuse?*

"Then I simply take it... which is more pleasant for me anyway."

*Stay away from me.*

With that, I moved away as fast as I could imagine myself, willing my body into the tight compactness that was able to streak to the Records before. But Beatrice was able to manipulate the environment in a way that I cannot describe. I only know that despite my frantic efforts to escape, she captured me in a sort of energetic trap that held me fast. I could move my body within this cocoon, but I could not move in any directional sense.

She approached me from behind and said, "Just relax. You might even enjoy it"

I felt a type of ecstacy building in my nerve center, followed by a release that was orgasmic in nature; with this, pure light flowed into the trap, causing it to glow brighter to the degree that I had grown dimmer.

"You see? That wasn't so bad, was it?"

The process was repeated, and this time it took much more effort for the buildup to reach its critical point; indeed, the second release left me feeling weakened.

*Enough.*

"Hardly. We have only begun."

The process was repeated, and was far more violating. It did not help that Beatrice had moved into my field of vision and was taunting me.

"If you had been man enough to satisfy my physical entity, we might not be here."

The buildup had become painful and I was certain I could not manage.

*I can't.*

"Oh, please. You would manage this for Liliana. And you managed to produce that wretched little Petra as well…"

The mention of those two entities caused a sudden sharpening of my will, and my energy pulsed in a way that the buildup proceeded quicker.

"Yes…"

My nerves became taught with energy and the point of release was reached and surpassed. I sharpened and concentrated my anger.

"That's right…"

Focusing on my love for Liliana and Petra, and my absolutely sickening fear of not seeing them again, I tensed all of my energetic pathways and released a furious burst of anger that caused Beatrice's apparatus to loosen. Still "screaming", I shot forth from the construct and discovered that I had a type of bludgeon in my grasp. I turned it onto the energetic siphon that had been draining me and swung at it with all of my will. The construct broke apart with the force of my blow, and Beatrice was momentarily stunned.

I turned on her and swung the weapon with all the will I could muster and with the full intent of destroying her. But she had recovered from her shock and the blow I had aimed at her center was stopped in midair. The weapon was rendered from my grasp and disappeared in the void separating us. Beatrice was no longer in her physical form, but had transformed into her energetic body. She towered far above me.

"I could easily finish you."

*You will not!*

"You fool. The only reason I do not-"

A piercing beam suddenly delved into my midsection, draining my energy in a way that made me yearn for and welcome the concept of oblivion. I watched in detached fascination as she robbed me of my lifeforce; in so doing, she grew in dimension and degree of brightness until she was gigantic.

Finally she relented, and the utter horror ceased.

"The only reason I do not continue," she said, "is utter boredom."

I was unable to articulate thought or movement as blackness enveloped me.

**Chapter 25**

I do not know for how long I was immobile.

I only know that from time to time a passing entity would linger nearby. Some were benignly curious and would eventually continue on their way. Twice, however, I was forced to repel the tentative grasps of entities that seemed to thirst after the energy pool I had become. These instances rendered me listless, and for long periods I was left alone.

Eventually I found that I was able to will myself into motion. It was very slow at first, but at great length I attained the speed I had managed before Beatrice intervened.

Entering into the black realm, I concentrated so hard that I forgot to be afraid and I passed through without incident.

I again found myself in the presence of the towering but benevolent entity I had met while giving Jake his reading.

She nodded in recognition and again my heart sang – she told me that the attack had lessened me, but had also allowed me to concentrate in a more coherent manner.

Without being asked, she produced a large, bound volume opened to the beginning. A jumbled mass of luminous characters floated out and coalesced into a message.

*The body must heal itself.*

I nodded.

The message dispersed, then re-arranged itself into another.

*The ribcage is broken and pressing on the heart, rendering it dormant. The heart must be translocated.*

I nodded again.

The glowing characters then melted away and danced chaotically. No further message could be divined. They eventually returned to the volume, which closed itself and faded away.

I had begun to lose coherence.

The being continued to regard me until I heard it "speak".

*You are... unable to do this.*

I slumped, feeling dread at the prospect of not seeing Liliana – or Petra – again. I raised my eyes and beseeched her.

*Please.*

An eternity passed. Then she slowly nodded.

*But you must return. There is much to do.*

*Yes. Anything.*

She continued to regard me.

*You are certain?*

With all of my willpower, all of my concentration, and all of my love, I said, *I promise I will return.*

☯

Somewhere far away, I awoke in a brilliantly white room. Liliana's worried beauty was hovering over me.

"Hey…," she said, and began to cry.

With all of my willpower, all of my concentration, and all of my love, I said, "I promise I will return."

Liliana's crying smile was the last thing I saw before I slipped into bliss.

†

# Inspirational readings

The Active Side of Infinity by Carlos Casteneda

The Alchemist by Paulo Coelho

The Bhagavad-Gita

The Bible

Desolation Angels by Jack Kerouak

Divine Interventions by Dan Millman and David Childers

Edgar Cayce Companion by B. Ernest Frejer

Edgar Cayce on the Akashic Records by Todeschi

Everyday Enlightenment by Dan Millman

The Four Agreements by Don Miguel Ruiz

The Gift of Gabe by Brian Joseph

In Search of Stones by M. Scott Peck

Memories, Dreams, Reflections by Carl Jung

The Razor's Edge by M. Somerset Maugham

The Road Less Travelled by M. Scott Peck

Sacred Journey of the Peaceful Warrior by Dan Millman

The Screwtape Letters by C.S. Lewis

Siddhartha by Hermann Hesse

Tao te Ching by Lao Tzu

Way of the Peaceful Warrior by Dan Millman

# About the author

Together with his wife, Jim has lived in various European countries exploring the challenges and glories of the expatriate lifestyle.

Along the way Jim has worked as an actor, English teacher, summer camp counselor, editor and writer.

Further writings, including the book titled Stories from elsewhere, as well as the podcast titled It's Those Foreigners, can be explored at www.jimcurtiss.com.

www.ingramcontent.com/pod-product-compliance
Lightning Source LLC
Chambersburg PA
CBHW020605260626
47157CB00003B/868

* 9 7 8 0 5 7 8 0 1 6 6 8 9 *